"There it is!" hissed Dall. The younger elf pointed across the basin to the opposite ridge, and Kagonos saw it, too: a glimmer of silver, as Kyrill reached the saddle on the opposite rim and flashed his blade in the sun.

Kagonos threw back his head, lips taut as he put the spiraling horn to his mouth. He blew a harsh, strident blast that carried clearly to the ears of all the elves—yet was virtually inaudible to the ogres, who heard merely a fresh ripple of mountain wind.

To the hundreds of Elderwild warriors waiting among the trees, the Ram's Horn sounded a clarion call to battle.

Saga

From the Creators of the DRAGONLANCE® Saga

**THE LOST HISTORIES**

### The Kagonesti
Douglas Niles

### The Irda
Linda P. Baker
*Available June 1995*

### The Dargonesti
Paul B. Thomson and Tonya Carter Cook
*Available October 1995*

**The Lost Histories
Volume 1**

# The Kagonesti

A Story of the Wild Elves

**Douglas Niles**

**To Alaina**

DRAGONLANCE® Saga
The Lost Histories
Volume One

**THE KAGONESTI**

All characters in this book are fictitious. Any resemblance to actual persons, living or dead, is purely coincidental.

This book is protected under the copyright laws of the United States of America. Any reproduction or other unauthorized use of the material or artwork contained herein is prohibited without the express written permission of TSR, Inc.

All TSR characters, character names, and the distinctive likenesses thereof are trademarks owned by TSR, Inc.

Random House and its affiliate companies have worldwide distribution rights in the book trade for English language products of TSR, Inc.

Distributed to the book and hobby trade in the United Kingdom by TSR Ltd.

Distributed to the toy and hobby trade by regional distributors.

Cover art by Larry Elmore. Interior art by Jeff Butler.

DRAGONLANCE is a registered trademark owned by TSR, Inc. The TSR logo is a trademark owned by TSR, Inc.

First Printing: January 1995
Printed in the United States of America.
Library of Congress Catalog Card Number: 94-60834
9 8 7 6 5 4 3 2 1

ISBN: 0-7869-0091-1

TSR, Inc.
P.O. Box 756
Lake Geneva, WI 53147
U.S.A.

TSR Ltd.
120 Church End, Cherry Hinton
Cambridge CB1 3LB
United Kingdom

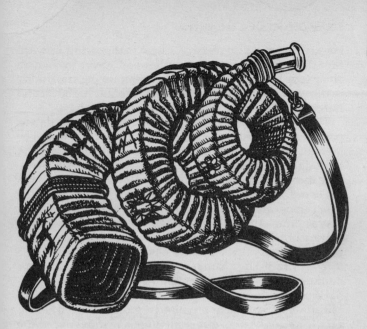

# Prologue

# Darlantan, of Dreams and Light

*3811 PC*
*Southern Khalkist Foothills*

The naked figure sprinted up the silent streambed, bounding from rock to rock, leaping stagnant and muddy pools. A flying spring, one leg kicked out for a graceful landing, spanned twenty feet of jagged boulders. Black hair trailed in a long plume, soaring with each jump, now streaming behind as the slender form reached a smooth stretch and sprinted like a deer.

Kagonos ran for many reasons. He relished the joy of motion for its own sake, his body fleet and powerful, his reflexes reacting to each challenge of the makeshift trail.

He savored the discovery of a new path, racing upward into these hills along a route that had never known an elven footstep. He loved the all-encompassing tranquility in the wilds, a peace that descended around his spirit and transcended the petty concerns and fears of others.

These motivations had all been on his mind, two dawns past, when he had awakened in the sprawling encampment of the Highsummer council. He had emerged from his lodge, located in the honored center of the tribal congregation, and spoken to no one while he trotted through the camp. His departure had drawn the attention of the tribal chiefs and shamans, but none had tried to delay or distract him—they all knew Kagonos often ran to a pulse that no other Elderwild could hear. Indeed, some of the priests looked relieved as the naked elf vanished up the forested trail. The shamans remembered more than one outburst from Kagonos that had disrupted a bonding ritual or communing attempt. The upcoming ceremony of Midsummer Starheight promised a greater level of solemnity if Kagonos was out somewhere wandering in the wilderness.

For his part, Kagonos had no patience for silly rituals of stars, sun, or seasons. The diamond speckles that brightened the night sky were best viewed alone. Truly, the stars did seem like magical things—they were masters of the heavens between sunset and sunrise—but how could they be honored by an elven ceremony or the recognition of any other mortal?

The wild elf had run for a day and a night and, now, through the morning of the next day. Still each breath came easily. Only the thinnest sheen of sweat slicked his bronze skin with a cool embrace. Gradually, hour by hour, he loped toward a state of spiritual intensity, an undeniable, consuming, and vibrant sense of life.

A thought flickered through his mind, and he knew the truth: one day soon he would leave the tribe forever, coming into these hills to dwell in solitude. He would be master of himself alone, beholden to none, a being fervently, totally attuned to this majestic land of forest and mountain.

In truth, he didn't know why he had stayed with the tribes so long. With his fanatical single-mindedness, his intolerance of any kind of weakness, Kagonos knew that he frightened the chiefs and veteran warriors. A stranger to his own parents, the Elderwild had even angered the shamans by declaring that love, among many other things, was a weakness to be scorned and avoided.

The wild elves, for the most part, were a happy people —playful, innocent, and careless. Kagonos did not hesitate to display his anger with that childlike naivete, for he knew that the tribes faced enemies on many sides. Why could not his people see those threats?

None of the braves could match Kagonos, physically— perhaps because his body seemed to thrum constantly, at the very brink of explosion. They treated him with respect, allowed him to come and go, and for the most part listened politely when he spoke. In different decades he had lived with each of the tribes—the Black Feathers, the Silvertrout, the Whitetail, and most recently the Bluelake clan. When danger from ogres or humans had threatened, no warrior had fought more savagely than Kagonos, and his efforts had helped to win many battles.

Kagonos often warned his tribemates about the threat of the House Elves, but here the Elderwild were less receptive to his strident admonitions. Under Silvanos, the golden-haired elves had formed their clans into mighty houses, then created literally that: tall buildings, crowded together into cities, in which they enclosed their lives. To Kagonos, these self-made prisons symbolized with shocking clarity the danger represented by the wild elves' numerous cousins. At the same time, he knew that other Elderwild were curious about, even attracted to, these garish constructions.

The lone warrior's mountain run was the perfect opposite to those House Elf desires, and even to the more limited society of the wild tribes. Now Kagonos knew pure, unadulterated freedom, as he escaped the constraints of other elves, of garments, of any edifice or tool showing the bend of a mastering hand—whether human, ogre, or elf. He desperately needed these hours, these days of solitude, in order to keep his internal tension from tearing him apart. Finding this path, racing upward with the wind blowing through his thick, black hair, the fullness of life soothed his tension and gave Kagonos profound joy.

And there was another, even greater reason that had drawn him from his lodge, from the summer gathering of the tribes—a knowledge that, by itself, would have compelled him to race into these hills.

Kagonos believed that today, once again, he would glimpse the Grandfather Ram.

Twice before Kagonos had encountered the mighty creature. Always the ram had been perched on the side of one of the highest mountains in the Khalkists. Kagonos had been below, trekking along a path none other had trod. And each of those times, as now, the tribes of the wild elves had been gathered for Highsummer council, and Kagonos had grown tired of the ceaseless discussion and frequent complaints of his clansmen.

On those occasions he had run for days before the Grandfather Ram had appeared. The magnificent animal, horns curling a full three spirals on each side of a broadskulled head, had regarded Kagonos from on high. It remained lofty and distant, yet a searching presence in the huge, golden eyes had been undeniably close, intimate.

The Elderwild wondered if anyone else had ever seen the ram. He didn't think so, though he wasn't sure why he should believe this. True, there had been something about the expression in the magnificent animal's eyes, something so profoundly personal that Kagonos believed implicitly that it had been a message intended for only him. And surely, even if others had seen the animal, they had not been the beneficiaries of that knowing, soothing gaze.

A shadow flickered across the wall of the gorge above Kagonos, and he flinched, knowing it was too late—he must certainly have been spotted by some flying creature. He spun to look at the sky, realizing that the shade had been far too large for a vulture or eagle. Quickly he saw the broad wings—a span easily twenty feet across—and the bulky body, four legs sweeping backward, confirmed his original impression. A griffon!

Instinctively the wild elf ducked beside the shelter of a large boulder. The hawk-faced creature must have seen him, but it would probably not attack—not unless it was starving, and even from below Kagonos could see that this was a sleek, healthy specimen.

Then he got the real shock. As the griffon flew onward, Kagonos saw a trailing plume of golden hair flowing freely above an armored shirt—a rider on the griffon's back! Appalled, the wild elf realized that a House Elf had somehow captured and tamed one of the beasts. Kagonos grimaced. It was bad enough that the elves of the house clans should master and saddle horses—must they now bind even the savage flyers of the skies?

As the griffon and rider disappeared around the shoulder of a looming mountain Kagonos resumed his run, but in the flash of that brief encounter his exertions assumed a bitter, fatiguing edge. He no longer felt the tingling joy of pathfinding, not now, when another saw his route before he did. His sense of solitude had been violated in a way that stirred deep resentment in his soul, bringing outrage to the forefront of his emotions. What right did a House Elf have to these heights? The fellow didn't even sweat as he traveled here—he merely sat on his saddle and discovered places, overlooked paths that should have been the province of the lone Elderwild runner.

Another jolt shook Kagonos as he remembered the Grandfather Ram. Would the mighty mountain sheep show himself to this House Elf? Would he be spotted inadvertently? The thought sent a bolt of alarm through his cloaking fatigue. A deep and fundamental fear drove the wild elf upward with renewed strength, his momentary lassitude forgotten as he all but flew over the jagged rocks of the steeply climbing riverbed.

For hours Kagonos hurled himself higher into the mountain range, through rough gaps in the foothills, over granite, crested ridges, along trails that no elven foot had ever before trod. He ran without thought of direction, yet he knew exactly where he was going. Always he climbed, pressing ever higher, working toward the loftiest peaks in the range.

When he emerged onto a high mountain ledge, coming around the shoulder of a looming peak, he was not surprised to see the griffon of the flying elf tethered in the valley beyond. A saddle of supple leather, studded with gold and gemstones, covered the creature's back, and the beast's hawklike face remained fixed on a scene below.

Next Kagonos saw the House Elf creeping downward. The intrusive rider was a hunter, to judge from his bow and arrows, but a wealthy one—perhaps even a noble. He wore pants of golden silk and gleaming black boots, with a tunic of bright white wool. The fellow's bow was strapped across his back, and in his hand he bore a long-shafted axe with a blade of silvery steel. Carefully the hunter descended, looking toward something in a dip of the mountainside below.

Even before the wild elf stepped forward, he guessed the nature of the House Elf's quarry.

Then Kagonos saw the white fur of the Grandfather Ram, showing in stark contrast to the gray rocks. From a hundred paces away Kagonos could see the crimson stain blotting the animal's heaving flank. The feathered shaft of an elven arrow jutted upward from the wound.

Springing forward, Kagonos took vague note of the ram's proud head, flanked by its triple-spiraled horns. The animal kicked its feet, its long tongue trailing from its mouth as it labored for breath. The elven hunter was barely a dozen paces away, advancing with the axe upraised, fully focused on his prey.

The griffon shrieked a warning—the sound something like an eagle's cry, but bellowed with the force of a roaring lion. Immediately the golden-haired elf spun, his blue eyes flashing as he spied the naked figure lunging toward him.

"Hold, Wild Elf!" shouted the warrior.

Kagonos slowed his advance to a walk, studying the other. The House Elf hunter wore a steel breastplate and carried a small dagger in his left hand. In the right he brandished a long-bladed axe—a mighty weapon. Emblazoned on his armor was a golden shield marked with the crossed claws of a rampant griffon.

"Leave the ram. Go." Kagonos spoke sharply, without considering the possibility that he would not be obeyed.

The House Elf threw back his head and laughed, a mocking, bitter sound. "Leave? This is a trophy more splendid than any I have seen. I intend to take this head, use it as my standard!"

The Elderwild did not reply, though he continued his measured advance. He didn't understand what the other meant about a standard, but Kagonos knew that a great wrong was being enacted before him.

"Stop there. Come no closer!" barked the golden-haired elf.

"Who are you?" Kagonos asked, halting ten paces away.

"I am called Quithas Griffontamer! Remember that name, savage—I sit at the right hand of Silvanos, and when the great war comes it will be I who commands his armies, who defeats the ogres and their dragon-spawn allies!"

"Leave the ram, Quithas Griffontamer. He is not your trophy."

Quithas laughed again. "Do *you* intend to stop me? A naked boy, no weapon, no armor? I do not wish to kill you, Wild Elf, but if you try to claim my rightful prey, I shall."

Kagonos moved with the quickness of thought. His sleek body flew toward the other elf, then tumbled to the ground as the keen axe blade whooshed through the air above him. The wild elf hit the hunter hard, both of them going down in a tangle of limbs. Kagonos grunted as the metal hilt of the dagger smashed against his forehead, but the fury of his onslaught sustained him. He threw his fist into Quithas's flank, avoiding the metal breastplate, driving the breath from the House Elf's lungs. Staggered by the impact, the hunter tumbled sideways across the loose rock of the mountainside.

The axe skidded away, and Kagonos leapt forward, stomping one foot on the weapon's long wooden shaft. Up the mountainside, the griffon shrieked in agitation, but the tether prevented it coming to its master's aid. Slowly, precisely, the wild elf reached down and picked up the axe. The weapon was surprisingly heavy, though the edge had been honed to a razor's sharpness. Holding it upward, brandishing it toward the elf who still sprawled, speechless, on the ground, Kagonos trembled under the onslaught of an almost uncontrollable hatred.

"This is a bad thing you have done, to hurt the Grandfather Ram. You said that I could not stop you, for I had no weapon. Now I have a weapon, Quithas Griffontamer, and I send you away." The wild elf reached forward and snatched the arrows from the other's quiver. Contemptuously he snapped them, casting the broken pieces at the House Elf's feet. "Mount your animal and fly, or I shall kill you."

Sputtering in fury, his eyes flashing a hatred that matched Kagonos's, Quithas nonetheless scrambled backward, rising to his feet beyond the range of the axe.

"Give me my weapon!" he demanded harshly. "It is more precious than you can know—forged by the master smiths, enchanted by Silvanos himself!"

"The axe shall be *my* trophy!" retorted the wild elf, tautly. "Now leave, before I claim your head as well!"

The House Elf's eyes flared, burning into Kagonos like a physical assault. Full of menace, the Elderwild raised the weapon, his own eyes narrowing as he watched Quithas back toward the prancing, agitated griffon. The House Elf spoke no further as he climbed onto his gilded saddle, seized his reins, and rode the beast's powerful spring into the sky.

Kagonos watched until the flying creature disappeared over the rim of a nearby mountain. Then he turned to the Grandfather Ram and knelt beside the stricken creature's head. His heart nearly burst with sorrow as he saw the growing crimson stain on that glorious white fur, saw the pleading expression in the gold-flecked eyes, the tongue lolling carelessly on the rocks.

"Water. Bring me water."

Kagonos blinked, then nodded. He had leapt to his feet and sprinted toward the stream at the base of the slope before it fully dawned on him that the animal had spoken. When he reached that clear brook, he knelt and, lacking any vessel, filled his mouth from the cool, sparkling flow. Racing back to the ram, he allowed the water to trickle over the animal's tongue, watching in wonderment as a trace of luster returned to the eyes.

"Shelter . . . we must find shelter. There is . . . a cave nearby. Carry me there."

The Grandfather Ram spoke haltingly, but Kagonos sensed this was due to the creature's wounds more than to any awkwardness with speech. The voice bore a suggestion of deep resonance and timbre, wrapped richly around his sparely chosen words.

The elf knew that the creature must weigh several hundred pounds, but Kagonos nevertheless reached under the ram and gently eased it upward, careful not to prod the flesh around the arrow. Surprisingly, he lifted the animal with ease. Following the ram's directions, he soon carried it to a small niche in the rocky mountainside—a "cave" only in the loosest sense of the word.

"The arrow . . . can you remove it from my side?"

Kagonos worked the missile gingerly, wincing every time the ram grunted in pain, but eventually he pulled it free of the deep wound.

"It's out, Grandfather. Rest now—do you need more water?"

The ram shook its head. "That's better. I fear some enchantment, some lethal elixir was laid upon the arrowhead—else it would not have felled me so readily."

With a grunting effort, the mountain sheep rolled onto its stomach, legs curled underneath. Already the bleeding from the arrow-wound had slowed to a trickle, and the animal's breathing grew stronger, more regular.

But was it an animal at all?

"I have seen you before, Pathfinder," spoke the sheep. This time those luminous eyes—the orbs that twice before had touched Kagonos from mountainous heights—seemed to penetrate through to the wild elf's soul, and he could only nod at the words.

"You travel the mountains with the grace of one who belongs here. You seek the trails, and you discover them—places where neither elf nor man, not even ogre, have trod before. You are a worthy chieftain of the Elderwild."

"I thank you, Grandfather—but I am no chieftain. Indeed, there are some in my tribe who think me mad, others who wait only for the time I depart my people and go to live in the hills. Perhaps my true worth may be measured in the tending of you. Can you tell me who you are?"

"Outside. Now I must come out of here," the sheep declared, standing weakly and taking several steps from the mountainous niche. The ram settled to rest on a smooth patch of shale, looking at Kagonos with a suggestion of amusement.

The wild elf gasped and stepped backward, startled by something he couldn't explain—the ram was *changing!*

Silver gleamed where that white pelt had been, as if a shimmering cascade of metal coins had suddenly spilled forth. At the same time the creature grew with impossible speed, extending incredibly. A long, sinuous tail curled outward, shining silver like the rest of the suddenly huge body. The already broad skull lengthened, the snout growing fearful, into a monstrous maw that bristled with sharp, curving fangs. The twin horns fell from the ram's head, tumbling onto the shale as the last vestiges of the mighty sheep vanished, replaced by leathery—but still silvered—wings and powerful, crouching legs. Hooked talons, like silver sword blades, curved from the massive fore and rear paws.

By the time the transformation was complete the serpentine body coiled in a great arc, half-encircling the dumbstruck wild elf. Kagonos felt no fear—just an incredible sense of awe, a knowledge that he beheld a miracle. He sensed, too, that his life from this point on was irrevocably changed.

"You ask who I am, Pathfinder? I am known by many names in the world, but you may call me Darlantan."

"Yes, Lord," Kagonos replied, dropping instinctively to his knees. The Elderwild had never bowed to anybody or anything in his life, yet now as he knelt he did so not only willingly, but with a sense of profound joy.

"I name you, Kagonos, as the true Pathfinder of the Elderwild. Your people shall need you in the centuries to come. If they are to survive, it will be because you have shown them the way."

"But . . . but how will *I* find the path?"

"Have faith, my brave son. I do not charge you with an easy task—it will be more difficult than you can ever know. But I know that you have thought of leaving your tribe, of becoming a lone elf in these mountains. A hermit."

"Yes, Lord. My time to do this is—*was*—soon." Even as he spoke, Kagonos realized that he would not become a lone elf. Had not Darlantan told him that his destiny lay with his tribe?

"I believe you to be worthy, Pathfinder. But know this: If you are to lead your people through the age to come—an age when the House Elves will grow mighty, will seek to seduce your tribesmen into their cities, an age when danger will soar from the skies on wings of red and green and blue—you must be faithful to me, and to me alone."

"You have my pledge, Lord."

"As Pathfinder, you are a leader greater than a chief, a spiritual counselor above any shaman. Your task will take all of your life, all of your soul. Take no wife, for she would distract you from the importance of your tasks. And never venture to the cities of the House Elves, for they will know you, and seek to enslave you."

"As you command, Lord."

Darlantan looked down, and for the first time Kagonos saw a hint of sadness in those golden eyes—the eyes that were the same as the ram's eyes, though everything else about this mighty creature had changed.

Following the glance, the elf saw one of the triple-spiraled horns lying on the stones at his feet. Like the ram, the horn had changed—though it retained its original shape.

Kagonos hefted the coiled object, feeling from its lightness that it was hollow. The wide end flared into an open bell, and the pointed end was carved, or somehow shaped, into a mouthpiece. Without being told, the elf knew he should raise it to his lips.

Placing the narrow tip between his teeth, Kagonos blew a long breath, feeling the mournful notes emerge from the horn, hearing the music keening through the mountain valley, a portent of danger and fear—yet a song that ended with a high note of hope and triumph. He had never played an instrument such as this, yet the notes came to him with intuitive clarity, and he raised his song with the fluid grace of his thoughts.

"This Ram's Horn is my gift to you," Darlantan said. "It will be heard by me, or my people, and if there is a way that we can aid you, we will.

"Play it in times of joy or sorrow, and it will speak to your people of hope and promise and pride. Play it in times of danger, and it will show you the path to safety.

"I shall keep the other horn," Darlantan continued. "And forever may these two spirals be a symbol of the bond between our peoples. Their sound is a thing beholden to your people and to mine, heard by none except a silver dragon or a wild elf."

"This is a precious thing," Kagonos declared. "But why do you bestow it upon me?"

"You are the Pathfinder," replied the dragon, and his powerful voice took on a firm sense of command. "Your people shall depend on you—and this horn is a sign of your high station. Even the shamans will hear your song of faith, and through it they shall better know their gods. Return with it to your tribes, to the council of High-summer. When the Elderwild hear your song, they will know the truth."

"I shall do this thing—though I still do not understand why."

"That is of no matter. You need most to remember the two Ram's Horns, Pathfinder. When either is played alone it may bray a song of hope and friendship, a lasting bond between our peoples. Either horn may cry for aid or offer comfort, and their songs will ring through the centuries of our lives.

"And someday in the future, perhaps, the two horns may be played together. The song they raise will be an anthem of hope and promise for the future of the world."

# PART 1

## Kagonos

*3357 PC*
*Khalkist Mountains*

# Chapter 1
# Meeting at the Edge of the Sky

The wooden skis rasped across the snow, barely marking the icy crust. Kagonos worked his way between frosted pines, carefully remaining below the knifelike crest of the high ridge. On the sunny northern slope the surface already grew soft and slushy, threatening a deadly avalanche, but here on the southern face the snow remained hard, crisp.

The lean, sinewy wild elf skied with steady urgency. Despite the chilly air, Kagonos wore only a pair of leather leggings and a buckskin vest. At his side he carried the three-spiraled Rams Horn, suspended by a sturdy thong. Stiff moccasins, lined with fur, protected his feet. Currently devoid of warpaint, Kagonos's skin was a rippling surface of gleaming, almost metallic bronze, shiny with a sheen of sweat and oil. His black hair fell in a long, thick coil down his back, wrapped into a single braid with a feathered thong.

Hissing softly, the skis glided down the incline into a deep, wide ravine. With a leaping turn at the bottom, the wild elf aided his momentum with plunging stabs of his poles, smoothly coasting halfway up the opposite slope. Kicking hard, still poling, he pushed himself quickly through the last, steep stretch.

Beyond the ravine, the wild elf picked up speed. Climbing gradually, he remained near the summit of the ridge, skimming over the snow with the combined force of his kicking feet and steadily poling arms. When he reached a clump of rocks that had been blown free of snow by the steady wind, Kagonos paused. He kicked off his skis and dropped to his belly, ignoring the icy surface against his naked arms. Crawling slowly, he worked his way between the boulders, carefully raising his head just high enough to see into the broad valley beyond.

His caution may have been extreme—the nearest ogres were at least a dozen miles away. Still, there was no other way Kagonos could have approached this lofty horizon. To the wild elf, there was no such thing as "unnecessary" caution, for once one became used to taking chances, discovery and disaster were inevitable.

His hazel eyes flashed at the sight of the huge army sprawling across the plain in an irregular column. For many days the Dark Queen's horde had followed the fringe of the Khalkist foothills, closing in on the army of Silvanos, which remained out of sight somewhere to the south. The ogres were creatures of lofty places and would have preferred to march in the heights, Kagonos knew—it was only the commands of their dragon masters that brought them down from the mountain summits.

Of those masters, it was hard to believe that only one clan of evil remained to menace the world. For more than a century and a half Kagonos and the Elderwild had been unwilling participants in the battles against the five children of Takhisis, Queen of Darkness. These dragons—of green and black, of blue and white and red—had plundered Ansalon for most of those decades, bringing death and destruction to elvenkind and humanity.

The tide of evil had been stemmed, finally, when three gods had conspired to bestow potent gifts upon the elves. These artifacts were the five dragongems—magical stones of life-trapping. During the most recent years of the war, Silvanos and his legions, aided by warriors mounted on flying griffons, had created clever traps. In their great, flying wings, evil dragons had fallen to the elven ambushes, until the greens, reds, whites, and blacks had all been ensnared, their lives trapped within the potent gemstones—the stones then buried in the depths of the Khalkist Mountains.

Finally only the blue dragons remained, and the great leader Silvanos had planned for his final victory. Before the battle could be joined, however, disaster had struck in the form of an ogre raiding party— the Bluestone was stolen! Vanishing into their mountain fastness with their priceless trophy, the ogres had taken from Silvanos his only effective means of fighting the blue dragons.

Recriminations had been many, with the House Elves of Silvanos blaming humans, and the humans—so recently escaped from ogre-bound slavery—quick to turn the blame against the elves. Word had reached the Elderwild through several routes—a trader of beads and steel arrowheads had come from Xak Tsaroth, trembling with predictions of doom, and several wild elves had come north, refugees from the House Elf compounds, carrying the tale of consternation among the Elderwild's kin.

Kagonos believed that the ogres were more to blame than either humans or elves, for they were the ones who had actually stolen the precious artifact. He had been amused to hear the tales of bickering and blaming, none of which changed the central fact that the Bluestone was missing.

The blue serpents, in many ways the most evil and malicious of the five children of Takhisis, had plundered, raided, and ravaged all the north coast of Ansalon during the winter. Now, with summer arrived, everyone knew they were winging toward the central plains. When they arrived, the damage they might do would be beyond measure—and without the Bluestone, the forces of Silvanos had no way to stand before the potent, massive wyrms. The great elven army would be dispersed, Silvanos's power broken, and the survivors of his legion scattered across Ansalon.

Reflecting on the potential for disaster, Kagonos wondered about his own, private knowledge—the secret he now carried to the top of the mountain. It did not seem possible that he and his braves could change the course of fate, yet he had to hope that they might do just that.

The elf squinted into the distance. Tall, billowing clouds rose into the skies over the plains, towering like mighty marble columns. Sunlight reflected from these alabaster pillars with a brightness that almost forced the wild elf to look away. But still he stared, shifting his eyes only slowly among the great cumulus.

Finally he blinked, satisfied—for the moment, at least—that the blue dragons did not soar above the marching army. They would come, he knew, and probably soon, but he drew some satisfaction from the knowledge that they had not yet arrived. The two armies on the ground were still many miles apart, so it seemed that the battle would not occur for several days.

He thought for a moment of the Elderwild tribes, gathered only a day's march from here in a deep, sheltered valley. His people had come when Kagonos had summoned them with the Ram's Horn. As always, even the chiefs of the different tribes turned to their Pathfinder for hope in time of danger—yet never in their history had the threat of destruction been so imminent and so complete. For the most part, since the Dragon War had raged, the Elderwild had dwelled in small bands, rarely venturing from beneath the protection of their treetop canopies. Only the command of the great horn could bring them into a large gathering, and only the secret knowledge Kagonos now possessed could have motivated him to make that summons.

Of course, the elves of Silvanos had developed another tactic during the course of the war—one that enabled them to dwell in large tribes, and even to defend themselves against the dragons. They had fortified their great cities as bastions against evil. When a dragon flew against one of these walled enclaves, it was forced to do so without the ogres who formed the other potent club of the Dark Queen's hordes. Thus unsupported, the tough-scaled serpents proved slightly vulnerable to elven arrows—to the extent, at least, that the steel-tipped weapons fired in volley struck the dragons as a barrage of vexing stings. Ultimately, though cities had been ravaged and many elves slain within them, the evil wyrms had learned to avoid the House Elf strongholds. The great serpents were basically cowards and preferred to work their villainy in ways that brought little risk to themselves.

Looking toward the vast plain, Kagonos could not see Silvanos's army, but he knew that his golden-haired cousins were there. All the houses had gathered for this final confrontation, and the wild elf knew that a great deal of the future history of Krynn, for good or ill, would be decided on that barren flatland sometime within the next few days.

However it came out, Kagonos thought wryly, the histories would ensure that Silvanos got most of the credit. The Pathfinder had personally met the lord of his kin on a few occasions, and always Silvanos had impressed him as an elf of wisdom, patience, and almost palpable leadership. Although, remembering his pledge to Darlantan, the wild elf had never visited any of those crystal cities, many stories reached him from those Elderwild fortunate enough to escape the bonds of House Elf servitude. The city clans hailed Silvanos as the font of all wisdom, the holder of highest elven honor. His virtues—of honor, grace, and patience—were raised as the ideal for all his subjects.

"Claim as well that he invented food or sleep," Kagonos had muttered on hearing these tales, and that opinion had not shifted in the years since. Perhaps he wasn't being entirely fair—after all, Silvanos was undeniably a leader who was wise and just. His feat in uniting the squabbling houses of elvendom—all the tribes save the Elderwild—was certainly no little accomplishment, though Kagonos still could not understand the benefits of this great melding. After all, why would any chieftain choose to subordinate himself to a greater chief?

Yet another thing about Silvanos he respected very much. The elven leader was strong, both in his own physical presence and in the use of his mighty army. Strength was a thing Kagonos understood and valued. Indeed, it seemed possible that Silvanos's strength might be the hammer that finally smashed dragons down from their cruel mastery of the world. That was a result the Elderwild could only embrace.

Wriggling back from the ridge, the elf tucked his moccasins into the bindings of his skis and once again started along the icy crust. He continued to work his way steadily upward, poling strongly toward a steep-sided dome crowning the end of this winding elevation. A quick glance at the sun showed him that he still had plenty of time, but now there was a new urgency to Kagonos's rhythmic strides.

Soon he reached the base of the great summit, and—still gliding smoothly among the trees—checked the encircling woods for signs of a potential trap. Not only did he see no evidence of a current trespasser, but the snow hadn't been disturbed since long before the crust had formed. This place would work well.

At the base of the precipitous slope, the Elderwild removed his skis, lashing the boards and poles to his back—they would be of no use on the steep climb, but they would greatly speed his descent. He started upward with the same grace and fluidity that had marked his progress across the snow. Even when he was forced to grip an outcrop crusted over with glare ice, his fingers and toes were firm, his attachment to the mountainside never wavering.

In an hour, Kagonos had reached the rounded summit, and here he walked carefully across the windswept, rocky ground. To three sides the soaring peaks of the Khalkists challenged the sky. In the fourth direction sprawled the barren plains of Vingaard, where it was left to the mortal armies of elf and ogre to do the challenging.

The Elderwild circled the promontory, confirming that no marks had been made in the snow anywhere atop the mountain. On the lofty slopes overlooking the plain Kagonos moved from barren rock to patches of stony ground, ensuring that he never silhouetted himself against the snow for the benefit of a distant watcher below.

Returning to the point of his original ascent, Kagonos at last raised the horn to his lips. Closing his eyes, turning the mouth of the instrument toward the highest peaks of the range, he blew a long, clamorous blast. The wind took his song, carried it upward and away—but only to those ears sensitive enough to hear it. Patiently the elf stared eastward, visually tracing the long, twisting valley leading toward the heights.

The Pathfinder's hazel eyes darkened as he squinted across the miles. Raising a hand to his forehead, he shaded his vision against the bright sunlight, his focus extending far, far into the distance.

Minutes passed, and then silver glinted, blinking the reflection of sunlight with each powerful stroke. Darlantan's mighty wingspan stretched outward in a broad embrace of the air, shimmering even across a score of miles. The silver dragon flew low, ensuring that he was not visible to anyone beyond the confines of this high valley.

Kagonos smiled tightly as he watched the gleaming serpent glide along the curve of the descending vale. Flying, he thought, must be the only type of movement more

serene, more fluid than skiing. As always, the majesty of
the airborne serpent all but took his breath away. The elf's
throat tightened with the familiar, warm emotion as Darlantan drew nearer to the mountain and gained speed.

Finally those wings hooked outward, rigid sails in the
wind, as the momentum of the dragon's flight swept him
upward. Always Darlantan kept the bulk of the mountain
between himself and the ogre army—the monstrous
troops would not observe his presence on their flank.

Nearly stalled in the air, the dragon reached out with
huge paws, driving his wings powerfully downward for
one last stroke as he settled gently to the rocks of the
domed mountaintop. He shook his head and snorted a
blast of frigid air, as if clearing the reverie of flight from
his ancient, wise brain.

"Greetings, Pathfinder." Darlantan nodded elegantly,
dipping his head as the silver scales rippled along his serpentine neck. "I am glad that you summon me."

Darlantan's body shimmered and twisted, shrinking
more quickly than the elven eye could follow, and in a
blink Kagonos was looking at a long-bearded, spry old
human, who wore a bright cotton tunic that matched the
pure white of his flowing beard. His eyebrows and the
thick mane of his hair were tinted with silver, and his
eyes—gleaming from deep-set sockets—were a vibrant,
fiery yellow. Though the wrinkles across his forehead
showed a visage that could be stern, now Darlantan's face
beamed as he reached out to clasp his friend's hand.

"Tell me," Kagonos asked. "Why do you take the shape
of a man when you could be something so much more
handsome—an elf, perhaps?" He was used to Darlantan's
shapeshifting by now—during previous meetings the silver dragon had appeared as a man, an ogre, an elf, a bear,
an eagle, and a host of other creatures. Still, the Elderwild
knew that Darlantan favored the shape of this human
sage, and had never figured out why.

Darlantan laughed, a sound that was kind and compas-
sionate as well as heartily amused. "I am whichever serves

me best at the time," he replied—his typical evasion. "As to this body, there may come a time when your people develop an appreciation of human wizardry!"

"The House Elves, perhaps—but the Elderwild have no need of humans, nor any desire to learn from them."

Darlantan nodded, a noncommittal glitter in his eye.

"Have you flown over the plains?" asked Kagonos, with a look toward the flatland and the distant ogre horde.

"Aye—in the guise of an eagle, so as not to alarm the ogres. The two armies vie for position on the field. If Talonian is not careful, he will find that Silvanos has him trapped against the Vingaard."

"Good. Perhaps the House Elves can win their victory, even without the power of the Bluestone."

"That is the hope of us all," the human sage replied. "But I fear that the blue dragons will arrive any day—and when they do, it will take more than an army to defend Silvanos and the elven houses." He looked shrewdly at the wild elf, as if he had a premonition of Kagonos's secret news.

"There is a reason I asked you here," said the Pathfinder slowly. He continued, as Darlantan made no reply. "I believe I have located the Bluestone."

"This is very good news—if you are right. You have not seen the stone itself?"

"No—but I have discovered an encampment of ogres near here. They have selected a defensible hilltop, but it is not a place they would normally choose to make a camp. I believe they guard something there."

"That makes a great deal of sense. The Bluestone is the last of the Five Talismans—they will go to every length to ensure that it remains in their hands. The entire army of Talonian, on the plains before us, maneuvers only to divert attention from the real object."

"And what word of the blue dragons?"

"They departed inland several days ago. Even if they do not fly at top speed, they will reach the central plain within the next three days. Unless Silvanos has the stone by then, his army is doomed." Darlantan looked to the north, as if he sought a sign of those serpents against the horizon. Then he turned back to the elf.

"Where is this ogre camp?"

"Not far from here, though it will be difficult for my warriors to reach. The camp is on an island in a lake, secured within the crater of a high peak. Now, of course, the place is surrounded by snow and ice. I imagine they think it will take any attack a long time to develop."

"But you will try this attack?"

"Yes. I have gathered the tribes in the mountains and shall ask all the braves to join me. Can Silvanos prepare to face Talonian and the dragons in time?"

"I will carry word to him. He has been contemplating dividing his force, seeking shelter in the southern forests—but I'm certain that, with this hope before him, he will stand firm. How long will it take?"

"Our attack will be made the day after tomorrow—it will take that long to gather the warriors, to climb the outer mountain. It will take another day, perhaps a day and a half, to carry the stone to the plains."

"It may be that we can reduce that latter delay. I depart at once, for I know that Silvanos will be elated by this news."

"Will we have time?" Kagonos asked.

"Only the gods know. If the blues come too soon, I shall try to hold them at bay until the stone arrives—but it will have to be soon, for I cannot stop them all."

"Then we should go quickly from here and meet again on the field of victory. Thank you for coming to the summons of the Ram's Horn."

"I could do nothing else—but hold a moment. There is another thing you should know."

Kagonos waited.

"Silvanos wants you, wants all your tribe, to join him in the south after the war is won. He would raise you to the status of a house, and bring you into his new nation."

The Elderwild shrugged. "He can ask—but I shall not go."

"That is as it should be." Darlantan was pleased. "Now, go to the dragongem—and may this accursed business be put behind us! Do you know—even the gods themselves have paid a price in this war?"

"What do you mean?"

"Three children of Paladine—Solinari, Lunitari, and Nuitari—stole the power of magic, that the dragongems might be made. Those gods have been punished for their theft, in a manner that will soon be made apparent to all."

"What punishment is of avail against a god?"

"Look to the night sky, after the last battle—whether the result be for good or ill. There you will see the proof, outlined against the stars."

Darlantan explained with a slow nod. Long tendrils of silvery whiskers curled outward from his jaw, and now that fringe flickered slightly in the growing wind. That same breeze brought the sounds of a distant pulsation.

"The drums have begun," Kagonos observed.

"In three days at the most, Talonian's ogres will be ready to attack. The blue dragons will be near, and the time of resolution falls upon us," agreed the elderly human. Though his body seemed frail, he stood firmly against the force of the wind, and in his yellow eyes glowed a glint of very youthful determination.

"Good luck, my friend," Kagonos offered, placing an affectionate hand on the man's shoulder. Already the human shape began to change, shifting and expanding into the form of the great serpent.

"And you," replied the dragon, with a serene dip of his head. "May victory soon be ours."

The Elderwild turned back to the slope and jammed his feet into the bindings of his skis while Darlantan spread his broad silver wings. In moments, they were flying— one through the air, the other over the snow—as they swept downward from the mountains, toward a battle that would shape the future of the world.

# Chapter 2
# The Mountain

---

Three wild elves leaned into the wind, climbing steadily along the knifelike crest of ridge. Sweeping onward in a graceful arc, the mountains rose ever more steeply toward the curve of barren, windswept summit. The tracks of the three climbers dwindled into the distance below, trailing all the way down the ridgeline to the forested foundation of the massif.

A week earlier, Kagonos had climbed the other side of this mountain to discover the ogre camp within. Today, the Pathfinder chose this route for the second exploratory climb to the top. He remained aware of the mountain as a whole, though from this angle on the shoulder he could neither detect the full sweep of the circular summit, nor see the snow and ice-filled caldron within. A singular, crumbling notch broke that encircling crest at one point, allowing a tiny stream to flow through a narrow gorge, giving outlet to the lake within the mountain's crater.

Instead of looking over the great slope before him, Kagonos allowed his eyes to sweep outward, inevitably drawn to the descending sweep of the mountains and the dusty plains beyond.

In the lead of the climbing trio, the Pathfinder paused to catch his breath while he looked under his shoulder at his brothers, who climbed steadily behind and below him.

Dall looked back, his dark face split by a fierce grin of elation, the circles of his war paint exaggerating the smile into a fierce leer. Behind Dall, Kyrill frowned with intense concentration. Like their elder brother, the two wild elves wore leather breeches and thick, deerskin cloaks to protect them from the biting wind. Still, their hands and heads were bare, except for the whorls of black paint with which the Elderwild warriors had marked their skin.

The other warriors of the tribe waited, concealed beneath an overhanging cliff in the valley at the mountain's foot while the Pathfinder, aided by his two younger brothers, sought this second route to the summit. Kagonos pushed forward with urgency, knowing that two of them would have to descend with the summons to attack before the rest of the braves ventured onto the slopes.

After a pause while each elf caught his breath, Kagonos again rose and turned his face toward the crest. One foot after the other, he started upward, following a line that angled toward the right, where the Elderwild had seen a shadow along the mountain's surface. True to his suspicions, he located a narrow ravine there and led Dall and Kyrill into the scant shelter offered by its cracked and jagged walls. Here they were protected from the wind and more secure from observation by any ogres that might be posted on the heights above. Even though Kagonos had seen no such scouts on his first climb, the Pathfinder wasn't inclined to take any chances.

"Why don't we just sneak in through the stream outlet?" Dall asked as he joined his brother beside a snow-streaked boulder. Once more the three climbers halted to catch their breath, Kyrill sweeping the snow off a rock and sitting down, while Dall and Kagonos leaned easily against the rough walls of the narrow ravine.

"That's the obvious route—so it's the only one we *can't* take," Kagonos replied. "It's essential to approach an enemy from a direction he does not expect you to come."

"Besides," said Kyrill with a sly grin, propping one foot on a craggy rock as he leaned against the ravine wall, "the view's a lot better from up here!"

"No city can offer a vista like that," Kagonos agreed, reverently allowing his eyes to sweep across the expanse of mountains and distant plain. From this height, the silver ribbon of the Vingaard River was barely visible, many miles from the foothills.

"Why is it that Silvanos and the House Elves seek to hide themselves within walls?" Dall asked, showing the naivete of his youthful eighty-four years. "Are they all cowards?"

"Most likely," said Kyrill. At two hundred, he had seen enough of life to make him, in his own eyes, an expert on most topics. "Either that, or they're afraid that if they wander into the forest, all their women will come running to us!"

Suddenly Kagonos felt very tired—tired of war, tired of climbing, tired of watching out for the lives of the brothers who, since the death of his parents early in the war, were the only family he had on all of Krynn. Other warriors, by the time they had earned the right to paint the spirals of paint on their chests, had taken wives. Some even had children, a legacy to extend into future centuries. But for Kagonos there was none of that, not for the centuries since he had become the Pathfinder, the hope of his people.

"Many geese flew over this spring," Dall said quietly. "The hunting in the fall will be rich, don't you think?"

"Aye," Kyrill agreed, grateful for the change of subjects.

"If the war's over, we'll have our pick of the marshes—and I intend to find the one where they're packed so close that each arrow will bring down two geese!"

"Wishful thinking, my keen-eyed brother," Kagonos said, forcing a chuckle. "Though if there is an archer among the Elderwild who could do it, it is you."

"Do you really think the war will end soon?" Dall asked, shaking his head in wonder. "The shamans say that it might—that the gods will so decree. And for years Balif's legions have pounded Talonian, with the cavalry and griffons of General Quithas riding all across Ansalon—but still Silvanos has not been able to win ultimate victory over the ogres."

Kagonos spat at the mention of Silvanos's commander of cavalry, the renowned griffon-rider himself. "Quithas is not as great as they say. Even he would bleed red blood if cut."

"But all the tales . . . I've heard that his legion can ride a hundred miles in a day and then attack an enemy army during the night. And *still* he wins the battle! Are these exaggerations?"

"Perhaps, or perhaps not. But no single general, no one army, can stem a tide of evil that has flowed for a hundred and fifty years. And, for all his arrogance, Quithas is but a single elf—even if he does augment his speed by riding a horse, or a griffon!"

Kyrill could not miss the bitterness in his older brother's tone. "This Quithas . . . he is the same you met in the mountains, before I was born. The hunter?"

"Quithas sought to kill the Grandfather Ram—he whose horn I keep at my side. But I took the Griffon-tamer's weapon—this axe I still carry—and he fled from the valley."

Eyes wide, Dall looked at Kagonos. "You challenged the mighty general—and he *fled?*" he asked, awestruck.

"Like the wretched cur he is," the Pathfinder replied grimly, his jaws tightening at the memory. "Though he was not Silvanos's general at the time—indeed, that was before the war. Though even then, Quithas seemed hungry for strife. He told me that he would one day lead many elves in battle."

"And so he does—and will, until we can end the war," Kyrill noted.

"Which might be today!" Dall exclaimed.

"*If* we can capture the Bluestone and take it to Silvanos—or to Darlantan," Kagonos agreed cautiously.

"Are you certain the stone lies beyond this summit?" Kyrill inquired.

"As certain as I can be. Darlantan thought that my intuition was correct," Kagonos snapped.

"That's good enough for me," Kyrill said with a shrug.

"But what if the blue dragons or the army of Talonian destroys Silvanos on the plain? Then what will happen?" Dall pressed.

"What if the face of Krynn splits apart and we all fall into the hole?" demanded Kagonos. He knew that such questions were part of elven nature, but why could such elves not remain silent? Roughly he forced his temper down. "Then we die, and evil holds sway across the world! Darlantan says that the blue dragons will not be here for two days, at least. Furthermore, I do not think Talonian can defeat Silvanos. Apparently, the ogre chief has his own doubts—else why would he conceal the dragon talisman so far from the main body of his army?"

"Perhaps because he *doesn't* fear the Elderwild," Kyrill said.

"Then let us make him pay for his mistake," Kagonos replied as he climbed to his feet and turned once more toward the ascent.

The gorge continued steeply upward, and the three nimble elves leapt over the snow-covered boulders that littered its floor, moving quickly after their brief rest.

Kagonos, still in the lead, felt a growing sense of disquiet. He wanted to protect his brothers—for many decades he *had* protected them—from the terrible violence of war. The tribe had dwelled in the forest, moving often, never camping under the open sky, and it had been years since the Elderwild of his or any other band had been swept into a major battle.

The chieftain's thoughts returned to the present as he saw blue sky yawning beyond the next curve of the gorge. "Careful," he whispered. "We're almost to the top—don't reveal yourself over the horizon."

Ignoring the chill of the snow, Kagonos dropped to his hands and knees, creeping forward to the crest of the mountainside. At the top, he very slowly lifted his forehead until his keen eyes could see into the vale beyond.

It was as he remembered. The circular crater in the center of the summit was steep-sided and broad, a dazzling bowl of snow-lined whiteness. A wide expanse of flatness formed the bottom, several hundred feet below. Though it was featureless now beneath winter's blanket, that flat area could only be the frozen surface of a lake. The island rose as a cone in the center, barely two hundred paces from the shore, and atop that rise he clearly saw ogres. In the week since his first discovery, the brutes had cleared away the snow from their camp and had spent some time piling rocks around the perimeter to form an improvised wall. Kagonos saw no sign of any lookouts on the mountain's rim, or even of any organized attempt to keep watch beyond the makeshift wall.

"They're still here," he told his brothers, before fixing his eyes on Kyrill. His plan, which had begun to form with his first reconnaissance, now fell into place. "Get the warriors and bring them to the top. Dall, bring Chief Barcalla and the warriors of the Silvertrouts, Whitetails, and Bluelake here. This is where we will make our attack.

"Kyrill, I want you to take forty braves and circle around the mountain. Go with Chief Felltree and some of his Black Feather braves. When you get to that notch over there, wave your sword—let the sun flicker off the blade. I want you to start the attack, to divert the ogres toward the west. Then the bulk of the tribe will come down from this side, gaining some measure of surprise."

Kagonos took his brother's arm and stared into his eyes. Kyrill's face was flushed with excitement, and his hands tensed around the hilt of his weapon. Once again the Elderwild Pathfinder felt that stab of regret and apprehension, but with action so close he had no choice but to force it away.

"Kyrill, listen," he ordered tautly. "When you draw close to that island, bring your warriors around the lake and join the attack from this side. I don't want the forty of you trying to climb that hill in the face of all the ogres in the camp. Do you understand?"

For a moment the younger elf looked as though he wanted to argue. Abruptly he nodded, and with a last look at the ogre hilltop, Kyrill turned back toward the gorge and started down the mountain.

# Chapter 3

# Contest in Blood

The ogres continued their disorganized attempts to fortify their hilltop camp, piling boulders into a ring around the periphery of the crest to form a barrier of irregular height and loose, haphazard construction. The makeshift wall had numerous gaps, and nowhere was it higher than the top of an elf's head. Kagonos saw that most of the ogres already grew bored with their labors, and dozens of the brutes lolled about their camp or engaged in listless bickering and brawling. This lassitude served to reassure the Elderwild that the monsters were unaware of the imminent menace to their camp—and to the Bluestone.

What if he was wrong—what if the stolen artifact was not kept there? Kagonos could only dismiss the thought, unwilling even to consider the prospect, knowing that if it was true, all hope was lost.

While waiting for his warriors, Kagonos had spent hours scouring, with his eyes, the hilltop camp, seeking some sign of that powerful talisman of dragonkind. He knew that the stone cast a powerful illumination, so that even if he couldn't see the magical gem itself he hoped to catch a glimpse of its emanations. His search had proved fruitless, but that did not change his mind. Very likely, he told himself, the Bluestone was concealed in a cave, or had perhaps been buried somewhere.

Thus far, however, the Pathfinder had been unable to locate a cave mouth. The hilltop was fairly smooth, and though, because of the crude wall, he couldn't see all of the enclosed area, Kagonos had begun to form a suspicion. In the center of the fortified clearing rose a small cairn of boulders, no taller than an ogre. The top of the pile had been smoothed into a platform, suitable for a lookout to see over the walls, but during the time the elf watched, no ogre had climbed onto that cairn for so much as a glance at their surroundings. It seemed to him, then, that the boulders had been piled there for some other purpose.

A purpose such as concealing the mouth of an underground hiding place. The more he thought about it, the more convinced Kagonos became that this cairn marked the place where he would find the Bluestone—after, of course, the Elderwild entered the crater, crossed the lake, climbed the hill, and breached the ogres' impromptu wall.

He heard the sounds of climbers only as Dall came into sight below. Quickly the young elf rejoined his brother, creeping to the edge of the crater, while a file of warriors advanced behind him. Another wild elf crept forward, and Kagonos nodded to Barcalla, chief of the Silvertrout tribe. Each of the Elderwild warriors bore a pair of skis strapped to his back, with both hands free to hold weapons. Kyrill would take longer to reach his position across the crater, but he, too, should soon be getting into position.

"They don't look like they're expecting trouble," Dall whispered. The young elf's voice trembled with excitement, and his hand shook as it clutched the slender steel sword that, today, he would use for the first time in anger.

Dall's face, like his brother's, was painted in the charcoal black stain favored by the tribe as war paint. Since this was his first battle, the younger elf's skin was marked by circles of black, instead of the winding, spiraled ram's horns that denoted the more experienced braves. Dall, like Kagonos, bore the insignia of an oak leaf design enclosing his left eye. This was their family sign, unrelated to any of the tribal symbols.

"Ogres never *look* alert," Kagonos replied, "but they react very quickly when trouble shows its face."

"I know," replied the younger elf, eager to demonstrate his readiness for this battle.

Kagonos sighed, wishing there were another way—futilely cursing the necessity that brought even the youngest males of the tribe into the battle. But there was no alternative. If they won this battle, the Elderwild could live in peace and flourish. If they lost, and the blue dragons remained free to terrorize Krynn, the end of the wild elves would be an inevitable and probably imminent development.

"Is Kyrill over there? Is he ready yet?"

"Patience, my brother. Kyrill will signal us when he's in position."

Kagonos allowed his eyes to drift upward, away from the snowswept island in its vast bowl of snow, until his gaze swept across the rock-fanged ridge on the opposite side of the frozen lake. Though the Pathfinder could see no sign of movement, he knew that Kyrill must by now be leading his detachment of warriors through those rocks. Moving invisibly among the snow-draped crags, the Elderwild across the mountain would be nearing their starting positions. Kagonos studied the small saddle, marked by a distinct pillar of rock, where Kyrill was to signal his readiness. He saw no sign of the elf yet, but

Kagonos forced himself to be patient. He knew that his brother wouldn't make him wait much longer.

The high, steep ridges encircled the lake almost completely—only the narrow notch broke the crest at one point, plunging into a canyon where the stream of the lake's outflow passed toward the plains. Now that waterway, like the lake itself, was frozen. Several ogres stood sentry duty in the foot of the gorge, diligently observed by Elderwild warriors who remained out of sight among the rocks above.

The snow on the rugged heights, on the other hand, showed no sign of drawing ogre curiosity. Many trees dotted the crater's slopes, and deep drifts of powder rendered the ground into a deceptively smooth incline. Hopefully, the snow would provide the means for a quick and startling attack by the elven braves. Certainly the soft powder made it difficult for the lumbering monsters to get around, but their carelessness still astounded Kagonos. Surely they were aware that the Elderwild could travel here?

Perhaps they were too busy worrying about Silvanos, he reflected. That must be it: why would they worry about a few hundred savage elves—elves who didn't wear armor of metal, who shunned horses and lances and the steel-coiled longbows of their city-dwelling kin—when faced with the threat of an entire, well-disciplined army marching along the fringe of the mountains? The wild elves would take grim satisfaction in proving them wrong.

Kagonos's eyes swept back to the camp, where the work on the wall had ceased altogether, though the barrier remained irregular and slipshod. Most of the ogres relaxed under the afternoon sun or bickered and gambled in small groups.

"There it is!" hissed Dall. The younger elf pointed across the basin to the opposite ridge, and Kagonos saw it, too: a glimmer of silver, as Kyrill reached the saddle on the opposite rim and flashed his blade in the sun.

Kagonos threw back his head, lips taut as he put the

spiraling horn to his mouth. He blew a harsh, strident blast that carried clearly to the ears of all the elves—yet was virtually inaudible to the ogres, who heard merely a fresh ripple of mountain wind.

To the hundreds of Elderwild warriors waiting among the trees, the Ram's Horn sounded a clarion call to battle. Garbed in fur cloaks, wearing skis, the elves turned their feet downhill and began to move.

Kagonos led the warriors attacking from the south. Here the trees were dense, and he cut back and forth between them, rapidly gaining speed. The snow had melted even in the shade, making the initial maneuvering slow and clumsy. Soon, however, he slashed downward, the wind burning his face and stinging tears from his eyes while his increased speed allowed him to turn smoothly, gracefully to avoid the trees.

Silent except for the hissing passage of their skis, the elves glided down from the highest forests. The Pathfinder could hear them behind, knew that his warriors used every ounce of their skill as the descending onslaught continued to gain speed.

Kagonos stole a glance across the valley and saw a rank of Elderwild come into view—Kyrill's northern attack swept downward precisely on time. The tree line was higher over there, but those elves had the shortest stretch of lake to cross before the ogre encampment.

The shriek of the eagle split the air, then resounded dozens of times over as the Elderwild of the northern rank raised their voices in the shrill war cry of their people. Kagonos held his breath—would the ogres react as he had hoped?

One of the brutish warriors roared an alarm, spotting Kyrill's elves sweeping downward. That small band of elves continued to shriek like furious birds of prey, crowing crude insults at their enemies or shouting valiant boasts of their own prowess. Ogres raced toward the sounds, quickly gathering at the north wall of their camp to await the attack.

Now, however, skiing warriors came into view to the south as Kagonos led his own shrieking party—much larger than Kyrill's forty braves—toward the base of the steep slope. On the open snow he crouched for speed and balance, dimly aware that he had never traveled so fast. In the corner of his eye he saw an Elderwild break a ski on a hidden obstruction—the wild elf went down in a tumble of snow and flailing limbs. Risking a quick look behind, the Pathfinder saw that his warrior lay motionless at the end of his fall.

Now the skiers raced onto the frozen surface of the lake, rasping across the crusted snow at high speed. A few ogres scrambled back to the unprotected walls on the south, but most of the brutes still stood ready to face Kyrill's onslaught. The rising bulk of the island blocked Kagonos's view of his brother's band, but he knew that the northern attack must already be sweeping around the sloping hill. Kagonos quietly repeated his command, hoping Kyrill remembered—come here to join us! Don't storm the wall alone!

His own momentum held all the way across the lake, propelling him halfway to the crest of the island's slope. As soon as Kagonos ceased moving, he kicked his feet free of the skis and sprinted up the hill, driving his moccasins into the crust of the snow with each bounding footstep. The eagle's shriek rang all around him, echoed by his own lips without accompanying thought.

The Elderwild Pathfinder bore two weapons: in his right hand the long-hafted axe with its steel blade, sharp as a razor, in his left a thrusting javelin with a head of sharpened flint. Both had served as ski poles during the descent, but now he shifted his grip, brandishing the axe upraised while he held the spear ready for jabbing. The Ram's Horn was as safe as he could make it, tied snugly against the small of his back.

Worry tightened a grip on his heart as he looked around —there was still no sign of Kyrill. Clearly the young brave led his warriors in a valiant attack on the north, continuing the diversion at the risk of their lives.

Unwilling to wait for Kagonos's braves, a lone ogre scrambled over the ramshackle wall, raising a club and bellowing in fury. The monster charged forward, heavy boots immediately breaking through the crust of the snow. Sunk to its thighs, the monster flailed madly at the charging Pathfinder.

Kagonos paused for a fraction of a second, allowing the club to whoosh harmlessly past his face. Then he stabbed with the spear, driving the tip into the shoulder of the monster's weapon arm. The ogre bellowed in pain, dropping its club and twisting away from the elf. Kagonos charged past, slashing a blow with his axe that elicited another groan of pain. Knowing other warriors would finish the monster, the chieftain sprinted onward, leaping up the piled boulders of the wall.

Atop the ring of rocks, Kagonos cried out with savage delight. He saw pandemonium in the ogre camp as the brutes ran toward the unprotected sections of their wall. Many Elderwild warriors scrambled over the granite rampart, adding their own triumphant cries to the din.

Only across the compound, where Kyrill's courageous band had indeed made the initial attack, did the enemy meet the onslaught with a firm defense. There ogres massed behind the wall, while several of the monsters lunged over the top, charging into the press of the attackers. None of the elves on that side had yet made it onto the wall.

Another ogre charged, roaring, toward Kagonos. With one leaping bound, the elf jumped from the top of the wall, landing lightly in the monster's path. Startled, the ogre skidded to a halt, but when it blocked the steel head of Kagonos's axe with a stout club, the Elderwild jabbed the monster's bulging gut with the javelin. Groaning, the ogre collapsed.

"To the Bluestone! Find the stone!" cried the Pathfinder as more and more of his warriors sprang from atop the wall. Dozens of clashes whirled around the camp as elves in ones, twos, and threes turned their weapons against the disjointed ogre resistance.

More bird-cries came from the right as cawing Elderwild surrounded a hamstrung ogre, stabbing the hapless creature with their weapons. Other monsters charged to their companion's rescue and the elves turned with shocking speed to meet the new attack—but not before one of them sliced the throat of the unfortunate brute who had spurred the rescuers.

Two ogres rushed at Kagonos, and he fell back, parrying the blows of a club and a huge, bronze-bladed sword. Abruptly the sword-wielder shrieked and twisted. In the gap of a second the chieftain saw Dall there, jerking back on the short-bladed sword he had stabbed into the monster's thigh.

It was a painful wound, but not crippling, Kagonos saw with dismay—obviously the young warrior had underestimated the monster's speed of response. Dall tripped and sprawled on his back, but when Kagonos leapt to his brother's aid, the club-bearing ogre smashed his weapon straight toward the Pathfinder's head.

Barely raising his axe in time, Kagonos blocked the attack, the force of the blow staggering him. Quickly recovering, he drove in hard and fast, underneath the ogre's clumsy backswing. The bloody tip of the javelin drove upward through the gristle of the monster's neck, slicing through its mouth and finally lodging in the hateful brain. Slain instantly, the ogre toppled backward, pulling the javelin from Kagonos's fingers as it fell.

"Look out!" cried the Pathfinder, leaping past the corpse. Dall rolled across the ground as the second ogre raised the huge bronze blade for another blow. Gashed deeply on his arm, the young warrior clawed for purchase on the slippery rocks as the wound spurted blood.

Kagonos swung, all the supple force of his long arm packed into one powerful blow. The gory axe head slashed through the air, toward the thick, muscle-bound neck—a blow that would cut through bone, slice the spine, kill with ultimate and undeniable authority.

But as he knew all this, Kagonos also understood that his kill would come too late.

Dall's eyes widened in terror and comprehension as the bronze blade plunged earthward. The barbed edges of the heavy weapon tore a cruel hole in his chest, and the weight of the metal did the rest.

Howling furiously, his voice more like a wildcat's snarl than an eagle's shriek, Kagonos chopped the head from the ogre's shoulders. The sounds emerging from the Elder-wild's mouth twisted and wailed in the air, a rising song of unspeakable grief, as the headless monster tumbled to the side.

His brother's eyes dimmed as Kagonos knelt at Dall's side. The younger elf stared desperately at the Pathfinder, and for a brief moment his gaze seemed to hold the wisdom, the serenity of countless ages. Then Dall relaxed, slumping backward, eyes half-closing. Knowing death, Kagonos gently reached out and closed his brother's eyes fully. Despite the gaping hole in his chest, the younger elf looked oddly peaceful, as if he'd grown tired and simply lain down for a few minutes.

Vaguely Kagonos remembered that battle still raged. He blinked and looked around, thankful that several warriors had held a pair of nearby ogres at bay during his brief moment of grief. Now the Pathfinder sprang to his feet, axe held high.

As if they sensed his grim purpose, the two ogres stepped backward, but too slowly. Kagonos leapt like a striking snake, his slender axe head lashing out to cut the throat of one ogre while the other was borne to ground by two leaping Elderwild, eager to avenge the death of their Pathfinder's brother.

"The Bluestone—it must be here!" shouted Kagonos, staring across the battle-scarred hilltop, trying again to divine a hiding place. The mound of boulders still seemed the most likely location, though the monsters made no particular attempt to defend that locale—at least, no greater effort than they made everywhere else. Yet Kagonos had to believe that the rocks mounded into a flat-topped cairn concealed the hiding place of the Bluestone.

Howls of wounded ogres mingled with the shrieks of attacking Elderwild. Those elves who suffered hurt, conversely, bore injury in stoic silence—indeed, many wounded elves limped in the rear of the attack, ruthlessly finishing off any ogre stragglers that had survived the first rush.

"Follow me!" Kagonos rushed forward, amid the chaos of the shattered camp. Many ogres—and nearly as many elves—lay bleeding and motionless across the expanse of rocks and snow. A band of the monsters still stood clustered at the north wall, though now it seemed as though the ogres sought to flee, no longer interested in defending their mountaintop retreat.

The potent gemstone was large, the elven Pathfinder knew, but it could possibly be concealed in an ogre belt-pouch or satchel. "None may escape!" cried Kagonos. "Surround them—cut them all down!"

Whooping in fury, the elves closed in. Ogres trampled each other in their haste to escape, darting this way and that in a futile effort to avoid the stone and metal weapons of the Elderwild warriors.

Kagonos reached the large cairn and quickly scrambled to the top. There, among the piled rocks, he saw the outlines of a shadowy niche. He began to kick stones free, sending the boulders tumbling down the pyramidal sides of the rock pile. A quick look across the hilltop showed him that Kyrill's band still massed at the wall, blocking the ogres who so desperately tried to flee.

Then rocks shifted beneath his feet, and Kagonos tumbled backward as a huge, yellow-tusked ogre burst upward from a suddenly revealed cave mouth. Spittle flew from the monster's roaring jowls, and in its burly paw it clutched a huge, hook-bladed sword. The weapon flashed, and a lightning blow whistled toward the Pathfinder's head.

# Chapter 4
# The Guardian and the Stone

Kagonos jumped back, feeling the swish of air as the mighty weapon slashed past his torso. The blade clanged against a rock, bouncing back in a lightning-fast parry—even before the wild elf could raise his axe for an attack. The huge ogre lunged forward to block the cave entrance, and the Elderwild had no choice but to fall back another step, though his eyes probed beyond the brute's shoulder, looking for some telltale gleam of blue. For now Kagonos saw only blackness, though he got an impression of shadowy alcoves and twisting passages. Certainly there was more to this shelter than first met his eye—but he wouldn't be able to explore it unless he disposed of the menacing ogre.

The monster roared, fetid breath washing over the elf as Kagonos ducked into a fighting crouch. His axe, normally such a potent and deadly weapon, seemed a frail counter to the ogre's crushing blade—one solid parry, he knew, and the wooden haft would splinter like kindling.

The ogre's face twisted into a mask of hatred, bloodshot eyes glittering wickedly as it sensed the elf's weakness. The brute took another step forward, pushing rocks out of the way with its shoulders as it forced its way through the narrow cave mouth. A grotesque tongue licked across the ogre's sagging lips, while its twin, yellowed tusks gleamed with drool.

Kagonos retreated again, forced backward by a slashing blow. The monster sensed an advantage and lunged outward, shaking dust from its shoulders and roaring in fury and anticipated triumph. The sword slashed again, and the Pathfinder used his axe in a parry—fortunately the steel head deflected the great bronzed blade, the shaft holding firm.

This time the ogre overreached and the elf hacked a return stroke, carving a bloody gouge in the monster's shoulder. Howling furiously, the beast whipped around with a savage backswing. Kagonos ducked, knowing that the blow had enough force to hack his head from his shoulders. Springing upright again the elf chopped with the spiked reverse side of his axe head, driving the sharp steel tip into the ogre's knee and drawing a shrill bellow of pain and outrage.

Shaking free of the enclosing boulders, the ogre climbed out of the narrow cave entrance, stabbing its sword at the dodging, dancing elf. Kagonos chopped, bashing away the thrusts of the off-balance ogre, while the beast limped on the weakened knee, fury undiminished.

Once on the open ground of the hilltop, the ogre stood tall, seizing the hilt of the sword in both its mighty hands. Kagonos realized with a jolt of surprise that he had never seen such a huge specimen of the brutal warriors—the monster loomed half again as high as the elf, and the

Elderwild's arms could not have come close to encircling the girth of the mighty beast's muscular shoulders.

The ogre, too, seemed to sense its immense physical advantage. The thick lips curled upward in a cruel sneer, while the yellow tusks gleamed—as if anticipating the taste of its victim's blood. With a grunting curse, the brute raised the sword over its head, bringing the weapon down in a crashing blow.

Feinting to the right and then rolling left, Kagonos saw a boulder crushed to gravel as the monstrous blade smashed into the ground to the elf's side. Bouncing to his feet, the Pathfinder slashed at the ogre's unprotected flank. The monster spun with surprising agility, however, and Kagonos tumbled backward, barely avoiding a wicked sideways slash as he landed heavily on the rocks.

The ogre lunged closer as Kagonos frantically rolled to the side again, then reversed his evasion as the monster once more chopped savagely in the direction of the elf's feint. The diversion gave him enough time to leap to his feet, though the wild elf was again forced to dance sideways to avoid the brute's pressing attack.

For a moment, the two combatants circled each other. Countless savage melees raged around the hilltop as individual ogres and elves remained locked in mortal combat, while the cries of wounded ogres and the clash of steel against bronze rang through the air. Kagonos knew that none of his tribesmen could come to his aid. The ogre sensed this and lunged eagerly after the light-footed elf.

Kagonos feinted left, this time following with a tip of his head to the right and then a full-fledged dive back to the left. The ogre was shrewd enough to anticipate the first fake, committing all of its force to a crushing blow against the rocks where it expected the elf to go.

The warrior's evasion was so successful that Kagonos bounced to his feet behind the monster's right shoulder. Sensing disaster, the ogre tried to spin, but it was no match for the wild elf's speed. Kagonos hacked with the blade of his axe, chopping into the monster's neck. With a groan, it stumbled to one knee, struggling to rise as blood spilled down its chest in a growing apron of gore.

The Pathfinder chopped again, reversing his weapon to drive the spike of his axe head into the base of the ogre's skull. The monster stiffened soundlessly, twisting away from the blow to sprawl, dead, on the rocks of the hilltop.

Kagonos didn't waste time looking around the perimeter, where he could hear that numerous individual battles still raged. Instead he all but dove through the mouth of the unconcealed cave, tripping on the loose rock in the entryway and then crouching in sudden caution. He realized belatedly that, had a second ogre been hiding in the shadowy interior, the sun-blinded elf would have been an easy kill.

The only sounds came to him from the desperate skirmish outside. Though the cave's interior was shrouded in shadow, Kagonos trusted the sensitivity of his ears in assuming that he was alone within the darkened interior. Besides, any lurking ogre would have been shrewd enough to attack him immediately, not giving him the time to adjust to the darkness.

Probing with his left hand and feeling cautiously along the floor with his feet, Kagonos worked his way along a shadowy passage. Elven eyesight is keen in the dark, and he quickly discerned additional details about his surroundings. Several small passages branched to either side, but all of these would have been a tight fit for even a slender ogre. The wild elf, assuming that the brutes would have spurned these tight squeezes in favor of the more spacious central corridor, continued to advance.

Heart pounding, Kagonos darted around a corner, seeing nothing but the continuance of the winding passage. Where was the Bluestone? He scarcely dared to breathe, so intent was he on the search—and so acutely conscious of the importance of the potent artifact.

Abruptly a flash of azure light caught his eye, and Kagonos knelt among the rubble within a narrow alcove. Desperately he clawed at the stones, pulling large rocks free with sharp tugs, excavating a steadily growing hole. The faint but noticeable illumination grew stronger, clearly blue. There was no doubt in his mind that he had found it: the thing that had made this attack necessary, and whose recovery would provide the means to win the Dragon War.

Grunting from the strain, he pulled a large boulder out of the way, and finally the treasure lay revealed. Kagonos paused, vaguely surprised—and disappointed. He had expected to find a magnificent jewel, smooth and bright, gleaming from a multitude of facets like the gems he had seen cut and polished by the jewelers among the House Elves.

Instead, he found himself looking at a stone of irregular shape, dirty and scuffed—an oblong rock that was nevertheless as large as his head. Though the azure illumination glowed from within the rock, the surface itself was dull, stained, and pockmarked. The Bluestone was a jagged, knobby stone that lacked the polish and glimmer of the carefully sculpted jewels used by elves and ogres for ornamentation. No jeweler had touched tool to this stone, and in places dirt and a crust of lichen tried to obscure its inner heart.

Yet in this they could not succeed, for the Bluestone pulsed with a light that would not be quenched. Carefully, reverently, Kagonos reached down and took the stone, surprised by its unnatural warmth. The hair on his scalp prickled upward as the stone's aura seemed to crackle in the air around him.

How many elves of his tribe had died that he might now hold this stone in his hands? He thought, with a bitter pang, of Dall, of his own inability to save his brother's life. It was a failure that would haunt him, he knew, for the rest of his years. Had it been worth the price—of Dall, and of all the other wild elves who would never descend, alive, from this bloodstained hilltop?

Countless ogres had died, too, in the fight. Would those monstrous warriors feel as though their lives had been wasted? The Elderwild shrugged away the question, telling himself that the thoughts of his enemies were of no concern to him. Still the wonder remained, tugging at his thoughts.

Cradling the precious artifact in his arms, Kagonos emerged from the narrow cave mouth.

Vaguely he heard the cries of battle still ringing around the camp and realized that the ogres had been prepared to flee and leave this precious artifact behind.

"Let them go," he said quietly, waving his hand dismissively toward the knot of terrified survivors. Scowling in perplexity, but not questioning their Pathfinder's command, the Elderwild warriors fell back. Like creatures of one mind, the ogres stampeded away from the cairn, scrambling over the crude wall and plunging through the deep snow.

Kagonos held the heavy gemstone, awestruck at its reputed power. Would they get it to Silvanos in time? He didn't know how the power of the stone was invoked, but he felt certain that the stone had to be nearby when the blue dragons arrived. If such an ambush could be arranged, the artifact would imprison the souls of the dragons within the stone—and the last wing of the Dark Queen's serpents would be vanquished. But it would take the rest of the day to march down from this mountain, and another day or more to reach the elven army on the plain.

Unless a faster means could be found.

Instinctively the elf raised his eyes to the sky. A speck appeared, soaring closer with powerful wing strokes, and with bittersweet satisfaction Kagonos saw that the transportation of the gem, at least, would be taken care of by an emissary of Silvanos.

The flying creature was a griffon, and the trailing golden hair of the rider clearly marked him as an elf. The great eagle wings spread into a soaring dive, while the beaked mouth of the griffon opened in a wide, shrieking cry. The animal's hindquarters, muscular and feline, covered with sleek brown fur, absorbed the shock of the landing as easily as a pouncing lion's. The griffon's forelegs, feathered and taloned like the limbs of a great eagle, came lightly to rest on the rocks. The creature pranced back and forth between these avian feet, allowing its powerful hind legs to absorb most of its weight.

Even before Kagonos saw the rider, he knew who it was. The wild elf struggled to swallow the hatred that had lingered from centuries before, though his emotions surged as strongly as if the enchanted arrow had pierced Darlantan's body only a week ago.

"Greetings, Quithas," Kagonos said stiffly. He did not bow.

The elven warrior, his golden hair flying in the breeze, his golden breastplate sparkling in the sun, dismounted and swept his eyes over the bloody hilltop. With loathing, the Pathfinder recognized the crossed claws of the griffon emblazoned on the gilded shield.

"Silvanos placed his army in considerable danger, based on the word of the dragon Darlantan. I hope that you have made the risk worthwhile."

"We did—if you can get him this gemstone before it's too late."

"You killed many ogres, I see—somewhat surprising, given your primitive weapons and tactics," Quithas remarked, as if he hadn't heard the wild elf.

"We regained the Bluestone—the gem that was lost by the House Elves. Now, take it to Silvanos before it is too late."

"The timing is good," Quithas allowed, reaching out and taking the gem. He barely looked at it before tucking it into a deep saddlebag. "The blue dragons winged into sight this morning, but that silver wyrm—Darlantan—went aloft to fight them. I should think he would be able to delay their attack until my return."

Abruptly the golden-haired elf spun around to face Kagonos. Face flushed, Quithas dropped his eyes to the silver axe, now cleaned, that swung at the wild elf's hip. The Pathfinder was strangely unsettled by the dramatic alteration in the House Elf's mood.

"I see that you taunt me with my axe. One day we will not be allies, Wild Elf. Then I shall kill you and take it back."

Without a backward glance the elven commander leapt again into the saddle of his proud flying steed. Sensing its master's tension, the griffon sprang upward, and the eagle wings quickly caught the wind and carried it aloft. Watching him shrink into the distance, Kagonos cursed Quithas for his arrogance, yet wished him all the speed in the world on his mission. Darlantan was powerful, but how long could he do battle with a host of blues, the immortal children of Takhisis?

"My Pathfinder . . ." The voice belonged to Felltree, the young chieftain of the Black Feather tribe. Kagonos knew that he had displayed a great deal of courage in the past. Now Felltree's voice was tight, his eyes wet with unshed tears.

Then, in a withering storm of despair, Kagonos knew why. The warrior bore a bleeding, lifeless form in his arms. The Pathfinder didn't need to look closely to recognize the body of his brother Kyrill.

# Chapter 5

# Council on the High Plains

More than two hundred of the tribe's braves had fallen during the battle. The slain Elderwild were buried collectively in a large cairn atop the hill, individual stones standing on end to mark each warrior. The surviving elves tumbled the dead ogres down the hill, then dragged them across the lake so that their rotting corpses wouldn't pollute the water with the coming of spring.

Afterward, Kagonos led the surviving warriors down the frozen stream, through the deep cut in the side of the mountain. The band of warriors moved quickly, in several long files, following the course of high, barren valleys until they reached the lower vale where the tribes had gathered. At the outskirts of the pastoral valley the

Pathfinder met several white-haired archers—braves too old to march to war, but who stood ready to guard their loved ones in the absence of the main body of Elderwild warriors. The older elves watched their tribemates' return, and tears streamed from their eyes as they saw the ragged gaps in the long columns.

Still, the survivors stood tall, marching proudly as the sentries fell into ranks behind them. They returned to the encampment, where hundreds of tents and huts had been erected along the shore of a deep lake. The warriors came to tell of a victory—but also with a toll that tonight would bring grief to many families.

Barcalla, Felltree, and the other chiefs went to their sections of the camp, while Kagonos sat alone before a small fire. Cries—hopeless, keening songs—began to rise from many of the lodges, as the names of the dead were tolled.

Kahanna, a young elfmaiden who had been sweetly, innocently in love with Dall, brought the Pathfinder cakes of corn and venison wrapped in crispy leaves, then hurried away as if she didn't want to intrude on his mourning. Kahanna had served Kagonos for many decades, tending to most of his household needs. Now he felt a sting of guilt—surely the young maid must grieve for the loss of her lover. Yet, because Kagonos was the Pathfinder, she bit her tongue and held back her own tears.

Dimly he heard the sounds of the shamans chanting, working the healing magic that might save a limb, or prevent a deep wound from festering. The worst of the wounded received the benefit of these merciful spells, and many lives were saved. But the tribal priests were too few, their powers too limited, to hold against the tide of suffering and death.

For the first time since the battle, he unlashed the Ram's Horn, raising the trumpet to his lips. For the hours of sunset and twilight he played a song of mourning. The notes carried clearly through the camps of the four tribes and rose through the forests into the mountain heights as well. In that music was comfort for all who grieved, and a measure of hope for those Elderwild who tumbled toward despair.

Finally the chiefs joined Kagonos at his fire, and they shared a silent pipe. Only after the last of the tobacco smoke had wafted into the wind did the Pathfinder look around the gathered elves. A part of him saw them as strangers, unknown to him. They needed him, he knew—but did he need them?

The answer to the unspoken question didn't matter. Kagonos must decide what to do now, and he knew this was a decision he could not make by himself.

Abruptly the Pathfinder remembered something that Darlantan had told him. He stood and turned his back to the fire, eyes seeking the eastern horizon. Then he raised a finger and pointed. The chiefs gasped collectively as a crimson orb climbed slowly into view, rising above the ridge and ascending into the darkening sky. Another moon, this one of brilliant, crystal white, followed the first. The third moon, the black one, was invisible when it came after—but the Pathfinder sensed its stark and ominous presence. And now he understood Darlantan's truth: even gods could be punished.

"The war is finished. The gods have banished their own kin, those who gave the dragongems to Silvanos. We see them entombed before us."

"The dragons—even the blues—have gone?" Barcalla asked hesitantly. "You know this from these moons?"

"Yes—but we must be certain. Tomorrow the tribes shall march from here."

"Where do we go?" asked Feldree.

"We shall march to the camp of Silvanos. There we will see what the future holds."

\* \* \* \* \*

From the top of a foothill ridge the wild elves could see the ogre army streaming toward the north—a ragged, panicked mob, leaving chariots, foodstuffs, and weapons strewn in its wake. The midday sky was clear, free of clouds—and of dragons. Along the southern horizon, four hours' march away, the army of the House Elves sprawled in a vast encampment across the plain.

Watching the flight of the ogre survivors, Kagonos finally knew that more than just the battle had been won. With dual victories, in the mountains and on the plains, the elves had prevailed over their enemies in the Dragon War.

Still, he felt a curious numbness as he led the Elderwild tribes toward the camp of Silvanos. From the crest the march took the rest of the afternoon, and with each step it seemed that the mass, the numbers of the House Elves, grew steadily larger. Cheers rang out as the wild elves approached, and the Pathfinder knew that their greeting would be warm.

But what lay behind that warmth?

It all depended on Silvanos, Kagonos knew. So much about the ruler of the House Elves was a great mystery to the Pathfinder, and it was not without trepidation that he took his warriors and their families among the much more numerous elves of the city-dwelling clans.

The House Elves had made their encampment on the heights overlooking the Vingaard River, within sight of the battlefield—but far enough away to avoid the stench of rotting ogre corpses. In the light of the setting sun Kagonos saw hundreds of vultures wheeling over the scene of carnage, while clusters of the birds already gathered on the ground, flocking like maggots around the multitude of gruesome remains.

The elven camp, conversely, was a riotous gathering of colored tents, crowded horse corrals, and brilliant banners trailing in the breeze. Many of these pennants blazed incredibly bright in the light of the setting sun, as if the flags themselves were living tongues of flame.

In the center of the gathering snapped the white crown pennant of House Silvanos, and Kagonos guided his column toward the patriarch's circle. Nearby waved the green-and-white birch branch that signaled the tents of the great Lord Balif and his attendants. The wild elf knew that it was Balif, even more than Quithas, who had planned and executed Silvanos's most stunning victories. Balif was the true war leader of the Silvanesti, a fact that Silvanos never failed to acknowledge. Now cheers and the sounds of a boisterous toast rose from that great captain's compound, and Kagonos guessed that Balif had played a part in yet another historic victory.

Nearby fluttered another banner, this one all too familiar to Kagonos—a golden field emblazoned with the crossed claws of Quithas's rampant steed. The Elderwild chieftain sensed with a sting of lingering hatred that the general of Silvanos's cavalry had not only survived the battle, but had showered himself with glory.

Now, as they welcomed the arrival of the Elderwild, the elves of Silvanos came forward with shouts and cheers, forming two broad columns to either side of Kagonos's march. The numbness in the chieftain's breast expanded into a sort of vague disbelief as he heard the cheers, felt the exultancy of victory surging over him, offered by the warriors who were of his race but not of his people.

Even in looking at Silvanos's troops, Kagonos could see the differences. The House Elves wore armor of silver, and all of them bore swords or daggers of keen steel. Their faces were unpainted, their boots firm and stout—at least by comparison to Elderwild moccasins—and their blond hair was bound carefully against their necks.

Most of the warriors, by now, had set their armor aside in favor of cloaks and tunics of bright silk and dyed cotton, while jewelry of silver and gold dangled or gleamed from wrists, necks, ears, and fingers. On many of the high-ranking elves, gems—diamonds, emeralds, rubies, garnets, and many others Kagonos didn't even recognize—sparkled in a brilliant affirmation of an individual's wealth, status, and power.

The elves of Kagonos's band, conversely, allowed their darker hair to flow freely across their shoulders, blowing in the wind with the same lack of constraint as the folk themselves cherished so deeply. The Elderwild were still painted in their swirling battle colors, with each tribe displaying the symbol that identified it—the antlers of the Whitetails, the curling wave of the Bluelake, or the hawk's beak sigil of the Black Feathers. Many wild elves displayed spirals of varying length, and while some of the warriors still showed the hollow circles of unblooded braves, these circles would be altered to spirals at the earliest opportunity. Of course, the paint would be washed off at the conclusion of the victory celebration, but during preparation for battle it served as a key indicator of an individual's station within the war party and the tribe. Now those symbols marked them as a proud and distinct people, obviously very different from the light-skinned House Elves.

The column of Elderwild marched steadily, warriors raising their heads and throwing back their shoulders as they walked among the ranks of their allies. Though every one of them had lost a brother, cousin, or friend in the fight, the survivors remained determined to present a proud and honorable face to their kinsmen from the city houses.

The cheers rose to a crescendo as Kagonos led his fighters among the tents of Silvanos's entourage. Before him crackled a huge fire, sending tendrils of flame dozens of feet into the night sky, and it was around this blaze that the leaders of the House Elves had gathered.

Despite his mental preparation, Kagonos was startled when, as he neared the fire, Silvanos himself came forward to greet him. As before during their occasional meetings, the Elderwild was struck by the youthfulness of the great leader and statesman. Since the first great council of the Sinthel-Elish, more than six hundred years ago, Silvanos had been the unquestioned leader of all the House Elf clans. He was, in some senses, the king of Silvanesti—but in every other sense he was very much more than a king.

Though his hair was as silver as spun wire, Silvanos's proud face was free of lines. His wide green eyes glowed with a depth of wisdom that never failed to unsettle the forest-dweller, and there was something about Silvanos's stature—removed from mere height or broad shoulders—that gave to the elven ruler an undeniable sense of destiny and power.

"Greetings, kinsman," declared the great leader. Silvanos halted and bowed deeply to Kagonos. The Elderwild returned the bow to the exact same depth.

"And to you, kinsman," the Pathfinder replied. "I see that your efforts were met with victory."

"And yours," Silvanos replied. "Quithas brought the Bluestone to the battlefield in the very blink of time that remained to us, before the blue dragons would have wreaked terrible havoc. Now the spirits of those serpents are entrapped in the stone, and it will be buried—as were the stones of the reds, greens, blacks, and white dragons before them."

"Then it was worth the cost of gaining it," Kagonos stated grimly.

"Before the battle, Darlantan told me of the stone's location, of the nature of your attack. Tales of your courage and triumph will be told through the ages."

The elven lore masters, Kagonos thought with surprising bitterness, will sing of your battle, of Quithas's flight. But they will have little to say about us.

Shaking his head, the Pathfinder fought off the resentment, the anger that had begun to seethe within him. Surely, after a victory like this, they could set aside their differences for a time. Then he thought of Dall, of Kyrill, and he was not so sure.

The esteemed ruler allowed his eyes to flicker across the column of Elderwild survivors, many of whom were bandaged or obviously wounded. "The cost to your tribe has been dear—I'm sorry for that."

"We all pay the prices we must," Kagonos replied, discomfited by his kinsman's sympathy. It was far easier for him to regard the House Elves as dangerous rivals than as friends. Now he could not relax from a sense of impending danger. However, decorum called for some sort of response.

"I am sure that many of your own tribe will not share the celebration of victory," he offered, with a stiff nod of his head.

"As you say, the price . . ." Silvanos was quiet, pensive for a moment. "But perhaps, kinsman, with today's victory further bloodshed can be banished to some point far in the distant future."

"There can be no greater reward—nor one more honestly earned," Kagonos agreed.

A file of warriors came toward them, led by a tiny, bareheaded elf whose unusually broad face was split by a great smile. He reached up to clap Silvanos on the shoulder in a surprisingly casual manner, and then turned to study Kagonos. The wild elf looked back stiffly, wondering if the short elf could actually be as friendly and guileless as his beaming expression indicated.

"You have not met my right hand, General Balif," Silvanos said, smiling without apparent discomfort at his lieutenant's bold friendliness.

"You and your warriors are a tribute to the elven peoples," Balif said, startling the Elderwild Pathfinder by reaching out and taking both of his hands. "Know that, in the new realms we open in the east, the forests will always be open to the wild elves."

"I thank you," Kagonos replied, liking Balif in spite of his un-elven lack of reserve. He turned back to Silvanos with a raised eyebrow. "What are these new realms?"

"Balif will take a number of the houses and settle the forest lands of the eastern shore. The ogres don't live there, and there are barely a few tribes of human savages in the woods. Balifor will become the second great nation of elves."

Another House Elf, this one dressed in a golden helm, stepped forward to the ruler's side. Kagonos recognized

Quithas, and the Elderwild's scalp bristled with instinctive antipathy.

Taller than the average elf by more than half a foot, his dark eyes glittering on each side of his hooked, hawklike nose, Quithas looked down at Kagonos.

Kagonos thought that the elven war leader looked darker and far more bitter than he had during their last meeting, which had occurred just two days before. Now Quithas fixed his gaze on the steel-headed war-axe at the wild elf's belt, then raised his gaze to stare into the Pathfinder's face.

"Dare you come here with my weapon?" he demanded.

"It is my trophy now—remember?" Kagonos retorted.

"So now you come to seek rewards for your contribution?" spat the general. "As if our sacrifices have not been enough, you seek the treasures of the House Elves?"

"The sacrifices have been made by all tribes," Silvanos interjected smoothly, ignoring the taut lines of anger suddenly etched into Kagonos's face. "General Quithas, perhaps you should see to the arrangements for the victory feast."

Now it was the city elf's face darkened by fury, but he dared not challenge his ruler. Quithas turned and stalked away, while Silvanos shook his head sadly. "His son was slain in the charge that broke Talonian's line—while Quithas himself was off retrieving the Bluestone. I fear . . ." The great ruler's voice trailed off, sad and pensive.

"Sacrifices have been made even by the gods," the patriarch noted abruptly. "Did you see the moons these last two nights?"

Kagonos nodded.

"Those are the remains of the three gods—those immortals who gave us the means to win this war."

"Why were they punished thus? Do the other gods favor evil?"

"I believe they regret that we mortals have gained the power of magic. Perhaps they should, though we shall endeavor to keep its use under control. But enough of that—suffice to say that the cost has been high to all."

Silvanos sighed, and for the first time Kagonos realized that the elven patriarch was actually subject to mortal failings. "It grieves me to see such divisions among our people, my friend," he told Kagonos. Though he did not want to hear the words, the Elderwild found it impossible to tear his attention away from the patriarch's charisma.

"We are all one folk, under the war paint and the golden cloaks," Silvanos continued. "I would like us to know that oneness through all aspects of our lives on Krynn."

"The hatreds of the House Elves will ever divide us," Kagonos suggested. "Those like Quithas, who cannot grasp the rightness of freedom."

"Do not confuse living in a city with slavery," Silvanos chided. "We, too, are free—in many ways freer than you of the woodland shall ever be." Kagonos thought there was a trace of genuine regret in the ruler's voice, though the Elderwild was truly mystified by Silvanos's concepts of freedom. How could any walled enclosure hope to offer the breathtaking and unfettered life that he knew in the forest?

"Tonight is not the night for such discussion," the Elderwild chief noted awkwardly. "We have won a victory—and must mourn our dead."

"Indeed. Death has touched us all. I grieve beside you over the loss of your brothers. They died as brave warriors, as elven heroes, and their courage will be a source of pride for many generations—in the cities as well as the forest."

Kagonos tried to suppress his astonishment—the only communication between the two armies had been the flight of Quithas, when he retrieved the stone. Certainly that dour elf had not carried word—had not even known—of the Pathfinder's personal tragedy.

"The grief you struggle so hard to conceal—it shows in your eyes, for one who knows what to look for," said the great patriarch gently. "I have seen that look many times today. My own nephew, Palthios, was killed leading a charge against the ogre flank; my brother's eyes were as haunted as yours. And General Quithas's loss was his *only* son, his only child. For a time I thought the darkness in his mind would consume him."

Numbly Kagonos nodded, wondering if Quithas might not yet yield to that ultimate despair. The Pathfinder was aware that some portion of himself was terribly racked by grief. Yet why was it, then, that he barely sensed the feeling?

"I invite you, as I have before, to come to the new land of Silvanesti with us," Silvanos declared earnestly. "There, amid the splendid valley of the Thon-Thalas River, we shall create the greatest city the elves have ever known, and we hope that your tribe shall stand at our side as we do so."

"We have no need of a new land, not now—not when the war is won, when all Ansalon beckons."

"But think of the might we could gather, centered in Silvanesti! All the elves together. Your people, too, as one of the great houses! We shall name you House Servitor, and your people will know lives of productivity and beauty!"

"That is no life for an Elderwild!" Kagonos's voice grew sharp with scorn. "House Servitor, you say—will you make us lackeys to your lords?"

"No—of course not. But tell me, Kagonos—why have you never accepted my invitations?" asked the great leader, ignoring the hostile tone of the Pathfinder. "Come, at least, to visit one of my palaces! Stay as my honored guest."

"It is impossible," Kagonos said with a firm shake of his head.

"But, why?"

"A vow—a pledge I made centuries ago." Kagonos recalled the scene as if it had been yesterday—the Grandfather Ram, suddenly become the dragon Darlantan, commanding his obedience and loyalty, compelling him to obey two rules. In obedience—and, fully in keeping with the Pathfinder's own wishes—he had never taken a wife, and he had never journeyed to a House Elf city.

Vaguely, he felt the patriarch's gaze on him, and when he looked at Silvanos he saw more, even greater, sadness. Instinctively, with a chill, he knew why.

"Darlantan?" asked the Elderwild. Suddenly the numbness was gone.

"He awaits you beside the river," Silvanos said. "He bade me speak to you first, before you went to him. You will find him there, where the twin cottonwood trunks cross."

The Elderwild squinted into the patriarch's face, certain that Silvanos knew more than he was telling—and equally certain that he would learn no more in this conversation.

# Chapter 6
# Passing of a Patriarch

Gripped by a dire sense of apprehension, Kagonos sprinted through the army of elves, drawing little more than curious glances—and an occasional curse if he came too near a fire, or startled some dozing sentry or grazing warhorse. Soon the darkness of the night surrounded him, but it was not the cool, still quietude of the mountains. Here in the plains the night air pressed against him, warm and stifling. The harsh grass was brittle underfoot, neither solid like the bedrock of a high ridge nor cushioning like the mossy loam of an alpine meadow.

The two trees indicated by Silvanos arched upward, silhouetted against the stars as they joined in a towering apex. Beyond them, glittering like pale crystal, rolled the waters of the eternal Vingaard, alternately silvered and red beneath the flickering reflections of the two visible moons. The great river was shallow here, the surface roiled by rapids across its breadth of perhaps three hundred paces. It had proven an effective backstop against the maneuvering of the ogre army.

And now, the elf saw with a sharp gasp of breath, the mud of the broad bank provided a soft resting place for a massive, terribly wounded figure.

Darlantan's great silver head rose from the mire, the luminous amber eyes blinking several times as Kagonos scrambled down the embankment and knelt beside his oldest friend.

"I am glad to see you alive, Pathfinder," said the dragon, Darlantan's voice a rasping shadow of its formerly powerful timbre.

"And you," Kagonos replied, trying to bite back the sadness that cloaked his words. "You fought the blue dragons, held them off—and lived."

"There is no need for deceit—I will not see the next sunrise," Darlantan demurred. "But that is of little consequence. My time is through, but because of our victory today there will be many families of elves and humans who will live out their lives in peace. That is a worthy knowledge to carry to one's death, I think."

"And I, too, Silver One. But I grieve that you, who have fought so valiantly, should not live to see that blossoming of peace."

"I have seen much in my time—though I did not see the two blue dragons come at me from below. That's when they rended my wing," the serpent declared with a wry chuckle that carried some of his usual resonance. "It was the fall—something more than a mile, I should think—that did the rest." The mild laughter faded into a coughing gurgle that left no doubt as to the severity of the wounds.

"Do not labor yourself with speech. Allow me to sit—to make vigil with you," Kagonos said.

"That would please me—but as yet I am not ready for silence. There is a thing I must say."

The Elderwild waited, squatting on his haunches, listening in desperation to Darlantan's labored breathing.

"Your people are strong, and proud, and beautiful." There was nothing weak about the dragon's voice now. As he spoke, his words struck to Kagonos's core. He knew Darlantan's words were more than an opinion, that they went beyond simple praise. The mighty dragon spoke a fundamental truth.

"More than all these things, you are wild—and that wildness lies at the center of your being. You must help your people remain wild, Kagonos Pathfinder—wild for all time."

For a long time the elf sat silently, formulating a reply. "I hear your words. Know that I desire for my people that we always remain free of the House Elves' fetters. But I fear that, as the centuries pass, the ways of the Silvanesti will draw more and more of my people from the forests—until there are none left to be wild."

"Your fears are real, but you—and you alone—can ensure that they do not come to pass. The horn will help to guide you—use it."

"But . . . how?"

"Let the music tell you that. Remember, too, that the second horn is safe, in the den of my wyrmlings. They will know its purpose and its importance. They know, and you should remember always, that the silver dragons and the wild elves will share a kinship, a bond that will last for all the ages of Krynn."

"Rest, now," urged the elf. "Save your strength, and you may well see the new dawn." In his heart he desperately wished he spoke the truth—but in his mind he recognized the lie.

"I shall have time . . . for rest," Darlantan murmured dreamily. "As do we all. One day even you, Kagonos, shall have to choose another Pathfinder, to pass along the horn of the Grandfather Ram. Elves are long-lived, but you shall not roam the forests forever!"

The massive silver body shifted, shrinking, and as the elf reached out he felt warm, coarse wool. He brushed his palm over a sturdy shoulder, his throat tightening in grief as he recognized the Grandfather Ram. Though Darlantan had appeared in many incarnations in the centuries Kagonos had known him, he had not seen the lordly ram since their first meeting. The white-maned head lowered, and Kagonesti thought he saw a shimmering of silver scales in the curling pelt—or was it merely his imagination? With a great exhalation, the ram dropped his chin to his shoulder and lay still.

"Dar—" Kagonos's throat choked the rest of the word. He blinked bitter tears, then grinned foolishly as Darlantan opened one bright, yellow eye. It gleamed at him with vast depths of wisdom.

"Your people . . . lead them. Find the path—and use the Ram's Horn to show them the way," whispered Darlantan. "Now, I go to rest. . . ."

This time, when Darlantan ceased speaking, Kagonos knew that his words were done forever. Sighing, yet possessed by a tingling sense of energy he had not known since before the battle, the wild elf rose to his feet—though his shoulders remained hunched in grief.

Now he had an important task. Kagonos found a sturdy, blunt-ended stick below the cottonwood tree, and used it to scratch a hole into the soft dirt. He knelt to pull the loose soil out of the hole with his cupped hands. The work was hard and grueling, yet the elf took a peculiar satisfaction from the blisters raised on his palms, the stiffening muscles that began to ache and complain each time he hoisted more dirt out of the hole. He felt that, in every way, this was the most honorable work he had done in a long time.

Finally the excavation was deep enough to protect Darlantan from scavengers and desecrators. As gently as possible the Pathfinder carried the ram to the grave, laid him with dignity along the soft mud in the bottom of the hole.

Murmuring a prayer for the creature's peaceful rest, the wild elf slowly, reverently, moved the dirt back into the hole. When he was finished, he washed himself in the river and spoke another prayer for the spirit of his friend. With a look at the sky, Kagonos had no trouble believing that Darlantan's light still burned brightly among the legion of twinkling stars.

Across the plain, huge victory fires blazed, spurting showers of sparks into the dark sky. Tinder, in the form of ogre supply carts, surplus spear shafts, and other debris, was cast onto the coals. Shouts and cheers arose around the fires—already the victory dances, with their attendant boasting and storytelling, had begun.

The Elderwild braves would figure prominently in the celebration, Kagonos knew. His people could brag as expansively as any other, and a wild elf warrior would not be shy about enhancing the drama and glory of his accomplishments. And in the recent battle those accomplishments had been truly legendary.

Still, the Pathfinder could find no enthusiasm for the celebration. If not for the need to tend his people's business, he would have started back to the mountains immediately. The solitude of the heights seemed likely to provide the only possible balm for his multitude of intangible wounds. He realized that all of central Ansalon was once again open to him, to all the wild elves. Yet what freedom was that when Dall, Kyrill, and Darlantan would not be there to share it with him?

Certainly the rest of the tribes would depend on him for leadership, for some sort of suggestion as to where lay the future of the Elderwild. Perhaps it was time for the multitude of small tribes to consider gathering again in larger clans. After all, the danger of the evil dragons was gone. He thought back to a long time ago, having difficulty remembering that the Dark Queen's wyrms had smashed the great councils that had been an annual feature of Elderwild life during the first centuries after Kagonos's birth. He remembered the time of Midsummer Starheight, when he had spoken to the Grandfather Ram. He had left the tribes, tired of their silly celebration—and had been given the Ram's Horn. Now the tribes would create a whole new series of such observances, based around the moons that appeared nightly.

Indeed, the idea of such communal celebrations tickled a favorable nerve—perhaps the idea had merit. If the tribes once again met in Highsummer council, if they talked with their brethren from across Ansalon, would not the wild elves grow stronger, develop the will to resist the encroachments of the followers of Silvanos? And they would all hear the song of the Ram's Horn and share in its wisdom and comfort.

The wild elf Pathfinder cast a last look at the grave of his comrade. The site, with its smooth, rounded dome of earth, seemed larger than was possible. Even in death Darlantan possessed a regal dignity, an awe-inspiring presence that seemed to cry out to any observer that this had once been a masterful being, lord of flatland, mountain, and sky.

Abruptly Kagonos froze, then slowly lowered himself into a flat crouch. He didn't know what had alarmed him—sound or smell, most likely, a sensory impression too light for conscious awareness. Nevertheless, he *knew* he was not alone. There was an intrusive presence nearby, someone who had arrived here with stealth and cunning. With that knowledge, Kagonos clearly understood something else, something important:

The hidden figure in the darkness was someone who intended him harm.

# Chapter 7

# An Accounting

Kagonos crouched soundlessly, responding by instinct to the sense of danger. He tried to absorb the subtle clues of the night, sniffing the air, trying to penetrate the shadows with his eyes.

Someone shared this dark riverbank with him—someone very close, someone dangerous. Kagonos was inclined to believe that it had been an odor, faintly borne by the night breeze, that first had triggered his subtle sense of alarm. He never questioned that his intuitive response had been a portent of real danger.

Silently the Elderwild crawled sideways along the riverbank, wriggling snakelike through the mud and grass. He strained to study the darkness, to break the veil of silence. His nostrils twitched, probing the wind, and then he knew: it was the scent of metal, tainted recently with blood.

The wind shifted, and the scent was gone, yet its passing gave Kagonos a better picture of his enemy's location. The threat lay along the bank, slightly downstream. Carefully, silently, the Elderwild worked his way along the mud flat bordering the great flowage, crawling against the direction of current until he felt safe from observation. He remained as low as a slithering animal when he climbed the bank and lay on the brittle grass of the plain. Against the horizon, the fires from the camp still surged, too far away to provide any illumination here.

Staying low, Kagonos crept along the bank, vision attuned to the darkness, nose twitching as he sought that faint, yet clearly definable, scent.

His elven eyes saw the threat first as a haze of warmth gathered between two juniper bushes. Creeping carefully closer, Kagonos discerned his quarry pressed to the ground, immobile, head raised to better see the grave site. Obviously, the lurker hadn't seen the wild elf make his way off to the side.

Kagonos observed the vague shape, gradually making out the cooler form of a longsword held ready in the fellow's hand. That blade was the source of the smell, he knew. The fact that it remained out of its scabbard seemed clear enough proof of this hidden figure's hostile intent.

Rising on his hands and gathering his legs beneath him, Kagonos prepared for the charge. His long-shafted weapon, the steel axe head gleaming coolly in the starlight, felt light and deadly in his right hand, while his left would launch the momentum of his charge. When the soft moccasins nestled into small depressions in the ground, the Elderwild waited a few heartbeats, ensuring that his quarry did not know he had been detected.

No sign of alarm disturbed the still watcher. The steel sword remained poised a few inches off the ground, the slender head—an *elven* head—fixed on the riverbank below.

With an explosion of speed Kagonos sprang, raising his axe and sprinting along the dry grass with no more noise than the rustle of the air around his body.

Yet that wind sound was enough. The other elf twisted on the ground, starlight reflecting with diamondlike glitters as that silver sword whipped toward the charging Elderwild. Kagonos pounced and swung, then cursed as the clang of metal rang loudly through the night—his target parried the blow with a lightning-fast twist of his blade.

The Elderwild tumbled away, hearing the *whoosh* of air as the deadly sword slashed past his ear. Bouncing to his feet, crouching for balance, Kagonos raised his axe and watched his quarry, ready to counter the swordsman's next move. As he probed the darkness to seek his enemy's intentions in his eyes, the tribal chieftain recognized the stealthy ambusher—without surprise.

"Quithas!" he spat. Though he had suspected this since his first tingling of alarm, the sight of his old enemy inflamed, and at the same time strangely gratified, Kagonos.

"Yes, Wild Elf. I have come to reclaim my axe—and to avenge myself for its theft."

"You lost it easily enough—against a naked, unarmed 'boy.' Do you remember?"

Kagonos watched the golden-haired general carefully. Quithas was taut, almost trembling with tension—but his hook-nosed face was twisted into an almost giddy grin. He leered at the Elderwild, his eyes glittering unnaturally, and cackled a laugh before he replied.

"I remember well. But I have killed many times since then," Quithas replied. "And with each death my skills have improved—and with each death I have brought myself one step closer to ultimate vengeance against *you!*"

"Why do you seek me now, when peace is here?" The Elderwild was disturbed far more by his opponent's unsteady demeanor than he would have been if Quithas had been grim and purposeful. Kagonos struggled to contain his own anger, understanding that careful alertness might be the only way to save his life. Forcefully he pressed aside an urge to throw himself wildly at the House Elf, swinging the axe in mad, furious swipes.

"There can be no peace for me, as long as *you* live!" Quithas declared. For a moment, his face became earnest, as if he really wanted the Pathfinder to understand his murderous intent. "There is more than vengeance in my mind, Kagonos. I shall kill you, but not *only* for revenge."

Kagonos ducked as the silver sword slashed forward. Skipping backward, the Elderwild parried a series of fast cuts, meeting each with the head of his long-hafted axe. He took great care to parry metal against metal, knowing that the keen longsword, if it met the wooden shaft, could possibly chop his weapon into two useless pieces. Deftly the wild elf backed away, watching his enemy expend energy on a series of futile slashes.

"What is this if not your revenge?" demanded Kagonos, falling back for a moment, trying to keep his enemy talking. He was surprisingly shaken by the House Elf's words.

Quithas barked a laugh. "Silvanos is speaking to the Elderwild. Under a banner of high honors, he has promised to lead them to his capital in the south, to fete them with gifts and treasure."

"They will not go!"

"Already they agree. Barcalla and Felltree have been dazzled by jeweled bracelets—the shamans are fighting over baubles," Quithas declared with a smirk. "I told the great ruler that I would seek you, persuade you of the wisdom of this course."

"He knew you would try to kill me!" Kagonos declared. The Pathfinder's rage expanded outward to include the elven patriarch in its embrace.

"Perhaps," Quithas noted with a shrug. "I don't think he really cared—he doesn't understand, as do I, that your people will be much more malleable without your disruptive presence."

"My people love the life in the forests—they will not turn their backs on it!"

"Silvanos can be very . . . persuasive. He has showered them with countless things they could never gain in their usual savage state."

This time Kagonos didn't hold back the fury. He exploded toward Quithas with a wicked slash of his axe. Drawing back before the griffontamer's parry, the wild elf reversed his swing, driving his opponent back toward the steeply dropping riverbank. One step from the edge, Quithas halted, defending against the attacks with skill that was the match of the Elderwild's. Finally Kagonos retreated, realizing that he would not yet find the fatal opening. Once more Quithas breathed heavily, drawing deep gasps through his open mouth even as he tried to grin triumphantly.

Within Kagonos's mind raged a storm of dissension and fear. Could it be as Quithas had boasted? Would the elves of his tribe turn their backs on the woodlands, choosing instead the "protection" of city walls? And what use would their polished cousins find for them— painted, unclothed, unschooled in matters of poetry and arts? As House Servitor? No! They must be wild!

He remembered Darlantan's commands—only Kagonos, the Pathfinder, could show his people the way.

Quithas moved so quickly that Kagonos barely saw the attack. One moment the swordsman leaned forward, gasping to regain his wind, and the next he burst into violence, silver blade lashing from the darkness like the tongue of a striking snake.

Again and again the axe bashed the sword aside, though the tip of Quithas's weapon gouged a stinging cut across Kagonos's chest. Now it was the wild elf who fell back, struggling to block each potentially fatal blow, striving to avoid the roots and branches that suddenly seemed to thrive on ground that had been smooth a few minutes earlier.

Then the House Elf stabbed with a lightning thrust that grazed the Elderwild's side as Kagonos twisted away. Grunting, Quithas twisted his weapon, carving deeply into his enemy's flesh. The Pathfinder gasped as cold steel ripped over his rib cage.

But this time Quithas overreached himself, though he realized the mistake immediately. Planting both feet, crouching, the swordsman jerked his blade back, flipping it upward to parry Kagonos's blow—which he expected from the left.

The Elderwild feinted with a drop of his shoulder, but at the same time he flipped the axe into his other hand. When Quithas raised his weapon to block the anticipated blow, the axe head swept inward from the opposite direction, striking the elf cleanly in the neck, slicing with cruel force, the blade coming free, emerging into the air above Quithas's opposite shoulder.

With a reflexive shiver, the House Elf's body flexed backward, the longsword flying harmlessly into the mud. When the corpse started to topple, Kagonos reached forward and grasped Quithas's head, seizing the locks of long blond hair. While the body flopped onto the ground, the head swung freely from the Elderwild's hand.

Instinctively Kagonos tipped back his head and raised the horn to the sky. He blew, and the braying wail carried across the plains, into the camp of the celebrating army, perhaps even to the distant stars themselves. He wondered if Darlantan heard—and took some comfort from the hope that he did.

Then Kagonos turned toward the House Elf camp. His fury pounded, and he held his grisly trophy up toward the sky. He would go there, carrying the head of Quithas Griffontamer, and present it to Silvanos himself!

Kagonos would speak to his people, would wrap them in his fury. They would fight if they had to, battling through the camp of the craven, villainous House Elves. He would show them the path with his rage, with his righteous condemnation of Silvanos. He would lead them to the wild places!

If they would come.

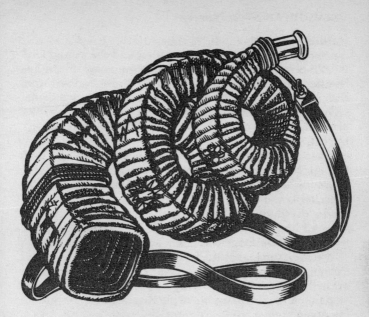

# Chapter 8
# Song of the Ram's Horn

As he trotted along, fueled by fury, the Pathfinder clutched the head of his enemy and grasped the smooth haft of his weapon. Only gradually did Kagonos begin to perceive the effect that his entrance to the camp—bearing the gruesome head—would have.

The grisly talisman would certainly have the power to inflame the elves of Silvanos, perhaps driving them to a frenzy of vengeance that would bring open warfare to the camp. The Elderwild, outnumbered and surrounded to begin with, would certainly lose—but Kagonos knew that none of his braves would shrink from such a battle. That was one way to bind them to their chieftain, and in a way that would allow them to fight in the finest traditions of warlike elven valor.

Of course, there were the women and the young and the old elves who were not warriors but would nonetheless be caught up in the slaughter. Or else, left without their braves, they would have no choice but to give themselves into the hands of the House Elves, joining the ranks of House Servitor. Was this not the fate that so many of them desired?

Yet even as the martial beat of his heart intensified, and though he did not waver in his direction or his pace, Kagonos began to question the wisdom of his tactics. Truly, he saw, if the tribes were to sunder themselves from the House Elves, they could only do so peaceably. The severed head of Silvanos's cavalry general would do nothing to make this easier.

With a scornful gesture, he threw the trophy to the side, cleaning his hands by wiping them on tufts of dry prairie grass. Then he resumed his rhythmic lope, stretching each step into a lengthy, gliding stride that betrayed his growing urgency.

He trotted into the camp, past armed pickets who stared at him in surprise, but made no effort to impede his progress. Kagonos continued jogging forward, ignoring the numerous elves who, apparently startled by the intensity of his gaze, scattered out of his way. The followers of Silvanos thronged to watch his arrival, gathering to form a long aisle for their leader. Steadily the wild elf continued along this impromptu passageway.

Before him the clans of the Elderwild chanted and sang, gathered around one of the largest of the victory fires. They cheered at the Pathfinder's approach, and Kagonos saw a look of relief on Barcalla's face as that normally reserved warrior raised his voice in a lusty shout. He saw others, including women and the children, and knew that he must not give way to the anger that once again began to burn within him.

Many of the wild elf warriors crowded forward as their chieftain approached. Still painted, their faces flushed with celebration, the braves held their weapons aloft and shouted a mixture of eagle and wolf cries. Kagonos smiled thinly as the cacophony washed over him. Finally the Pathfinder came to a halt, breathing easily as he stood before the great bonfire, letting the heat steam the sweat from his skin.

The crowd of House Elves parted, and Kagonos saw Silvanos, with Balif at his side, striding forward to greet him. If the great ruler was surprised to see the Elderwild alive, his face betrayed no hint—instead, the patriarch's expression seemed to be one of genuine pleasure.

"Welcome back, my kinsman," Silvanos said, before his eyes betrayed a hint of somberness. "Did you find Darlantan . . . in time?"

"Aye . . . though his time is now past."

"He is a hero unique among our allies—a dragon whom the elves will revere throughout all the coming ages."

Kagonos had his doubts about that, but he was touched by Silvanos's apparent sincerity. If Darlantan's name was not remembered by elves two thousand years hence, the Elderwild knew that it would not be because Silvanos himself had forgotten.

"Did Quithas find you?" Balif asked. Kagonos looked for a hint of conspiracy in the diminutive elf's eyes, but he could see only honest curiosity.

"He went to tell you of our council," Silvanos explained, looking over the Elderwild's shoulder as if he expected Quithas to come trotting through the camp behind.

"He found me, but he said little about your council," Kagonos replied, watching as Silvanos frowned in puzzlement. "In truth, he came to kill me—and he nearly succeeded."

"What?" The patriarch was clearly shocked. He squinted at the Elderwild in real suspicion. "I do not think you would lie to me, but I find this difficult to believe."

"*I* believe," Balif said softly. "There was a look in

Quithas's eyes when he departed. I thought it was grief over his son—but it seems, now, that it may have been murderous rage." He hung his head, then looked at Kagonos with genuine regret. "I'm sorry that I didn't send another to find you. We are all glad that he failed. You can trust that he will be punished."

Kagonos surprised them by laughing. "Your general will not be returning—not for punishment or for any other purpose," he declared, as the great leader stepped forward.

Silvanos sighed, his eyes narrowing. "Tell me everything that happened."

"General Quithas is dead. I killed him. His body lies beside the river. His head is somewhere on the plain."

Growls of outrage rose from the assembled elves. Silvanos grew suddenly pale, his voice tightening.

"I would have questioned him myself, seen justice served. Or has your own hatred made you mad? Do you commit murder, then come here to boast about it?"

"I defended myself—*Quithas* came to commit murder. He failed."

"But . . . *why?*" The elven statesman seemed honestly puzzled.

"It is proof of the divisions between your clan and mine—we are *two* peoples, not one!"

"No! There is time to change!" Silvanos disputed. "I have been speaking to your people of the benefits of life in Silvanesti, of the wonders of our cities. We shall set aside great preserves for you, where game dwells in plenty! You will have no need of your paint and your feathers—you will wear silks and perfume instead!"

"That war paint is our pride—it shows who we are," Kagonos retorted sharply.

"Your pride can rise to even greater heights with us! You elves, and your great clan—House Servitor—will become as mighty as any of—"

"House Servitor will lead us only to a future of humiliation and slavery! I will not take that road, nor will I lead my people there!" cried Kagonos.

Silvanos's face darkened. "Will you command them to follow you?" he demanded harshly, knowing the Pathfinder had no power to give orders his people must obey.

"I make no commands—but I will lead them from this camp. Those who do not follow me, you are welcome to take back to your cities."

He remembered more of Darlantan's words—he *must* show them the way! Then he knew, and he lifted the spiraled horn from its place at his side.

Kagonos raised the curling trumpet to his lips, eyes blazing as he stared across the upturned faces of his fellow Elderwild. The painted warriors shifted nervously, each dropping his own gaze rather than meet the burning rage of his Pathfinder.

The wild elf lowered the spiral instrument just a few inches, snapping his words in curt, decisive tones.

"I cannot—I *will* not—command you to follow me. Any Elderwild who chooses to accompany my esteemed kinsman to Silvanesti should do so! Fly to the walls of the cities—fly to the tables and windows and floors that will, for the rest of your days, form the borders of your lives!"

Again he raised the horn, and as he touched it to his mouth music began to flow. Notes rolled into the night with deep and resonant force, a sound unlike any horn ever carved. Indeed, it was more like the mournful, somber chant of some monstrously great creature.

A creature like a dragon.

He blew into the instrument, and the powerful sound rose, sweeping across the stunned Elderwild, washing over the suddenly stilled masses of the House Elves. Could they hear the music? Certainly they saw its effects. Silvanos himself, eyes wide with wonder, took a step forward and reached out a hand, as if he would hold and caress each blissfully poignant note.

The Pathfinder played without conscious thought. He did not know what he did to make the sound—rather, it was a kind of instinct that guided his music. The heart of the song, it seemed, came from the horn itself.

Kagonos paused for breath, and the notes died away, but again he touched his lips to the mouthpiece. As he blew, the sound rose anew, gaining pulse and tempo, surging upward from its minor key into a challenging chorus of a climbing scale. But still it did not make the sound of a horn.

The song had no words, but it painted vivid pictures in the minds of the Elderwild. The first notes created a background of trees, leafy branches rustling in the wind. A waterfall trilled somewhere, with music so cool that spray seemed to wash the skin of all the gathered wild elves.

Then the melody became a wind, singing of open skies, towering mountains, yawning chasms . . . and always new and wondrous trails. It was a song of endless pathfinding, tracks everywhere, choices unfettered by thoughts of borders, or houses, or cities.

Kagonos felt his skin tingling, as if the music had wrapped him into a cocoon of gentle, yet prickly, warmth. His war paint embraced him, emphasizing that heat like warm wax trickling, not uncomfortably, over his skin. With a sense of wonder, Kagonos lowered the horn and realized that the notes continued to expand, sweeping across the gathering and embracing all the elves—but most especially the Elderwild—in its subtle clasp.

The Pathfinder clasped the instrument as if it were his only anchor in a storm, and as the growing force of sound swept him up, he felt as though strong winds buffeted him, rendering his footing unsteady, his vision cloudy.

Why couldn't he see? Everywhere he turned Kagonos looked upon a bright aura, like a film of fire that sheathed him, screening him from observation. Only gradually did he realize that the flames were real, and that they were surging outward from *him*—from his skin.

Wonderingly, the Elderwild looked at his bare chest, seeing yellow flames licking higher, bright and lively as they sputtered from him. Still he felt no pain, but instead his sense of wonder seemed to grow. Gradually he understood that it was not his entire skin that burned, but only the places where war paint had been smeared upon his body.

As the flames died, his body rippled under dark, permanent tattoos—stains that perfectly matched the hawk and oak leaf pattern of Kagonos's war paint. His paint had become a part of himself, indelibly burned into his skin—marks that would, for the rest of his life, show him as a member of a different people than the House Elves of Silvanesti.

The flames, Kagonos saw, did not die away entirely. Instead they swirled outward, rising up in a great archway before the awestruck faces of his people.

Barcalla was the first to advance. The warrior held his head high and stepped through the archway. Immediately the paint on his dusky skin flared into life, the flames singing upward like the highest notes of the Ram's Horn. Before these flickering fires died away, others of the tribe had advanced, in pairs and trios, then as a great column, proudly walking through the fire, letting the tongues of flame embrace them.

By the time Barcalla's halo of fire died away, Kagonos saw that the warrior, too, had been permanently marked— also in the pattern of his war paint. As each wild elf advanced, the gentle cocoon of brightness took him, kissed his flesh, and left him with the marks of distinction that would forever show the rest of Krynn that this was a tribe of forest-dwellers, wild elves who shunned the enclosures of their kin. Kagonos knew that even if more nations of House Elves were formed, if Balif made his kingdom in the east, if other clans moved to the Kharolis forests in the west, the wild elves would remain wild and free.

The elves of Silvanesti stood aside to let Kagonos past. He looked once at Silvanos, and he did not see an enemy— but neither did he see a being who had any further meaning for him or for his tribes.

"Go, then, Kagonos," the patriarch said quietly, and even now the force of his words arrested the Elderwild chieftain, compelled him to listen. "You have made your choice, and I must trust your wisdom. You lead your elves as one clan, now—a greater tribe than they have been before. No longer are you the Elderwild.

"In our songs, you shall be called the Kagonesti—and you shall ever be known as our kin."

The name was good, thought the Pathfinder, though its portent sent a slight shiver of apprehension along his spine. If he had not fully grasped the momentous nature of his decision, Silvanos's words made it quite clear.

Raising his head high, shouldering his weapon and letting the horn fall comfortably back to its position at his side, Kagonos felt a pleasant warmth from the tattoos that now marked his skin. The Pathfinder turned his face to the north, where the tree-lined foothills rose gently against the night sky.

And Kagonos led his people back to the forest, and to the woodlands beyond.

# PART II

## Ashtaway

*1019 PC (Third Dragon War)*
*Woodlands of Central Ansalon*

# Chapter 9

# Forest of Fire and Fury

The dappled pattern of black ink on bronze skin rippled through shadowy underbrush. A very keen observer might have discerned the shape there, but only after careful scrutiny— and in the time needed for such an inspection, the stealthy figure would have vanished, moving smoothly on.

Ashtaway glided through the roughly wooded country-side. The Kagonesti looked upward, hazel eyes sweeping the surrounding crests of tree-lined bluffs and broken, rocky cliffs of granite bracketing these lower valleys. His skin, patterned in dark tattoos, blended with the under-brush even as he moved—he was an intrinsic part of the forest. Yet, for three days he'd been on the hunting trail, and it galled him now that he was still empty-handed as his steps carried him back toward the village.

Indeed, these valleys showed not the slightest promise of game—no tracks in the muddy trails, no padded bower where a doe and her fawn had bedded down, or even any sign of grazing on the supple spring shoots that began to green the woodlands. Shaking his head in frustration, Ash decided to climb, hoping that the increased vistas along the rippling bluff line might give him the chance to see something, *anything*, that could offer a suggestion as to the whereabouts of game.

The rocky heights, in the foothills of the Khalkist Mountains, had been the hunting grounds of his tribe since the time, more than two thousand years ago, when the Kagonesti had split from the elves of Silvanesti in the Great Sundering. The warriors of the wild elves tattooed their skin in black ink, as a sign of their permanent removal from the ranks of their civilized kinfolk. Ash bore a vivid imprint of an oak leaf enclosing his left eye, while on his chest was emblazoned the wide-winged silhouette of a hawk. He carried several weapons, including the strung bow in his hands, with a quiver of arrows and a long-hafted axe slung over his shoulder.

The wild elf reached the mouth of a scree-filled ravine and turned upward, grasping branches with his wiry hands, unerringly finding with his moccasins those rocks set securely in the midst of the loose gravel. Breathing easily, his longbow and quiver resting on his back, Ashtaway glided toward the ridge with the same fluidity of movement that had carried him through the forest shadows.

A wall of rock, perhaps thirty feet high, blocked the crest of the gully, and here the elf's progress slowed—but only slightly. Without halting, Ash started up the sheer face, picking his route as he went, seizing with his fingertips narrow holds, or perching his toes on outcrops barely a fraction of an inch wide.

Reaching the top, he jogged through open woodland, but despite the increasing vistas surrounding him, he saw no indication of any game worth his sleek, steel-tipped arrows. He passed through a sun-speckled meadow, barren of deer or wild pig. No elk grazed in the marshy saddle between two crests, nor did he hear or see sign of the great flocks of geese that were overdue to make their springtime migration.

Ashtaway thought of Hammana and felt a sense of urgency—he would love to impress the elfwoman with fresh game, to see her eyes shining at him during the celebration feast, while Iydaway Pathfinder played his horn in joyous affirmation of the kill. Tomorrow, perhaps, she would consent to walk with him beside the lake—nothing in his knowledge could be finer than a few uninterrupted hours with the serene, gentle elfmaid.

Though she was younger than Ashtaway by several decades, Hammana had already proven herself to be a healer of great skill, renowned among the four tribes. Her father, Wallaki, was the shaman of the Bluelake Kagonesti, and he had shared his priestly arts with his daughter. Hammana had used her natural talents to ease the sufferings of countless wild elves afflicted by illness or injury. Despite her youth, Hammana possessed maturity and inherent grace in measures far beyond the other women of the tribe, and Ashtaway's heart pounded faster at the memory of her soft, impeccable beauty.

Hammana would indeed be proud if he brought back a fine deer or pig, but would it be more than pride that gave her eyes that alluring light? In the corner of his mind, Ashtaway hoped that another emotion dwelled there as well—and, slowly, over the course of the past few seasons, he had begun to believe that it did. The feeling between them was a truth pressing with increasing force toward the surface of his and, hopefully, her awareness.

Abruptly a shiver of alarm rippled along Ashtaway's shoulders and, for the first time in several hours, he froze.

He looked around at the steep bluffs rising in leonine majesty from the surrounding woods. Something unseen, but powerfully menacing, threatened to trouble this pastoral place. He thought he knew the nature of the threat, and he was afraid.

Ashtaway stood atop the summit of one of the granite precipices, concealed by lush undergrowth and a few large boulders. The place was familiar to him—indeed, the bluff's top had been one of his favorite overlooks since he had discovered it as an exploring youth nearly a hundred years before. Crouching, he examined the valley floor, and almost immediately the glint of sunlight on metal caught his eye. Expressionless, he watched a file of armored riders pass along a lowland trail, moving at an easy walk. Often the treetops concealed the horsemen from his view, but occasionally they passed through a meadow or along the shore of a rock-bordered lake, giving him ample time to study the interlopers.

He was very interested in the humans, but as he remembered his ripple of apprehension, he knew that they were not the thing whose presence had troubled the forest itself. Yet they still deserved watching. All of them were cloaked in metal clothes and rode steeds much larger than the other horses the Kagonesti had seen. The man in the lead carried a pennant bearing an insignia of a red rose.

Ashtaway suspected that the men might be Knights of Solamnia. During his rare contacts with the Qualinesti elves he had heard of the knights, surprised that even the haughty, long-lived House Elves spoke of them in not uncomplimentary terms. Tales of knightly discipline, bravery, and loyalty to an altruistic cause had impressed the young Kagonesti warrior, and now, given the chance to watch the mounted, armored warriors, he seized the opportunity with all of his woodland skill.

Of course, humans in general were the traditional enemies of his tribe. Ash had never personally battled them, but for centuries the older warriors had ceaselessly driven men from the forests whenever they had tried to build their towns or to cut their long, unnatural roadways. Many men had fallen to Kagonesti arrows, and not a few braves had felt the cut of human steel.

Ashtaway wondered about the purpose of this company's presence here. The column numbered several dozen men, each mounted on a horse the size of a bull elk. Clad all in metal, except for visors raised to expose their faces, the knights must have been stiflingly hot. Yet none seemed to object, and indeed they held to that steady walk.

Again the Kagonesti felt a shiver of alarm, and now the menace had a familiar taste. Ashtaway looked skyward, let his eyes sweep toward the distant horizons.

The first tangible sign of approaching danger was the shade flickering across the ground, dappling the sun-speckled waters of a lake where only a cloud shadow should be. Looking farther upward, Ashtaway saw a pair of young red dragons—not as massive as the hugest of their kind, but still terrifying. The wyrms searched for the knights, he sensed, and flew on a course that would take them directly over their enemies.

Ashtaway watched, fascinated, as the dragons swept closer. The knights had not observed the danger yet—a fact that could only test their mettle to the limit when battle was ultimately, suddenly, joined. As the file of riders entered a broad, wet clearing, the Kagonesti knew that the mutual discovery would soon occur.

The wild elf had experienced the awesome horror of dragons, and he fully expected the knights, when they saw the serpents, to tumble from their saddles and writhe in abject horror as the crimson wyrms dove toward them.

Of course, if the targets of the ambush had been Kagonesti, Ashtaway would have warned them of the danger. He could have shouted, tumbled free some large rocks, or flashed the silver-steel head of his axe in the sun.

Since these riders were only humans, however, the elven warrior decided to watch and see what would happen. True to his suspicions, the dragons and the knights quickly spotted each other. With a shrill screech of triumph, the two reds tucked their wings, racing downward in an awe-inspiring dive.

Expectantly Ashtaway turned back to the knights, wondering if they would topple from their horses in panic or simply flee headlong through the woods. Surprisingly, they did neither. The first of the men shouted a harsh command, audible even to the distant elf—indeed, Ash was impressed by the lack of hysteria in the sound.

Immediately the knights scattered, individual riders racing toward the scant shelter of nearby trees. As the lead dragon, still shrieking, plunged landward, silver shafts sparkled in the sun. Some of the knights had crossbows, and they released their missiles with uncanny speed and accuracy. The serpent's cries took on a shrill, painful note, and the broad wings shifted to carry it off to the side. Flying awkwardly, the wyrm settled with a splash of muddy water to the marshy ground in the center of the clearing.

The second dragon, even larger than its mate, cried out in fury. Huge jaws gaped, and Ashtaway felt a tremor of sympathy as he saw a great fireball explode outward, sweeping around several tree trunks—and consuming the horses and riders who sought shelter there.

Ignoring the death screams of their comrades, a dozen knights charged with leveled lances toward the dragon as the serpent landed in an open space between several trees. The wyrm reached out, crushing one rider with its great claws, then incinerating several more with another firestorm. At the same time, sharp steel lance heads pierced the dragon's flanks, drawing a shrill cry of pain. The serpent struggled to break free, flapping its wings frantically as the knights plunged their long-shafted weapons deeper.

Several men drew huge swords and chopped into the monster's flesh as it flailed. Ash was deeply impressed by the force behind these blows. He watched the steel weapons plunge deep through the monster's scaly skin. Blood flowed from the wounds as the dragon bellowed, pivoting through the midst of nearly a score of dead knights.

The dragon tried to raise its head, jaws gaping, for another explosive breath, but now the surviving knights drove in, chopping and hacking at the exposed neck. One man in particular, bearing a two-handed sword with a golden hilt, threw all caution to the wind as he stood before the writhing wyrm. With a mighty, shuddering stab, he thrust the weapon through the red-scaled breast, all the way into the serpent's corrupt, seething heart. The beast reared and then, serpentine body shivering with tremors, collapsed forward in one dying lunge. The monster's death shriek turned to a gurgle as it convulsed and died, fully burying the courageous knight beneath the crimson bulk of its body.

The first dragon, during the death fight of its companion, struggled through the sticky muck, flapping and clawing desperately. Many arrows, which to Ashtaway looked like tiny darts in the distance, glittered from its right wing. Apparently the knights had been trained to concentrate their shots, and to good effect—obviously the beast had been too badly injured to fly. The Kagonesti reflected, grimly impressed, that crippling one wing of a flying creature was every bit as effective as injuring them both.

But the crimson monster could still breathe, and when its companion fell, fatally pierced, the survivor erupted with a screech of pure hatred. Fire exploded once, twice, and again from those widespread jaws, incinerating the remaining knights even as the humans turned to meet the new threat. Even in the face of certain death, the men remained steadfast—not one threw down his weapon or turned in a useless attempt at flight.

Ashtaway continued to watch, awestruck, as the wounded dragon crawled away from the bloody battle. Dragging its useless wing in the dirt, it disappeared into the forest. The Kagonesti warrior remained immobile and silent for several minutes after the last scarlet scales on the serpent's tail had vanished into the shadows.

Finally he moved, though he didn't take the trail back to the village. Avoiding the scene of the battle, Ash worked his way along the high crests. All the while, the moves of the combat replayed in his head like the steps of an elaborate dance. The battle offered by the knights had been the greatest act of courage he had ever witnessed. Furthermore, the fact that the heroes had been humans now forced him to reexamine a number of previously held beliefs and assumptions—obviously, short lives did not equate to a craven existence.

A sound reached his ears and sent a jolt of alertness through Ashtaway's body—a tingling sense of delight that took him completely by surprise. The noise was repeated, and the wild elf recognized the distant blaring of a horn, its music impossibly sweet, delightful.

He was reminded of the three-spiraled Ram's Horn that his uncle, Iydaway Pathfinder, played on important or ceremonial occasions. The sound of this distant music was similar, yet even more grand—fuller of body, more resonant in tone. And despite its distance, something told the elf that this horn played a song for him, and for him alone.

Even as he wondered about the sound, he began to run, not consciously aware that he had been summoned.

# Chapter 10

# Lectral

Ashtaway ran tirelessly, coasting down from his lofty vantage, sprinting along flowered meadows and down shaded forest trails. Like a deer he flew over shallow streams, darting around thickets, speeding dizzily when the undergrowth thinned. He raced for hours, unaware of time or distance, knowing only a joyous sense of anticipation.

Finally his footsteps faltered. The wild elf's forest senses suddenly signaled an alarm. He slowed to a trot along a narrow deer trail, then stopped altogether, listening.

Other footsteps thudded quietly through the woods, but not silently, like the running of a Kagonesti brave. Crouching, Ash melted into the brush beside the path. Someone else came along the same trail—and ran with a great deal of grace and speed, to judge from the sounds.

Abruptly she came into sight around a bend, and when he recognized Hammana, Ashtaway's heart trilled with delight. The elfwoman's slender body was garbed in a gown of soft doeskin, her black hair braided into a single, lush plait that usually lay over her shoulder—though now it trailed behind, flying from the speed of her run. Her beaded moccasins glided lightly, making little sound—for the Kagonesti women were nearly as adept in stealth and woodcraft as were the men.

She was a healer, not a warrior, and she did not have the warrior's constant alertness. Her bright, hazel eyes were downcast, her face wrinkled in concentration as she raced closer to Ashtaway.

When she was still a dozen paces away, he stepped into the trail and called her name, wanting very much not to frighten her. She gasped slightly and pressed her fingers to her mouth as she suddenly stopped, but Ash thrilled to the realization that she concealed a sudden, secret smile. She was not displeased to see him!

"Greetings, Warrior Ashtaway," she said formally. Then she frowned. "Did you hear it as well?"

"The horn? I am on my way to find its source."

"I heard it calling, and I had to do the same. But what do you think it is?"

Hammana came closer, and Ash was once again struck by her beauty and serene grace. Since childhood she had possessed that sense of self-assurance he found so refreshing and impressive. Perhaps because she was blessed with her unusual skill, she lacked the self-effacing shyness that characterized so many young Kagonesti women. Often Ashtaway had watched her in the village, and sometimes had even gone into the woods to spy on her as she wove nets by the marshy edge of the Bluelake. The few times they had walked that shoreline together were experiences burned indelibly into the young warrior's memory.

Now fate had drawn them both to this compelling sound, and this fact excited and disturbed him. Surely that was a portent of destiny—that the two of them were meant to be together. Only as these thoughts filtered through his mind did he remember her question.

"It—it sounds like the Ram's Horn, or a bigger version of it," he suggested. "I've heard my uncle play it many times."

"I, too," she reminded him. "Though this did not sound like the signal of our Pathfinder."

They fell into step side by side, jogging along quickly—though not so fast that they couldn't converse. "Where were you when you heard it?" he asked.

"At the lake shore," she said. "There were fishers there, too, but none of them noticed the sound—I asked them."

"Only you . . . and me," he said, his tone serious, the significance of the fact not lost on either of them.

She started to ask something and then, as they came around another bend in the trail, halted with a gasp of breath.

Ashtaway protectively took another step before he, too, ceased moving. The woods opened into a wide clearing, with a cliff of black rock rising steeply beyond. He could only stare in awe at the creature that lay, coiled, in the center of the open space.

Silver scales rippled in the sun, though in many places the argent surface was broken by cruel cuts and ugly, bleeding gashes. One leathery wing, also silver, was half-spread onto the grass, while the other was twisted awkwardly at the great creature's side. The serpentine neck curled through a full circle, and the broad snout was turned to face them—though both silver eyelids remained close.

The dragon was big—larger than the two reds Ashtaway had seen before—but terribly rended by battle. At first the elf thought it was dead, until he noticed the slow, rhythmic pulsing of one wounded flank.

"Look!" Hammana whispered, her voice taut—but with excitement, not fear. "There, held in the forepaw."

Carefully Ashtaway stepped forward, looking down to

get a clear look at the object held by the dragon.

"It's the Ram's Horn!" he replied. "Or one very much like it."

"Yes—but it's not the tribe's horn. Look, it curls in the opposite direction . . . as if it came from the same ram, but from the other side of its head!"

They looked at each other, awestruck. The legend of the second Ram's Horn was a part of Kagonesti lore, familiar to them both. At the time Darlantan bestowed the powerful talisman upon Father Kagonesti, he had claimed that the second horn would be held by the silver dragons, a symbol of the bond between wild elf and those mighty serpents. Yet it had never been heard in the dozens of centuries since, so the Kagonesti had come to view the story as a mystical legend.

"The second Ram's Horn. The tales are *true*," Hammana breathed, taking Ash's hand as she stepped to his side. He welcomed the touch, feeling this as a moment of wonder, not danger. "Is it dead?"

"Not yet, thank you." The words rumbled from the great mouth, though the jaws barely moved. With a grunt of effort, the silver dragon lifted its huge head from the ground and blinked with a pair of luminous yellow eyes.

Hammana rushed forward, kneeling before the great head as Ashtaway stepped more deliberately behind. "You called us, and we have come! How can we help you?" she asked, gently placing her hands to either side of the mighty jaws.

"Who are you?" asked the Kagonesti warrior, squatting before the silver dragon's head.

"I am called Lectral among my people, and it would please me to be called that by you as well." The dragon dipped his head, formally polite. "And you are of the wild elves?"

"I'm Hammana, and this is Ashtaway, a mighty warrior!"

"A mighty warrior of the Kagonesti. I am indeed honored."

"My friend is overly kind," Ashtaway declared, shaking his head in embarrassment. "I have only recently spiraled my tatoos, and my prowess is far from legendary." In fact, while Ash had accompanied war parties against humans and House Elves, his only kills had occurred in a few fights against the scaly, lizardlike bakali—evil creatures that sometimes penetrated the Kagonesti woodlands and were slaughtered by the wild elves whenever they were encountered. While he had fought well, there were many other braves in the tribe who had earned higher battle honors.

"Perhaps not legendary yet, but you will be." The dragon said this with a shrug, as if it were a statement of fact, not conjecture. Ashtaway felt a shiver of apprehension tinged with profound wonder.

"Who hurt you?" the warrior asked protectively, as if he himself was ready to avenge the attack.

"Four red dragons fell upon me, just two days since. I killed two, but I'm afraid the other two got the best of the fight. They must have been in something of a hurry, though—they left me wounded, when they could have finished the job."

"Are you badly hurt? The cuts look deep," Hammana observed.

"It will be long before I fly again." The dragon wriggled his mangled right wing, but the leathery membrane barely twitched weakly. "And some of these bites, I fear, may begin to fester."

"Hammana is a healer of much skill," the warrior said hurriedly. He turned to the woman. "Can you help him?"

"I need mud, for poultices—and bring me strands from the inner bark of young pines. I saw some mushrooms beside the trail that I'll fetch, and I think I noticed the smell of lilyweal. I'll gather some of that as well."

Leaving the dragon, who seemed not the least bit concerned by his grievous wounds, the pair scoured the woods for a time, gathering the items Hammana needed. While he searched, Ash located a deep, dry cave in the base of the sheer obsidian cliff. He returned to Lectral, who was intrigued by this suggestion of shelter and limped after the warrior to the foot of the black stone wall.

"This will do quite nicely," the silver dragon admitted.

Hammana, bearing an armful of herbs, roots, and tubers, found them at the cave. Ash built a small fire—for roasting some of the herbs—while the woman began applying poultices of mud and leaves to the worst of the dragon's hurts.

"That feels much better," Lectral allowed, stretching his neck around to let her swab a wound in his shoulder. "Now, if only you had a deer, perhaps, or a wild pig?"

Ashtaway shook his head, shameful. "This has been a hard time for hunting. I had stalked for three days when I heard your horn, and had not even seen the spoor of game."

"It is the war," Lectral said with a shrug. "With dragons in the air, the forest creatures must resort to extreme caution—those who survive, that is."

"Aye. And the dragons fly closer than ever," Ash noted. He described the encounter he had witnessed, carefully relating every detail of the red dragon attack and the heroic defense of the knights. "You told me of battling four, killing two. Perhaps they were the survivors." Lectral listened in silence until the tale was fully told.

"This is both bad and good," the great silver serpent declared sagely when Ash had concluded.

"I understand the bad—but how can it be good as well?" wondered the Kagonesti.

"The sending of her scouts this far to the south is a sign that the Dark Queen grows desperate. For too long her armies have been held in bloody stalemate on the Plain of Solamnia, at the brink of the Kharolis Mountains, and perhaps she begins to fear that victory may yet elude her. She must strike at the forces of Paladine in Palanthas, and until she breaches that range she cannot bring her army to bear."

"I have heard of these mountains—but they are terribly far away, beyond the broad plain of Vingaard," Ash said skeptically. "What importance can those battles have to these southern forests?"

"There has come a warrior, a knight called Huma. It is said that through him the forces of Paladine may yet find a way to defeat Takhisis, and to reclaim the plains they call Solamnia. The Queen of Darkness must have heard these tales as well—and she is frightened. Since her armies are held at bay, she no doubt seeks another way to strike at the knights in Palanthas."

"But surely she will not find such a route through these southern forests? Only Silvanesti lies beyond."

"Perhaps it is not attack, but defense, that is now on her mind," Lectral suggested.

"Defense from what? We Kagonesti? Or does she fear that the arrogant House Elves of Silvanesti will take notice of her war and march forth to do battle?" The scorn in Ashtaway's voice clearly showed his own estimation of that likelihood.

"I doubt she fears the elves. Surely Takhisis knows that if she leaves them alone they will not interfere with her plans for the human realms. Still, as her armies and arms are depleted, she must take steps to guard her base of power and supply in Sanction."

"I have seen Sanction from the mountain heights. It is a smoky, miserable place—why must she guard it so carefully?"

The silver dragon was silent for several minutes, gathering his thoughts. Ash waited patiently until his companion once again spoke.

"For two reasons. Sanction holds the great forges where all of the dark army's steel is smelted, and is the place where weapons that carry the war forward are forged. Her losses have been heavy, and it is known that her slaves are driven hard to hammer new steel, to forge weapons to replace those broken and abandoned on the fields. Sanction is where all this labor occurs. Great mounds of coal are stored there, as well as fields of iron and nickel from which that steel is forged. If she were to lose Sanction, her armies would be left without the lifeline of their power—the materials that allow her to wage this war.

"And second, the city is the site of countless huge storage barns—the food that will keep her army in the field through the upcoming year. Were those to be destroyed, much of the evil strength would be dispersed by the need to forage."

"Cannot the knights attack the city and destroy these forges?" Ashtaway wondered.

"I am certain that they would like to, but the city is guarded by walls and armies against attack from the west. Any attacking force would have to penetrate many barriers in the face of much resistance. Though they might desire to do so, I doubt that even the bravest warriors could succeed."

"What does this have to do with dragons flying over the forest?"

"Just this, I suspect: As I stated, Sanction is secure against attack from the *west*. But as her situation grows more perilous, perhaps Takhisis worries about attack from some other quarter. True, Sanction is guarded by mountains to the north, east, and south, but the Dark Queen is fearful, and no doubt seeks to reassure herself that these avenues, too, are protected."

"This knight called Huma must be a great man," Ashtaway suggested, "for his presence to cause the Queen of Darkness such concern."

"I am told that he is," Lectral agreed. "And, no doubt, if there was any way through the mountains, the knights would make every effort to strike at Sanction. I suspect her fears on that score are groundless, but she will nevertheless make effort to patrol these forests, just to make sure."

"I wonder what it is that brought the knights into the woodland. The force was too small for a battle such as you describe. This is far from their domain, as well," the elven warrior mused.

Lectral shrugged a great shoulder. "Humans think that all Krynn is their domain—but who can guess why they ride where they will?"

"My fellow warriors have slain many humans. When they fight us, they seem crude and vicious, not at all courageous. Though I admit that these knights were different—"

"Isn't this enough talk of war?" Hammana interrupted. She looked at Ashtaway pointedly. "Can you find some food?"

"Perhaps you might look along the valley below here, just to the north of my cave," Lectral suggested. "I caught the scent of deer only yesterday. It may be that you will find food for your village—and, perhaps, a haunch that you could spare for your silver friend."

"I go there immediately," Ash declared, rising to his feet with dignity. "And if I meet with fortune, know that I will soon return."

"Splendid," Lectral said, pleasantly blinking his large yellow eyes, allowing Hammana to massage a blend of herbs into a raw patch between his nostrils. "I shall take a nap while you hunt, and dream of awakening to the smell of venison."

With a deep, reverent bow, Ashtaway stepped to the mouth of the cave. By the time he started down the trail, the crippled dragon had already drifted off to sleep. Hammana, however, looked after him—and in her eyes he saw the glow of pride . . . or something more.

# Chapter 11

# Smoke on the Bluelake

True to Lectral's word, Ash found deer in the marshy vale. The warrior stalked during a long, moonless night, bringing down two plump does with a single arrow apiece. In the dawnlit hours he left one whole carcass before the cave in repayment for Lectral's suggestion. Hammana announced that she would stay with the dragon for a few days, and Ash promised to carry word of her decision to her father, Wallaki.

Pledging to return soon, Ashtaway hoisted the other deer to his back and started toward the village. The gutted doe was heavy, but the weight felt good on the wild elf's shoulders—and even under the load he maintained a steady, loping jog along the forest floor. The village beside the Bluelake was close, barely a dozen miles away, and he looked forward to returning there by midafternoon. His arrival, he knew, would be greeted with great happiness among all the villagers—it had been many months since a Kagonesti warrior had returned to the village with such a prize.

Ashtaway's supple moccasins glided softly across the carpet of pine needles, moss, and soft loam. He drew his breaths in long, rhythmic inhalation—once for each four steps—and then exhaled in the same measured pattern. Sweat slicked his bronzed, tattooed skin, but the cool wind of his movement evaporated it quickly, bringing welcome relief from the oppressive summer heat.

He ran with trancelike concentration on his silent, measured progress, yet at the same time his mind remained alert to the forest all around. He listened for the cry of the hawk, or the cawing of angry crows—for any of the usual sounds of woodland life. As he drew nearer the Bluelake, with the morning's mist burned away by the climbing sun, he grew mildly concerned by the extent of the silence around him.

One possibility, he knew, was that the creatures sensed *him*, and in their fear they held close to their dens and nests. But Ashtaway knew a great deal about the sensory capabilities of his fellow forest-dwellers, and he felt fairly sure that most of them were not aware of his stealthy passage. After all, he ran facing into the little breeze there was, ensuring that his scent did not precede him. Too, his footsteps were as silent as a stalking cat's, such that even animals who might be cowering nearby would not hear him go past.

His conclusions did not cause him an overwhelming sense of concern, though they did serve to heighten his alertness. After all, the scarcity of game had not been the only effect of the war. Perhaps another flight of dragons had soared overhead during the night. If the creatures had flown over this stretch of forest, the lingering awe of their presence might be enough to hold the lesser creatures trembling in their nests for a day or more—even lesser creatures like elves or humans, Ashtaway reflected wryly.

The warrior was grateful that his village, though spacious and open on the ground, was screened from the sky by its verdant canopy of vallenwoods. The elves were careful to leave no sign of their presence along the shore, where the Bluelake sparkled at the foot of the steep bluff. Even alert dragons, flying slowly, would be unable to spot the Kagonesti community from the air.

Now, as he jogged beneath the fine weight of venison and diligently probed his surroundings with eyes, ears, and nose, another part of his mind reflected on the battle between the knights and the red dragons. It remained much on his mind, and not just because of the valor displayed by the doomed Knights of Solamnia. There was also the indication, by the presence of both the human and dragon combatants, that the scourge of war might be drawing nearer to the Kagonesti wilds than ever before.

He recalled Lectral's words about Sanction. That smoldering city, nestled in the valley between three rumbling volcanoes, had seemed to him a hellish place on the lone occasion when he had observed it. At that time Ashtaway had discovered a winding, narrow valley leading up to the saddle between two of the smoking mountains. The finding of paths had long been a skill of his people, and Ash had initially been pleased in his discovery, for the mountainous trail was apparently known to no other. His disappointment had been keen when he learned that it led to such a useless place.

The miles passed beneath his leather soles, half a dozen, then ten, and soon he knew that the village was near. His heart lightened, anticipating the joy that his burden would bring to his villagemates. His uncle Iydaway, Pathfinder of the tribe, had grown too old for the hunt himself—but Iyda would no doubt compose a song for the occasion, probably to play on the Ram's Horn around the feast fire tonight. Old Iydaway had been a great hunter and warrior in his prime, and now the venerable Pathfinder took great pride in the accomplishments of his elder nephew, even going so far as to give Ash his keen steel axe blade upon the young warrior's initiation to manhood.

Now, the Kagonesti hunter thought with a thrill of pleasure, his uncle would be very pleased—

Abruptly Ashtaway froze, his reveries interrupted by an acidic, reptilian smell. Bakali! The lizardlike humanoids served the Dark Queen with ruthless loyalty in her war, and twice before Ashtaway had fought—and slain—individual bakali who had wandered too far from their tribes. In each of those occasions he had been repelled by the characteristic stench now wafting through the woods before him.

Yet the scent reaching his nose was far more powerful than he had felt even when in the clasp of a bakali's slime-coated limbs. There must be a large number of the lizardmen—a war party—that even now could be encircling the Kagonesti village.

Ashtaway lowered the deer to the ground and shrugged his bow off his shoulder in one smooth, soundless gesture. Nocking an arrow, he resumed his advance as soundlessly as before. Still he moved with fluid grace, but the sinew of his muscle rippled through his skin, as taut as his bowstring. Even as he took each step with precise care, his eyes flashed constantly to the left and right. His nostrils twitched, desperately sampling the air for further information about the menace.

He moved along the gradually descending floor of a narrow valley, with two hilltops rolling irregularly to the left and right. Less than two miles ahead the valley emptied into a lush vallenwood grove along the shore of a pristine lake—the site of Ashtaway's village for the last century. Since the lingering stench was carried only by the air—there was no spoor of the bakali on the trail or underbrush—the Kagonesti suspected that the lizardmen had crept into the valley at some point ahead of him.

The tribe always kept a warrior on lookout in these hills, but they had never been menaced by attack here before, so the sentry duty tended to be casual. Still, if the elven warrior—whoever he might be on this day—happened to be alert, there was a good chance that the village could be warned.

Ashtaway tensed, instinctively drawing back the bow as another alarming scent came to him. His nostrils sampled the air, found the fresh smell of blood—*elven* blood.

In another dozen steps the wild elf made a gruesome discovery. Though the corpse's scalp had been torn away and the body horribly mutilated—by talon and fang, it looked like—he recognized his tribemate Warrican. The youngster had earned his first tattoos just the previous winter and took his duties as a warrior very seriously. Yet he had not been prepared for the stealth, the savagery, of the bakali.

And now there was none to warn the village of danger.

Running again, Ashtaway risked minimal noise as he raced along the winding trail. Still he probed the surroundings, wondering if the bakali might have left a sentry to watch their rear. At least Ash could hear no sounds of disturbance—and if the attack had begun, he would certainly have heard it from here.

The stink of the lizardmen grew stronger, and finally the Kagonesti warrior turned from the valley floor, gliding smoothly between the trees of the forested hillside, climbing toward the rounded crest. He darted from tree to tree, staying low, seeking those frequent vantages where curves in the hilltop gave him a look at the valley below.

The lake came into sight, immaculate, blue, sparkling like millions of gemstones in the sunlight. The lofty vallenwoods screened his view of the near shore, but then the featureless expanse of water swept away to a distant, tree-lined fringe.

Ash saw movement around the bases of the nearest trees. At the foot of the slope before him, scaly humanoid shapes slipped through the shadows under the leafy canopy. The lizardmen crept forward, intent on the lodges that stood, still unseen, within the grove. Greenish brown, the monsters blended well with the underbrush. They crept on all fours into an expanding arc around the Kagonesti settlement. The bakali bore crude weapons of stone and bronze, but each of the brutes was much larger than an elf, and was naturally armed with powerful, fang-studded jaws and nimble forepaws tipped with sharp, hooked talons.

Pressing forward, over the rim of the hill, Ashtaway suddenly came upon three bakali crouched in a dip on the descending slope. One of the lizardmen was bedecked in feathers and bore a stout staff topped with a crystal totem in the image of a grotesque beast. The wild elf guessed immediately that this was the chief. The two other lizardmen were garbed as typical warriors, belts of skin supporting loops for their weapons, decorated by one or two dangling osprey feathers. The two spearmen looked to each side while their leader examined the developing ambush below.

In the instant of discovery Ashtaway knelt and drew his bow to full tautness, aiming at the base of the bakali chieftain's neck. One of the bodyguards turned his snake-like face upward, spotted the elf, and hissed a warning— but not before the Kagonesti had released his missile.

The shaft flew straight, the steel arrowhead plunging through the gristly mane of the hulking lizardman, razor-edges cutting the creature's throat before it even knew that it had been shot. As his first target fell, Ashtaway drew another arrow. He shot one bodyguard through the heart, dispatching the second immediately afterward.

Only then did Ashtaway throw back his head and utter the alarm—the sharp, keening cry of the hunting eagle, repeated three times. Several voices rose from the village in answering cries: the warning had been received.

The bakali ambushers below whirled toward the hilltop, their attention drawn by the sudden sounds. Ashtaway stood there in full view, and when he had the attention of the lizardmen, he raised his arms over his head, shook his bow and arrows, and whooped jeeringly.

Many of the brutish reptiles charged the lone warrior, while others vanished into the vallenwood trunks, grunting and barking aggressively. Ashtaway heard screams from the village, but the sounds of clashing metal weapons were also audible and he knew that the Kagonesti had not been taken completely by surprise.

But now he was faced with immediate problems of his own. Ashtaway had a dozen arrows left, and twice that many lizardmen rushed toward him, leaping and springing over the ground with shocking speed. Catlike, racing on all fours, a few of the bakali scampered ahead of their fellows up the steep hillside.

Slowing his breathing to the rhythmic pace of perfect concentration, Ashtaway drew back another arrow and let fly, dropping the leading lizardman with a clean shot to the neck. He shot again and again, each missile claiming another one of the attackers—and by always killing the one closest to him, he gained the time to shoot until his feathered shafts were all expended.

Throwing down his bow—he would return to get it later if he was still alive—Ashtaway pulled the long-hafted axe from his belt and raised the gleaming, steel-headed weapon over his head. Though the shaft had been made by Ash himself, Iydaway had told him that the axe head was a venerable artifact. The Pathfinder claimed that the weapon had been in the tribe for generations—legends held that it was handed down from Father Kagonesti himself. Whatever the weapon's past, Ashtaway suspected that the keen steel blade was no stranger to bakali blood.

A lizardman rushed up the hillside, leaping over the bodies of the chieftain and bodyguards. The creature sprang at the elf, jaws gaping like a crocodile's. With a single downward swing of the axe, the Kagonesti split the monster's skull, using the creature's reckless momentum to amplify the force of the blow. Slain instantly, the beast fell atop the corpses of its comrades.

Ashtaway surprised the next bakali by rushing forward, swinging the axe in a dazzling array of slashes. The first two chops nicked the lizardman's arms, sending it skidding into retreat. With a nimble leap, the Kagonesti swung again, wielding the axe as if he assaulted an ancient vallenwood trunk.

But the pale white skin of a bakali's belly was no equal to that legendary hardwood. Ash's blade slashed halfway through the monster's torso, sending it tumbling backward in a writhing mass of gore. The following lizardmen slowed their pace, suddenly alarmed by this deadly elf.

The Kagonesti did not give the bakali time to consider a revised plan. He rushed first at one, crippling it with a downward slash of the axe, then followed up against another, driving it to the ground and then killing it.

More than a dozen of the lizardmen swarmed to the hilltop. Ash risked a quick glance into the grove—he still couldn't see any of the village, but several ominous wisps of smoke emerged from the upper levels of the leaves. All he could hope was that his desperate warning had given most of the villagers time to escape. He knew that every adult, male or female, who could wield a weapon would be covering the flight of the children and the infirm.

He could do nothing for his people by dying on this hilltop. Instead, he spun and raced along the crest of the twisting ridge, darting through the trees with the grace of a deer, flying like a bird over the far side of the slope, diving toward the denser woods at the bottom. He paused in the shadows of a fallen vallenwood, where a cluster of roots extended overhead like a miniature cave. Far behind, still near the top of the hill, he saw several lizardmen cautiously advancing. The creatures darted back and forth, checking behind every tree trunk. Ashtaway smiled grimly—obviously he had taught them great respect for his fighting prowess.

Moving with caution and utter stealth, he worked his way along the foot of the ridge, steering clear of the bakali who had fanned into a long line to pursue their search. The lizardmen at the downhill end of the rank came within a dozen paces of Ashtaway, never suspecting that the patch of darkness beside the base of a great fir tree was anything other than afternoon shadow.

The searchers safely past, Ash sprinted along the forest floor. The smell of smoke was strong in his nostrils. The picture of the sturdy lodges—leather-bound houses that each sheltered a wild elf family—ravaged by the invading bakali nearly blinded him with fury.

Then he was in the midst of the vallenwoods, the great trees rising like pillars from the soft, brush-free ground. Each trunk was larger around than a chieftain's lodge, the upper branches so dense and so far above that they filtered the bright sunlight into a kind of vague and perpetual twilight. Ashtaway ran like a ghost along pathways that yesterday had chuckled to the tread of children's feet but now festered under the lingering stench of bakali.

Even before he emerged into the encampment, the smoke began to sting his eyes, and when he burst from between the last vallenwoods he could not stifle the wail of despair that rose from his lips. The lodges, the huts, the drying-racks for hides and jerky, *everything* was in flames. Lizardmen ran to and fro, forked tongues flicking menacingly from their jaws.

Yet, as the creatures piled more and more of the tribe's possessions onto the bonfires, Ashtaway sensed a frustration, a bitter sense of failure in the monsters' demeanor. Heart pounding, the Kagonesti warrior looked around, realizing with a glimmer of hope that there were no *bodies*! The villagers, most of them at least, must have escaped.

At the moment of his realization, one of the bakali warriors spotted Ash and uttered a shrill warning bark. Immediately several reptilian warriors converged.

But this was the grove where Ashtaway had spent the greater portion of his life. He didn't need to look overhead as he thrust the axe haft through his belt and leapt, strong hands closing around the limb he remembered. Nimbly swinging upward, Ash rose to his feet on the sturdy bough, some ten feet above the ground. One of the lizard-men prodded upward with a spear, and Ashtaway reached down with lightning quickness, snatching the weapon away.

Standing again, he raised the shaft to his shoulder and threw it at its original wielder. The crude flint spearhead gouged a painful wound in the monster's side and sent the other bakali scrambling backward.

With another upward leap, Ashtaway seized a second branch, scampering along this one until he reached the deep shadows near the tree trunk. The lizardmen scrambled toward the bole of the mighty vallenwood, jabbing upward with their spears.

A few of the monsters leapt, grasped the lower branches with their clawed hands, then scrambled up toward the waiting elf. Ashtaway met the first of these with a slashing blow of his axe, chopping off a forepaw that reached too far upward. Another bakali tumbled backward, bleeding, and the rest of the monsters paused.

Ash cawed at them like a taunting crow, dancing rudely back and forth on the limb, just out of reach of the lizardmen's crude weapons. He watched the slitted yellow eyes narrow hatefully, saw the tongues flicking in and out of the scaly jaws as more of the monsters raced to the tree.

When a large crowd of the brutes had gathered, Ashtaway leapt upward again, pulling up to the next limb, then bounding still farther above. Soon dark shadows cloaked him as the branches pressed closer, and he knew he was fully masked from below. At the same time he heard the snapping of branches, and the muttered cursing of his enemies—obviously the mud-dwelling bakali had entered the foreign realm of the treetops in their search for the vexsome Kagonesti.

Balancing with easy grace, Ash stepped away from the thick tree trunk along a slender but sturdy limb. Pacing his steps carefully, he was able to move without causing the rustling sounds that accompanied each lizardman's presence. The branch began to sag as he neared the end, but from here he could see the stout limb of a neighboring tree, extending to within a dozen feet of his position.

Hurling himself into space, Ash felt the stinging passage of branches whipping across his skin. For a brief moment he flew between the trees, and then his hands unerringly seized the supple branches of the next vallenwood. As the limb bent downward, the Kagonesti swung into the concealment of enclosing branches. In a few seconds, he dashed all the way to the tree trunk, where, once again concealed by shadows, he stealthily worked his way upward.

Shouts and barks rose from the ground. Ash knew that his leap had been observed, but the lizardmen would have trouble catching him no matter which tree protected him, and sooner or later the elf would find an escape route concealed from below.

High in the sheltered boughs, Ashtaway threw himself flat on a broad limb—a branch that had been one of his favorite vantages since the village had been here. Crawling outward like a snake, keeping his body atop the thick branch, he remained invisible to the watchers below. The sturdy wood bent only slightly from his weight, and soon he emerged from the thicket to get a good view of the clearing on the lake shore.

The heavy cloak of leaves concealed any glimpse of the sky overhead. So dense was the foliage that the smoke had begun to collect underneath it, just as a smoldering cook fire obscured the ceiling of a lodge. The edge of the bluff dropped toward the lake beyond the far line of trees. The lone pathway to the water followed the floor of a narrow, steep-sided ravine descending from the edge of the village clearing. Two Kagonesti warriors lay, cruelly hacked, at the mouth of this ravine. Obviously they had been a rear guard, holding so that the rest of the villagers could escape.

Ashtaway saw no sign of the rest of his villagemates, which he took as good news. It seemed that most of the Kagonesti had escaped. His heart burned with hatred as he watched the lizardmen ransack and destroy the village. Yet everything, from houses to drying racks to the furs, pots, and spices that were the possessions of each family, was replaceable. It was the lives of his people for which he felt the most fear.

Peering into the grass choking the upper end of the ravine, Ashtaway saw a telltale bending of the long-bladed plants. Someone—several people, actually—concealed themselves there, where they, too, could watch the destruction of the village. Some of his fellow warriors, he suspected, had returned to spy on their enemies. The Kagonesti braves should be safe, since the minor waving of the reeds was not likely to attract the attention of the brutish bakali.

Then Ash's heart almost stopped beating as he saw a tall, proud figure stand among the long-bladed grass. He recognized the hawklike features, the feathered ceremonial cape of the Pathfinder—but why would Iydaway expose himself? Other Kagonesti—a half dozen young warriors—rose behind Iydaway. Resolutely, the small band of elves started from the ravine into the smoky clearing. They had not yet been observed by the plundering lizardmen, but Ash knew they would inevitably be seen—probably in a matter of seconds.

Ashtaway released his grip on the branch, rolled to the side, and plunged downward with dizzying speed. Shouts of triumph rose from below, bringing a grim smile to the falling elf. With precise timing he seized a lower limb, arresting his fall and swinging himself back into the concealment of the vallenwood greenery.

Again he raised his head and taunted his enemies with the cawing of a crow—the most insulting sound in the long list of Kagonesti malignery. As if they sensed his scorn, the bakali grew frantic, howling and snapping ferociously. Several of them threw spears into the tree. One of the weapons *thunked* into the bark near Ashtaway, and the elf quickly pulled it free, hurling it firmly toward the chest of its caster.

But now whoops and shrieks rose from across the clearing, and Ash knew that Iydaway's small band had been discovered. "Why?" he groaned aloud. Why did his uncle risk his life like this?

Dropping lower, Ash got a look at the courageous, futile charge—six Kagonesti warriors and an old man, brandishing a mixture of swords, axes, and spears, charging into a camp occupied by perhaps a hundred savage lizardmen. Howling madly, the elves attacked with such valor that, at first the bakali scrambled to get out of the path of these mad fighters.

Iydaway was not as quick as he had been three centuries before, but the Pathfinder still flew over the ground with grace and balance. The old elf feinted a charge directly across the camp, then turned and led his small party toward the smoldering wreckage of a large, ceremonial hut.

The bakali closed in, and two of the younger warriors halted, meeting the charging lizardmen with steel swords, holding them at bay while Iydaway and the other warriors raced toward the ruined hut. Reaching the smoldering wreckage, the venerable elf plunged into the hot coals, kicking his feet through the ashes on what had once been the floor of his home.

Ashtaway cried out in fury as he saw the pair of rear warriors fall, rended savagely beneath the talons and fangs of the bakali. Dropping to the ground in the midst of his enemies, Ash struck this way and that with his axe, carving painful wounds into several of the lizardmen before he again leapt upward and pulled himself to the minimal safety of a tree branch.

But now, at least, he had begun to guess at his uncle's motives. There was only one possession of the tribe that was truly irreplaceable, a treasure that would always be passed from generation to generation. It had been entrusted to Iydaway before Ash had been born, and often the young warrior had watched as his uncle made music or ritual with the celebrated artifact.

Now, the young warrior knew that Iydaway had gone to retrieve the Ram's Horn.

One of the Kagonesti protecting Iyda fell, pierced by a bakali spear, while the three who remained fought desperately to screen the elder. None of the lizardmen seemed willing to brave the heat of the coals in pursuit. They would wait for the old warrior to burn, or to emerge from the ruins into range of their weapons. One, then another of the warriors fell, cruelly slashed. Many more bakali had gathered in a ring around the base of Ash's tree, fully encircling even the vast sweep of the vallenwood's branches.

Ashtaway moved with the speed of thought, flying like an arrow from the limb, driving his head into a lizardman's back. The creature went down, its spine shattered, and the Kagonesti rolled away from the body, bouncing to his feet beyond the enclosing ring of bakali.

Racing toward the ruins of his uncle's lodge, Ash chopped down the only reptilian warrior who tried to stand in his path. He saw the last warrior of the Pathfinder's escort die, pierced by a stone-tipped spear. Iydaway, a blackened shape in his hand, abruptly threw his hatchet, dropping one of the lizardmen standing warily beyond the coals. Ash shrieked like a hunting hawk, racing at the other two, madly brandishing his bloodied axe. A crowd of howling lizardmen pursued the fleet Kagonesti.

The elder warrior snatched up his weapon and leapt into step beside his nephew, sprinting for the largest of the village vallenwoods. Ash didn't risk a glance backward, but as he slowed his pace to match Iydaway's he knew that the enraged bakali had begun to close the gap.

Their pounding feet carried them across the empty ceremonial circle at the center of the village. Since a mighty vallenwood stood beside this circle, steps had been pegged into the trunk and a platform of branches had been erected some twenty feet off the ground. It was one of the few Kagonesti sites that had not yet felt the scorching flames of plunder.

At the foot of the tree, Ash whirled, crouching with his axe upraised. He heard Iydaway scramble up the wooden steps as the young elf slashed his weapon through the air, so fast that the steel edge vanished in a blur. The bakali had learned to respect that razorlike surface. In one mass, the pursuing warriors skidded to a halt, the mob expanding to encircle the tree and try to rush at Ash from the flanks.

Ashtaway gave his uncle two heartbeats to get up the steps, knowing that a moment longer would give dozens of lizardmen time to overwhelm him. Springing upward and back, still slashing with his long-shafted axe, the warrior retreated up the steps. The wooden pegs were too narrow to support more than one foot at a time, but he held his balance long enough to reach the first of several handy branches.

A bakali leapt at the elf's foot, but tumbled back with a bloody gash in its forepaw. Others barked and howled at the rear of the mob before turning about and racing to a nearby lodge. Drawing partially burned sticks from the blaze, the lizardmen waved them through the air until yellow flames crackled and trails of smoke dwindled in the air. Bearing their makeshift torches, the creatures hastened back to the tree.

By this time Ash had joined his uncle on the ceremonial platform. Above them the bole of the tree rose into the limitless heights, challenging the clouds and leading through innumerable pathways into a dozen neighboring trees. Still clutching the blackened horn, Iydaway started upward. His nephew followed, waiting only long enough to cut the lashing of the platform and drop the heavy wooden structure onto the dozen or so bakali foolish enough to stand directly underneath.

# Chapter 12

# The Pathfinder

"Your warning gave us time to flee the village," Iydaway explained. "We made many of the lizardmen pay for their cruelty, but brave elves gave their lives in that cause."

"I found Warrican at his post, slain by surprise attack," Ashtaway said.

"Palqua and Thyll held at the mouth of the ravine for a long time. They gave the rest of the villagers time to reach the foot of the bluff and make their way along the shore."

The two Kagonesti padded silently along the forest floor, a mile from the ruined village. They made their way toward a grotto in the heart of the vallenwood forest. Years ago it had been selected as the tribe's gathering point in the event of disaster.

"And more died to regain the Ram's Horn," Ashtaway noted. "Is it so precious, Uncle, that six warriors should perish to save it?"

Iydaway sighed and shook his head. The spiraling tattoos on his cheeks and chin masked his grief, but Ash knew that the question had hurt the elder warrior, and with that knowledge came regret that he had asked it. But his uncle held up a hand as if to dissuade the younger elf's guilt. The leafy pattern inked onto Iyda's palm had a soothing effect on Ash, and again he breathed deeply as he awaited a reply.

"It is not, in truth, worth the sacrifice of a single life— at least, not that we can say with certainty," Iydaway declared, his voice rhythmic, almost songlike. "But in the same truth it may be worth the saving of a hundred lives, of the whole tribe. And then who knows? If I had known that those young braves would die—or that I would live—would my decision have been the same?"

Ash waited, knowing that this was not a question he could answer.

"In truth, I *had* to go and get the horn. As long as I live, it is not a thing I can abandon. Were you to throw it into the deepest sea, I should be compelled to dive in after it, drowning in the attempt to plunge the depths. Should you cast it into the fiery crater of one of the Lords of Doom, I must need pursue it, walking through fire as long as blood flowed in my veins. I am the Pathfinder, and such is my destiny and my fate—a destiny that I willingly bear."

Iydaway paused, shaking his head sadly. Ash was surprised to see tears in his eyes. When the old elf spoke, his voice had returned to its natural tone.

"To answer your question, if I had known that my protectors would perish in the attempt, I would have ordered them to remain behind."

"And perished by yourself," Ash confirmed.

"And the horn would still be lost to the tribe," agreed the elder.

Ashtaway took the sooty spiral and tried to wipe it

clean with his hands, succeeding only partially. Still, the shine of the smoothly curled horn seemed to gleam through the dirt, as bright as sunlight in the shadowed forest depths.

"Is it truly made from the horn of a great ram?" Ash asked skeptically. Though he had enjoyed the music of the horn at village ceremonies and knew that his uncle cherished it above any other object, the young warrior realized that he knew very little about the treasured item. At the same time, with a shiver of portent, he remembered that he had to tell the Pathfinder about Lectral.

Iydaway shrugged. "That is what Callista Pathfinder, my granduncle, told me, and his predecessor—the Pathfinder Barcalla—told him. The legend declares that, in the Age of Dreams, the Elderwild Kagonos carved it from the horn of the Grandfather Ram—the creature he met, as you know, among the highest peaks of the Khalkists."

"Uncle, I heard the second Ram's Horn." Iydaway's eyes widened, but he made no reply. With careful attention to detail, Ashtaway told the tale of his summons from Lectral, and the subsequent encounter with the wounded dragon. Iydaway nodded sagely, clearly unsurprised by the information—a fact which, in itself, surprised Ash a great deal.

"It is fitting that you were the one who heard," Iyda said, smiling gently.

"Myself—and Hammana," Ash noted.

"Yes, and Hammana. That part puzzles me."

"Her healing has been a great help to Lectral—some of his wounds might otherwise have killed him."

"Indeed." Iydaway walked in silence for a time. When he spoke, his question took Ashtaway by surprise. "Does it seem as though the mantle of Pathfinder is a burdensome thing, Nephew?"

"No—well, perhaps yes. It is an important task, I know. And no wild elf should find it difficult to stay away from the House Elf cities. But for a man to go through life without taking a wife . . . that, it seems, might be a lonely choice."

"The Pathfinders of the wild elves, from Father Kagonesti on, have been solitary elves, true. Perhaps, because of this, we have not felt that lack as much as another might."

"I know that they have been great leaders, Uncle, and a strong bond to unite all the tribes."

"Indeed, it was Father Kagonesti who gave birth to our freedom. Without our first Pathfinder, there would be no tribes today."

"And you, Uncle, have shown the tribes the way to survive the Dragon War. Finding the paths deep in the forests, seeking these glades where the trees shield us from the sky . . . we owe you much."

"Ah . . . but that is a sadness, that we must forever hide from the sky. At least we, at the Bluelake, have the best of the deep forest—for our shore gives us a glimpse of open waters and sky."

"When the war ends, then perhaps we'll seek the high valleys again, where the wild elves lived for hundreds of years," Ash mused. He himself had always loved the heights and had spent much of his youth exploring the mountains within a fifty-mile radius of the Bluelake. Yet, despite these sojourns, Ash was not by nature a solitary elf and always rejoiced when he returned to the company of his villagemates.

"It will be the task of the Pathfinder to lead us there," Iydaway agreed. "Though I have found the path may best be chosen through discussion among the people, perhaps spiced with a bit of persuasion by myself. In this, I am different from Callista or Barcalla. My predecessors—following the example of Father Kagonesti—would show the path and expect the tribe to follow. For me, it is better when we talk first, then move."

Ashtaway nodded thoughtfully, curious that his uncle chose to explain this philosophy to him.

The two Kagonesti continued in silence, remaining alert for pursuit. Once they heard the hoot of an owl and looked up to see a tattooed warrior waving them on. A few minutes later, they joined the rest of the tribe in the shadowed depths of the vallenwood grove. A pool of still water reflected the darkening sky, and Ash's heart broke at the sight of the many frightened faces peering out from behind the mighty trunks.

The elves would not risk many fires tonight, but they felt secure for the moment from bakali pursuit. A dozen warriors stood duty in the woods, posted in pairs and observing from the treetops fully a mile away from this secret grotto.

The rest of the tribe, save for the nine warriors who had fallen during the battle, now awaited the communal decision as to their next course of action.

Ashtaway quickly sought out Wallaki, Hammana's father. The old shaman, a respected figure in the tribe, had been given a straw mat underneath a lush vallenwood, where he would be as comfortable as possible. Resting a small gourd over a patch of glowing coals, Wallaki mixed some kind of medicinal brew with herbs and water. The shaman raised his darkly tattooed face hopefully as Ash approached, though his eyes seemed to search beyond the warrior's shoulder.

"I—I had hoped . . ." The shaman's voice choked, and Ash was grateful that he could ease his fears.

"Hammana is safe, not near the village," Ash said, explaining the summons that had drawn the two of them into the foothills. "Now she remains with Lectral, healing his wounds, which are many and deep."

"Hammana tends a silver dragon?" The shaman nodded without surprise, studying the strong-smelling brew that bubbled over his fire. "That is a wondrous thing for anyone, and the highest honor of all to a Kagonesti healer! But are you sure she is safe?"

"Safer than beside the Bluelake," Ash said wryly. "But, in truth, Lectral is a fine dragon, and grateful for her attentions. And though he cannot fly, he can certainly protect her from any other threats that might lurk in the woods."

"That is very well, then," Wallaki agreed, before turning back to his potion and beginning a mystical chant.

Ashtaway joined the warriors who gathered around the Pathfinder and his spiral Ram's Horn. Iydaway played the instrument slowly, mournfully, the music cushioning and echoing the grieving of the tribe for its lost warriors. He ceased playing long enough to recount the story of Ashtaway's attack, and other warriors—who had seen parts of the battle from distant treetops—chimed in with further praise. Ash sat tall and proud, deeply warmed by the praise of his comrades. Warrican's father recounted a list of the dead, and after each name, the warriors chanted a pledge, promising that the deaths would be avenged.

Finally the Pathfinder lowered his horn. The other braves waited expectantly until he spoke. "Our homes are destroyed, and the hated enemy camps in the ruins of our lodges. Some of us have died, but many more still live. Now we must decide what to do."

"Let us return to the lake shore during the night. We'll kill the lizardmen and reclaim our village!" spat a young warrior, Ampruss, whose father had been one of the first warriors to fall.

"Already the bakali have given me cause to grieve," argued Maggera, newly widowed mother of Ampruss. "Let us escape with those lives we have saved."

"Perhaps we can muster other tribes to aid our attack," suggested an older warrior. "The Whitetail village is but two days away, the Silvertrouts barely another day beyond. Shall we get them to help?"

"It would take too long," Ash suggested. "These bakali came to raid our village. I don't think they want to live there."

"We should attack quickly! The lake shore has been our home for a full century," stated Faltath, a veteran warrior and lifelong friend of Ashtaway. "Are we such cowards as to be driven away by a single attack?"

"It is not a matter of cowardice, but perhaps destiny," Iydaway demurred. All the other arguments ceased as the Kagonesti waited for the honored Pathfinder to continue.

"We know that war has blackened the northern plains

and extended far into the mountains and forest lands as well. The dragons of the Dark Queen fly ever farther, it seems, always seeking to extend the range of her deadly servants.

"Now we can go back to the village and kill many bakali," Iydaway continued, the firm resolve in his voice indicating that he, personally, would derive great satisfaction from this bloodletting. Then his tone took on a sadder, more wistful sound. "But I fear we may not be so lucky when the lizardmen come again. If Ashtaway had not been returning from his hunt, we would be weeping for many more of our people tonight."

"The bakali never came before! Why do you say that they will come again?" persisted Faltath, who had earlier counseled attack. He was a huge elf, nearly as big as a human, and had been Ashtaway's main rival in the arts of the hunt and battle during his early years. Though they had become different as they matured, Ash still admired Faltath's strength and his determination when faced with a course of action. The big warrior's face was obscured by spiraling whorls of black ink, so that his eyes flashed from the middle of an apparently spinning vortex. Now they glowed with anger, an accusation against any brave unwilling to join his proposed attack.

"Because that is the way of wars," Iydaway responded, "of all great wars, at least. And the war that plagues Ansalon now is such a war. This I know. It is a great monster whose reach has been sweeping ever closer, until today we were grazed by a single talon on the far fringes of its great body, well removed from its dark and bloody heart.

"Yet the talon has learned that it can reach us, and when next it strikes it will be with the full force of a paw, or a mighty leg. The next time perhaps the bakali will have time to surround us, or they may come with ogres, even dragons. Then the killing will fall upon us."

"Dragons do not care about the forest floor," argued Faltath, his fist clenching around the heavy hilt of his longsword.

"This is not true, not anymore," Ashtaway declared. He told of the battle between the twin red dragons and the armored knights. His wonder at the knightly courage choked his voice, and for the first time he profoundly regretted his silence, knowing that he should have warned the humans of the impending attack. Understanding that the other braves regarded the presence of the knights to be as great a threat as the red dragons, he tried to reach them with his eyes, to show them that, somehow, these humans were *different* from the land-stealing men who had been the lifelong enemies of the tribe.

As he spoke, his listeners remained silent. "Not only were human riders patrolling this part of the forest, but the dragons who flew overhead were also searching the ground. If they had spotted the village, it is foolish to think that they would not attack, simply because they haven't done so before."

"But the lizardmen must be taught a lesson, just as we would slay the humans if we found them near the village!" Faltath argued furiously. "We know that Ashtaway fought and killed many bakali, while the rest of us fled! How can we let them think we run with our women and children at the first sight of an enemy, not daring to exact revenge?"

"We cannot let them think this," Iydaway declared bluntly, momentarily silencing the belligerent warrior. Faltath eyed the Pathfinder carefully, waiting to hear his next suggestion.

"The lizardmen must be punished for their attack. But we, the Kagonesti of the Bluelake, must also find a new home. It is clear that the war will no longer leave us in peace—and it is equally clear that, though this is not our struggle, it has the power to sweep us into its grip and destroy us."

"How will the bakali be punished?" demanded Faltath, as if he had not heard the rest of the elder's pronouncement.

"We will make an attack, savage and unrelenting, that slays many and drives the rest from our village. They shall know it as a place of defeat and death—but even so, we shall no longer live there."

"But . . . where do we go?" asked Ampruss.

"We shall move south, past even the village of the Silvertrout, into the heart of the woodlands between the two great mountain ranges of the world. There we shall find a new lake, and there we will make our new home."

"It is decided, then," said Faltath bluntly. "We march to the south, but not until we have slain many, many bakali."

"Indeed," Iydaway said. "And that is enough talking for me. I shall leave it to you warriors to plan the attack."

## Chapter 13

# Vengeful Arrows

Ashtaway looked to his right, across the space between the lofty vallenwood trees. Faltath, his tattooed face locked in a grimace of fury, signaled that he was ready. With a look to the left, Ash saw Balkas, a young archer with a patient and deadly eye. The bowman had an arrow drawn back to his cheek, and Ashtaway knew that his tribemate already had a bakali in his sights.

"The braves are almost ready," Ash whispered to Iydaway, knowing that the warriors on the flanks were still moving into position.

The Pathfinder nodded. "Soon," he replied, his words as soft as the night breeze.

Ash deeply regretted his uncle's presence in the tree,

with the battle so imminent. The Pathfinder had been a mighty warrior in his day, but Ashtaway would have been much happier if the old elf had consented to wait with the other elders, safe in the forest grotto, until the attack was over. He knew better than to argue with the stubborn Pathfinder, however—all he could do was resolve to keep an eye out for him as much as possible.

The ruined village sprawled below them. Lodges and huts still smoldered, but no trace of their wooden frameworks jutted from the soft ash. The central circle, beside the greatest vallenwood, was strewn with rubble and debris. In the fullness of the predawn dark, the shapeless bundles that were sleeping bakali lay haphazardly about the village, exhausted from their battle and its subsequent revelry. The lizardmen were not totally careless. They had posted several guards around the periphery of their captured glade, but these sentries had been no match for Kagonesti stealth. Now, each of those guards was dead, throat slit by an elven warrior.

More Kagonesti, about four dozen in all, still climbed into the trees that were out of sight to either side. Though elven eyes were keen in the darkness, even the Kagonesti could not see all the way across the darkened camp, so it was hard to know how many of these had taken up their positions.

Ashtaway knew that the bakali would have discovered the ravine to the lake shore. He had suggested that a small force try to block that escape route, but Iydaway and Faltath had both vetoed that idea, pointing out—justifiably— that the warriors in that party would have little chance of surviving the battle. The tribe would attack from the woods and hope to kill as many of the enemy as they could before the rest made their escape.

Faltath hooted softly, like a contented owl, but the sound carried obvious urgency to Ash's ears. The Kagonesti were tightly wound, ready to fly against their enemies like the arrows that would signal the start of the attack. Yet Ashtaway still found himself vaguely reluctant to initiate the ambush, for reasons that he couldn't understand. Certainly he had no hesitation about slaying bakali. Indeed, his sincere hope was that none of the scale-skinned humanoids would escape the killing ground of the former village.

Shaking his head, biting back an unbidden cough of anger, Ashtaway forced aside his indecision. Pursing his lips, he made ready to whistle the distinctive cry of the whippoorwill. The sound would not be unnatural in the summer dawn, though the birds themselves would not speak out for another hour or so. That minor inaccuracy was enough to conceal the code from the dimwitted lizardmen.

Before Ash could signal, a shaft flew from a nearby tree. A bakali shrieked as more arrows sliced into the lizardmen. But now the scaly defenders leapt to their feet, racing madly about the camp.

A heartbeat passed as four dozen bowstrings quivered under full tension, four dozen sleek-shafted arrows sighted upon their targets. The missiles flew, and immediately the bakali camp echoed with shrieks and yowls of pain. Many lizardmen thrashed madly, while others lay still—slain in their sleep, or the first few moments of wakefulness. A hundred or more of the reptilian invaders raced about, weapons raised, staring frantically into the enclosing forest.

Another volley of arrows sifted silently into the horde, and then another. Helpless against the attack, which came from three sides, the mob of bakali milled about, small groups rushing toward individual trees. Some lizardmen dropped to all fours and galloped toward the vallenwood occupied by Ashtaway. He shot one, his arrow joined by a volley from several surrounding trees. The small band of attackers, in unison, flopped to the ground and lay still.

Ash looked for another target. Some of the lizardmen had begun to back toward the ravine leading to the lake shore, and the others instinctively followed. Silver arrowheads shot from the woods around the ravine, but Ashtaway wasn't certain the retreat could be stopped by arrows alone. Still, the tribe sought to attack without taking losses themselves, so the Pathfinder had urged the necessity to stand off and shoot for as long as possible. Thus far, it seemed no Kagonesti had been hurt, while numerous bakali lay still and bleeding on the soot-covered ground.

Abruptly the darkness was shattered by the cry of a diving hawk. Faltath, who, like Ashtaway, could no longer find a bakali in arrow range, leapt from the lower limbs of his vallenwood and started across the clearing, longsword upraised in his clenched fist. The warrior's cries took on a fiercely triumphant sound as he sprinted toward the enemy.

Other elves echoed the bold shrieks—Ashtaway didn't hear himself crying out until he noticed the tautness of his lips and mouth—and in one savage wave the tribe converged on the retreating lizardmen. Even Iydaway sprang like a young warrior, cawing wildly. The bakali pounced over each other in sudden panic, surging into the narrow ravine that seemed to offer the only possible escape.

Ash struck down a crocodile-faced warrior with his axe, and it seemed as though he had stepped directly from the earlier battle into this one. His weapon rose and fell like an intelligent thing, choosing its targets quickly and then striking with unerring accuracy. Part of Ashtaway's attention remained on Iydaway as he sought, with limited success, to prevent the Pathfinder from throwing himself fully into the melee. Fortunately, so pervasive was the panic among the lizardmen that the elven warriors faced only a few hurried return blows.

Several of the scale-skinned creatures suddenly stopped their flight and barked furiously. They charged en masse, viciously hacking their swords into a Kagonesti warrior, slaying the wild elf as Faltath and Ashtaway leapt forward. The hulking warrior bore one of the monsters to earth, twisting its head in his hands, while Ash chopped savagely into first one, then the other bakali's face. Groaning piteously, the two reptiles fell. Whooping Kagonesti warriors stabbed the writhing forms as Ash continued forward.

The ravine provided an easy route to the lake shore, and Ashtaway worried now that many bakali would escape. The creatures teemed onto the trail, crowding down the narrow gully. Still more of the lizardmen halted their flight, turning to meet the pursuing elves with their weapons, and the Kagonesti realized that something must be halting the enemy's retreat.

He thrust at two monsters with one swinging slash, and they both cowered away. Whatever held up the flight, Ash knew that it wasn't a sudden development of courage. Demoralized by surprise and the slaughter of so many of their fellows, the craven bakali sought only escape.

The ringing of steel clanged through the night, in a sound more brash than any light Kagonesti longsword. Puzzled, Ash stepped back from the melee, struggling to hear.

From somewhere up ahead, bakali screamed in panic, and their terror was mingled with many a dying gurgle. That steel blade rang again, and the mob of lizardmen actually surged back, toward the weapons of the waiting Kagonesti.

"By the Oath and the Measure!" came a cry from the darkness, in a language barely recognizable to Ashtaway.

But he recognized the heavy, nasal tone—a human! A *human* stood in that ravine, blocking the flight of the terrified lizardmen.

Bakali crowded into the gully, clawing at each other, trying to hack and prod through the press. Behind them the Kagonesti closed in, blades slashing.

Perhaps there would be no escape for the hateful creatures, Ash thought with grim satisfaction. But it was knowledge underlaid by a deep and substantial fear—a fear triggered by this inexplicable arrival of a human.

Trotting along the top of the ravine now, Ashtaway struggled to penetrate the darkness with his keen eyes. Below him, dozens of bakali squirmed and struggled, some trying to press down the floor of the ravine while others scrambled, with equal vigor, to get back to the clearing in the vallenwoods. None of the lizardmen so much as tried to climb the rough, crumbling walls, though any wild elf could have scampered up and down in a dozen places.

Ash stepped with care as he worked along the upper edge of the ravine, knowing that a misplaced foot could send him sliding into the midst of the bakali. At the same time, he hurried as quickly as he dared, trying to imagine what he would find.

The terror of the fleeing lizardmen was an almost palpable force, rising out of the narrow ravine like a stinking cloud. Ash again heard the human's voice bellow amid the clanging of steel. The elf came around the bole of a large tree and saw him: a strapping fellow bearing a great sword in both hands, standing in the narrowest part of the ravine. Swinging the weapon through a dazzling series of slashes and parries, he completely blocked the escape route of the panicked lizardmen.

Now several of the bakali tried to scramble up the steep walls of the gorge, falling backward after they got a short distance above the ground. One made it far enough to snap at Ashtaway's foot, but the Kagonesti chopped downward with his axe and sent the monster tumbling into the press of its comrades.

Even through the darkness a flash of recognition struck Ash—something about the human's huge, golden-hafted sword seemed vaguely familiar. The man stood with unfaltering courage, shieldless, clutching the hilt of his weapon in white-knuckled fists. Sheer rock walls rose to the man's right and left, and the sweeps of that mighty sword came within inches of each cliff. A lizardman dove to his belly and tried to squirm past the knight. The creature died quickly, its heart pierced by a blow from above. Two more of the scaly humanoids hurled themselves at the lone fighter, but the man cut them down so quickly that the two stabs seemed almost simultaneous to Ash's astonished eyes.

Movement to the side caught the elf's attention, and he

turned to see Faltath following him. The elven brave's longsword was streaked with bakali blood. Behind the inward spirals of his facial tattoos Faltath's eyes were alight with the glory of battle. Every Kagonesti brave knew that heady rush of battlefield energy, but somehow the appearance was magnified by the intensity of the sword-wielder's fury.

Ashtaway gestured silently as his villagemate joined him. The human swordsman continued to battle, though he stepped backward in the face of the lizardmen's relentless pressure. The ravine widened gradually as he retreated, and even that long-bladed sword would not long be able to block the passage.

"A human . . . he dies well," Faltath observed.

"Perhaps he shall not die," Ash suggested, watching the other Kagonesti.

Faltath snorted contemptuously. "Even if he kills a hundred bakali, a single Kagonesti arrow will see that he does not return to the plains."

Ashtaway nodded, not surprised by the reply. He *was* surprised, however, by a feeling within his own breast—an urge to help this human, to give him a chance to live. The notion was contradictory to everything in his life, and at first he couldn't explain it. Then he remembered.

"The wyrm of fire!" he whispered, shaking his head in awe. "I saw this same man stand before a red dragon, facing the creature with that sword. I thought he perished in the fireball."

There was no shred of doubt in his mind. The heavy sword had the same golden hilt, unique among the knights he'd seen, and this fellow fought with the same unbending stance, with identical fury and concentration. Ash vividly remembered the scene of the dragon attack, and tried to imagine how this man could have survived. Too, he felt his growing guilt over his failure to warn the knights of danger, and made a silent, grim promise that—for this man, at least—he would try to rectify that mistake.

"The dragon he killed—the beast fell on top of him

before the other serpent breathed. Could it be that he was protected from the fire by that corpse? And that he then crawled free of the mire?"

Faltath's laugh was bitter and cold. "If he did, then he has already lived longer than any man has a right. Let him be content with that."

Suddenly Ashtaway needed to know more—what had the man done then? How had he come to the Bluelake? And why now did he risk his life in such a mad, pointless fight?

"He must not be killed!" he declared, ignoring the scowl of suspicion that darkened Faltath's features. "I'm going to help him!"

The bakali pressed against the walls to either side of the gorge. The knight held at bay those monsters directly before him, but now he had a hard time fully blocking the ravine. He was forced to step back quickly in order to protect his flanks—but each retreat carried him farther along the ever-widening channel.

Ashtaway skirted the rim of the ravine until he had passed the valiant knight. Picking a smooth patch of dirt for his landing, the elf sprang lightly to the floor of the gorge. He landed almost soundlessly, the din of the panicked lizardmen surely swallowing any slight noise—but the knight nevertheless whirled, bringing his sword around to meet the threat he had somehow sensed behind him.

Ignoring the threatening parry, the Kagonesti sprang toward the bakali and swiftly killed two with sure-handed strikes of his axe. Smiling grimly, the knight pivoted back to meet the scaly warriors. For long, bloody minutes the pair stood firm, blocking the channel with their courage and skill.

The rest of the tribe closed in on the rear of the fleeing horde, with many elves advancing along the tops of the ravine. These showered the lizardmen with arrows, logs, rocks, and anything else that came to hand.

Finally, crouching and tense, Ashtaway dimly realized

that there was no one left to fight. The elf and the human knight looked around in amazement until their eyes met in frank appraisal.

The human, impatient in the way of his race, spoke first. "Thank you. I think the buggers would have had me there if you hadn't dropped in when you did."

Ash nodded, squinting as he concentrated on the words. The dialect was thick to his ears, but discernible—it was similar to the Qualinesti trading tongue that he had learned early in his life.

"You fellas put up quite a fight," the man continued, wiping his blade with a square of dirty cloth. He seemed uncomfortable by Ash's silence, as if it would soothe him to have the night filled with sounds. "Do you understand a word I'm saying?" he finally demanded, exasperated.

"Yes. Come with me." Ash started down the ravine, noting for the first time that dawn's pale blossom had begun to spread across the sky. Shrugging, the knight fell into step behind him. They descended the stone steps near the end of the rocky cut, as the walls that had bracketed them gradually gave way to the rolling earth of the surrounding forest.

So effective had been their blocking maneuver that none of the lizardmen had escaped. Several braves probed through the gory mess in the ravine, chopping or stabbing wherever they found a sign of life. The others, Faltath in the lead, gathered on the lake shore at the mouth of the gully.

When Ash and the knight walked toward them, a grim silence fell across the warriors of the tribe. Hazel eyes glared, unblinking, and the Knight of Solamnia stood a little straighter, walked a little more firmly. Ashtaway noted the change in the man's demeanor, not surprised to observe that the fellow had a strong underpinning of pride.

Faltath stepped forward, speaking rapidly to Ash in the tribal tongue of the wild elves. "It is bad enough that you do not slay this human. Why did you tell me that he should remain unharmed by the others of the tribe? Do you deny that he is a human?"

"He is a human."

"Perhaps you have forgotten the tales of our fathers—of the humans who scoured the forest for our people? Who slew them without compunction, that they could torch the woodlands and create their abominable fields?"

"I remember the tales," Ashtaway replied. "But I remember other, older stories as well—legends of another dragon war, when elves and knights fought together to bring evil to its knees. I am wondering if Krynn is not facing another such time. We know that a deadly war rages, and that we are no longer free from its reach."

None of the Kagonesti replied. For several minutes, the braves scowled at the knight, who stood rigidly beside Ashtaway. The elven expressions remained unchanging, but Ash knew that they were considering his arguments. Finally he judged that enough time had passed for him to continue.

"This knight, in particular, slew many of our enemies. His actions in battle ensured that our victory would be complete—more complete than we could have hoped. I offer him my protection—it is the very minimum of the debt we owe him."

Ashtaway said the words bluntly, and no physical reaction showed on the faces of the warriors. Still, he was somewhat surprised at his own temerity. His fellow braves, impassive though they were, must be shocked, Ash knew—by offering his protection, the elf had declared to his lifelong companions that they would have to kill him before they would be able to harm the human.

Another long silence followed. The human's eyes flicked from Ash to the rest of the tribe, and the elf sensed the man shifting his weight from foot to foot—so gradually that the movement was practically imperceptible. The Kagonesti was grateful that the fellow had the good manners not to interrupt the meditative silence of the band.

"You, Ashtaway, have earned a great measure of this victory for our tribe. We should respect your words, and your wishes. But now tell us: Is there something about this human that leads you to extend him your protection?" Balkas, the eagle-eyed archer, scowled in concentration as he spoke to Ashtaway. Clearly the young warrior was puzzled, but Ash was gratified to see that he was also willing to listen and consider.

"In the forest camp I told you of the dragons I had seen, and their battle against human knights. This man was the leader of those knights, and though I thought I saw him perish in flames, he still lives. I would find out his story. And, too, it seems that a man who has faced dragons and countless bakali deserves a better death than an arrow in the back."

"Shoot him from the front, then," growled Faltath menacingly.

The knight understood the warrior's hostility and stiffened reflexively. Yet he made no move to draw his weapon or to speak. Instead he waited with patience that, Ashtaway guessed, must require a great amount of effort from the human. After all, everyone knew that mankind's world was a place of frantic pace and impatient activity. The Kagonesti had no regrets about his decision. With every passing moment, the feeling that this human was worth Ash's protection grew stronger.

And even the angry Faltath, Ash knew, would not challenge the protection extended by his friend. Because of Ash's simple statement, any aggression against the man would constitute a great taboo against the tribe's traditions and customs.

"Let us return to the village," Ash suggested. "There we can make a dawn fire and smoke the pipe of victory."

"That is a good idea," Balkas agreed, stepping forward and scrutinizing the man. The elf lapsed into the tongue of the traders. "I would like to know what it is about you that has caused my old friend to act like a madman."

Chuckling easily, Ash felt the tension drain away. His step was light, relaxed, as he led his new companion back toward the woods.

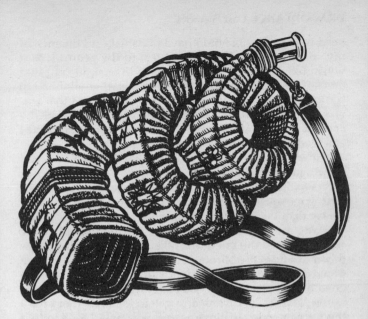

# Chapter 14

# The Younger Pathfinder

"I am called Ashtaway," the warrior offered as he led the human toward the village clearing.

"Sir Kamford Willis, Knight of the Rose, at your service."

"I recognized you from your sword, though, of course, I did not know your name."

"Recognized me from where?" the human asked, puzzled.

"I witnessed your fight against the red dragons—you and the men who rode with you." Ash described his vantage of that heroic, doomed skirmish. "When the dragon's breath swept across you, I felt certain you must be dead. Perhaps I should have looked more closely."

"It was the mud," Sir Kamford explained, shaking his

head in wonder. "I should have perished—all the men of my company did. But when I fell to the ground, that wyrm fell on top of me and pressed me right into that muck—it was quite wet in that clearing, after all. I had to squirm out before I suffocated, and I assure you that was no easy task. A small dragon it may have been, but plenty enough weight to trap a man for good! Then, by the time I emerged, the other dragon was gone."

"How did you come to the Bluelake? And why did you stand against the bakali?"

"As to the first question, I was lost. The mountains kept forcing me south when I wanted to go west—traveling a lot slower than I would have liked, since I lost my horse. I was working my way along the shore, hoping I could swing westward past the tail of the lake. Then, yesterday, I saw the smoke from the burning village, and I got close enough to see the lizardmen—no friends to any knight. I found a good hiding place under the bank, right at the foot of the ravine. Naturally, I wanted to get an idea whether or not this force intended to move against Solamnia." Sir Kamford continued to explain as they reached the edge of the vallenwood glade, where Kagonesti warriors halted their labor of removing bakali bodies to watch the human's arrival with cold, impassive eyes.

"Then, when you launched your attack and took them by surprise, I saw the chance to trap the scaly fellows right here. But I did wonder why you didn't send some of your braves to seal off the escape route."

Ash shook his head, unwilling to admit that his own suggestion for that tactic had been vetoed. He could clearly imagine the mass bakali escape, however, if Sir Kamford had not arrived when he did.

"The aim of our attack was to drive them off. Thanks to your help, the victory is—"

Ash froze, paralyzed by a look of alarm on Ampruss's face as the young brave dashed up to him. "It's the Pathfinder! You must see him—before it's too late!"

Panicked, the warrior raced to the ruins of his uncle's

lodge. Ampruss ran beside him. "It was a bakali—it came out of the woods when the battle was almost over. I . . . I killed it, but too late!" The young warrior's voice choked, and Ashtaway sensed, with pain of his own, Ampruss's grief and guilt.

Iydaway lay on a straw mat just outside his former front door. Ash knelt beside him, sickened to see a deep, bubbling wound in the Pathfinder's frail chest.

The old elf's lips gasped reflexively, but no sounds emerged. Ash leaned close as his uncle desperately tried to speak.

"Here . . . take . . ."

At first the warrior didn't understand what Iydaway meant. The old elf's hands trembled, seemed to flail meaninglessly. Or perhaps, Ashtaway didn't want to understand.

"The Ram's Horn, Pathfinder," Iydaway gasped. "It is yours now—yours as long as the gods allow."

"Don't talk!" urged Ashtaway, desperately frightened by the old man's weakness, and by his words as well.

"I . . . had hoped to teach you longer. But I have always suspected you would be the one—then, when you heard the second Ram's Horn, I knew."

"Please, Uncle—"

"Listen . . . no time . . . you are the Pathfinder. Go, now, speak to the tribe. . . ."

"But—what can I say? Why should they listen?"

"Use the horn . . . it will know . . . play the horn, and Father Kagonesti will show you. . . ."

For a time Iydaway was silent, and Ash feared he had died. Finally the wounded Pathfinder opened his eyes, inhaling a deep, bubbling breath.

"Take the tribe south . . . the central woodlands . . . find the path."

With a gurgling exhalation, the elder Kagonesti shuddered and lay still. Tears stung Ash's eyes, and he looked, with something like loathing, at the spiraled horn in his hands.

Then he thought of Hammana, of the potent force—he knew, now, too late, that it was love—growing between them. He truly hated the horn, hating even more the bonds of pledge and responsibility that were its potent companions.

But he could not ignore the command. Blindly he rose to his feet, stumbling away with a hand in front of his face—the hand that brandished the Ram's Horn. Vaguely he became aware that many eyes were turned to him. He blinked, and forced himself to stand tall.

"You are the Pathfinder," Faltath declared, his voice emerging from the mass of tattooed braves. Ashtaway didn't see his old friend, but he wanted, desperately, to argue with his words.

Ashtaway thought: My uncle has made a mistake! The young warrior wanted to shout the news to the tribe, to hold out the spiraled horn for any who would take it. But he couldn't do this any more than he could disobey Iydaway's command.

"He gave it to me because I heard the second Ram's Horn. Let us gather in the council circle, and I will tell the tale."

The wild elves ringed the central fire pit of the village. They listened raptly as Ashtaway told of the summons from Lectral, of the silver dragon that Hammana still tended. His voice tightened reflexively as he spoke of the beautiful healer, of her tender ministrations toward the mighty serpent.

After a time, one of the older warriors produced a pipe, and for several minutes the braves smoked, passing the ritual bowl from one to another—waiting silently while the young Pathfinder suspended the telling for his turn to inhale the aged tobacco. Ashtaway gave it to Sir Kamford and admired the human's fortitude as the knight drew in the harsh smoke and allowed it to breeze easily outward from his nostrils.

Pensively, Ash's mind returned to Hammana. More than ever before, he wanted to see her, to talk to her. But he had other things to do now, and to say.

"The tribe must make ready to depart," Ashtaway declared. "Such was my uncle's last wish, and it shall be done."

"You won the battle, and you're still going to *leave*?" The knight spoke more bluntly and hastily than an elf, and Ashtaway paused, startled.

"The village has never been attacked here," the Pathfinder explained shortly. "Now the bakali, and doubtlessly other minions of the Dark Queen, know that we are here. We fear for the lives of our elders and our children. Also, it seems that the war is creeping steadily closer."

"Aye, my friend. Those are good fears, right and proper. But as to the war, if you find a place where it's *not* encroaching, I wish you'd let me know. There's people all over Ansalon wishing for the same thing, but not one that I know of's been able to find it."

"We will move south, into the heart of the forest lands that divide Silvanesti and Qualinesti."

"Forests? Maybe in your granddaddy's time, I'll guess," Sir Kamford disputed, with a wry chuckle that struck a dissonant note in the contemplative elves. "True, I'd heard tales going back to the time of Vinas Solamnus himself. Said that there used to be woodlands filling the whole gap between the Kharolis and Khalkist Ranges. Not anymore, I'm afraid. You're talking of migrating into some prime farmland now."

The Kagonesti warriors remained silent, but uneasy glances flickered among the tribe. None of them was prepared to believe the word of a savage human, but neither did any of the elves have personal knowledge of the southern forests. Not since the Kinslayer War had any of the wild elves dwelled there, and that was a thousand years in the past.

"It's not a surprise, I guess, that the lizardmen should have found you down here." The human rambled on with a garrulousness that rendered meditative discourse practically impossible. Ashtaway, however, was curious to hear what the man would say.

"The Dark Queen's armies are starting a big push to the west this year. By high summer, there'll be battles waged from here to Palanthas, if she has her way. It's only natural that she send some of her lizards into the forest, looking for a way around the knights."

"I first observed you with a small company of knights. Did you then seek to block this maneuver?" Ash asked. He began to wonder if, behind the knight's undeniable courage, there lurked the mind of a mad fool. His force of two dozen men seemed far too small to accomplish such a bold mission.

"We were not here as an army, either of invasion or defense," the knight assured him. "Our primary task was to explore the valleys in the foothills, to seek a route into the mountains."

"Not to defend Palanthas?" Ashtaway tried to picture a reason for the human's strategy.

"No, but, perhaps, to make the Queen's attack against Palanthas less successful. Takhisis, you see, has sent practically all of her dragons with the strike force of her armies. They make a formidable force, and we know their target is, eventually, Palanthas."

"Then the war may indeed be approaching its end," declared Faltath. His tone made it clear that he viewed the defeat of the knights as a thing of precious little consequence to himself or the tribe.

Once again, Ash found himself disagreeing with his lifelong friend. The prospect of dragons soaring over the woodland, of bakali legions roaming and plundering wherever they wanted to go, seemed like a chilling legacy for the years of his children and grandchildren—and then, with a cold shiver, he again felt the weight of the Ram's Horn. There would be no children for him.

"Don't hold a victory celebration for the Dark Queen. Not yet!" snapped the knight, with appalling rudeness. Faltath flushed, but Sir Kamford continued speaking without a pause. "There's hope for the knights in several straws, slender though they may be."

"Do you speak of ways to defeat the Dark Queen and her dragons?" wondered Ashtaway. Often he had remembered the savagery of the dragons he'd seen. An army of the creatures seemed almost incomprehensibly powerful.

"It's not so unthinkable," the man replied. "There are, after all, dragons who fight as our allies. The golds and silvers make a formidable armada when they take to the skies, and thus the Dark Queen needs always to guard against a surprise attack against Sanction, where lies the root of her strength."

The young Pathfinder remembered Lectral saying much the same thing. "Then why not strike at Sanction from the plains, where your army is?" Ashtaway asked.

"Because the queen's armies—and her dragons—block our passage across those plains," Sir Kamford said grimly. "We couldn't attack from there until we defeat those armies. And unless we can burn the depots of Sanction she'll be able to keep her army in the field for ten more years!"

"I have seen Sanction, from a distance," the young Pathfinder noted. "There seemed ever to be a black, angry cloud about the place—it seems a fitting abode for the Queen of Darkness."

The knight chuckled, and even Ashtaway was set aback by the man's lack of manners. Suppressing his own temper, aware of the other warriors' displeasure behind their stoic expressions, Ash forced himself to remember that Sir Kamford was a stranger to proper society—indeed, there seemed to be no rudeness intended in his expression of humor.

"She doesn't actually *live* there, of course—nor anywhere else on Krynn. But it's rumored that her serpents have their lairs in the volcanoes around the city, and that's where she's assembled the supply depots to run the war."

Ashtaway was intrigued, remembering what the knight had said earlier. Lectral's speculations in the cave, which had centered around the importance of Sanction to the

Dark Queen, came vividly back to him. "And while her dragons are in the west, menacing Palanthas, you seek to find a way to strike at Sanction? To cripple her village while her warriors are out on the hunt?"

"In a manner of speaking." There might have been a trace of amusement in Sir Kamford's voice, but it seemed as though he was making a conscious effort, now, to mimic the serene expressions of the Kagonesti. "Of course, the central plains are too dangerous. Any party of knights caught by dragons, miles away from shelter, would be doomed. And if we tried to march directly, there's no doubt that we would be caught."

"So you were planning to attack along an indirect route?" Ashtaway surprised himself again, this time by speaking so abruptly on the tail of his companion's words. He could sense Faltath staring at him in disbelief, but he was very curious—and a little awed—by the human's audacity.

"The company you saw last week? No, we were just a scouting party. The Lord Knights won't even consider launching an attack unless we could return with word of a route through the mountains."

The elven warrior nodded.

"My party had been scouting since the snow melted in the lower valleys. Unfortunately, every time we found a promising path, we ended up in some box canyon or confronted by a ring of tall peaks. Places even a *man* couldn't go, to say nothing of our horses."

"You would take your horses to this battle?"

"A knight without his horse is like . . . is like one of you without his legs," Sir Kamford said seriously. "Yes, we would ride our horses into battle. The Knights of Solamnia, in charge rank, are a force to make even ogres quail."

The Kagonesti remembered the small company battling against the red dragons, and he had no doubt that Sir Kamford spoke the truth.

"Yet the charge against Sanction, it seems, will never be made," the knight declared sadly. "Even if I live to return to Solanthus, I will not be able to offer the lords any hope. There was no route in the mountains, and across the plains lies only death."

Ashtaway nodded solemnly, as if in sympathy with the human's despair. It was a warrior's tragedy: brave men on a desperate mission, slain by crimson death on wing. This lone survivor, a valiant knight to be sure, the only one left to carry the tale of failure.

At the same time, the elf's mind churned with a knowledge that he suspected he would not be able to contain. Should he speak? There was really no choice involved.

"There is, possibly, another way," Ashtaway said deliberately. "Perhaps . . . even a way that the tribe could remain beside the Bluelake, to live here in safety."

Even the human remained silent, waiting for him to continue. Ash took a long time to think, collecting his thoughts before he spoke.

"There is a route through the Khalkists, leading up from the south. It is a narrow pass that winds high among the peaks, but I believe it would be passable even for horses."

"A route that leads to Sanction?" asked Sir Kamford tautly, after a barely respectable pause.

"I have seen the Three Smoking Mountains from the crest of the pass, and looked down upon the city in the valley of fire beyond."

"The Lords of Doom! So there is—there *might* be—a way! Tell me, where is this pass? How can I find it?"

"I doubt that you could," Ashtaway said, without rancor. "I discovered the place myself only by accident, after many seasons of hunting in the high mountains."

For a moment, the Kagonesti paused. He felt a sense of portent, and knew what he was about to say even before he articulated the words. At the same time, he realized that his tribemates would react with shock and dismay— yet Ashtaway could not, *would* not pull back from his decision.

"I will show you the pass," he said quietly. "You must

return to Solamnia and gather your force of knights. I will lead you through the mountains, so that you may strike at the Dark Queen's village."

"What treachery is this?" demanded Faltath, his face taut behind the whorls of his tattoos. "You would lead a force of humans through the heart of our woodlands?" The elf's fist closed around the hilt of his sword, and for a moment Ash wondered if his old friend would draw his weapon and violate the protection extended to the human.

"We aren't coming to invade!" declared Sir Kamford.

Faltath raised his hand from the hilt of his sword and crossed his arms firmly over his chest. "Do you mean that we should *welcome* humans into these forests?" he demanded, his tone edging on mockery.

"Perhaps you would prefer to welcome red dragons, or ogres, into the woodlands," suggested Ashtaway tightly. He felt his own temper rising. Why couldn't Faltath *understand?*

"That's just the point!" Sir Kamford's voice was full of persuasive enthusiasm, though it sounded harsh and strident to the elven ears. Still, their attention was bound by the force of his conviction. "I can't promise that if we strike at Sanction, we'll win the war. Indeed, I suspect the issue will be decided in the west, dragon against dragon, in the skies over Solamnia. But our attack can weaken the Dark Queen's army just when it is most in need of strength!

"And make no mistake, my elven friends." Now the knight's tone dropped to an ominous timbre so portentous that none of the Kagonesti reacted to his categorization of them. "The victor in this war will have strong bearing on the future of Krynn—for *all* races, *all* peoples. It is an effect that will outlast the lifetime of even the most venerable elf."

"I have seen the dragons," Ashtaway noted. "If they return, the forests will not be safe for elf or man. Far better to cast our weight before the war is resolved, that the dragons of evil may be defeated."

He looked at Sir Kamford, and his hazel eyes were flat

and cold. "*After* this war," he added meaningfully, "we can decide what to do about the humans."

"Fair enough," agreed the armored knight. "I offer my word—I shall describe your contribution to my lords, as well as your desire that we leave you alone. We pass through your realm only because it offers the best—the *only*—path against the Dark Queen's bastion."

Ashtaway felt a surge of apprehension. Was he doing the right thing?

If he made the wrong decision, and the village was attacked again, could they hope for a repeat of their recent good fortune? Or might they be attacked by dragons and ogres as well as by the dimwitted bakali? If so, Ash knew that it might mean the end of the tribe.

Yet if they left this place, they had no guarantee that they would find another site half as good—perhaps there would not even be woodlands, a range of pastoral forest in which to hunt and live. He knew how quickly humans bred and multiplied, about their insatiable thirst for land. It did not seem inconceivable that during the last thousand years they had claimed great sections of what had once been forest.

Finally Ashtaway sighed and opened his eyes, which he fixed upon the face of Sir Kamford Willis. "How long will it take you to reach Solamnia and return to the woodland with this army of knights?"

"Two weeks to walk home, a week to gather the force, and another week to return with riders—and myself back in a saddle. In four weeks, you could show us the way into Sanction."

"I do not know these 'weeks,'" replied the venerable Kagonesti. "What does this mean in the cycles of Krynn?"

Sir Kamford frowned in thought, then looked at the dawnlit sky. The sliver of Lunitari, barely past new, had just risen in the east. "When Lunitari grows to fullness, then fades, and then returns as a crescent such as it is now, I shall arrive with my knights."

"Very well. I will tell you of a place we can meet, in the

foothills north of here," Iydaway agreed. "The tribe will remain beside the Bluelake for at least another season. By that time we should know if the menace of evil has been defeated or merely enraged such that we will need to flee."

"Splendid!" declared the knight. "I depart at once!"

"First, you must stay and eat with us," the young Pathfinder declared. "For it is bad fortune to start a journey on an empty stomach."

# Chapter 15

# A Cycle of Lunitari

The tribe remained at the Bluelake as the early summer advanced. The young Pathfinder suggested that they increase the number of warriors guarding the approaches to the village, and his tribemates welcomed the idea. The knowledge that he could help them pleased Ashtaway, but he missed his uncle greatly, seemingly more with each passing hour.

Geese had flocked to the shoreline marshes two days after the battle, winging from the south in great, cackling formations. Most of the tribe's hunters went out in search of game, and it seemed that, for the present, lack of food would not be a problem.

Ashtaway did not accompany the archers on the great

stalking. Assured that the tribe would eat well, he left the village, climbing away from the lake and into the wooded foothills. He departed with a strange reluctance, as if he neglected a responsibility. Though he knew that Iyd-away—and the earlier Pathfinders—had often vanished into the wilderness for months, even seasons, at a time, Ash felt the spiral horn as a surprisingly heavy weight at his side, an anchor that seemed to hold him close to the tribe. He missed the smiles, the jokes, and the boasts of his fellow warriors. Yet he loped easily through the forest for hour after hour, as cool morning passed into sun-soaked afternoon.

His mind, freed from battles and choices, dwelled on Lectral—and Hammana. It would be very good to see the dragon again, he knew. As to the elfmaid, he desperately *wanted* to see her, but because of the horn at his side, he was terribly afraid.

He reached the glade where, by Lectral's suggestion, he had earlier taken the deer, and was fortunate enough to bring down a young buck with barely an hour's stalking. Slinging the gutted carcass over his shoulders, he continued on, climbing through the cut into the rocky crest, seeing the obsidian cliff rising beyond.

Shortly before dusk, he approached the sheltered cave where he had left Hammana and Lectral. Slowing to a walk, he followed the same trail on which he had met the elfwoman on their first visit to the silver dragon. Even before she came into sight, a waft of breeze carried Hammana's scent to him, and Ash knew that she was in the woods—no doubt gathering more medicinal herbs for her huge patient.

He found her kneeling in a meadow of columbine and honeysuckle, digging at a stubborn root. So as not to startle her, he coughed gently from the edge of the clearing.

Hammana leapt to her feet, whirling to face him, looking at once frightened, embarrassed, a little angry, and far more beautiful than his imagination had remembered. Her face flushed as she wiped the dirt from her hands and smoothed the supple doeskin of her skirt.

"I'm glad to see you again," Ash said, stepping toward her. For a moment, he was the young warrior again, carefree and confident—the Pathfinder's job was a task for someone else, someone wise, like his uncle.

"I—um—Lectral will be happy that you're back," she stammered, still startled by his sudden appearance. He dared to hope that the blush rising across her cheeks was a sign that their meeting brought her as much joy as it did him.

"I told your father that you would stay here for a while. He was worried, but he trusts you."

"Thank you. Lectral's much better. I think the poultices have helped a lot."

"There's not another in all the tribes who could tend him so well," Ash declared.

"And how fares the village?" she asked, allowing him to fall into step beside her as they started toward Lectral's cave.

"There was trouble," he admitted. He started to tell her about the bakali, but abruptly she froze, her eyes locked on the spiral horn at his side.

"No!" she gasped, her face numb with shock. "Iydaway Pathfinder . . . ?"

"He was killed in the battle. Before he died, he passed on the Ram's Horn—"

"To you." Hammana completed his statement bluntly, though all the color had washed out of her face. "You are the new Pathfinder of the Kagonesti."

For the first time since his moments of doubt on the night of Iydaway's death, he wanted to deny the fact, to refuse the calling that had given him the Ram's Horn. Hammana's soft eyes, her serene, vibrant strength, suddenly seemed more precious to him than anything else could possibly be.

But already she had stiffened, withdrawing a half step from his side, restoring the formal reserve that was the norm between unmarried wild elves of opposite sexes.

"I am sorry about your uncle," she said quietly.

He told her of the others who had perished, and of the great victory the tribe had won, thanks to the intervention of Sir Kamford Willis, the human knight. By this time, they had reached the cave, and the great silver head, supported by the serpentine neck, emerged to greet them.

"Welcome, Pathfinder," Lectral said, his fangs glistening in a crocodilian smile. "I see that you bear the horn of the Grandfather Ram."

"And dinner as well," Ash said, dropping the buck's carcass outside the cave.

"You are ever welcome here, but most especially when you come with meat," the dragon noted.

Hammana sat silently beside a flat rock and began pounding her herbs with a stout stick. Ashtaway wanted to talk to her, but she avoided his eyes with fierce determination. Instead, the young Pathfinder described for Lectral the developments in the village by the Bluelake. He declared his intention to meet the Knights of Solamnia when Lunitari next waxed crescent—and when he said this, Hammana stiffened almost imperceptibly. Ash was heartened by this proof that she did not ignore him entirely.

"This is a proper and important thing you do," Lectral agreed, nodding sagely. "The knights are good men— among the best—and this Sir Kamford seems to have proved his worth twice over. If you can aid them to strike at Takhisis, you will do a service for all of Ansalon."

"It seems a strange way to make war," the wild elf admitted. "But if the armies of the Dark Queen cannot subsist without their food and weapons, then it may be that by destroying those we can greatly weaken her troops."

The silver dragon nodded, grunting contentedly as Hammana changed the dressing over several of his wounds. Ash noticed that the serpent's scales gleamed much brighter now, and his yellow eyes reflected the waning daylight with a pleasant luster.

"She has helped me very much," Lectral said, slowly. His hooded eyes shifted from the warrior to the woman, as if probing at the tension between them.

"I have done what I could. He is very strong," she replied, intent on her work.

"Alas, I'm afraid this old flap is never going to lift me into the air again," Lectral noted with a grunt of disgust. He twitched his left wing, showing that the leathery surface was pitted, scarred, and twisted. "Still, there are things other than flight to keep a dragon happy. Wyrmlings, for example. Did I ever tell you of Saytica, my daughter?"

Ash shook his head.

"She flies in the wing defending Palanthas. I have even heard that she bears a great captain of the knights on her back—one of the lords of the knightly orders."

"It is a thing to make one proud," Ash agreed, trying to picture the might of an armored knight mounted on one of these great serpents. How could the Dark Queen's forces hope to destroy an army such as that?

"Alas, there are but few of us," Lectral continued, answering the wild elf's unspoken question. "The reds and whites alone outnumber us, and then there are the blues, the blacks, and the greens. It is a desperate struggle we wage."

Ashtaway could only agree and silently pray that the dragons of silver could hang on long enough to prevail. He hoped that the strike at Sanction would make a difference.

But there was another thing on his mind.

"We each bear a Ram's Horn," he said after a respectful silence. "Can you tell me how you came to possess yours?" he asked. "There have long been legends among us of the second horn, but not since the time of Father Kagonesti has anyone seen it."

"It was given to me by my sire, Callak, who got it from Darlantan himself."

"Are you a Pathfinder of the silver dragons?"

Lectral chuckled. "We have no such title, really, but you might say that I am the Hornkeeper."

The dragon drew a deep, pensive breath before he continued. "The silver dragon, Darlantan, is the father of our people, and in his wisdom he saw that even we dragons had weaknesses. He knew that, through the coming centuries, it was important that we have friends, allies, among the peoples of Krynn.

"Of course, the only of those peoples whose lifetime even begins to approach our own are the elves. Yet Darlantan could see that the House Elves—who have many fine qualities, though you raise your eyebrow in skepticism—would become a potent and aloof society, with little need of alliance. Too, the elves of Silvanesti are ever concerned with their own mastery and would have been difficult partners in any endeavor."

"And so he came to Father Kagonesti, in the guise of the Grandfather Ram?" Ash wondered, knowing the answer as legend, but awed to hear it from Lectral as truth.

"Darlantan saw, in your first Pathfinder, that pride, that self-reliance that drew him to the wild elf first as a friend, then as an ally. He bade Kagonos to remain apart from the Silvanesti and laid a heavy mantle on that Elderwild's shoulders. The twin horns of the Grandfather Ram would be the symbol of this bond, and of the Pathfinder's burden.

"Kagonos bore that burden well, and when the First Dragon War raged across the land, he brought his Elderwild into the struggle and gave all the people of Krynn a hope for the future.

"Before Darlantan perished—at the end of that war—he gave the Ram's Horn to his wyrmling, Callak, who protected it for thirteen centuries. It was during this time that the dwarves, with their infernal greed, dug up the magical dragongems and unwittingly released the evil serpents into the world. As an ancient wyrm, Callak passed it to me when I was but a fledgling flyer, and for ten centuries it has been my task to keep it safe. For most of those years, it was protected deep in our lair, among mountains inaccessible to any land-bound creature."

"Yet you carried it from that lair . . . ?" Ashtaway, mystified, reminded Lectral.

"Indeed. Now a cruel Dragon War rages again, and those who battle the Dark Queen have fared badly. Remembering that the Elderwild aided us to win the first war against evil dragonkind, I wondered if perhaps their children—the Kagonesti—could do so again. Thus, I winged toward these woodlands, on my way to seek your people, when the reds fell upon me, ending my flight here."

"You sought our aid in the Dragon War?" Ash asked, surprised. "Surely you knew that we would never agree to enter such a . . . ?" He trailed off as the realization dawned.

Darlantan smiled a crocodile grimace of sharp fangs. "It seems to me that, even without my beseeching, you already *have* agreed," he remarked gently.

Pondering the irony of this fate, Ashtaway built a fire while Hammana sliced meat from the carcass of the buck. They ate, the two wild elves cooking their meat over the low blaze while Lectral contentedly gnawed at a haunch. Afterward, they slept, and Ashtaway woke with the first cool light of dawn. Hammana was already up, grinding at her herbs, brewing a thick tea in a gourd that sat on the banked coals of the fire.

At first he had thought that he might stay here for several days, but one look at the elfwoman's rigid back, then the sound of her stiffly formal greeting when he bade her good morning, convinced him that his presence here—at least, for any longer—would be a mistake.

As soon as Lectral awakened, Ashtaway announced his intention to return to the village. He promised to return with game as soon as possible, though he warned this might not be until after he journeyed to Sanction and back.

"Good luck," the dragon declared. "These knights can hurt Takhisis if only you show them the path."

"I will do that." Ashtaway paused, then drew a breath. "Hammana?"

"Yes?" She rose and accompanied him from the cave, though she did not meet his eyes.

"Is—is there anything I should tell your father? When will you return to the village?"

"I . . . I don't know. I'll stay here awhile. Lectral still needs me." Was it his imagination, or did she emphasize the dragon's name, pounding home the fact that a Pathfinder had no need of a woman, of anybody?

The Kagonesti wanted to tell her that it wasn't true. He wanted to confess his own need, which he felt more strongly than ever before. He, Ashtaway, needed her at his side! Couldn't she see—couldn't everyone see—that a partner such as Hammana could only make him a *better* Pathfinder?

But then she raised her face, and when he saw the fierce anger in her eyes, he felt a strange catch in his own throat and could only hold his tongue.

At last, when the cool cloak of the forest surrounded him, the isolation came almost—but not quite—as a relief.

# Chapter 16
# Mountainous Meeting

Ashtaway approached the rendezvous from the east, going many miles out of his way. He trusted Sir Kamford as much as it was possible to trust any non-Kagonesti, but his natural caution required that he take every measure to guard against betrayal. Thus he crossed two low, wooded ridges and traversed a shallow marsh just to ensure that his route could not be anticipated or intercepted. This legacy of caution seemed more important to him than ever before, perhaps because of the spiral horn he bore at his side.

Moving through the pine woods of the mountain valley, Ash scanned the skies, the ridgetops, and the surrounding slopes for any signs of danger. He saw a small herd of deer grazing near one of the crests. This was a good sign. The animals certainly would have sought shelter if they had sensed humans in the vicinity. Still, the elf did not relax even as he ascended back to the ridge and looked toward the deep, bowl-shaped valley where he had arranged to meet Sir Kamford and his force of knights.

The familiar basin sprawled before him in apparently pristine solitude. A wide fringe of flower-speckled meadow surrounded a grove of towering cedars, with another small meadow visible in the center of that grove. Though the dense needles of the upper limbs created a barrier to any observation from above, the wild elf knew that the floor of the grove was smooth and comfortable. No underbrush grew in the dense shadows, and the large trunks were well separated. Even a good-sized company of men and horses would be able to conceal themselves there, camping in relative comfort.

A spring bubbled from a stony embankment on the opposite side of the grove, providing plenty of fresh water. The encircling meadow bloomed with ample pasture for the horses, while the shallow outflow of water created a stream stocked with plump trout. On several occasions Ashtaway had eaten well here—simply by lying beside the narrow brook, carefully reaching in with his hand, and flipping out as many of the tasty fish as he desired.

Now the whole scene looked as peaceful and undisturbed as he remembered. Located far from any communities and from the eastern trade routes, the valley made an ideal rendezvous. Sanction lay forty or fifty miles to the north, with numerous sheer, sharp ridges rising throughout the intervening distance. Over the past six or seven decades, however, Ashtaway had discovered routes around the most precipitous of these heights, as well as the best routes of ascent and descent to the multitude of passes.

The sun had barely reached noon on the day of the meeting when the elf settled in to watch. Also near zenith, preceding the sun as if it lured the fiery orb across the sky, the sliver of the moon Lunitari gleamed against the pale blue background, as it had one cycle earlier when Ash and Sir Kamford had arranged this rendezvous.

Careful to remain below the crest of the ridge, the wild elf found a shaded, rocky niche, where he was fully concealed from observation above or below. With patience only another Kagonesti could have matched, he lay prone, peering outward between several low bushes, his hazel eyes flashing back and forth through the depression.

To the north he could see the rocky outlines of the pass leading to Sanction, and for a while he reflected on that which he was about to do. Though his intervention in a war of humans and dragons was a thing that would have astonished him if another elf had proposed it, or even if he had thought about doing it as recently as half a season before, now he had no regrets. The Dark Queen was an enemy far more deadly than all the teeming numbers of humankind, and there was no question in his mind that he should offer his knowledge to aid in striking a blow against her.

For a while he wondered about that great war. What was it like to see thousands of troops surging into battle? He tried to picture a sky filled with sweeping, wheeling dragons, and found that he couldn't do it. Someday, perhaps, he would see for himself—though it was a thing he would neither seek nor hope to find.

The knights' manner of waging war against this threat seemed curious and foreign to him, oddly removed from the vital fury of battle that lay behind every Kagonesti attack or defense. He could see the logic of an attack against foodstuffs, against coal and steel and corrals and forges, but as a purpose for attacking it did not ignite any martial fires in his breast. Yet if that was the way these humans wanted to wage war, so be it—he would hope that the Dark Queen could be sorely hurt by their sudden onslaught.

Late in the afternoon, he saw a sparkle of sunlight and

knew that something metallic moved over the opposite rim of the valley. Squinting, frozen with concentration, he stared until he saw that the sun had winked off the silver bridle of a great warhorse. Ash winced unconsciously. Didn't these humans know that shiny metal might make them visible to an observer many miles away? Immediately his musings were forgotten and he stared, rapt, at the human riders slowly coming into view. Similar in some ways to the wild elf's own approach, these knights moved with caution. Ash watched a preliminary party of four cross the ridge and move downward toward the grove Ash had described to Sir Kamford.

From his vantage, the Kagonesti saw that another knight remained on the ridge, crouched among a cluster of thick brush—though he was quite conspicuous by wild elf standards. Still, Ash approved of his new ally's caution and was also pleased to see the sentry adjust his position over the next few minutes until he had vanished into the ground cover almost as effectively as an elf.

The four knights of the advance party split up as they approached the valley floor, a pair riding slowly through the pine woods circling the base of the depression while the other two advanced straight toward the grove of tall cedars Ashtaway had described. A stag and two does burst from the near side of that clump, bounding toward the heights, and the Kagonesti welcomed this sign that all was well.

Still, the humans took their time, the two riders on the slopes making a full circle around the basin as they searched for danger. Below, the pair who had disappeared into the grove remained for nearly an hour before they emerged and waved to their fellows on the slopes.

Only then did the rest of the knights come into view, riding in single file through the narrow gap and following the beckoning waves of their scouts. Ashtaway was impressed in spite of himself as he counted nearly one hundred huge chargers, each mounted by an armored human warrior. He saw that the glint of sunlight that had first attracted his eye had been unusual. For the most part, the Knights of Solamnia had dulled their armor, many even attaching leaves to their helmets or obscuring metallic sword hilts with mud and clay. He was relieved that they had at least made an effort at elementary concealment. Ash would make sure, before they left the valley, that their efforts were rendered fully effective.

By the time the band of knights had entered the cedar grove, the sun had set and the sliver of Lunitari neared the western ridge. Ash waited a few more moments, watching the crescent slip from view. With the whole crest around and above him in full shadow, the Kagonesti emerged from his hiding place and carefully started down the slope.

He moved slowly, always advancing from one piece of cover to the next—slithering like a snake in those places where he was forced to cross open ground—and by the time he reached the floor of the valley, the stars had sparkled into life.

Still he moved with care, crouching low as he moved toward the grove. Near the edge of the clump of trees, he paused while a gust of wind swirled outward. He smelled humans, knew that at least two of them were very nearby, probably posted as sentries on this side of the grove. Good. Like himself, the humans knew the need for caution.

A tight smile creased his lips as he crawled under the canopy of the first pines. Although he was pleased with Sir Kamford's alertness, it would please him even more to demonstrate wild elven proficiency and stealth. Ashtaway saw the boots of a knight no more than five paces away, but the man had not noticed him in the gathering darkness. Silently the Kagonesti moved from tree trunk to tree trunk, using his keen night vision to spot each of the pickets before the men had any idea that he lurked so closely among them.

A horse stamped nervously, and the elf froze, chagrined at his own carelessness. Rigidly he watched the beast's clomping hooves, noting the shaggy fetlocks, the span of the legs. Though he had little experience with horses, he guessed with a fair degree of certainty that the steed before him was an unusually large specimen. Too, he should have guessed that the great beasts would possess a wild animal's keen senses of smell and hearing. No doubt the steed had picked up his scent. Still, after that momentary restlessness the horse snorted several times and went back to placid grazing.

A few more minutes brought Ash to the brink of the grove's central clearing, where most of the knights were preparing to bivouac for the night. Several staked out horses, while others sharpened weapons, mended saddles, or cleaned dust and mud from their boots. Again the elf was impressed—though the night was chill, the humans showed no inclination to build a fire. Neither did they make any unnecessary noise during their activities.

"D'you think he'll show up?" The voice came from a group of knights gathered at a ring of boulders—a circular space Ash had used as a campsite on his previous visits to the grove.

"If he don't, we've taken a hundred lances out of the lords' army fer nothin'!" groused another knight.

"He'll come." Now Ash recognized Sir Kamford's voice. The knight stood in the center of the circle, an undeniable figure of command. The other knights fell silent as he spoke. "There was something about him—a kind of wisdom that I've rarely encountered. He gave me his word—"

"And I have honored it," concluded Ashtaway, stepping into the circle. He enjoyed the consternation of the knights as they scrambled to their feet or instinctively reached for weapons, held back by Sir Kamford's chuckle of amusement. The knight bowed his head in a gesture of respect and appraised Ash for a moment before speaking.

"Welcome. Were my pickets sleeping on the job?" asked Sir Kamford with good-humored amazement.

Ash repeated the respectful bow, and he, too, paused to meet the other's eyes before he spoke. "No, they are alert and would doubtless have discovered any human who sought to intrude—or an ogre or Silvanesti elf, for that matter."

"I believe you," Sir Kamford said with a nod. "It is good to see you again, my friend—and ally."

"And you, human. I see that you bring many warriors."

"You are the elf who will show us the road to Sanction?" inquired one of those knights, quite rudely, thought Ashtaway. Below his large nose this fellow had a curving red mustache. The human fixed the Kagonesti with a look of frank skepticism and not a little hostility.

"I would not call it a road," he replied stiffly. "I made it clear that it is but a hunting path. It does, however, cross the lower slopes of the smoking mountains and leads to the valley you call Sanction. And I believe that your horses will be able to cross."

"*Believe?* You don't know?" demanded the red-faced warrior.

Ashtaway stiffened, forcibly holding his hand away from the hilt of his axe. This knight's lack of manners offended him deeply, and for the first time he wondered if he was making a great mistake by coming here.

"How could I know?" he replied curtly. "We Kagonesti have no need of animal slaves in our efforts at war. We do well on our own feet." Ashtaway sensed that his own words were inflammatory, but he found it impossible to hold his tongue. The blunt conversation with the red-faced man seemed to arouse an instinctive antipathy.

"Animal *slaves?*" The knight's mustache quivered in indignation, and his fists clenched into firm knots. "These steeds are the boldest warriors on four legs! *Never* insult them—for to do so is to insult the men who ride them! To do *that* is to die."

The words hit the Kagonesti with the piercing force of a hot lance. "If there have been insults uttered, it was not I who began the exchange," Ash replied grimly, his own fingers curling inward. "I was led to believe that my services would be of some aid to the knights, and to my friend, Sir Kamford Willis. If that is not the case, I will go—or I will fight, whichever you choose."

His hazel eyes, darkened in the night, remained unwaveringly on the face of the belligerent knight. A small voice grew louder within him, suggesting that perhaps his coming here was a mistake, that humans and wild elves could not work together.

"Patience, Sir Blayne." It was Sir Kamford who cut through the tension with a soothing voice. "As I told you—and told the lords of the orders as well—Ashtaway has hunted over this trail on foot. But if he suspects that our horses will pass, I'm prepared to believe him."

"He passed our pickets, all right. He must know a little something," murmured another knight, not unkindly.

The one called Sir Blayne made a visible but only partially successful effort to relax. "Very well." He addressed Ashtaway. "Your offer of help is not unwelcome. You should know, however, that these hundred knights could be very useful on the plains during this summer. If our mission here comes to naught, the loss could be catastrophic."

"I cannot control the success or failure of your mission, but I can see that you will be able to approach Sanction from the southeast. The rest will be up to you."

Ashtaway felt the flame of his anger slowly doused. As the hazy sense of instinctive rage faded, he wondered about its sudden force and fury, and he told himself that he would have to work hard to hold that tendency at bay.

"That is all we ask," Sir Kamford declared, silencing Sir Blayne with a firm look. "Can you tell us what we will do from here?"

"In the morning, we leave this valley, crossing the north ridge. In four or five days, we should reach the summit of the pass, and from there you will be able to see your destination."

"Up the north ridge of this valley?" Another knight spoke, faintly skeptical. "That didn't look like any kind of slope for riders."

Ashtaway shrugged. "If the little climb out of here is going to stop you, then I can say with certainty that your horses will never make it over the pass. I am sorry."

"We can make it!" Sir Kamford snapped. "We'll dismount and lead the horses on foot over the rough parts."

"I still say we'd be more use forming a line of charge on the plains, fighting beside Lord Huma in the battle that will decide this war!" Sir Blayne, apparently, could not keep himself quiet.

"Why aren't you there, then?" Ash asked in genuine confusion. "Are you not your own master?" He couldn't understand why the man had joined this mission if he was so doubtful of a positive outcome. Certainly no Kagonesti would ever consent to such behavior.

"Orders," growled the knight, as if begrudging the word. "I am a loyal knight who follows the commands of his lord."

"But if you do not wish to attack Sanction, then don't," argued the brave. "I do not wish to lead any warriors where they are afraid to go."

"How *dare* you—a painted savage—question my courage?" snarled Sir Blayne, and this time his fist closed around the hilt of his sword.

"Enough!" barked Sir Kamford, stepping between the elf and the angry knight. He fixed Ash with a level gaze. "There is none who may question the courage of any of my knights without questioning my own. And Sir Blayne is right. We will not tolerate such insinuations."

Ash remained silent as the leader of the humans turned to his companion. "And I remind you, good Knight of the Crown, to remember your oath. It is unbecoming that we bicker thus in the presence of one who may help us to a spectacular victory. Neither should we make slander against his motivations or his noble people."

Sir Blayne stood stiff and tall, and for several moments Ashtaway wondered if he would be able to control himself. Finally he exhaled and bowed his head stiffly. "You show us the way to Sanction, and our courage will be displayed before all."

Ash accepted the reply. "I will go to the ridge crest to sleep tonight, and return with the dawn. You should be ready to walk, then, if haste is of importance."

"It is," Sir Kamford declared.

The Kagonesti turned and vanished into the night, seeking his high ledge for a night's rest. He had a strong feeling that most of the knights were not disappointed to see him go.

# Chapter 17

# Sanctionheight

"That's the pass?" Sir Kamford was frankly dubious. He stood with Ashtaway on a promontory of rock, staring up at two sheer mountain faces. A narrow notch between them showed a gap of smoky sky, dark clouds roiling and seething in a fiery, unnatural manner.

"Beyond lies the place you call Sanction," Ash confirmed. "The clouds you see are not born of the sky, but of the earth—they are belched from the three great mountains of fire."

The elf looked up at the dark, heavy overcast, feeling as though the air itself oppressed him. This grim, omnipresent blackness was one reason, perhaps the strongest, that he had never liked this place.

Behind them, the file of knights waited in the shelter of a narrow canyon. For five days they had followed the paths of the Kagonesti, as Ashtaway had led them through the trackless heart of the Khalkists. Now, with the final barrier before them, the wild elf wondered how they would fare.

In truth, he had been favorably impressed by the knights. Of course, many were arrogant and rude, even hostile, but he was honest enough to realize that many Kagonesti were the same way. During the walk, he had remained separate from the bulk of the knights, though he spoke with Sir Kamford frequently, discussing possible routes and sharing some of his knowledge of these rugged mountains. He made particular effort to avoid Sir Blayne, for he sensed the sparking of anger within himself whenever their eyes so much as met.

The fact that all of these warriors obeyed the bidding of a single captain, Sir Kamford Willis, he found intriguing and, he had to admit, quite useful. To have an attack commence when all the fighters were ready, rather than when a single warrior could no longer contain his bloodthirsty enthusiasm, would be an effective tactic. He could see easily that human customs allowed an army to perform encirclements, traps, ambushes, and even retreats with an order and precision that the wild elves had never known.

Also, he had had a chance to examine the armor and weaponry of the knights, and found it to be remarkably impervious to harm, wear, or age. Of course, the keen head of Ash's axe, too, was made of a strong, hard metal, and it had lasted through many generations of Kagonesti. Still, such weapons were rare among the wild elves, while every one of these knights had a great steel sword, as well as a lance, a dagger long enough to be called a short sword, and a sturdy shield. The elf suspected that, between his shield and plate mail armor, a knight would be virtually invulnerable to the attacks of a single warrior.

He wondered what the knights felt about these wild places through which he took them, and about the wild elf who showed them the path. Did they distrust him? Fear or admire him? He couldn't know, naturally, and a voice within Ashtaway told him that he shouldn't care. Certainly most Kagonesti—and every previous Path-finder—would have been disinterested in the opinions of a human. Why should it matter to Ash? He couldn't answer the "why," but he knew that it *did* matter.

Of course, some of the humans—most notably Sir Blayne—had been sullen and hostile, but for the most part the riders had expressed wonder at the places to which he had taken them. They were a brave lot. Never had the humans showed any trepidation over the prospects of the upcoming attack.

Now, however, he would know for sure. Ashtaway started along the trail, hearing Sir Kamford fall in behind. In moments, the clopping of many hooves told him that the whole column of knights had begun to move along that narrow, steeply climbing route.

As they moved out of the fragrant pine woods onto the barren slopes of the steep mountain, they followed no trail to speak of. It remained for Ashtaway to select a path among the boulders and precipices, crossing back and forth on the slope to minimize the incline, working gradu-ally upward instead of striking directly toward the pass.

Sir Kamford followed, though he moved slowly in order to give his horse time to place each hoof with care. The other knights came in file behind their captain, and as Ash worked his way carefully up the slope, he stopped frequently to give the horsemen time to keep their ner-vous steeds in a close order. The horses whinnied and kicked, but, with calm cajoling, the men kept them mov-ing upward.

It occurred to the Kagonesti that if a single dragon were to fly overhead and discover the knights on the mountain-side, the entire mission could be ended in the space of a few heartbeats. He shook the concern away, hoping that Sir Kamford's belief—that the dragons had all flown westward for the decisive battle of the war—was correct.

There was nothing they could do about it in any event, since the treacherous climb would have been quite impossible in the darkness.

Ash used his hands to cling to a rough outcrop of rock, but as he worked his way around the obstacle he saw quickly that the horses would never be able to follow in his immediate tracks. Instead, he released his grip and backed along the trail for several steps. A narrow chute led upward, allowing him to scramble up to the relatively flat surface of a shoulder, where there was space enough for a dozen horses to stand and rest. He lent a hand to Sir Kamford, and with a clattering of loose rocks, the knight persuaded his mount to scramble up after him.

The elf moved onward and up while the captain of knights caught his breath. One after another, the human knights and their jumpy horses clambered onto the broad surface. When the shoulder's flat space became too crowded, Sir Kamford led his charger after the elven guide, with the next knights falling into file behind him. In this fashion, each of the humans and horses had a short chance to breathe, but then quickly rejoined the steady, upward progression of the march.

Soon afterward, Ash reached a section of loose rock. The pressure of his moccasin began a sliding, clattering cascade, and the elf sprang backward while a mini-avalanche of stones spilled down the smooth mountainside—fortunately to the side of the precariously balanced knights and horses below. Only when the tumbling had ceased did he again advance, this time finding the footing more secure.

He heard a shout of alarm and the panicked whinnying of a horse. Ashtaway looked down the slope and saw several knights hauling and straining on the lead of a great black charger. The animal's hooves had slipped from beneath it and it lay on the rocks, kicking frantically at any human who came close. The Kagonesti was certain that the beast was lost, and he only hoped that the riders would have the good sense to abandon it before any of the other mounts, or even a man, slipped downward to join it.

To his frustration, the knights wasted precious minutes coaxing and soothing the animal, helping it to get its hooves underneath its belly. Ash couldn't mask his surprise when the horse at last scrambled to its feet and once again resumed the climb, pounding upward as if anxious to make up for the delay.

The minutes dragged into hours, morning's light swiftly waning into late afternoon, and still the file of dismounted horsemen crept up the mountainside. Slipping and staggering frequently, the men somehow continued without a dangerous fall. Progress was slow and careful, though the knights instinctively picked up the pace as they sensed that they would, indeed, make it to their objective.

Ash reached the notch of the pass with several hours of daylight remaining. Towering heights rose to each side, and smoky fog obscured much of the valley before him. He remembered that the descending trail curved around the slope of a great mountain, and that the city itself didn't come into view until one walked some distance from the pass. Still, it was the perfect gathering place for the knights, since the geography and the air itself combined so effectively to screen them from observation.

As the wild elf looked at the winding column, which still extended nearly halfway to the bottom of the slope, he hoped that all the knights would reach the summit before nightfall rendered their task impossible. Still, as the file straggled into a long, sinuous formation, he wasn't at all sure that they would.

The summit of the gap was a broad saddle between two towering mountains. Here, one by one, the knights gathered in the shelter offered by several overhanging rocks. The humans stroked and spoke to their nervous steeds, while the horses stared in wild-eyed fear at the barren landscape, at the specters of smoke and steam spewing from several of the nearby summits. The elf was impressed by the way in which each rider seemed to understand his own horse's fears—the men clapped their steeds on the neck, or patted their muzzles and withers, soon able to restore their animals' calm.

Though Sanction was not visible from the notch of the pass, the knights, like Ashtaway, saw that this fact worked to their advantage. Steadily the humans assembled, resting and grooming their mounts without having to worry about observation from below.

"Which way to the city?" asked Sir Kamford when several dozen knights had gathered in the pass.

Ashtaway pointed. "The trail down is wider and more gentle than the climbing route. If you move slowly and stay alert for sentries, you should be able to spy your target without being observed."

"Very well." Sir Kamford, accompanied by Sir Blayne and several other knights, left their horses with the others and went off to perform a reconnaissance on foot.

One by one, the rest of the knights made their way into the cold, bare shelter of the pass. Each human reacted differently—some with obvious relief, others with swaggering bravado, still others with a pause for reverent thanks to the gods of good. All of them looked at the tattooed figure of the wild elf, with wonder, respect, and perhaps a little bit of suspicion on their faces. Yet the men then looked past, staring into the smoldering valley below, as if reflecting with amazement that their mission was on the brink of decision.

Dozens of knights still remained on the mountainside when Sir Kamford returned. The knight's mustache bobbed up and down, and his eyes flashed with enthusiasm as he joined Ashtaway beside the trail.

"It couldn't be more perfect. The plateau on this side of the city is virtually unguarded. They assume any attacker would have to fight his way through Sanction to reach it!"

"And is this plateau worth attacking?" wondered the elf.

"Undeniably! I saw large wooden bins where they store

the coal for their forges, and the great barns, with their doors open, were full of grain. Those stockpiles would keep the army in the field over the entire winter if they get delivered—and if we're successful, they'll burn for days once we give them the spark. And they've built huge depots for weapons—spears, arrows, and the like. Those, too, we'll put to the torch! Then there are the corrals— huge things, really. They've got horses, mules, and oxen, a thousand of each if they have a pair. I don't doubt for a moment that we'll scatter the lot of them to the four winds!"

"I am glad the route might prove useful. Let us hope that the rest of your men can reach the crest by nightfall."

Sir Kamford, with a worried frown, looked over the tail end of his column. "Let's step up the pace there, lads!" he called. "Don't want to get stuck down there in the dark, now do we?"

Grumbling, the knights who were within earshot pressed ahead, while the last few struggled as quickly as they dared to close up the gaps. Even so, the sun had set before the final knights reached the pass, though enough daylight remained for even these last humans to see the path barely a few feet in front of their faces.

"That's the lot!" cried Sir Kamford when the full company of men and horses had gathered in the pass. The warrior's elation had continued to grow with each new arrival, and now Ashtaway marveled at the keen energy that seemed to possess his human companion.

"You will attack tomorrow?" asked the elf.

"As soon as we can get down there—I want to start the descent before sunrise," Sir Kamford asserted.

The human looked again at the sweeping mountainside they had ascended during the day, then turned to fix his dark eyes on the wild elf's face. "I wasn't at all sure we could do it, you know. When first you showed us the path, I thought we were doomed. Now here we are—and without losing a single horse on the climb!"

"Would that the battle be so kind," Ash remarked.

Sir Kamford's expression sobered. "It won't be," he acknowledged. "But, thanks to you, we'll have the chance to strike a solid blow in the name of the Oath and the Measure."

# Chapter 18
# Rank of Charge

In misty purple light, an hour before dawn, Ashtaway started down the smooth path toward Sanction. The knights were already active in the mountain camp, brushing and feeding the horses before cinching saddles and bridles into place. As if sensing the impending battle, the animals snorted softly and pawed the ground with barely contained tension. Still, secrecy was paramount. By the time the elf had moved fifty paces from the camp, he could hear no sounds of humans or horses.

Instead, he was bombarded by a sensory onslaught from the city that gradually came into view. Sanction expanded to fill the horizon as steady progress brought Ashtaway around the great bulk of the volcano. Even in the predawn darkness the city was alight, illuminated by glowing fissures in the bedrock. Flaming rivers of lava spewed heat and fire into the air, washing the entire, crowded valley in erratic pulses. Now, as dawn diffused the harsh, fiery illumination, Sanction promised to remain a place more of smoke and shadows than of daylight.

One of the Three Smoking Mountains—the peaks the knights called the Lords of Doom—belched forth a river of molten rock. This flowage blazed and hissed across the face on the opposite side of the valley, and Ash could see the course of the lava stream as it sputtered through the heart of the city.

Despite the destructive forces raging around the valley on the ground and in the air, to the wild elf the city of Sanction seemed an ancient, timeless place—a place where the works of nature ruled with far more authority than the audacious constructs of humankind.

Ashtaway got a clear view of the plateau, with its smooth eastern approach and the scattered clusters of buildings, corrals, and storage depots. As he moved farther, he saw the teeming slums come into sight, buildings sprouting like weeds on every patch of level ground and some places that were very steep as well. Narrow, twisting streets forced their way through these packed structures, and the wild elf could only wonder at the kind of desperation that would compel free creatures to dwell in such squalid, tightly packed surroundings.

Many towering edifices of stone rose among a tangle of lesser buildings, and wide avenues cut through the chaos to link numerous teeming alleys and lanes. The whole of the crowded metropolis blocked the valley between two huge volcanoes, with the broad expanse of the Solamnic Plain extending beyond. Where the city met the plain, the high wall of stone had been erected, and though it was pierced by numerous gates, Ash could see that it presented a daunting obstacle to anyone attempting to attack the city from the west.

Finally the mighty temples, grand structures that

flanked the city on three sides, came into view. Even these left him cold. How could their grandeur hope to compare to the majesty of even the smallest mountain peak? Beyond the farthest temple stretched the high wall, studded with towers, bristling with parapets, screening Sanction against any army that dared to approach it from the plains. For the first time, Ashtaway began to see the true potential of Sir Kamford's plan, suspecting that the knights might meet with bold success even though they attacked a place where, all told, they might be outnumbered by something greater than one hundred to one.

The mountain trail led down from the east, and from his vantage the elf got a better look at the broad clearing on this side of the city. Many corrals had been erected there, and though some were empty, others held large herds of horses or oxen. He could also see the tents and barns, lined in neat rows, where Sir Kamford had said they would find the accumulated weapons and stores of the Dark Queen's reserve.

Ashtaway wondered briefly about his own presence here, on the fringes of a place that would soon become a savage battleground. On his previous visit to the pass, when he had discovered the trail, he had ventured only far enough through the saddle to get a look at the city. This was not a place he had any desire to explore. Yet even with that memory—and the same feeling now, only much stronger—he continued to creep toward Sanction's festering and polluted fringes.

Certainly, the knights no longer needed the Kagonesti's help to reach their battle. The trail down the mountain was smooth and wide, aided by the fact that the slope was far more gradual within Sanction valley than without. Still, Ashtaway never considered departing before the charge. He had been impressed by these serious warriors with their great steeds, and he was very interested in seeing their attack.

He knew that the column of horsemen must have started down the trail, though they remained out of sight behind him. Sir Kamford was determined to commence his attack with the earliest hours of full daylight, while sleep still dulled the senses and impeded the reactions of the snoring garrison troops.

Nearing the bottom of the slope, Ashtaway felt his scalp tingle with a sudden sense of alarm. He wondered, briefly, what might happen if the dragons came back. It did not take a great deal of imagination to see that, if Sir Kamford was wrong about the strength of Huma's campaign and several of the serpents returned to Sanction to keep an eye on their precious reserves, a military disaster was inevitable.

Concealed by a knobby outcrop of rock beside the trail, Ash studied the smoke-screened skies. He saw no sign of anything flying there, not even a bird, and gradually convinced himself that his alarm had not been triggered by the arrival of evil dragons. It was probably just the pungent smell of this place, the elf told himself, as the bitter air stung his nostrils and wisps of sulphurous smoke brought tears to his eyes.

As he moved along the foot of the mountain, leaving the path to take advantage of the concealment offered by the rough ground at the base of the slope, he saw that the plateau of Sanction was terribly vulnerable to attack from the east. At this early hour even the slaves still slept, and the great racks of weapons—as well as the bins of coal and the stone-walled edifices of the city's great forges—stood for the most part undefended. Animals rustled and paced in the crowded corrals, bellowing and lowing as if they sensed the danger of which their masters remained blissfully unaware.

The listless sentries Ash saw included many humans and a few bored, lazy ogres. The guards on duty seemed more concerned with finding a comfortable place to rest than in protecting their precious stockpiles. And even when one of them did sit up and look around, the elf noticed that the guard paid a great deal more attention to the city beyond than to the smoldering mountain rising so close by. Obviously, the notion of an attack from the east was a thing that these guards—and, by inference, their commanders—had long since discounted.

Dawn seeped veins of crimson light through the smoke, bringing an otherworldly glow to the mountainous horizon. Whips cracked, and hulking ogres urged columns of slaves from their barracks to the mines and forges on the plateau. Ash saw these miserable laborers marching dully forth, responding only to the extent necessary to spare the sting of the lash. What must life be like for them, he wondered? How could any sentient creature surrender to such an existence? He knew that he, or any Kagonesti, would sooner accept death than allow himself to be compelled into a life of servitude.

He heard the clanging of a heavy metal object and ducked once more into a crevice between two lava-scarred rocks. Several ogres appeared, apparently marching right out of the mountainside, clomping within a stone's throw of the concealed elf. Only then did Ashtaway notice that they had emerged from a tunnel, leaving a pair of great iron doors standing open in the mouth of their subterranean passage.

Squinting in the growing light, the Kagonesti observed that the file of ogres numbered at least a dozen. The brutes were coated with black dust and tromped along slowly, with an unmistakable air of fatigue. They wore large swords at their sides and dented, battle-scarred helmets on their heads. Obviously these were not workers, but warriors.

"Good to see sky again," one grunted, coughing with an exhalation of dust.

"Tunnel's too blasted long," another groused. "Too many days underground."

"But at least we get to Sanction," a third growled. The latter seemed to be some sort of commander. He cuffed the two complainers across the backs of their heads. "Straighten up! March good-like!"

Still muttering, the rest of the monsters took steps to

obey, brushing the heaviest layers of dust from their arms, adjusting their swords at their belts so that the weapons hung straight. They even tried to collect their file into a double rank, but in this they were less than successful. The elf watched as they marched out of earshot, discerning that the ogres veered sharply left, apparently heading for the city and not the labor fields of the broad plateau.

Ash took careful note of the concealed entrance, wondering if his knowledge of yet another path might prove useful in the immediate future. Sidling sideways, darting from one cluster of rocks to another, he sought to get a look inside.

The tunnel opened into a low cut in the rocks, which helped to conceal it from outside observation. The two large doors must have weighed many tons each, and for a moment Ash couldn't understand how anyone could have opened them. Then the elf saw a curious wheel, set on its side with spokes extending out beyond the rim. Around the axle below the wheel was a tight coil of rope, and though he couldn't understand how it worked, the Kagonesti guessed that this mechanism was the means of opening and closing the door. Leaning farther, he saw a second, matching wheel beside the other door.

Movement within the tunnel caught his eye as several figures advanced from the shadows. He heard the cracking of a whip and a sudden yelp of pain.

"Move, you toads!" growled a deep voice—a sound that could rumble only from an ogre chest.

Ash crouched just a few feet outside the still opened doors and observed a number of small figures scrambling and tumbling toward him. The whip snapped again, and the small figures scattered to all sides.

"Get back here! Turn that capstan! *Now*, by the Dark Queen, or dere'll be no gruel for you!"

Whimpering pathetically, the little fellows gathered, cringing, around one of the curious wheels. Seizing the spokes where they emerged beyond the rim, the dwarflike figures began to pull. With a creaking groan, the nearest door began, very slowly, to move.

Now Ash saw the overseer, who was indeed an ogre. The monster wore a black tunic of stiff leather studded with nails. An old specimen, the brute had lost both his tusks, but his bloodshot eyes still sparked with evil and cunning. He raised a clublike fist, and the elf saw the supple strand of the whip lash back, ready for another strike at the tiny, pathetic slaves.

That blow would never land, as a steel-tipped arrow flew into the cavern mouth with silent accuracy, slicing through the ogre's neck. The brute, retching and gagging, stumbled backward, far too slowly to avoid the tattooed figure that plunged through the door.

Ashtaway raised his axe with cold, deadly efficiency. The ogre, both hamlike fists grasping the shaft that emerged from its throat, gaped stupidly at impending death. The axe swept downward once, and again, leaving the monster as a gory corpse on the tunnel floor.

The slaves, each of whom was as filthy and disheveled an individual as Ash had ever seen, gaped up at him. Slack jaws distended, eyes as wide as saucers, the little fellows looked from the dead ogre to the tall, garishly tattooed elf.

One of the slaves left the wheel and stepped to the side of the corpse. He sniffed the brute, then prodded with his toe. Finally he hauled back and delivered a sharp kick into the monster's unfeeling knee.

In an instant, the rest of the group, which numbered perhaps ten, scrambled all over the body, spitting, kicking, pinching, punching, inflicting all manner of vengeance over what Ash had no trouble believing had been very rough treatment.

"T'anks, Mister!" declared the first of the slaves to inspect the corpse, leaving to his fellows the meting out of revenge. "You kilt ol' No-Teeth, but good!"

"You're welcome," Ash replied, struggling to understand the slave's thick accent. The Kagonesti leaned forward to get a better look at this curious laborer.

The little fellow, as if sensing that he was under inspection, stood up straight and thrust his chest out so far that a seam ripped along the side of his filthy tunic.

Ashtaway had encountered dwarves before, though he had never spoken to one—and never would, if he had a modicum of choice about the matter. He knew there was something vaguely dwarflike about this wretch, but at the same time no dwarf he had ever seen had been as scrawny, as filthy, and as abject as this slave and his fellows. A beard that was really no more than a few straggling hairs curled outward from the runt's receding chin, and he casually picked his nose—even as he continued to stand at attention.

As they finished their gleeful vengeance, the other slaves, one by one, marched over to stand beside their leader. Ash sensed that the fellows actually tried to form a straight line, though the formation assumed more of an **S** shape as more and more of the slaves joined up.

"Ogres find ol' No-Teeth, they gonna be right mad," one mused, not displeased by the notion.

"*Real* mad," another declared sagely—or at least, he would have sounded sage if he hadn't belched immediately following his pronouncement.

"You better scram," the leader suggested, winking at Ashtaway. "When more ogres come, we'll tell 'em No-Teeth fell down, say he couldn't git up. They just give us a new boss."

The Kagonesti was touched by the courageous, if misguided, offer to cover for him. He looked at the corpse, with the arrow jutting from beneath its chin, the two gruesome axe wounds that had only now ceased to bleed. "I, um, I think they'll see that No-Teeth didn't just have an accident."

The spokesman for the slaves sniffed, insulted by the suggestion. "I'm Highbulp Toofer—I'm a *good* liar! You think I'm no-good liar or sumthin'?"

Holding up a placating hand, the elf shook his head. "No! I'm sure you're a very good liar! But tell me, what are you? Are you a dwarf?"

"You betcha! Gully dwarves, all of us is! We the bosses of these tunnels—'til the ogres come, anyway."

"Are there more ogres coming? Do they live down here somewhere?"

The highbulp looked at Ashtaway, apparently wondering if the elf could possibly be as ignorant as he seemed. Deciding, obviously, that he could, the filthy dwarf spoke with great seriousness.

"Nobody lives down in these here caves—they's just roads to here and there. 'Ceptin' us and No-Teeth. We live here, so's we can open da gate."

An idea began to tug at the edge of Ashtaway's consciousness. Perhaps it had started even before he had shot the fateful arrow. "These tunnels—do they go a long way?"

Highbulp Toofer nodded vigorously, causing his dirty braid of hair to flop up and down over his face.

"Do they come out only in Sanction—or do some of them go under the mountain, come out somewhere else?"

"They goes all over the place. Under mountain, over mountain—even to different mountains!"

"You seem like a terribly wise Highbulp—but do you know these paths? Could you show a person the tunnel, say, to the other side of this mountain?"

"*I* kin show!" boasted one of the gully dwarves, shoving Toofer aside.

"Boodle gets you lost, right quick!" Toofer snapped. "But *I* knows the ways!"

"Look!" cried another gully dwarf, who had crept toward the still-opened doors and looked out on the plateau beyond. "They're doin' a parade!"

Ash remembered the knights and vividly pictured what the dwarf imagined as a "parade." The elf sprang back to the doorway, stepping out just far enough to get a view of the wide, flat ground to the east of the city.

The first thing that caught his eye was the rank of knights. True to his plan, Sir Kamford had led his company down the trail in the predawn shadows. His stealthy approach had no doubt been aided by the darkness cloaking the west-facing slope of the descent. In any event, the knights had apparently arrived at the foot of the mountain without being detected.

Now, as Ashtaway watched the last of the horsemen take up positions in the center of the line, they formed into a long, single rank. Lances raised, horses prancing anxiously, the Solamnic riders sat straight and proud in their saddles—as if they held themselves aloof from the chaos they were about to bring upon this valley.

An ogre sentry near one of the grain barns shouted, voice shrill with panic, and others took up the cry as the dawn mist parted to reveal the line of steel and flesh. A battle horn brayed somewhere in the midst of the labor camps, and the elf saw small groups of ogres lumbering toward the field. Many more figures—most of them slaves, no doubt—streamed out of the camps, toward shelter in the fiery, tangled city below.

The sun crested the ridge behind the knights, piercing beneath the heavy layer of overcast with shocking brilliance, like a wave of fire sweeping from the heavens into the seething hell of Sanction. Sunlight glinted like diamonds off the silver armor of the horsemen. Ashtaway realized that the knights had scrubbed the clay and the mud from their armor, discarding the leafy camouflage they had worn during the mountain trek. Polished, gleaming, and immaculate, they rode horses brushed sleek, with silken manes flowing in the wind.

For the first time Ash understood that it was more than vanity that had caused the knights to spend so much time cleaning and polishing their equipment. The pristine rank, appearing as if by magic against Sanction's unprotected flank, must have seemed to the enemy like some ethereal strike force dispatched by Paladine himself to smite his enemies.

Now the men put their heels to the horses, and the long line of steeds commenced to advance at a slow, deliberate walk—a pace that was, by its precise and unhurried nature, in some ways more frightening than a thundering gallop. Lances raised high, the riders quickly accelerated into a pounding, steady trot. Ash was particularly impressed by the way in which the rank never wavered—each of the horses moved at exactly the same pace. Spread across the broad field, the line of the charge stretched for nearly half a mile—a startling breadth of frontage for the relatively small number of attackers.

Ashtaway knew that no Kagonesti advance could ever be so precise, so well ordered, and he briefly regretted the chaotic impulses of his own braves. Certainly those urges led to many acts of individual bravery, but at the same time they served to dissipate the concentrated force of the tribe's warriors as a whole. He remembered the attack against the bakali beside the Bluelake. If all the braves had shot their arrows together, the shocking effect of the initial volley would have been greatly magnified.

The horses broke into a canter, and the thundering of their hooves pounded audibly to Ashtaway on the mountainside—and, no doubt, throughout Sanction as well. Still, somehow, despite their speed, the knights maintained a precise line. Lances that had been upraised were now lowered, couched in the riders' flanks, silvery tips angling toward the pockets of ogres and other warriors who scrambled to form some kind of desperate, makeshift defense before their precious forges, barns, and arsenals.

Finally the attackers broke into a gallop, and here the slightest variations opened in their lines as the fastest horses pulled slightly ahead of the slowest. Even so, the knights and their chargers advanced as a wall, bristling with razor-sharp lances, fueled by a grim desire for victory.

The initial groups of defenders raised their weapons, some ogres displaying heroic courage in standing to meet the charge. Screams of pain rose from the field, mingled with the splintering sounds of spear shafts breaking and the shouted battle cries of the charging knights. Yet the horsemen swept past without pause, the straight line barely rippling over each pocket of defenders, and Ash was awed to see that not a single ogre remained standing once the rank had passed them. The knights and their horses, conversely, did not falter in the precise formation of their advance.

Other groups of defenders—ogres, bakali, and numerous human warriors—scrambled to raise weapons, to join ranks in the face of the thunderous onslaught. Unarmored, clapping helmets on their heads, breastplates hastily fastened over their cotton tunics, these ragged, frightened warriors emerged from the barracks and forges, urged toward the sounds of the charge by the profane exhortations of their captains. One by one the companies were pounded into the dirt by the inexorably advancing knights, until those that had not yet joined the battle turned and fled in a desperate attempt to avoid the crushing wave of death.

One or two horses fell, gutted or hamstrung by desperate ogres. Ash saw a knight climb to his feet beside a writhing mount. The man shook his head groggily, then drew a mighty sword. He cleaved a nearby ogre who showed signs of stirring, then looked around for further victims. When none showed, he raised the weapon and trotted, on foot, behind the rank of his fellows.

By the time Sir Kamford's charge swept fully across the vast plateau, the horsemen had smashed every defender who had dared to stand in their way. A few ogres still moved, but these were stunned by the shock of the attack. Ashtaway saw one of these stagger to his feet, look at the devastation around him, then collapse in apparent despair. Others tried to fight, but could offer only feeble resistance to a few dismounted knights who now charged forward in the wake of the horses. Most of the riders had discarded their lances, and now the riders chopped, slashed, and stabbed with cold efficiency.

The knights broke into smaller groups as the charge was segmented by the looming piles of coal and the block-like structures of the forges, storage barns, and arsenals. Around the corrals, where horses bucked and snorted, fences went down under the hooves of chargers. More knights dismounted, smashing additional fences and prying open steel-barred gates. Like water flowing out of a breached reservoir, the horses streamed through the openings, while shouting knights, brandishing flaring torches, urged the frightened beasts into a raging stampede.

In Sanction itself, bright banners now flew from many staffs, while brassy horns brayed a constant summons to arms.

Ash saw troops streaming upward from the city, impelled by brash trumpets and hysterical cries of warning, but he could also see that these reinforcements would be too late. Flames spurted upward from one pile of wooden sticks—sticks that would never become the spear shafts that had been their destiny. Seizing the makeshift torches, the knights plunged through the camp, throwing flame at the stockpiles of coal.

Some of the men dismounted, smashing down the doors of forges and storehouses, charging inside with swords drawn. Soon smoke puffed from the broken doorways, and by the time the knights emerged to seek their next targets, orange blossoms of flame had begun to surge upward. A few more pockets of defenders tried to stand against the knights, but these were quickly ridden down and smashed.

More corrals collapsed under the onslaught, and herds of oxen lumbered in panic. Ashtaway had a brief picture of the food that stampeded away from them, thinking that a small portion of the herd would be sufficient to feed his tribe for years.

Frequently, now, the defenders of Sanction showed no heart for this battle. Ash watched with cruel pleasure as a whole company of human pikemen threw down their weapons and fled toward the city, only to be trampled beneath the hooves of the vengeful cavalry.

When bands of survivors did reach the broad roadways leading down into the city, their terror was a palpable force. Fleeing headlong, their shouts of panic audible even to the distant Kagonesti observer, these men piled into the wave of reinforcements that was trying to climb up the same road down which the routed defenders fled. Even when the fresh troops raised sword and spear in the face of their fleeing comrades, they couldn't bring the rout to a halt—the panicked survivors simply parted like water, scrambling through ditches and over rough slopes in their haste to escape the killing ground.

The combination of gravity, a lack of knowledge about their foes, and the palpable fear of the retreating troops gave pause to the fresh warriors. Many of the reinforcements stepped off the road to allow the running men to pass, while others actually turned and joined the flight. It amused Ashtaway to observe the contagious nature of this panic. Soon hundreds, then thousands, of men ran from a fight that they had yet to see! Of course, Ash thought with a tight grin, when these veterans later gathered around a bivouac's campfires, their roles in this furious battle would undoubtedly be embellished.

Much of the plateau was obscured by smoke now, as more and more fires erupted from the Dark Queen's arsenals and strongholds. Knights rode back and forth, many bearing torches, chasing the fleeing animals, trying to infuse even greater panic to the stampede. Sir Kamford, Sir Blayne, and the other leaders shouted and waved their arms, seeking to collect their men into companies, reforming the ranks to pursue the attack.

Once again Ash felt the tickling sense of alarm that had disturbed him earlier in the morning—hairs prickling upward at the nape of his neck. He looked to the west, suddenly fearful, and observed a serpentine shape, ghostly white, gliding below the clouds. Other mighty, winged creatures soared just beyond—another that was white, and several of rich blue. Broad wings stroked the air, and the deadly forms gained speed as they plunged downward from the overhanging pall of clouds.

With a pang of dread, Ashtaway knew what he was seeing: the dragons of evil had taken wing and were but moments from the fight.

# Chapter 19

# Into Darkness

Ashtaway acted with the speed of thought, throwing back his head and drawing a deep breath. His lips stretched taut across his mouth as, cupping his hands, he released a piercing shriek. The urgent cry of the eagle keened across the valley, ringing even over the sounds of battle. Several of the knights raised their heads, looking about for the source of the sound.

Instead, they saw serpentine death, plunging from the heavy layer of cloud. A white dragon in the lead shrieked in fury, and behind it other white and blue shapes thundered downward from the glowering clouds, horrific merchants of violence and death.

Again Ash sent out the cry, drawing his axe and waving

it above his head. Would they see him? One of the knights looked in his direction and shouted something, spurring his horse toward the wild elf. Several others wheeled to follow, and he knew that the humans had at least seen the hope he offered. Whether they could reach it in time was another question.

Casting a glance over his shoulder, he saw that the iron doors to the tunnel remained open. He expected that the gully dwarves would have vanished deep into the passageway and was startled to see the group of them clustered at his feet. The little wretches had crept forward soundlessly and now eagerly observed the battle from behind the shelter of the elf's legs.

Quickly Ash sought out Toofer, fastening his gaze on the Highbulp's grimy face. "Go back. Get ready to close the doors when I tell you to! Will you do that?"

"You betcha!" Toofer's head nodded eagerly, though he made no move to return to the tunnel.

Desperately Ash looked back to the battle, where most of the knights had remounted their chargers. In small groups they galloped toward the mountain, where the Kagonesti again waved his axe.

Looking skyward, the warrior saw three white dragons, diving in the lead, and at least a pair of blues coming close behind. The knights separated, scattering not from panic, Ashtaway sensed, but training. This way they presented the fewest targets to the horrific, death-dealing breath weapons of the vengeful serpents.

"Go inside! Now!" Ash repeated, his voice a desperate growl as he saw Toofer and the other gully dwarves still watching the battle.

The Highbulp scowled suspiciously. "You want us to miss best part of fight?" he demanded.

"I want you to stay *alive!*" Ashtaway snarled, furious. "And just maybe, to save some of my friends! Now, *go!*" He punctuated the command with a menacing wave of his axe, and that was enough to send the dwarves tumbling like ninepins back toward the tunnel mouth.

They took up positions at the great closing-wheels, but fortunately did not yet draw them shut.

"Wait till I tell you to close the doors!" the elf shouted, before turning back to the deadly fight.

The leading white dragon belched a cloud of frigid, killing frost. The white blast exploded downward and out, expanding across the ground, sweeping several riders and their plunging horses into the deadly effect—not to mention a few craven ogres who crouched nearby, apparently having realized they could never outrun the horses.

Dissipating almost as quickly as it had formed, the frost revealed the motionless figures of horses, knights, and ogres in its wake. The victims had not been frozen in the postures of the battle. Instead, the force of the frosty blast had sent the knights tumbling from the horses, smashing the unfortunate steeds to the ground with fatal, crushing power. The dead lay still, rigid, in postures suggesting the extreme agony and horror of their last moments.

More of the riders began to retreat, dodging through the dense clouds of smoke spewing from the coal piles. The white dragons soared after them, breathing their deadly frost, but nowhere could they catch more than two or three victims in any single explosive burst.

Breaking out of the enclosed buildings, the riders lay low across their saddles, lashing every bit of speed from the plunging mounts. The horses needed no encouragement; nostrils snorting, eyes wide with panic, the animals galloped in a desperate lather, keenly aware of the doom that soared just behind their tails.

One of the blue dragons swooped in from the flank, gliding low across the path of the knights. The monster's jaws gaped, and Ash blinked against the bright flash of lightning that burst forth—a killing bolt that seared two riders, instantly killing men and horses. The dragon slashed with its front foot, striking another armored rider from his horse as the azure wyrm swept upward for another pass. The man writhed in the serpent's crushing grip until, a hundred feet in the air, the dragon released its helpless victim. Ashtaway clenched his fists in barely contained fury as he watched the man plunge to his death.

Now the first of the riders neared the tunnel's mouth, and the Kagonesti Pathfinder gestured with his steel-headed axe. "In here! Keep going—get out of sight!"

A white dragon soared low, the cloud of his deadly breath trapping a number of riders as they crowded toward the tunnel entrance. Ashtaway tried to ignore the cries of agonized men as the killing frost embraced them, turning his eyes instead to the dozens of knights still struggling to reach shelter. Lightning crackled through the air, and more clouds of frost swept the ground, but now a steady file of horsemen galloped through the widespread iron gates, disappearing into the shadows below the mountains.

Ash recognized Sir Kamford, with Sir Blayne galloping at his side. A monstrous blue swept toward the two knights and in an eye blink the Kagonesti raised his bow and let a steel-tipped shaft fly. The arrow struck the dragon in its face, and with a roar of irritation the creature jerked its head to the side, spitting a hasty lightning bolt into the rocks before the elven archer.

Tumbling backward, Ashtaway smelled the acrid scent of the lightning strike, but realized that he was still alive. The flying dragons had all swept past, and though they quickly swerved around for another pass, most of the riders had gained the shelter of the tunnel.

Staggering to his feet, the wild elf looked back across the field. Kamford and Blayne waited beyond the gate, holding their wild-eyed, snorting horses in place with firm tugs at the reins. Apparently unconcerned with their own safety, they waited to watch the last of their men flee toward shelter.

"Start closing the gates!" cried Ashtaway, fixing his eyes on Highbulp Toofer's awestruck face. Blinking, the dwarf squinted in concentration, then shouted something to his fellows. Grunting from the effort, but working with surprising unity, the little fellows began to turn the great wheels. Ash saw the doors swivel inward, though he was dismayed by the slow progress of their movement. The gap remained plenty wide enough to allow a dragon, on foot, to press inward after the retreating Knights of Solamnia.

A trio of knights, fleeing from the far end of the camp, seemed like the last of the riders. Ash looked at the doors, which still closed with painful slowness, then back to the three knights. Lying low across their horses' necks, the men kept their eyes fastened on the refuge, refusing to look at the death wheeling through the skies, diving toward their tails. Kamford and Blayne reined in their horses just outside the gate, staring in desperate hope at the last of their fleeing companions.

Ashtaway heard Sir Kamford's groan of dismay as two dragons, a white and a blue, dove toward the three knights. Lightning crackled, the bolt of energy vanishing into a sudden cloud of frost with an intense hiss. The stench of burned flesh rose even above the stink of the lightning, and the cloud dissipated to reveal the garishly frozen, incongruously blackened corpses of the three men and their horses.

The blue dragon swooped toward the tunnel mouth as the white tried to pull up and away, but the frost dragon moved too slowly. The trailing coil of its tail struck the blue's wing, sending the creature careening off to the side. The two serpents crashed into the ground with a shudder that Ashtaway felt through his moccasins.

Still another dragon, a white, dove toward the iron doors that gradually inched shut as the last of the fleeing riders disappeared inside. Sir Kamford and Sir Blayne were the only two knights still exposed to danger.

"Go!" cried Blayne, suddenly leaping down from his saddle. The knight drew his monstrous sword and slapped the flat of the blade against the flank of Sir Kamford's horse, sending the animal galloping inward, carrying its cursing rider into the darkness of the tunnel.

Ashtaway leapt to the doors, seeing that they were

about halfway closed—still not enough of a barrier to halt a plunging dragon.

"Go, elf!" cried Sir Blayne, stepping away from the doors to face the diving dragon with his upraised blade.

Words caught in the Kagonesti's throat as Ash tried to urge the knight inward. He understood the man's sacrifice, knew that it was necessary, but in that instant wanted desperately to change his mind. Blayne had been an arrogant boor, he remembered with a pang of guilt, but there would be no faulting the man's courage.

Ash dove through the narrowing portal, hearing Sir Blayne's voice rise in a roaring challenge. "For the Oath and the Measure!" he cried, stepping forward and chopping savagely at the white's looming snout.

The serpent reared back, avoiding the blow, and the elf waited for the killing blast of frost, hoping that the deadly chill did not penetrate too deeply into the shelter of the tunnel. Curiously, the beast did not belch its murderous breath. Perhaps the monster had expended all its frigid exhalations against the fleeing knights outside.

In any event, the creature closed on Sir Blayne with wicked talons and crushing jaws. The knight's blade flashed again, and then, finally, the closing of the tunnel doors blocked the scene from view.

\* \* \* \* \*

Gully dwarves clustered around Ashtaway, clinging to his leggings, grasping for his hands. The little creatures stared upward, horrified, at the snorting horses and grunting, cursing knights, who tried to dismount in the utter darkness of the tunnel.

"Why you bring *them* here?" Toofer asked in a hoarse whisper—a voice loud enough to resonate through the enclosed tunnel.

"These are my friends—and yours. You helped save them," the wild elf explained.

"But horses, *too*?"

Ashtaway wasn't listening. He saw Sir Kamford, numb with shock, staring at the huge doors, where the faintest trickle of light spilled through the crack in the center. Somewhere behind the elf another knight groaned as two comrades worked to set his broken arm.

The Pathfinder stepped to Kamford's side and, hesitantly, laid a hand on the man's shoulder. The knight sighed, shook his head in resignation, and turned away from the heavy iron doors.

"Our fight will make the lords proud," declared Sir Kamford wearily.

"And you? Should it not make you proud as well?" asked the wild elf.

"Aye, my friend, but with the pride comes a weighty measure of grief."

"Was this a victory against the Dark Queen?" Ashtaway asked, remembering the great fires, the scattered livestock—and the fallen knights.

"A bloody fight, but a victory indeed," Kamford agreed. He blinked, trying to see into the depths of the stygian tunnel. "At least, a victory if we can get out of here. Do you know? Are we in a trap or an escape tunnel?"

"Come over here. There's someone you have to meet. I think he can show us the way."

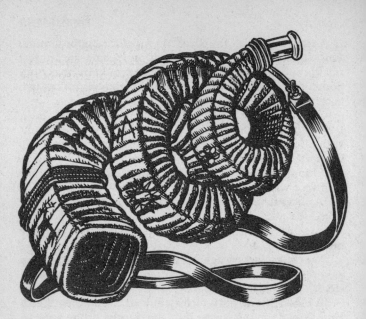

# Chapter 20

# A Parting of Friends

"Go out here," Toofer said, pointing to a pair of large iron doors blocking the end of the roughly carved tunnel. The gully dwarf halted in his tracks, arms crossed firmly across his chest, as if he couldn't wait for the elf and his human companions to be gone.

Ashtaway stepped forward, Sir Kamford at his side. The knight held aloft the last of the sputtering torches that had illuminated their world during the long, often confusing march through the tunnels under the great mountain.

The portals before them resembled strongly the doors Ashtaway had discovered in the valley above Sanction—though the elf sensed that their long subterranean march had carried them well south of that dark and smoldering city. They had been underground for approximately three days, Ash guessed, though they had seen no glimpse of the sky in that time and thus had no real grasp of the duration of their sunless trek. The wild elf also deduced, based on long stretches of gradual downhill slope, that the war party had descended a considerable distance from the entrance on the mountainside.

"Go on. Git," urged the Highbulp, all but pushing the knight toward the door.

"What's outside?" Ash asked suspiciously.

"Usual stuff. Air, mountains, sky. Ground where horses can poop and not stink up tunnel."

The latter concern, the elf thought with a smile, was strongly on Toofer's mind. Though the gully dwarves had displayed a remarkable lack of fastidiousness in all aspects of their lives, the presence of the knights' mighty steeds in these enclosed tunnels had apparently proved too much for even their less-than-delicate sensibilities.

Sir Kamford called several of his men forward to work the door-opening mechanisms—capstans, he called them. The first glimmerings of daylight soon crept through the opening portals, causing the men to blink and shield their eyes until they could adjust, once again, to bright illumination.

"Your help has been very valuable," Ashtaway said to the gully dwarf Highbulp, who had begun to tap his foot in agitation.

"Never mind about that. But t'anks for killin' ol' No-Teeth. We never liked him so much."

"You're . . . welcome, I think," Ash said with a grin. "But to be on the safe side, I wouldn't go right back to Sanction if I were you. No-Teeth might have had some friends, and I bet they're not too happy right now."

"No friends. But still, we go to different tunnel for a while. Was getting boring, just 'open door,' 'close door' alla time. Toofer *real* Highbulp, gonna get me a tribe. Maybe even make a army, like you got. No horses, though."

The gully dwarf wrinkled his face and held his nose as one of the great warhorses made another contribution to the floor of the tunnel. "Canya open that door faster?" he asked.

The knights ignored him, and in truth the iron portals swung open fairly quickly. No doubt, Sir Kamford's men were as eager to get outside as the gully dwarves were to see them go. Against the brightness of a cloudless day they saw tall, leafy trees, the edge of a forest beginning a few paces beyond the tunnel doors.

"You've been a true ally," Ashtaway solemnly told Highbulp Toofer. "Among my people, we have a term of honor. We bestow it on some of our great warriors, and those leaders who have an impact on our history. We call such a hero 'Pathfinder.'"

The Kagonesti took a tiny feather from his belt pouch, a tuft of ruby-bright crimson fading into an iridescent green. He placed it behind Toofer's ear, entangling it in the loose curls of oily hair.

"Highbulp Toofer of the Smoking Mountain, I name you 'Pathfinder.'"

The gully dwarf blinked in surprise. His chest puffed outward as he stood up to his full three-foot height, beaming.

"No worries about ogres chasin' you," he said. "Highbulp Pathfinder gets 'em going on the wrong way!"

"Thanks, my friend." Ashtaway was touched by the little fellow's heart.

"And our thanks, too." Sir Kamford joined them as the knights, leading their horses, began to file out of the doorway. No more than sixty of the original hundred had survived, but they knew that—without the discovery of the tunnel—all the knights would have perished beneath frost and lightning or fang and talon. "Sorry about the mess. I suggest you leave it for the ogres to clean up," he suggested with a chuckle.

Toofer brightened still further. "That's a *good* idea," he agreed before turning to the dozen members of his clan who had watched, awestruck, the bestowing of the colored feather.

"C'mon, you louts!" he shouted, pulling a forked stick out of his voluminous pouch. A string of rubbery, flexible sinew linked the two split ends "We got new game wit' ogres. Everybody got a flinger?"

The Highbulp commenced describing what promised to be a very elaborate tactical plan as Ashtaway and Sir Kamford finally passed through the doors. Breathing deeply of the fresh air, the elf looked up and saw close-pressing ridges, thickly covered with broad-leaved trees. A waterfall streamed, a plume of white mist, into the head of the valley, and nearby they could hear the splashing of a shallow but fast-flowing brook. The smells were summery and the air thick enough to confirm that they had indeed descended far from the mountainous heights.

"We must be very near the plains," Ash guessed. "If you follow the stream down from this valley, I suspect you'll be out of the foothills by the end of the day."

"Then westward, toward Solamnia," Sir Kamford agreed. "I need to learn how Huma's campaign fares— and let the lords know of our success."

"Was it worth the cost?" Ashtaway wondered. Throughout the long, dark march, his mind had replayed the glorious images of the charge. He remembered the inexorably precise advance, the way that no ogre or human could stand in the face of those raging horses.

Then had come the fires, when so much of the enemy's stockpiles had burned. This still seemed, to Ashtaway, a curious way to fight. It made sense when the knight described it—the Kagonesti could understand that the weapons and food would benefit the Dark Queen's army for some months—but it was not the kind of thing any wild elf chieftain would try to do. After hours of subterranean meditation, Ashtaway had finally understood why: When the Kagonesti went to war, they expected to win or lose on the day the battle was joined. This planning for battles that would not occur until the next season was a thing that seemed pointless, even defeatist.

"I believe it was," Sir Kamford declared, though he shook his head with a weariness that belied his words. "To lose Sir Blayne . . . to see so many other good men fall, never to rise. Who can say? If those arrows, that steel, were destined to kill a hundred men in the future, the cost was just. If they never were to have been used. . . ."

The knight lapsed into silence, and only after a moment's reflection did Ash realize that the human was patiently, elven-fashion, awaiting the Kagonesti's response.

"Even so, many ogres were slain. And some slaves were freed. I think that those are good things," Ashtaway replied.

"And I would like to think that the knights have made a friend—a *good* friend—among the proudest, the finest elves on all of Ansalon."

The Kagonesti Pathfinder, deeply moved, touched his hand to the knight's shoulder. "You have," he promised, knowing that Sir Kamford Willis was a warrior as courageous, as mighty—in his own way—as Faltath, or any heroic wild elf brave.

Ashtaway stood still, remembering and meditating, while the knights allowed their horses to graze and drink. He still hadn't moved when they mounted, though he finally raised a hand in farewell as Sir Kamford, riding at the rear, disappeared into the trees.

After a few brief minutes spent rigging several snares, Ash spent the rest of the day swimming in the stream and sunbathing. The snares provided him with two plump rabbits for dinner, and afterward he slept under the stars. Every time he awakened, he rejoiced to the array of lights that gleamed and twinkled at him from the moonless vault of the sky. He felt newly alive, as if he had emerged from the tunnels a different person, a different kind of Pathfinder.

He took five days in returning to the south, following valleys that became steadily more familiar as he moved closer to the Bluelake. All the while his mind worked, as he wrestled with an expanded view of his world. For the first time in his life, he considered the notion that there were good people in the world—people who were not of the Kagonesti. Sir Kamford, and even Highbulp Toofer, had forced Ashtaway to reconsider the traditions that had kept his tribe in an almost constant state of war. Surely some enemies, such as the ogres and the bakali, were worthy foes. But perhaps it was wrong to assume that humans, that dwarves, were enemies, simply because they were humans or dwarves.

Ashtaway even speculated about the Silvanesti—might the Kagonesti learn that the ancient clans of the House Elves were not filled with the despicable villains that Ash had always been taught resided there? He had known Kagonesti who had been killed by Silvanesti swords, and of the deadly traps laid by the House Elves to protect their precious cities. He had seen Silvanesti slain by arrows fired from wild elven ambush. He sensed that such depths of hatred could not be wrong. The House Elves and the wild elves were forever destined to be foes.

As he traveled through the eternal woodland, Ashtaway discarded some of his earlier beliefs and embraced others. He reflected on war and peace, on the worth of life and death when a hated foe stood before one's blade or bow. He wondered about the nature of hatred, such as that which had raged between his people and humankind through all the ages of Krynn. And still the inner torment raged within him. It was not until he had reached a familiar valley within a day's march of the village that he understood why.

Turning to the side, he made his way toward the foothill valley, climbing through the rocky notch to see the black, obsidian wall. He wished he had the time to hunt, to bring fresh game with him, but his urgency wouldn't allow delay.

Once again he found Hammana in the woods—though this time he didn't surprise her. Instead, she stood in the midst of the clearing, watching the woods as he emerged from the underbrush.

"Hello, Pathfinder," she said quietly. Her hazel eyes shined as she looked at him, her chin held proudly raised.

"Hammana. . . ." He crossed to her in long strides and took her hands in his.

"No." She pulled back, and he saw that the shining in her eyes came from unshed tears. "I cannot let myself love you."

He didn't pursue, though his hands remained outstretched, reaching. "I am the Pathfinder now. I didn't ask for the horn, but it's a destiny that came to me—and I shall bear it, I hope, well.

"But I know already, Hammana, that I'm a *different* Pathfinder than those who came before me. I am not Iydaway or Barcalla or Father Kagonesti. Just as Iydaway changed the tasks of leadership by speaking and persuading rather than guiding in aloof silence, I, too, shall change. I will not make war against the humans, simply because they are human. Already I have done a thing unlike any other Pathfinder of the Kagonesti."

"You . . . you will be a great leader of our people. This I know." She seemed proud when she said this, and sad as well.

"But this peace with humankind is not the only way I will be different," Ash persisted. He stepped forward and took her hands again, holding too tightly for Hammana to easily pull away. "Other taboos, too, date from an earlier time. They may have been right in the past, but I know they are wrong for me."

She looked at him intently now, surprised and wondering.

"I will also be the first Pathfinder who takes a wife . . . if she will have me."

For a moment, he didn't know what she would say. The tears spilled down her cheeks then, overwhelming her efforts to blink them away.

"She will," the elfwoman said, and his arms wrapped her as she fell against him.

"This is a wonderful development, truly splendid!" Lectral declared when, hand in hand, they went to the cave and shared their news. "A bit of departure from tradition, though, isn't it?"

"It is," Ashtaway agreed. "We live long lives, your people and mine, but I have learned that times can change, peoples can change—*many* things change."

Lectral blinked sagely. "Even for elves and dragons," he said with a contented nod.

# Chapter 21

# A Final Parting

The two wild elves returned to the village together. As they entered the vallenwood glade, Ashtaway saw Faltath, bearing the fresh, plump carcass of a wild pig on his shoulders, emerge from the forest on the opposite side of the clearing.

"Ashtaway!" cried the delighted brave, casting his prize to the ground. "I thanked the gods for sending me this gift of game—and now I know the cause of our joy! We shall have a feast to celebrate your return!"

"I thank you, my friend. And know that there is even more to celebrate—on this day I shall speak to Wallaki about the taking of his daughter's hand."

Faltath's eyes widened, then he threw back his head

and whooped in delight. "You *are* the Pathfinder!" he declared heartily. "And you are sure to show the tribe some very interesting trails!"

The tribe immediately set to the preparations for a feast. Older women took Faltath's pig and began to skin it, while several braves laid a bed of hardwood on the base of the fire pit.

Ashtaway crossed to the bark lodge where Wallaki, Hammana's father, sat outside the door, enjoying the afternoon's warmth. Blocked by the hut, the elder Kagonesti had not seen the pair return to the village.

"Welcome back, Pathfinder. Come sit with me and rest your feet after your long march. Do you have any further word of my daughter, or have you come straight from the Three Smoking Mountains?"

"Thank you." Ash squatted beside the old warrior. "Hammana has returned to the village with me. She will come to see you soon."

"But first . . . ?"

"I would speak with you." Ashtaway drew a deep breath and told Wallaki about the changes that he would make in his time-honored role. "I shall bear the Ram's Horn as long as the tribe wants me to have it," he concluded. "But, also, I will take a wife."

Now Wallaki's eyebrows raised and he looked at Ashtaway with keen interest. "Hammana is a precious girl, and a wonderful prize for any brave. She knows the arts of curing in ways that many healers who have studied for centuries can never master. Too, she is an elf of wondrous beauty, with many other talents as well. But I do not know how I should survive without her to tend to my needs."

Ash might have pointed out that Wallaki had survived quite nicely while his daughter had been caring for Lectral, but he did not. Instead, he spoke with respect. "Perhaps two doeskins and the down of fifty geese would make your loneliness more comfortable," he suggested.

Wallaki nodded. "That would help. But see these old fingers? They are too gnarled for proper fletching. I can still shoot, but I have no arrows."

"You will soon have one hundred of the finest shafts that I can feather," Ash promised, bowing his head. The dowry price was very high—and he was elated to pay it.

"Ah . . . that will do much to soothe my despair!" It was all the old shaman could do to keep from cackling in delight.

"We shall be wed with the autumn harvest," Ash told the beaming priest. The Pathfinder rose and bowed respectfully before he went to spread the word through the rest of the village.

Ashtaway stood beside the slowly roasting pig, far enough away so that he didn't get burned—but close enough for his silhouette to darken against the backdrop of brightness, as he looked across the faces of his people. The young Pathfinder felt a vague, unidentifiable sense of disquiet, wondering what unease lurked at the back of his mind. He wished that Iydaway could be here—and he wondered what his uncle would say about his break with tradition.

Then he realized another thing: He wished that Lectral, too, could share in this feast—that they could really celebrate the end of the Dragon War. But did he dare to hope that Huma's victory over Takhisis would occur, that the scourge of evil dragonkind might be lifted from Krynn?

"What is it, my Pathfinder?" He felt a gentle hand in his and looked down into Hammana's bright, penetrating eyes.

"I'm thinking of a friend," he said quietly.

"I think our friend will come."

Ashtaway patted her hand, appreciating her optimism even as he couldn't share it. But she was no longer looking at him—instead, she raised a hand and pointed toward the forest encircling the village.

"Look!"

Shiny silver rippled through the trees, and Ashtaway and Hammana raised shouts of greeting as a broad snout poked out of the forest. Kagonesti voices shouted in alarm, mothers sweeping children into their arms as warriors raced toward the dragon that had suddenly appeared in their midst.

Ashtaway raised the Ram's Horn to his lips and blew a joyful blast. "Hold!" he cried, as the warriors turned to look at him. "This is a friend—a very welcome friend!"

Stepping forward, Hammana at his side, he advanced to greet the mighty dragon.

The serpent, dragging his injured hind leg, limped into the clearing and coiled himself, smiling gently, at the edge of the village. Remembering Ash's tale of the great silver dragon, Lectral Hornbearer, the Kagonesti gradually overcame their awe and came forward to regard the dragon, who returned their dignified inspection with a serious and serene expression.

Children stared at the dragon wide-eyed, but without fear. Some even ventured to approach, and soon Lectral was entertaining them by lifting them up on his broad snout and letting them slide, squealing, down his smooth, curling tail.

"It is a time for changes of many kinds," Ashtaway observed solemnly.

"Aye, and friendships of many kinds as well," the dragon replied as a giggling tot tumbled from his tail into the dirt. Children clamored for more turns, but Lectral gently disengaged himself—after each of the youngsters had had a ride—and limped to the central clearing. The Kagonesti hurried about, cleaning dirt off the children, getting ready for the feast.

"It is good to see you so happy," said Lectral. "For this alone I would have come to the village."

Ashtaway didn't miss the dragon's meaning. "There is another reason that you came, then?"

"Yes. It is to make my farewells to you and Hammana, who have cared so well for me."

"Farewells? But surely you're not going anywhere? Not with the battle won, perhaps even the war! You must stay with us and celebrate the peace!"

"Alas, I cannot," sighed Lectral with genuine regret. "For, as you suspect, the war is won. But the price of that victory is the departure of me, and my kind."

"What do you mean?"

"They are winging to me, tonight. I came here to say good-bye to you and await Saytica—for the two of us will fly together."

Saytica, Ash remembered, was one of Lectral's female offspring—now a huge silver dragon in her own right. Her proud father had boasted that she was one of the foremost fighters in the dragon wing defending Palanthas.

"You're going to fly? Fly where? And *how?*" Ashtaway couldn't believe what he was hearing. He gestured at the scarred mass of the dragon's once-mighty wings. "Saytica may be a mighty dragon—but do you think she's going to *carry* you?"

Lectral smiled tolerantly, even puffing a brief snort of amusement.

"As to the where: We go to a place called the Isle of Dragons, a place beyond Ansalon. We—the dragons of silver and gold—are going there, and there we shall live out our days, and our generations."

"How do you know this?" Ashtaway challenged.

"Peace is a thing of which even the smallest birds take note—it has been the song on the wind for these past days. It is a music that spreads across the world, a tale of hope and mystery that an ear as sensitive as mine cannot help but sense."

The dragon smiled more broadly, mocking himself.

"Of course, it helped this morning that one of Saytica's children—a nestling, barely, but a fast flyer—came to my cave and told me to make ready."

"But Lectral—without wings, how will you fly?"

If the dragon had heard the question, he made no indication of the fact.

"They say that the Isle of Dragons is a splendid place, idyllic, bountiful to a dragon's needs," Lectral continued, his voice soft, dreamy. Ashtaway sensed that the great serpent did in fact relish the prospect of a pastoral life there.

The Pathfinder raised the horn to his mouth and began to play. He didn't think about the notes, but let the music rise from somewhere within his soul. Lectral half-closed his eyes, listening dreamily, while the rest of the Kagonesti sighed softly with the poignancy of the melody.

The notes of the horn, this time, were fuller and more profound than could possibly have resonated in that slender tube. Ashtaway recognized great, keening chants in the rich melody and understood that the instrument played a song of dragons. He did not, could not, know that these sounds had not rung from the horn in more than two thousand years, but he sensed their historic portent as he heard them now.

Lectral raised his own horn, and these notes joined Ash's in rising toward the sky, singing through the night. The elf had a strong feeling that Father Kagonesti himself hovered there, looking down at his people, his tribe. Ashtaway wondered what Kagonos thought about the changes in the world—and in the Pathfinder—that had come about during this portentous season.

In a flash of insight, he knew that the Elderwild was pleased.

At last, the big silver dragon lowered his horn and raised his eyes to the canopy of leaves over their heads. "They come," he said softly.

Limping awkwardly, the great serpent hobbled through the village, and made his way between the vallenwoods that stood at the top of the lakeside bluff. Emerging from the trees, he looked toward the northwest, where Lunitari had just settled below the horizon. The Kagonesti came behind, reverently gathering along the crest of the precipice, looking across the star-dappled pattern of the Bluelake.

The tribe settled into silence as the wild elves waited, following the direction of Lectral's gaze. Ashtaway still played, and still the notes of the horn keened impossibly deep and broad, and now the song expanded to fill the night.

The dragons came into sight first as silhouettes against the starlight, but as they flew lower the metallic glow of their wings shimmered even in the night sky. Many silver dragons circled overhead, most of them wheeling tirelessly far above the lakeside camp. A few dove, however, and one of these settled toward the great vallenwoods of the bluff's top, spreading her wings to land in a gush of wind beside the gathered elves and the great, crippled serpent.

"Greetings, Honored Father." Saytica, proud and beautiful, bowed to the great silver dragon. Her body was not as huge as Lectral's, but Saytica was supple and slender in a way that suggested deep and abiding power.

"Welcome, my daughter." Lectral's voice, firm with ritual, was nevertheless warm with the depth of his love.

"I am glad to find you," she said respectfully. "The time for flying is now."

"Farewell, my friends," Lectral declared with a bow of his head. Ashtaway watched in disbelief as the dragon's body abruptly shimmered and shifted, shrinking rapidly until he stood before them as an old human man. Shaggy white eyebrows concealed his yellow eyes—though Ash could still see those eyes flash in amusement at the elves' consternation.

"A—a human?" stammered the young chieftain after he regained his voice. "Why not take the form of an elf?"

The old man's face wrinkled into a smile. "Tradition, really. You see, my grandsire favored a body such as this. There were those who believed it to be his true form. In any event, I find that these whiskers, this old and wrinkled shape, suits me well."

The old man hobbled to Saytica's side, and the sleek silver neck bent low to allow him to mount. Seated between her wings, the man gave a single, regal wave, and Ashtaway felt a brief tug of melancholy. It seemed that more than a part of his life was closing—indeed, it was the conclusion of an epoch of Krynn. A world without dragons . . . what would that mean?

Then Saytica took to the air in a downrush of wings and a powerful spring. The elves watched for several minutes as she and her rider climbed into the sky, until the pair merged with all the other shadowy outlines there. In a sweeping, grand formation, the serpentine shapes turned to the north, slowly winging toward the horizon.

Gradually Ashtaway become aware of Hammana's hand in his. Together they watched the dragons wing northward for many long minutes, until their shadowy forms disappeared over the distant horizon.

# PART III

## lydahoe

*14 PC*
*Northern Silvanesti Borderlands*

# Chapter 22

# Whitetail and Silvertrout

A bit of jealousy whispered in Iydahoe's ear, though the emotion was far from a consuming blaze. Instead, the warrior wrestled with a sense of unfairness, spurred by the envious knowledge that his older brother, Kawllaph, was a very lucky wild elf. Trotting through the woods on this mission for his brother, Iydahoe really wished that he, himself, would soon know good fortune in equal measure.

Kawllaph had asked Berriama to marry him, and she had agreed with almost shameless eagerness. Now Iydahoe ran to fetch Washallak Pathfinder from the village of the Silvertrout tribe, so that the muted notes of the Ram's Horn could signal the solemnity, the timeless commitment, of the wedding vows.

When he thought of his brother's good fortune, Iyda-hoe felt that pang of envy, the feeling that Kawllaph had all the luck. Iyadahoe himself would like to court a maiden —indeed, lovely Moxilli, of the long, silken hair, came immediately to his mind. It would be splendid to have her as a companion, a lifemate. A wife was the perfect thing to make his life complete.

But then Iyadahoe's thoughts became more practical. He became painfully shy and tongue-tied whenever he so much as greeted Moxilli. And he looked more carefully at his brother's situation—Berriama was certainly not the bride that Iyadahoe would have chosen! Like so many wild elf females, Berriama had a noted tendency to nag, as well as a distressing sense of the importance of her own opinions.

Iyadahoe felt that a true warrior should be vexed by such assertiveness. He remembered the tales of his grand-father's father, of the dangers that had menaced the tribes during the Dragon Wars, and the courage with which the warriors met multitudes of threats. For a thousand years since then, the wild elves had enjoyed the peace that had reigned across Ansalon. Young warriors like Iyadahoe yearned for earlier times, and strong-minded females like Berriama became all too willing to unleash their tempers and their tongues.

Still, Kagonesti life was not bad—in fact, Iyadahoe could imagine nothing better. They had the vast wealth of untrammeled forest, the lakes and the heights. . . . They had the freedom to go where they wanted, to take the food that was offered everywhere by bountiful Ansalon.

His regrets vanishing in the cool stillness of the woods, Iyadahoe raced easily along the forest trail, skirting the deeper woods to run among widely spaced pine trunks. This was the second day of his journey, and he would need to travel all day tomorrow before he reached the Silvertrout village.

Iyadahoe tried to play over his arrival in his mind. The Pathfinder was a revered figure, after all, and the young warrior wanted to convey the invitation with proper formality. He would greet Washallak Pathfinder at his lodge on the low hillock, politely asking if the bearer of the Ram's Horn would journey to the settlement of the Whitetail tribe at his earliest convenience to preside over the wedding of Kawllaph and Berriama.

Iydahoe welcomed his mission, grateful that his status as a warrior gave him the right to perform it. The stinging pain of the tattoo needle had faded weeks earlier, within hours after his father, the tribal shaman, had ritually marked him. Perhaps it was his imagination, but the twin symbols on his face still seemed to warm his skin in a way that was not a source of irritation as much as of wonder.

His left eye was encircled by the ornately detailed outline of a long-lobed oak leaf, with extensions reaching around his forehead and a stem that trailed down to one side of his chin. A plain circle enclosed the other hazel eye, and though Iydahoe would have loved to wear the spirals of a veteran warrior, for now he had to settle for the unadorned roundel of the untested but battle-ready brave.

A feather, Iydahoe thought, returning to the pleasant contemplation of his status. He would need to get one or two bright feathers to complete his adornment as a proud Kagonesti brave. Perhaps he would trek all the way to the coast and seek a snow goose. He imagined the pristine plumage against his black hair and tattooed, sun-bronzed skin. The picture was fierce and gratifying. Perhaps he would even tie one of the rare plumes to the haft of his long-bladed knife.

His thoughts wandering, Iydahoe was only vaguely aware of the mountainous shelves rising to his left, the great sprawl of the Solamnic flatland to his right. This was wild elf territory, well south of the Black Feather and Bluelake villages but still near the wild heart of Kagonesti forest.

Iydahoe recalled his surroundings quickly when he saw a rising, crested pillar of rock. The unique structure triggered one of his prouder memories—knowledge of a place that he alone knew. Along the crest of the foothills, just beyond the rocky pillar, a narrow gorge twisted into the sheltered depths of a granite ridge. Delicate mosses grew on the floor of the gorge and showed no sign that any elf or human had ever visited the shadowy cut or the shady grotto hidden deep within. Iydahoe had found that path when he was younger—a decade before he had gotten his first warrior's tattoo. He had shown it to no one, preferring to keep the place as his own private sanctuary. Now, as a warrior, he felt that it was right and natural to know of such a place.

Before sunset, he killed a grouse with a quick arrow, cooking the unexpected delight on a small, smokeless fire. He reflected with serene pleasure on the bounty that the vast forest so willingly provided to the tribes. For a thousand years, the braves of the Kagonesti had been the sole explorers of this vast realm of forest land. Since the departure of the dragons, the servants of the Dark Queen had mostly left the wild elves alone. The bakali had vanished into their swamps; some said that the race had been exterminated, though elder warriors cautioned against this rash assumption. Ogres still lived among the high valleys of the Khalkists, but these were many marches to the north. Iydahoe, like many other young warriors, had never even seen an ogre, much less been forced to battle one.

Humans, of course, remained the eternal problem. For the first centuries after the Dragon War, mankind had ignored this vast woodland. A hundred years before Iydahoe's birth, however, human emissaries had once again tried to claim portions of these wilds. They came from a place so distant that Iydahoe could not imagine it—a mighty city and palace they called Istar. Only a few of these humans had been bold enough to reach the deep forests, and Kagonesti warriors had wiped them out with a savage efficiency that should ensure against further trespasses.

Iydahoe knew that the warriors of the Kagonesti were smarter, faster, and quieter than any of their foes. The elves had better eyesight and a far keener sense of smell.

These facts, coupled with nearly endless patience and a complete familiarity with their woodland home, kept the wild elves confident that they could quickly terrify or destroy any invader.

The young warrior slept comfortably under the stars, then rose with the dawn as quickly as any awakening wild animal. Stopping only to drink fresh water from a splashing creek, he started the last day of his journey.

Shortly after noon, a waft of wind swirled around him and Iydahoe smelled the fires of the Silvertrouts. He sniffed again, surprised, then alarmed. The smoke had an acrid taint, and the odor was strong, yet the village of the Silvertrouts was still several hours away.

The fires that sent smoke to his nostrils must be burning somewhere else—or else they were much larger than any cook's blaze. He sniffed again, taut with alarm. Mixed with smoke of wood and charcoal were other things—the smell of wet leather, steaming . . . and the stench of charred, blackened flesh.

Iydahoe sprinted, racing like a deer as he curved along the narrow forest paths. The malodorousness increased, and he knew it originated in the Silvertrout village. But these were not the odors of cooking, of tanned hides and smoking jerky. Instead, Iydahoe knew that he raced toward a scene of destruction and death.

Yet even that foreknowledge could not prepare him for the horror that met his eyes when at last he broke from the woods into the once-familiar village of the Silvertrouts. He saw charred ruins, still smoldering, where huts had stood. Grotesque shapes sprawled everywhere. He had to force his mind toward the realization that these blackened forms were bodies, the corpses of brutally murdered Kagonesti.

Like all of the wild elves, Iydahoe had visited the home village of the Pathfinder on many occasions, and he knew well the orderly layout of lodges, the ceremonial ring in the middle, and the watch posts mounted high in the sprawling oaks surrounding the community. Now those posts—and even the oaks that had borne them—were gone, scattered in the wreckage of felled trunks, shattered branches, and more bodies.

Iydahoe walked through the village in a daze. He stepped over a ragged shape, only afterward realizing that it was—had been—a child. Some force of unspeakable evil had torn it nearly in half.

Nearby, another blackened form was sprawled with sticklike appendages—arms?—stretched toward the mangled child. A steel shaft emerged from the back of the larger form, and Iydahoe recognized it as the arrow that had brought the wild elf down, too late to help its tiny offspring.

All around was evidence of more killing, butchery on a scale that staggered Iydahoe's senses. Over where the ceremonial ring had been surrounded by the lodges of great warriors, he saw only charcoal and the irregular shapes that he had come to accept as bodies. The warrior was not aware of the trembling in his own limbs until he started down the steps into the ceremonial pit. Then his heel slipped off the ground and he tumbled heavily to his side, rolling the last few steps until he lay on his back.

The sky, at least, was normal. He saw white clouds scudding through a rich, creamy blue that seemed to belie the horrors on the ground. For a moment, he wondered if he had imagined it. Surely he had dozed off in some forest meadow and been visited by some gruesome dream!

But then an eddy of wind brought the smells to him again, and he knew that this was no dream, that the death of the Silvertrout village was a nightmare more chilling, more evil, than any sleep-bound vision. He forced himself to sit, then shakily climbed to his feet and stumbled up the steps leading from the ceremonial pit.

His numbness began to give way to grief as he started to grasp that an entire village—one of the four tribes of Kagonesti—had been exterminated. Tears stung his eyes, but very swiftly anguish fell away in the face of a rising, terrible rage. Who had done this? What enemy brought killing on such a ruthless, all-encompassing scale?

His warrior's instincts turned his eyes to the ground, and for the first time he noticed hoofprints. Horses had trampled back and forth through the village, yet so numbing had been his shock that he hadn't noticed the plain spoor when he had first entered the Silvertrout village. Now he saw that the horses must have numbered many dozen, perhaps a hundred.

His first thought, filtered with disbelief, was that the House Elves of Silvanesti had struck this brutal blow. Yet, despite the enmity that had lingered between the two elven clans for more than three thousand years, such brutality seemed incomprehensible. The House Elves drove the Kagonesti out of their heartland, but they had never pursued them this far north. Why, now, would they come with such a killing force?

He remembered the steel arrow shaft, and he knew that this massacre had not been the work of House Elves. Again he turned his attention to the prints in the dust and rubble. Iydahoe saw that the hooves were broad, shod with heavy metal rings. Some legionnaires of Istar rode great horses, he knew. But how could a force of clumsy humans have approached so close to a Kagonesti village? Surely they would have been discovered a day's march away, met by a deadly ambuscade that blocked them from any such attack! If the force had been huge—perhaps a thousand riders or more—they *might* have battled through the ambush, but they would never have found the women and children in the village when they got here! Yet, from the hundreds of corpses scattered all over the clearing, Iydahoe knew that the tribe had been taken by surprise.

Had anyone escaped? The young warrior's eyes ranged over the wreckage as he forced himself to study the ground with all his skill. The underbrush fringing the camp had been thoroughly trampled, but the branches bent *inward*, toward the village. It was the attackers who had done the trampling, and they had come from all four sides. Even the grassy hillock where the Pathfinder's hut had stood was smashed flat—it seemed as though a rank of horsemen must have ridden over it in tight formation.

A chill of panic shivered along Iydahoe's spine at another realization. He raced among the ruined huts, toward the gentle elevation where the lone lodge had once stood. He remembered well his first visit here, seven or eight decades ago, when Washallak Pathfinder had played the Ram's Horn on that rise. The surreal sounds had soothed Iydahoe and all the other young elves, filling them with a mystical sense of wonder. As he had grown older, the same music had blown soft breath on the coals of his warrior's pride, keeping his heart fire banked against the coming of danger.

Now the site of the Pathfinder's hut was a blackened splotch, flattened, burned, destroyed. The green grass had been trampled into mud, the lodge itself smashed into bits of charred kindling. A corpse, as blackened as all the others, extended half out of what had once been the doorway. No marks distinguished the pathetic remains from any other warrior in the village, but Iydahoe knew beyond doubt that this was the body of Washallak Pathfinder.

A curled piece of shell lay on the ground beside Iydahoe's moccasin. At first he paid no attention to this blackened litter—what was one more bit of debris among a scene of ultimate destruction? The numbness returned as the Pathfinder's death became further erosion of the foundation of the warrior's life. Encased in that shroud of stupor, Iydahoe started to turn away, wondering where he could look to spare his eyes a vista of horror, heartbreak, and despair.

But at the last minute, some glimmer of awareness pulled him back. He looked down at the blackened shard, saw that it was not in fact a curled shell. Instead, it was a piece of something larger, something that spiraled into a circle. Here was another piece, and several tiny fragments were nearby, flattened in the print of a mighty, steel-shod hoof.

Even as he looked at the pieces, as he felt the collapse of a way of life that had lasted for more than three millennia, Iydahoe struggled against the truth. Desperately he wanted to deny that which he understood, the evidence of which could lead to no other conclusion.

The Ram's Horn of the Kagonesti had been destroyed. Finally his despair rose through numbness, forced aside the anger that had yet to kindle into full rage. Iydahoe knelt beside the corpse of the Pathfinder, trying to gather as many of the pathetic shards as he could find, scraping through the dirt, discarding bits of bark and stone.

Finally, he lowered his head and cried.

# Chapter 23

# A Legion of Istar

Iydahoe ran for two days and nights, desperate to carry word to his people. He prayed that his father, Hawkan, would be there. The old shaman was the only person who might be able to explain the nightmare of the Silvertrout. Yet Hawkan had left only a fortnight before on a journey into the mountains, and the priest's meditative sojourns often lasted for several moons. The warrior feared that his father would still be gone.

The young Kagonesti runner reached the Whitetail village shortly after dawn, staggering with fatigue as he trotted into the compound.

Kawllaph, seated at his breakfast fire, sprang to his feet in alarm when he saw the grim, ragged expression on his younger brother's face.

"Iydahoe! What happened?" Kawllaph's voice was unusually deep for an elf, and now the barrel-chested warrior's words carried throughout the village.

"Has father returned?" gasped Iydahoe, vainly searching for a sign of Hawkan.

"Still gone," Kawllaph said tersely. He took his brother's arm. "We'll go to the council circle—there you must speak to the warriors."

At the edge of the ceremonial ring they were met by the village chief, Tarrapin, who had been drawn by the commotion. Tarrapin's face was locked in an angry glare, the bear claw tattoos across his cheeks seeming to reach inward, ready to rend.

Quickly warriors gathered as Iydahoe recovered his breath, wondering how he could possibly convey the sense of disaster he felt.

He told the tale simply, starting with the smells and progressing to the scene of utter destruction. In two minutes, he had related the important details, and he knew that he could speak for two years and never communicate the true horror.

Yet his description was shocking enough to stun the gathered warriors, until Tarrapin flew into a rage. The gray-haired warrior, his face framed by the bear claw tattoo, drew his steel sword and brandished the weapon in the air. Iydahoe wondered, with the beginnings of outrage, if the chief might turn his blade against the young messenger. Stomping back and forth, shouting skyward, Tarrapin angrily declared that no Kagonesti village could be destroyed by such an attack, certainly not when the attackers were mere humans!

Iydahoe stood stoically before the elder's rage. He wished again that Hawkan was present to hear and believe the tale—and to stand up for his son. Yet that was obviously not to be.

Instead it was Kawllaph who came to his younger brother's aid. The warrior stood up and faced the raging

Tarrapin. "Let him speak!" demanded the brave. "My brother knows what he has seen. Let him tell us!"

"I have proof. Here!" Iydahoe remembered his belt pouch and pulled forth the fragments he had gathered around the Pathfinder's hut. "This is what is left of the Ram's Horn and Washallak Pathfinder's axe!"

Iydahoe produced the blackened, broken pieces of the horn, and Tarrapin grew silent. The lean, scar-faced chief sat numbly staring at the shards, turning his glittering eyes toward Iydahoe as if he still sought a way to blame the young warrior for the disaster. Iydahoe pulled another bit of proof from his pouch—the grimy head of an axe. The blade was long and thin, and a narrow spike extended from the back of the head. Though the shaft had burned away in the ruins of Washallak's hut, Iydahoe had found the metal remains of the unique weapon that had always been the axe of the Pathfinder.

Finally, Tarrapin nodded gruffly and rose. He ordered Kaheena and Altarath, both young warriors, to carry word of the disaster to the Bluelake and Black Feather tribes. Then he ordered additional warriors to man the many watch posts located throughout the surrounding forests. Finally—and though it was still early morning— he returned to his lodge to smoke and meditate with a half dozen of the tribe's veteran braves.

Iydahoe knelt and again gathered the fragments of horn and axe. When he stood, he saw that Kawllaph had gone to comfort Berriama. She clung to his shoulders, weeping, and Kawllaph finally had to pry her away so that he could join the warriors' meeting with the chief.

Standing straight, Iydahoe concentrated on the banishment of any trace of emotion from his face. Acutely conscious that several of the tribe's young females watched him from across the compound, he knew that they would never mistake him for the feckless, playful boy he had been just a few short weeks ago. But then the girls, too, seemed more serious, less carefree than they were a few minutes before. His village could never offer the serenity, the peace, that Iydahoe had known here through all the decades of his life.

Would life ever return to normal?

The girls, he saw, had gone back to tanning a rack of doeskins, perhaps sensing the harsh glare of the matron Puiquill, who squatted beside the rack and critically inspected the maidens' work. She was a stern taskmistress, but skilled with the bone needle and gut-filament thread with which the wild elves had made their clothing since the dawn of time.

The young brave's mind returned to the horror of Silvertrout, beginning to seethe with thoughts of the vengeance Iydahoe would someday exact against the hated legionnaires of Istar. He himself would slay, would cripple and burn, with the same ruthless—

"Will you take us fishing, Iydahoe?" asked a young boy, shyly approaching the warrior from behind. Iydahoe remembered that the youth's name was Dallatar. "My father was going to show us the trout pools, but he has gone to speak with Tarrapin."

Iydahoe turned, startled. How could he be expected to do anything so mundane at a time like this? Then, surprising himself, he nodded. "Gather the youngsters. Make sure that each brings his spear. I will meet you at the head of the stream trail."

Delighted, Dallatar ran off. As Iydahoe watched, his heart suddenly pounded as Moxilli came around the great smoking lodge in the village's center. Unlike the tanning girls, but like Iydahoe, Moxilli had recently passed the rituals of adulthood. Over the past sixty years the two of them had been children and adolescents together, though only recently had the young brave become aware of just how beautiful his youthful playmate was.

Moxilli had the long black hair of all Kagonesti, though her flowing locks seemed more iridescent, fuller, and shinier than the hair of any other tribal female. Unconsciously Iydahoe strutted proudly, his chest thrust out, his arms pumping with relaxed precision at his sides as he strode toward his hut to get his fishing spear, then went to the willow tree marking the trail head.

He was quickly joined by Bakall, a young, serious fellow who showed signs of one day becoming a patient, skillful hunter and warrior. Now he scowled toward the stream, as if willing the trout to be ready for his spear. Iydahoe sensed that Bakall would do quite well.

Within minutes, a dozen youths had gathered beside the great willow tree that marked the path down to the river. Each of the boys had a three-pronged spear, which he had carefully whittled from a maple sapling. The tines had been hardened by fire, and on the shank of each prong the boys had carved tiny barbs, designed to keep the pierced fish from wriggling off the weapon. Iydahoe did not inspect the spears, knowing that for each boy the most important lesson would come from the successful landing of a tasty dinner—or the teasing flick of tail as the trout wriggled free.

The lads had been boisterous and playful in the village, but, following Bakall's intent example, they lapsed into stealthy silence as they followed Iydahoe. Extending into a long, single file, the boys soundlessly padded down the winding trail. Thick-boled trees rose on all sides, while the forest floor off the trail was choked with underbrush that often included hook-thorned vines and dense, tangled brambles.

A sound carried through the woods, rising from the direction of the stream—but clearly unnatural in origin. It was a metallic "clink," or else the sound of something very hard striking a rock. Iydahoe froze, the boys doing likewise. The brave looked over his shoulder and raised an eyebrow, and Bakall nodded back, before peering into the woods. Apparently the boy had heard the same thing.

The sound was repeated, a muffled noise that nevertheless came clearly to alert, elven ears, probably because its source was closer. In a flash, Iydahoe understood that whatever had made the noise was approaching them up this trail.

Urgently the warrior gestured for the boys to retreat back toward the village, though he didn't look around to see if they obeyed. Instead, he crouched, watching, among the branches, knowing that the whorls of his tatoos would make his face difficult to see for anyone who might come around the next bend of the trail.

The breeze, which had been listless all morning, suddenly picked up, carrying the unmistakable scent of horses to Iydahoe's nose. His hand tightened around his spear as the terrifying thought came: legionnaires! He stared at the trail with blazing intensity, but he saw nothing.

With a sick feeling in his stomach, he remembered the butchery worked against the Silvertrouts. Now, as he thought of the youths behind him, the girls at their tanning rack, and beautiful Moxilli, brushing her hair by the well, he almost groaned aloud.

He felt, rather than heard, the presence of Bakall close by and knew that they had to get back to the village, to carry the alarm. But an alarm of what? All he knew was that someone with horses and metallic equipment was creeping up the trail.

"Go back," Iydahoe hissed, holding his lips a few inches from Bakall's ear. "Tell the warriors there are horsemen coming up the stream trail. Now, go!"

Eyes wide, the young Kagonesti scrambled silently up the trail, urging the other youths before him. Iydahoe slipped off the path, ignoring the brambles that scratched his skin, and started to work his way downward, seeking a look at these intrusive horsemen. How could they have gotten so close to the village? Were all the sentries dead?

Within a few moments, he heard the sounds of hoofbeats, though the steps had a surreptitious quality—the riders were holding their steeds back in an effort at stealth. Peering from beneath a leafy fern, the Kagonesti looked down a straight stretch of trail. He saw branches moving, pushed aside by a solid presence—but it was a presence that Iydahoe couldn't see!

Hoofprints appeared in the dust of the trail, advancing steadily closer. The warrior stared, but he saw no horse, no rider—nothing! A faint shimmering obscured the trail, as more and more puffs of dust floated upward. But *how*—when there was still nothing to *see*? Yet something was undeniably there, advancing up the trail. Iydahoe caught the unmistakable smell of horses, and he knew that he couldn't be wrong.

But why couldn't he *see*? There was only that shimmering—like a cloudy presence, an essence of something that was solid but invisible.

Iydahoe stood, bursting upward from the concealment of the bush. He heard a horse whinny in alarm, a man's curse commanding obedience. The fishing spear seemed like a horribly flimsy weapon, but the warrior hurled it with all of his strength. The shaft flew outward, then struck something unseen and dropped to the ground.

The horse gave a shrill cry of pain, and more curses were added to the din. Iydahoe heard a sharp, powerful word cut through the chaos and, abruptly, the screening cloak was removed and a column of horses and riders blinked into sight. The lead mount had bucked off its rider, and now that skittish horse blocked the others from moving up the trail.

Second in line rode a strangely garbed man clad in long gray robes. That fellow pointed at the wild elf and shouted—"There he is! Kill him!"

Iydahoe recognized the voice, knew that this was the man who had spoken before, whose single powerful word had broken the screen of invisibility. With a shiver of apprehension, the warrior knew that he faced a wizard.

The first man struggled to remount, hampered because he had instinctively drawn his sword. Other riders pressed forward, tightly packed on the narrow trail. These Istarian legionnaires, wearing cloaks of red and breastplates of polished brass, formed a column so long that its tail was out of sight somewhere down the trail—enough soldiers to form a grave threat to the village.

Iydahoe slipped backward, rising to a crouch when he was out of sight of the trail. He raced through the underbrush toward the village. After two dozen paces he stepped back onto the trail, since the bends in the winding path would conceal him from the humans and the broad track would save him precious seconds on his race to warn the tribe.

Then sounds of violence rocked through the trees, and he knew he would be too late. Terrified screams rose from the unseen village, splitting the pastoral forest air, while hoarse shouts and the clash of steel against steel told him that there were more humans than just the party advancing up the trail behind him. Kagonesti war cries mingled with crude commands and grim shouts of triumph. Loud hoofbeats now pounded to the rear, and he knew that the horsemen had heard the sounds of battle and wasted no time as they raced to the fighting.

Iydahoe burst into the village clearing, his knife in his hand, a furious war cry shrieking from his lips. Yet his worst moments of bleak imagination could not have prepared him for the sight that met his eyes.

A line of legionnaires on foot, shields held across their chests, advanced from the forest across the village. Several braves leapt toward them, courageously attacking, but these wild elves fell quickly before the scythelike reaper of the close-packed footmen. Kawllaph, Iydahoe's proud, capable brother, raced to the attack and then fell immediately, his head all but slashed from his torso.

Other humans, carrying spears and swords, rushed into the village from the right, and, though Kagonesti warriors killed several of these, the others rushed headlong into the clusters of lodges, brutally cutting down those elves who tried to scramble out the low-arching doors. Berriama, she who was to marry Kawllaph, ran screaming toward the slain body of her beloved—then she, too, fell dead, pierced by a legionnaire horseman's lance.

Whooping madly, Tarrapin raised his sword and charged the line of footmen. His blade clanged off the armored shoulder of a human, and in the next instant the chief's body was pierced by numerous Istarian blades.

A number of elders sought shelter in the woods, but as the wild elves hobbled toward the trees many silvery missiles sparkled in the sun—steel-shafted arrows! A deadly volley slashed out, missiles ripping through many a frail and weathered body. A second volley rattled, and dozens of Kagonesti lay on the ground, dead or rapidly dying. More legionnaires charged from the trees there, and Iydahoe saw that they bore the crossbows that had launched the lethal volleys. Now the men slung the missile weapons over their shoulders, drew short swords, and charged with lusty yells. Iydahoe saw that many of them grinned broadly, relishing the prospects of close-in butchery.

Puiquill and a cluster of girls huddled behind the wreckage of their tanning racks, which had been knocked over in the chaos. Bakall and the boys of the fishing expedition charged in a knot, courageously raising their light, three-pronged spears. One fell to a legionnaire's sword, but the others knocked the man to the ground and pierced him.

"Bakall!" shouted Iydahoe, pointing toward the cowering elves at the tanning rack. "There! Help the girls!"

Staring wildly, either from madness or shock, Bakall saw a legionnaire rushing toward the Kagonesti females. With a shrill cry, the boys flew at the man, bearing him to the ground, then ruthlessly piercing him with their spears. Bakall himself picked up the fellow's sword, holding it over his head with a whooping cry.

Iydahoe heard a scream and twisted to see Moxilli running from her lodge, where two bearded humans had just chopped down another elf and were busy casting glowing brands onto the loose thatch of the roof.

"This way!" the young brave shouted, and the terrified maiden met his eyes with a look of frantic pleading.

In the next instant he heard the sound of a heavy crossbow. The bolt caught the young Kagonesti woman in the side, tearing through her chest, the bloody tip erupting from her rib cage. Flung off her feet by the force of the shot, Moxilli was cast to the ground where she lay motionless in a growing pool of blood.

Iydahoe wailed his fury, striking down a nearby human with the keen edge of his knife. Villagers ran toward him, toward the path to the marsh, and he remembered the horsemen pounding up the trail behind him.

"Not here. More humans come from the marsh! Into the woods!" he cried, desperately waving his arms.

Abruptly horses surged into the village and Iydahoe was knocked to the ground by a blow to his head. Stunned, he tried to rise to his knees, watching the riders swirl through the dust and smoke while the phalanx of footmen continued to press the survivors into a small pack in the center. Despite pleas for mercy and the fact that many of the elves bore no weapons, the Kingpriest's killers continued to hack at the remaining members of the tribe.

Bleak with despair, his skull ringing from the force of the blow, Iydahoe lumbered groggily to his feet and shook his head to clear the sudden fog. He looked toward the drying racks to see Puiquill stand courageously as a man charged forward. The fellow cut her down with a single blow, kicking her corpse to the side as he turned toward the huddling children. Bakall, with a shriek of rage, stabbed upward, but the man knocked the youth aside with a contemptuous laugh. Grinning cruelly, the fellow raised his gory sword for another fatal blow.

Somehow Iydahoe's feet obeyed his mind, and he sprang toward the drying rack, raising his knife in time to deflect the man's powerful blow. With a grunt of surprise, the legionnaire looked at the warrior, his red eyes gleaming with fury and hatred, but before he could raise his sword, Iydahoe had cut him down with a slashing blow to the neck.

More men turned toward the tiny knot of young Kagonesti, while horsemen continued to pour into the camp from the marsh trail. Behind the drying racks plunged a narrow draw leading down to the water, and though normally the ravine was too tangled for anyone to think of going there, now it seemed the only chance.

"Fly!" hissed the brave, urging the sobbing children into the shadowy depression. A girl, Ambra, clutched Iydahoe's leg, and he pushed her away, relieved when Dallatar helped her toward the underbrush. Several of the boys led the way, while Bakall stood beside Iydahoe, driving the first of the pursuers back. When the young elves had slipped out of sight, the warrior pushed Bakall after them, then dove into the brambles himself, Istarian swords slashing at his heels.

For desperate minutes the tiny band of survivors struggled down the tangled gully. The young elves, fortunately, were so small that they could wriggle under the worst of the tangle, and Iydahoe ignored the cuts on his own skin. Finally the group of terrified, weary elves collapsed, gasping for breath, in a deep forest grove. When Iydahoe backtracked to check for pursuit, he could hear nothing.

"We're safe, at least for the moment," he said, creeping back to the little band. He counted ten boys and an equal number of girls there and realized with a sickening sense of responsibility that he—who had been a warrior for less than a full season—was perhaps the senior surviving member of the tribe.

"Are we the only ones left?" asked Tiffli, a wisp of a girl who struggled bravely against an urge to cry.

"Is my mummy killed?" asked another waif, whose name Iydahoe didn't know. That lack of knowledge brought him a pang of guilt, and he wished he could give her a hopeful answer.

He remembered Moxilli, felled by the cruel steel bolt, and all the other elves who had been hacked to death by the swords of the human butchers.

"If we are all that are left," Bakall stated, the boldness of his tone not quite denying the quaver in his voice, "then we shall *be* the tribe. I am ready to be a warrior!"

"And I," declared Dallatar, looking much older than he had when he'd earlier asked Iydahoe to take them fishing.

Iydahoe nodded absently, despair rising in a wave within him. How could he be mother and father to these elves? He could teach them a few things, but so many things he wouldn't know. Would he have to do it alone?

Then the branches parted beside them and Iydahoe looked into the reddened, horrified eyes of his father, Hawkan. The elder Kagonesti stumbled into the little group, shaking his head in horror.

"On the mountaintop I saw a portent of evil—I returned at once, but never could I imagine anything like . . ." His words trailed off, and he looked at his son seriously. "I am glad you have saved some of the tribe."

"For what?" demanded the young warrior. "To die in the winter, or to hide from the legionnaire butchers? How can this be a tribe—?"

"Do not speak such dark thoughts," Hawkan said firmly.

"But the humans had a wizard! The men of Istar were invisible. We couldn't see them approach! How can we survive against powers like that?"

"We have life, still, and therefore we must have hope. Now, how many of you are hurt?"

With shame, Iydahoe realized that he had not even checked the young elves for injury. An older girl, Ambra, had suffered a cut on her leg, and Bakall had taken a deep slash on his arm. Hawkan's knowing fingers probed at the girl's wound as he murmured a quiet prayer to the gods of the forest. In moments, Ambra's bleeding had stopped, and in another minute, Bakall, too, had been healed.

"What do we do now, Father?" asked Iydahoe, still reeling at the brink of despair.

"We move from here, to the place for a new village, though where that should be I haven't decided." Iydahoe noted a strong hint of doubt in the shaman's voice, but now it was the younger warrior who offered a tiny flicker of hope.

"This way," Iydahoe said firmly. He remembered the little grotto, with its fresh water and almost invisible approach, which he had discovered many years before. "I think I know where we can go to hide."

# Chapter 24

# Road-builders

Iydahoe, bow and arrow in his hand, crouched in a thicket and trembled with fear. These days he was always afraid, it seemed, often nearly paralyzed by a terror beyond any he had ever known. He tried to remain motionless, to steady his weapon in case a deer trotted into sight, but still his hands shook with the tremors of his deep, abiding dread.

He did not shiver under a fear of pain, or of any suffering that might be visited upon himself. That kind of fear Iydahoe could face, could vanquish or ignore. The terror that gnawed at him now was deeper, a more fundamental and unanswerable menace.

It was the fear that he would fail.

If Iydahoe was not successful on his hunts, if he could

not return regularly with fresh meat, then the Kagonesti of his little tribe would become hungry. This was the fear that threatened to crush him, borne of the knowledge that a score of wild elf lives depended on his skill with the bow and arrow. Though three braves—Kaheena and Hawkan in addition to himself—had survived the massacre, Iydahoe was recognized by all as the only true stalker. In an earlier era this knowledge might have swelled his chest with pride, but now it made him only more afraid.

Iydahoe had learned that there was only one way to counter this consuming dread: he almost never failed.

Yet he had stalked this game trail for more than twenty-four hours, hidden upwind of the path, as silent as a ghost. The tracks in the mud had been plentiful—dozens of deer had come by here on the previous day—yet in all the time he had waited he had seen not even a tremulous fawn. The clear water hole in the nearby valley was one of the few good drinking places in this part of the forest, and the deer and other forest creatures depended on it. Yet many hours had passed without sign of his shy quarry. If no deer came this afternoon or evening, Iydahoe's worst fears would materialize—he would have to return to the little tribe empty-handed.

Of course, there was always the hope that Kaheena would bring in some game. Still, Iydahoe knew that his fellow warrior did not have the steady hand of the deadly hunter—and Kaheena lacked the patience to sit, motionless, as Iydahoe had been doing since before sunrise today.

But all the patience coupled with the steadiest hands on Ansalon could not avail a hunter who never saw any game. Now, in the grip of his fear, Iydahoe grew more and more convinced that no deer would walk down this trail in the foreseeable future.

But why not? The tracks from two days earlier were clear and frequent—what would cause such a dramatic change in the animals' grazing and drinking habits? He couldn't just sit here and wait to find out. He had to *do* something!

His suspicions at last quelled the trembling of his fear and Iydahoe cautiously rose to his feet. Nothing stirred in the woods as he stepped onto the trail and started the long, winding descent toward the water hole in the valley.

Even as his attention focused on the sights and sounds of the forest around him, much of Iydahoe's consciousness dwelled on the young Kagonesti waiting for him in the grotto. The pathetic little tribe now numbered less than two dozen souls—and of them, only Kaheena and Iydahoe were proper warriors.

Kaheena had survived because he had been making the journey to the village of the Black Feathers when Istar had struck the tribe. When he had arrived at the neighboring village, Kaheena had found the same devastation that had greeted Iydahoe at Silvertrout—and by the time he had returned to his own village, the battle there was over.

Iydahoe, after taking the youngsters to the hidden grotto, had returned to the village to see what he could salvage. This had been very little. After the fight, the legionnaires had soaked the bodies and the wreckage with oil, burning all trace of the village into blackened, wasted rubble. Amid this ruin Iydahoe had met Kaheena. Together they waited several days to see if Altarath, the warrior sent to warn the Bluelake tribe, would return. They never saw him and were forced to conclude that the fourth tribe of the wild elves had met the same brutal fate as the other three—and that their tribemate had been swept into the disaster.

During the long, dark season that followed, the young wild elves had all but despaired under the knowledge that they might be the last survivors of their people on the broad face of Ansalon. Only Hawkan kept their hopes alive, telling them of the old gods, repeating the tale of the Grandfather Ram—the wise, ancient animal who had dwelled in the highest mountains, who had guided Father Kagonesti during the first years of the tribe. Those tales had sustained the flicker of vitality in their young elven breasts.

Hawkan could wield a weapon as well, but his primary

skills were as shaman. Indeed, the old elf's healing and sustenance skills were all that had seen the survivors of the massacre through the cold winter following the coming of Istar's legion. Hawkan had known how to find food, or to summon it out of inedible roots and tubers by the use of his priestly magic. He healed the children when they became ill, had even nursed little Faylai—the tot whose name Iydahoe hadn't known at the time of the attack—through a fever that had threatened to consume her life in burning embrace.

Finally, then, with the coming of spring, Iydahoe had forced himself to hunt. During the summer and autumn, driven by that consuming fear, he had perfected his skills as a stalker, until nearly every time he ventured out he returned with a plump carcass of fresh meat. Kaheena had devoted time to nets and snares, and Bakall and the older youths had proved to wield deadly fish-spears, so between the two warriors and the younger males they had been able to adequately feed the tribe. By now, many strips of venison jerky had been smoked and dried in preparation for the winter. They would need still more, however, to get through the cold months that lay ahead.

Abruptly Iydahoe heard a foreign noise, a sound that riveted his attention back to his surroundings. The forest was mostly silent around him, but there it was again—a sound harsh, intrusive in origin.

It was the cold laugh of a human.

The noise brought back all the hatred, all the impotent fury that Iydahoe had buried since the day, a year earlier, when he had watched his village die. Since then he had avoided humans, and none had ventured near the grotto where the tribe now made its home.

The noise of the man seemed to come from the direction of the water hole, and Iydahoe began to understand the absence of deer. Soundlessly the warrior slipped into the forest beside the trail. He passed among the trunks and bushes without rustling a leaf, steadily advancing toward the valley bottom.

He found men very near the water. There were four: butchers, standing around the carcass of a doe that had been felled by cruel crossbow darts. Iydahoe watched the men build a roaring fire, roasting the tongue and several steaks, licking their bloody fingers and laughing while the rest of the deer was left to rot.

Iydahoe understood the benefits of remaining undiscovered. As long as the Istarians thought that the Kagonesti were all dead, they would send no more men to kill them. At the same time, he had chafed under the need for vengeance and against the caution that had forced him to hold his hand.

It was the laughter that forced his decision. Hearing these crude killers chuckling and joking over the remains of the deer was too much for Iydahoe to bear. His bow was raised, arrow sighted on the nearest human's back, before he even thought about the results of his actions.

The steel-tipped shaft flew true, piercing the fellow's tunic, spearing his heart. Too startled even to cry out, the dead man toppled over the remains of the doe as Iydahoe released his second arrow. That shaft took another human in the throat, while his third plunged into the next victim's heart. The fourth man, mad with fear, made a futile lunge toward his horse before Iydahoe's arrow brought him quickly, permanently down.

The young warrior didn't even look at the corpses as he passed through the camp, noting instead the litter, the chaos of garbage and debris left by the men's effort to clean the little deer. He claimed the doe's carcass, as well as some hardtack and salt that he found in one of the saddlebags. Hoisting his treasures to his shoulder, Iydahoe turned back to the forest, starting toward the secret shelter of the grotto.

A slash of white drew his eye to a nearby trunk. He saw that the humans had gouged a hatchet into this tree, and to many others extending in a line to the north. Apparently they had been marking a straight path through the forest, slashing the trees to show someone who came later exactly where they had gone.

Further angered by this encroachment, Iydahoe left the place. Some hours later, he entered the narrow gorge, passing between the tall trees, hugging close to the steep, rocky walls. He heard a sharp whistle, and Bakall dropped to the ground before him. As the eldest of the boys in the tribe, the youth took his sentry duties seriously. Now he helped Iydahoe with the food, stepping from rock to rock on the stony ground. Though the tribe had lived here for a year, they had taken care to make no trail that could show an enemy where the little village was hidden.

The floor of the little vale was a flat, mossy expanse of soft ground. A half-dozen lodges of bark and skin stood among the shadows of the larger trees. Gray-haired Hawkan looked up from his labors before the largest of these lodges, but only nodded at his son's approach before lowering his face back to his eternal labor.

In front of Hawkan, carefully arranged on the ground, were the fragments Iydahoe had brought from the Silvertrout village. The shaman spent most of his time trying to arrange those fragments in the pattern that might recreate the Ram's Horn. Iydahoe, privately, thought this was a fruitless venture. For one thing, he didn't know if he had found all, or even the majority, of the spiraled horn's pieces. Some of the larger pieces formed a portion of the great bell, and a few others were recognizable as parts of the arcing curve, but it seemed undeniable that many other parts were missing. Iydahoe had even made a return trip to the ruins of the Silvertrout village, but had found only a few tiny shards in addition to the pieces he had earlier salvaged.

Iydahoe himself had remade and now carried the great axe of the Pathfinder. He had whittled a haft of stout ironwood, and had fire-hardened the shaft before he mounted the long, narrow axe blade onto the wood. The steel had lost none of its edge, and when the warrior had cleaned the grime off it, it gleamed with the silvery brilliance that had marked it in ages past.

Dallatar took the meat from Iydahoe while several girls gathered wet wood for the smokehouse. Some of the venison they would eat fresh, but the rest would be smoked and dried as additions to their winter stores. The warrior squatted beside his father, silently watching as Hawkan meditated above the fragments of the horn. Bakall returned to his watch post overlooking the approach to the grotto.

The young elf had been gone for only a few minutes when Iydahoe heard the rattling whistle of a crane—Bakall's symbol that a member of the tribe approached with important news. The warrior picked up his weapons and trotted through the narrow cut leading out of their grotto. In moments, he met sweat-streaked Kagwallas, one of the boys a bit younger than Bakall. The younger elf staggered to a stop as he saw Iydahoe.

"I come from Kaheena," Kagwallas declared, forcing his words between deep gulps of breath. "He has taken a House Elf captive. He wants you to come to him."

"A captive?" Iydahoe was alarmed. What use did they have for a House Elf? He was relieved that Kaheena had not brought the prisoner toward the grotto, but nevertheless disturbed by the news of his presence.

"Where is he?"

"In the valley above the twin waterfalls, just beyond the pool where the trout swarm."

Iydahoe knew the place, for it was one of Kaheena's favorite fishing spots. It was only four or five hours from the grotto—distressingly close to have a House Elf. The warrior wasted no time in further conversation. Loping into the woods and maintaining a steady pace, he found the Kagonesti warrior and his prisoner exactly where Kagwallas had said.

The captive was a golden-haired elf sitting sullenly on the ground, hands behind his back. Kaheena squatted nearby, staring at the House Elf as if his hazel eyes would bore through the fellow's light-colored flesh. The warrior barely looked up as Iydahoe joined him in the small clearing.

"Who is he?" asked Iydahoe.

"He claims to be a trail finder. He says that the House Elves and the humans of Istar will make a great road through the forest. He scouts a path to mark the way."

The prisoner's eyes, glaring with hatred, flickered between the two wild elves. Remembering the humans he had encountered, and the strange way they had been marking trees, Iydahoe shivered apprehensively.

"Do the House Elves make peace with Istar?" he asked, suspicious.

The golden-haired elf shrugged. "Who can say what the Kingpriest will do?" He seemed bored, as if resigned to a brutal fate.

"Why do the Silvanesti want a road to Istar?"

Again the House Elf shrugged. "For the singers, perhaps. Every year we send a choir of our apprentice clerics. They sing at the high festivals in the Kingpriest's cathedral, and in return receive training from some of the human priests."

Iydahoe had nothing but scorn for elves who would thus submit themselves to human control, but he bit back his contempt as he pressed for information. "And this is to be the site of the road?" he asked, gesturing to the blazes made along several nearby trees.

"It is one place. In truth, we thought that you Painted Elves were gone, that there would be none to bother the caravans here."

Now the warrior's eyes flashed. "We will release you, House Elf—but when you go back to your city, tell your masters that the Kagonesti are *not* gone! Any men, any elves, who come to build a road here will be slain!"

The House Elf laughed contemptuously. "You may kill a few, perhaps even many, but if you think you will stop this road, you are a fool. The Kingpriest of Istar sends his men where he wants, with no care for how many of them die."

"Then we will kill them all!" Iydahoe's fury clouded his eyes, as the full memory of the massacre came back to him. He could kill many soldiers of Istar every day—and yet he would never fully avenge that brutal attack.

Perhaps it was his rage or the distracting image of his human foes, or the fear that again began to insinuate itself into the warrior's mind. In any event, Iydahoe was slow to see the House Elf's hand emerge from behind his back—unbound! In that hand was a tiny, silver-bladed knife, a weapon that Kaheena had somehow not discovered when he had tied the prisoner's hands.

The Silvanesti lunged upward, driving the blade toward Iydahoe, as the young warrior's mind froze under the strain of apprehension and responsibility. He didn't recognize the danger, couldn't move to respond.

But Kaheena saw. The brave leapt forward, trying to grasp the attacker's hand—and failing. The knife plunged into Kaheena's breast, and the wild elf grunted as Iydahoe finally reacted, raising his steel-bladed axe and slicing it through the Silvanesti's throat. The two elves fell together, blood mingling in the dust before it soaked into the ground.

"No!" hissed Iydahoe, shocked by the gouts of crimson liquid pouring from the knife wound. Kaheena looked very surprised, until his eyes half-closed. Except for the horrid pallor of his face, he might have been sleeping.

When he pulled the bodies apart, Iydahoe noticed a tiny scabbard at the back of the House Elf's belt—the place he had concealed the deadly knife. Iydahoe buried Kaheena where he had fallen, leaving the Silvanesti for the crows.

As the wild elf started back to the grotto, he all but wept at a sense of supreme loneliness and bitter irony. Two elves had killed each other, pouring their lifeblood together as a sanctifier or a curse on the route of the King-priest's road.

# Chapter 25

# Ambush

The Istarians spent four years on the building of their road. It was not an easy task. The woods were thick, the ground rough. Even worse, many workers died, pierced by black arrows released with deadly accuracy by an unseen archer in the forest—a bowman who melted into the woods, disappearing before any humans could locate him. Despite this harassment, the broad track was finally, inevitably completed.

For nine more years, caravans traveled back and forth between Istar and Silvanesti. Though Iydahoe never let one of these pass unmolested, his arrows were little more than pinpricks in the flanks of a great, all but unfeeling, behemoth.

During those years, Iydahoe perfected his skills as a hunter—of game, and of humans. The warrior labored to vanquish his fear of failure. Though he was the lone hunter of the tribe, he kept the others fed, and he taught the older youths, such as Bakall, Dallatar and Kagwallas, many things about the taking of game. Eventually the three of them did most of the hunting, allowing Iydahoe to devote his attentions toward his vengeance against Istar.

True, the Kingpriest sent companies, even full legions, on sweeps through the forest, but the village grotto was so well concealed that the humans never came close to finding it. Sometimes Iydahoe worried about the gray-robed wizard, wondering if the mage was powerful enough to find the tribe through some arcane means. A small part of the wild elf longed to see the man again, to punish him for all the hurts the elves had suffered.

He continued to ambush the caravans whenever he found them. Still, the amount of damage Iydahoe could do by himself was sorely limited, and he began to wonder whether Bakall was ready for his initiation as a true warrior. The youngster was unusually serious and intent, and seemed to be a good candidate for the tattoos of adulthood.

Indeed, all the younger Kagonesti had quickly learned the skills of the wild elves—at least, those that Iydahoe and Hawkan could teach. The older boys had been forced to act like men, the adolescent girls taking on the roles of the tribe's women—though, as yet, none of them had married. Ambra, however, showed every sign of becoming a desirable young elfmaid, and Iydahoe had noticed Bakall, Kagwallas, and Dallatar all preening and boasting for her benefit.

The combination of Iydahoe's hunting skills and Hawkan's knowledge and guidance had allowed them to build lodges and feed the twenty-two elves who made up the tribe. Iydahoe's energetic scouting, fueled by the bitter hatred that always simmered near the surface of his consciousness, ensured that any humans who dared encroach near the tribal grotto met swift and violent deterrence.

One of his earliest targets had been an Istarian arms trader on his way to Tarsis, a prize that had yielded several thousand razor-sharp steel arrowheads. The younger members of the tribe, boys and girls both, had become expert fletchers. Iydahoe himself stained the shafts with a mixture of charcoal and the snail-dye that the tribe used as ink. The black arrows had marked each of his kills during the last thirteen years.

On an afternoon in late fall, Ambra and Kagwallas were busy feathering more missiles for Iydahoe, while the warrior himself lashed the steel arrowhead onto each shaft after the younger elves had finished with it.

Dallatar, ever ready with a joke, approached. Ambra didn't see the frog in his hands until he dropped it in her lap, then laughed as she leapt to her feet and cast the animal aside.

The others laughed, too, while Ambra blushed furiously and then lunged for Dallatar—who skipped lightly out of her reach.

"Iydahoe! I have news!" Bakall jogged into the grotto, observing the antics of his tribemates with a disapproving frown. Ever serious, Bakall still scowled as he squatted beside Iydahoe and Hawkan.

"A big caravan comes," he announced breathlessly. "It has moved past the borders of Silvanesti and now has turned up the Istar road."

"How big?" wondered the warrior.

"Many hundreds of horses, and twenty great wagons." Bakall hesitated, then blundered ahead. "Warrior Iydahoe, cannot this be my time to help you in the attack?"

Iydahoe looked at his father, certain that Hawkan would say Bakall was still too young—but the shaman looked down at his mossy blanket, where he busily studied the shards of the Ram's Horn. The warrior knew that the decision was his.

He looked at the young elf. Bakall was lanky and tough, though he had not filled out his adult sinew. He was also quick, keen-eyed, and very patient—the most important attributes of a Kagonesti brave.

"Very well. If the shaman will mark your tattoos, you may join me in the ambush."

"I have collected more snails over this past season," Hawkan said with a nod. Iydahoe knew that the black dye used in the tattooing process was obtained from these dirt-dwelling slugs. "I have enough to mark Bakall as a warrior."

That night, the tribe gathered solemnly as the old shaman took a sharp porcupine quill and inserted bits of the black ink under Bakall's skin. He marked his chest with twin circles and his face with an oak leaf to match Iydahoe's. Bakall bore the painful procedure without complaint, and when Hawkan had finished, the young initiate raised up a steel sword and whooped, promising to continue the vengeance against Istar.

Iydahoe led Bakall onto the ambush trail two mornings later. Each of them carried a quiver full of black-shafted arrows. They made their way to a place Iydahoe had chosen years before.

Not once did the warriors pause to reflect on the fantastic odds against them. Indeed, Iydahoe had grown used to attacking enemies who outnumbered him, relying on stealth and his knowledge of the forest to escape after inflicting as much damage as possible.

Based on his experience, Iydahoe expected that the two of them would shoot many arrows from ambush, hoping that each missile claimed a legionnaire's life. Then he and Bakall would melt into the forest, leaving only enough of a trail to lead pursuers in a direction opposite that of the village in its tiny, hidden grotto.

They found the caravan on the road, and for a full day the two elves observed the long column from hilltops, lofty trees, even thickets of thorns within a hundred feet of the road. They watched the golden-cloaked riders file past, heard the creaking of wagons, the snorting of the laboring horses. The commander of the Istarian legionnaires rode a gleaming white stallion with gilded bridle to match his tunic. His broad buttocks rested in an appropriately resplendent gem-studded saddle. The officer's eyes looked neither to the right nor to the left, his chin held proudly outthrust, as if by his presence itself he dared the forest and its denizens to throw a challenge at the invincible might of Istar.

That challenge, Iydahoe thought grimly, would soon be forthcoming.

By late afternoon, they had taken shelter in a dense, nearly lightless thicket fifty feet from the trail. The two Kagonesti lay flat on their bellies and watched the column file past. From here they could get an accurate count of its numbers and even discern details about individual riders.

About a hundred mounted legionnaires led the way, riding two abreast. All these riders, the elves noted, were dressed in bright ceremonial colors and bore themselves with a rigid pride that seemed more suited to a parade ground than a forest path. Never mind the pretty posture, Iydahoe silently counseled the humans—soon you will be glad to get out of here with your lives!

Abruptly the nature of the procession changed, following the long file of immaculate horsemen. Now the Kagonesti watched ornate, gilded wagons trundle past, each pulled by a pair of sleek white horses. The drivers of these wagons, Iydahoe saw, were House Elves—Silvanesti. Each was a warrior, with a steel breastplate and a sword close at hand. Doubtless the elves had bows and arrows within ready reach inside the wagons' covered beds.

The wild elves' questions about the contents of those wagons were answered, startlingly, as beautiful female voices rose in song. The sweet melodies were carried from wagon to wagon until nearly a score of the lurching conveyances had rumbled past. Then more legionnaires brought up the rear, another hundred in immaculate uniforms and riding proud, prancing horses.

As the Kagonesti watched the humans make their evening camp, Bakall trembled with excitement, and Iydahoe touched the younger Kagonesti's shoulder, silently counseling him to be patient. Iydahoe looked at the whole circles, so recently tattooed across his companion's chest, and felt a momentary pang of bitterness. Bakall was so young, lacking a full ten years on the traditional adulthood age of the Kagonesti warrior. Yet he was about to embark on his first attack.

The great column of Istar made too tempting a target for Iydahoe to ignore. The company obviously made its way northward from Silvanesti to the fabled city of Istar itself. Already the column had passed the thorn-hedge border in departing the elven realm, and for days it had hastened along the winding woodland trail as if the legionnaires and their captains sensed the danger that even a single Kagonesti might provide.

For the thousandth time, Iydahoe remembered, vividly, the massacre that had occurred fourteen years earlier. As always, the familiar rage welled up, the bitter fury that had made it so easy for the young warrior to look at the symbols of Istar, and then to kill and kill again.

In those intervening years, the deaths of a hundred elves of his tribe had been repaid by Iydahoe two or three times over—and he was only beginning to collect a deep and bloody debt. His arrows had slashed from the forest into Istarian road-building and trading parties. Logging camps had been burned, individual lumbermen discovered horrifyingly posed, their throats slit into garish, bleeding grins.

In the misty light of dawn, Iydahoe watched the column of legionnaires break camp and file onto the broad trail. He was almost ready to strike. Finally the last of the column moved onto the trail, and the two elves emerged from cover to work their way to the top of a nearby ridge and then jog easily through the more open forest there. They roughly paralleled the course of the caravan, and Iydahoe knew that they would soon pass it and regain a position for ambush. Calling on his memory of the geography, he had decided on the perfect place to make the attack. It had the further advantage of being one place on this road where he had never before struck, so perhaps the humans would be less vigilant than when they trooped past the scenes of his earlier ambushes.

"Those singers?" asked Bakall, loping easily behind the older warrior. "Who do you think they were? Certainly not humans, were they?"

Iydahoe reflected on the glorious sound and shook his head. "They must be elves. A long time ago I heard that some Silvanesti might journey to Istar to sing. Why they would go, I can't imagine."

"Perhaps they were prisoners," the younger brave suggested.

"Perhaps." But Iydahoe was not convinced. "I can't believe that anyone—*especially* an elf—who was held against his will would be able to create such beautiful music. No—I don't think they were prisoners."

"But then *why*?" pressed Bakall.

Iydahoe's silence was his only reply, and his companion understood that the older brave had nothing more to say on the subject. For more than an hour they maintained the steady trot, moving swiftly along the ridgetop, until Iydahoe judged it was time to curve back toward the trail.

Now he led Bakall through slopes laden with sumac, already turned crimson as a harbinger of the coming season—Yule, as it was known to the humans. They skirted a rocky bluff, then found themselves on the height of a promontory, perhaps sixty feet above the trail. A sheer precipice of cracked and treacherous limestone formed an impassable barrier between the two warriors and the trail they could see winding directly below them. A hundred feet away, a similar cliff rose to an even greater height, and between them these rocky faces formed a canyon through which the Istarian procession would have to pass.

"This will give us vantage to shoot many arrows and still make our escape," Iydahoe declared, and Bakall nodded approvingly—as if he, himself, had sought those exact advantages in the site of their ambush.

Taking shelter in a shaded nook that afforded them a good view of the approaching trail, the two wild elves settled down to wait. They carried some dried venison jerky and ate with the accompaniment of a few swigs from their water sacks. All the while they kept their gazes on the approaching path, staring with the patience that was such a vital characteristic of their kind.

"There!" whispered Bakall, pointing at a golden cloak that shimmered through the trees. Chagrined, Iydahoe realized that his young companion had seen the enemy first.

The captain of the legionnaires led his riders toward the steep, cliff-walled gorge, then reined in his horse and brought the whole procession to a halt. The elves watched him scrutinize the heights to each side of the trail, and Iydahoe sensed that the commander had some misgivings about the route. Obviously, he was not a fool.

Turning to his following riders, the man spoke some orders, and four men dismounted. Two went to each side of the trail, disappearing into the woods—though Iydahoe easily guessed their mission. Each pair of scouts had no doubt been ordered to inspect the looming heights, seeking just the sort of ambush that the two elves intended.

Nevertheless, the Kagonesti warrior was not worried. The bluff's top was rough, with too many hiding places to yield to anything but a sweep by a whole company of men. He took care to see that the two braves were fully concealed in the depths of a cedar bush. The scouts would not discover them unless they actually parted the branches, and there were far too many bushes up here for the two men to make such an exhaustive search.

As silent and still as the rocks around them, the two warriors waited for the scouts. True to Iydahoe's guess, the men appeared about an hour later, carefully working their way along the bluff top. Though they could have dropped the pair with two quick shots, the Kagonesti held their bows in reserve, not wanting to spoil the ambush before it had time to develop.

Grumbling angrily, the two men stalked past within a dozen paces of the hiding elves, but didn't come near the cedar bush. Iydahoe sneered at the carelessness, listening with amusement to their litany of complaints.

"Stinkin' elves, anyway," one groused. "Why we got to risk our lives to guard a wagonload of Silvanesti wenches?"

"Because the Kingpriest likes to hear them sing," declared the other, in a tone of rebuke. "Are you going to argue with him?"

"Me? Are you nuts? Not now, especially—when everyone's talking about this great cleansing he's going to do. He'll banish evil from the world, they say."

"Don't believe everything 'they' say," cautioned the older legionnaire. "But remember, the elven chorus has been a hallmark of the Evening Prayer in his palace every night, and it's time for a new bunch of elves to get up there. And, besides, who do you think could sing as pretty?"

"Or look as pretty," the other allowed with a rude chuckle. "I tell you, there's a few of them little vixens I wouldn't mind one bit if . . ."

The men's lackluster search took them out of earshot before the elves could hear more. Another hour passed, with the two elves remaining as still as before. Finally the riders began to move forward, and they knew that the scouts must have signaled from the other end of the gorge.

Carefully, Iydahoe and Bakall moved into position. The first hundred riders filed into the shallow canyon, and the wagons trundled into view behind. Iydahoe saw the curtain tugged back on the compartment of the lead wagon, and he was startled as an elven maiden, golden hair flying in the breeze, leapt onto the ground.

"Vanisia!" came a stern voice from within, but the girl avoided the summons. A male elf, wearing the blue mantle of a priest, stuck his head out of the wagon and gestured the maiden back.

With a carefree laugh, she knelt beside the path and quickly picked a cluster of bright blossoms. Her face flicked upward before she jumped back to the wagon, and in that instant Iydahoe was stunned by an image of perfect, exquisite beauty. Not since he had shyly watched Moxilli, alive and carefree about the Whitetail village, had his heart pounded to the kind of excitement that suddenly rose, unbidden, within him.

"Now?" asked Bakall, holding his taut bowstring against his cheek and waiting for Iydahoe's command. With a start, the brave realized that the legionnaires had advanced to well within arrow range.

"Now," he agreed.

Both Kagonesti shot. Their sleek arrows flashed into the gorge, dropping the captain and his nearest attendant from their saddles. Consternation erupted as men shouted, horses bucked, and dozens of swords slid from oiled scabbards.

But already the elves had fired second and third volleys. The legionnaires milled about in panic, seeking escape from the deadly hail that had already dropped a half dozen from their saddles. The wagons blocked escape to the rear, and the facing walls of the gorge prevented any sideways movement, so the lead riders put their spurs to their steeds and charged headlong into the continuing canyon.

Iydahoe shot again and again, each missile claiming the life of a panicked rider. In earlier ambushes, he had vividly remembered the massacre of his village, drawing on the hatred fueled by that butchery to commit himself to his own killings. But by now the murderous tactic had become virtually automatic, with all his thoughts focused on the locating of his next target.

The wagons rocked forward, creaking and bumping over the bodies of slain legionnaires as their drivers hurried them through the gorge. The first wagon compartment's curtain pulled back, and again Iydahoe saw that beautiful image—the elfmaiden Vanisia staring upward, wide-eyed. Oddly, she seemed more curious than afraid.

Abruptly she was pulled back into the wagon, her place taken by the dour figure of the elven cleric. Iydahoe looked back to the legionnaires, having little interest in killing a Silvanesti when Istarians were within range of his bow. Carefully he released another shot.

The cleric raised a hand, and Iydahoe gaped in shock as his arrow suddenly became a long-stemmed flower, fluttering gently against the chest of the human it had been intended to kill. Bakall's shot, too, vanished into the shape of a harmless blossom!

Again and again Iydahoe released further arrows, altering his aim, seeking difficult targets, but each time the elven priest chanted his arcane command, and the arrow was rendered not only harmless, but beautiful.

Furious, Iydahoe changed his aim, this time drawing a bead on the cleric himself. But while the arrow started on a true flight, it suddenly swerved upward. Aghast, the Kagonesti saw white wings sprout from the shaft. Then, miraculously, the arrow was a bird, a snowy dove winging upward and away. Two more shots he released, and two more doves flew away.

The cleric fixed a burning stare on the cliff where the wild elves were concealed. His chant grew in strength, tugging at Iydahoe with a strangely compelling pull. Thwarted, the warrior backed away from the edge of the cliff.

"Come on. Let's give them the false trail," he hissed, turning to Bakall.

But the young warrior did not accompany him! Astonished, Iydahoe saw Bakall rise and step forward, exposing himself to plain view at the edge of the cliff. Then, before Iydahoe could do anything to stop him, the young warrior turned his face to the cliff and began to descend—straight toward the milling mass of the legionnaires and their Silvanesti allies!

# Chapter 26
# The Long Reach of Istar

Iydahoe lunged toward the cliff's edge, but his split second of astonishment gave Bakall time to slip down the steep slope, dropping out of the older warrior's reach. Below, legionnaires raised crossbows, drawing a bead on the young Kagonesti's unarmored back. Apparently oblivious to his companion above and his enemies below, Bakall resolutely worked his way down the precipice, choosing his toeholds with almost reckless haste.

Carefully creeping forward, Iydahoe peered through a narrow crack between two of the rocks at the lip of the cliff. He saw legionnaires with their crossbows sighted upward, yet for long seconds they held their fire. Iydahoe couldn't see Bakall, but from the lowering of the cross-

bows, he deduced that the young elf had not been shot—
for the moment, at least.

Only then did he hear the other voice—first stern and
commanding, then softer, more convincing. Iydahoe saw
the elven cleric he had observed earlier. Now the priest
stood atop the seat of the wagon, addressing the legionnaires with words Iydahoe couldn't understand. Their
captain and officers slain by the first of the elven arrows,
the men-at-arms wavered between vengeance and the elo-
quence of the cleric's arguments. Ultimately they held
their fire, watching carefully as the young warrior reached
the foot of the cliff and advanced toward the Silvanesti
who still exhorted from his wheeled pulpit.

Iydahoe's bow and the dozen arrows remaining in his
quiver were forgotten in the wild elf's wonder at the scene
below. He saw Bakall reach the side of the wagon, taking
the cleric's extended hand to step upward. As the young
brave disappeared into the curtained interior, the cleric
shouted something to the legionnaires.

Another man emerged from a different wagon—Iydahoe felt a mixture of horror and fury when he saw the
dark gray robes of a wizard. He was out of arrow range,
or the elf would have shot immediately. The fellow set a
small, iron brazier on the ground and squinted upward,
beginning to chant something aloud.

Even at this great distance the wild elf felt the flash of
cold recognition. This was the face he had seen on the
robed rider, fourteen years before. Flinging himself flat on
the rocks, Iydahoe took shelter against the unknown
threat of magical attack. His mind seethed with the hatred
that had so long burned for this magic-user, the man who
had enabled the armies of Istar to reach the wild elf villages undetected. If there was one man, beside the Kingpriest himself, who was to blame for that butchery,
Iydahoe knew this wizard was that killer.

The mage shouted something, his words crackling in
triumph. Iydahoe, peering around the rock, gaped in
astonishment as the wizard's pot of coals suddenly

spewed out a great column of flame. The fire crackled upward and out, like a living being—a creature cringing before the commands of its human master. The twisting, blazing shape broke away from the brazier. The wizard shouted again, pointing up the bluff, and the fiery creature followed the magic-user's command. Bushes and trees crackled into flame as it moved, but the fire-being didn't pause. When it reached the base of the precipice, it began to surge upward, bounding with a series of uncanny leaps.

Abruptly the legionnaires kicked spurs to their horses, while the wagon drivers shouted, unsparing in the use of their lashes. Hooves pounding, wheels rumbling, the procession clattered along the floor of the gorge. Dust swirled into the air, pushed by the breeze into a choking cloud that billowed upward in the canyon like muddy water flowing through a stone-bound channel.

At the same time, fire crackled higher on the cliff side as the blazing monster flew upward. Dozens of newly-kindled blazes added to the smoke and terrified the horses. The first band of riders, less the several dozen who had fallen to Kagonesti arrows, galloped past, with the wagons clattering behind. Shortly afterward, the final rank of legionnaires came into view, staring with fear and fury at the cliff from which death had rained—and where, now, the animated figure of the wizard's fire reached the lip of the precipice.

Iydahoe was unaware of the fleeing legionnaires as the towering fire beast surged into sight. The creature had a broad torso mounted on a circular base of flame. Two blazing arms extended from its upper body, while a head—complete with two charcoal-black eyes—surmounted the entire horrific form.

The thicket concealing Iydahoe erupted into fire. Heat singed the wild elf's skin, raising blisters on his arms. Behind him, a dry tree exploded into flame, blocking the Kagonesti's retreat. With no alternative, the warrior raised the silver axe and lunged forward, slashing wildly at the belly of the monstrous creature. Surprisingly, the axe head ripped a great gash through the pillar of flame.

Then a fist of crackling heat smashed into the wild elf's shoulder, sending him staggering backward. With shocking speed the fire monster leapt—but Iydahoe flailed with the mighty axe blade, knocking the beast aside. More bushes ignited, and sweat dripped in the warrior's eyes. His retreat blocked by flaming brambles, Iydahoe again hurled himself at the blazing apparition, hacking with the axe from the right, from the left, then chopping with brutal, overhand slashes. Parts of living fire fell away, flickering weakly on the ground, and the elf pressed his advantage. Finally the monster broke apart, balls of oily fire dropping over the cliff, spattering into smoke on the rocks below.

The wild elf turned and sprinted through the blazing tinder, ignoring the sparks that stung his skin, the blisters that had begun to ripple along his legs. Real fear gnawed at him. How could he battle a man who could wield the forces of the very elements themselves? At the same time, Iydahoe imagined shooting an arrow into the wizard, putting an end to his evil, and the thought brought his hatred to a tight, burning focus.

Iydahoe was as frightened by Bakall's strange departure as by the wizard's magic. The brave raced along the high ground, striving to catch sight of the procession. His chest rose and fell from the easy effort of his breathing, and finally he got a glimpse of the rear guard. From there he held a steady pace with his quarry, taking care to remain back from the lip of the cliff. Fortunately, the hastening procession made enough noise that he found that he didn't have to see it in order to follow it. Soon, afternoon shadows lengthened around him and, based on his limited experience with humans, he felt it likely that the Istarian party would soon camp for the night.

The power the cleric had used to compel Bakall mystified Iydahoe—and, he was forced to admit, frightened him more than a little. How could the wild elves fight this kind of magic? Yet he couldn't abandon the young warrior, not while there was a chance that he lived and could be rescued.

Another part of him could not deny a feeling, however slight, of gratitude. The mysterious elven cleric, after all, must have gone to great lengths of persuasion to spare Bakall's life. Why would he deprive the legionnaires the vengeance they so obviously had craved? Dozens of their number had been slain, and one of the killers had emerged into plain view. What sort of discipline could have held their hands? Another question arose, pestering: For what purpose did the priest want a Kagonesti prisoner?

Soon the gorge walls opened up, the pathway meandering through a series of hardwood groves mingled with a number of small meadows. A clear stream splashed through the center of the valley, providing fresh water along the entire route. The procession made camp around the largest clearing they could find, but even so they were forced to picket the horses and halt the wagons under the boughs of many tall hardwoods. As the sun set and stars sparkled in the sky, large blazes crackled upward from a number of campfires. The humans seemed jumpy, and even from a distance the wild elf heard men bickering, shouting, and cursing at each other. Unsettled by the ambush, the men obviously suspected that additional danger lurked in the surrounding darkness.

Iydahoe approached the bivouac with every bit of stealth in his warrior's and hunter's repertoire. During the first two hours of full darkness, he circled the place, locating the numerous and well-placed sentries by their dull outlines, the warmth of their bodies illuminating them in the darkness to his elven eyes. The men had formed a ring of steel-armed vigilance around their camp, but it was a circle with an inherent weakness: All the sentries stood on the ground.

Climbing into the branches of a widespread oak fifty feet outside the ring of sentries, the wild elf was careful to keep the heavy bole of the tree between himself and the wagons. With silent care, he hoisted himself from limb to limb until he was several dozen feet above the ground. Here, the boughs of the tree were still thick and sturdy, but a lower, leafy level of branches provided him good concealment from the human men-at-arms below.

Climbing from tree to tree, moving along one limb to the next with patient deliberation—more like a snake than a monkey—the Kagonesti brave approached the camp of the humans. A guard stood beneath the third tree Iydahoe reached, and he crept with ultimate stealth along the limbs and around the trunk of the forest giant. He heard the man sniff his nose and spit, but by moving with incredible deliberation the elf passed overhead without making a sound audible to the watcher below. It took him the better part of an hour to traverse that tree, but by the time he slipped into the next, the wild elf was within the perimeter of the procession's camp.

He waited for a long time, watching. His bow and arrows were ready to hand, and he desperately hoped that the gray-robed magic-user would wander into sight. Though he saw dozens of legionnaires among the campfires and corrals, there was no sign of the wizard or the House Elves.

Iydahoe had marked the wagon holding the cleric and Bakall by its blue canopy, which was embroidered on each side with a series of silver discs. Now the Kagonesti was not surprised to find that wagon near the very center of the bivouac—yet even here the humans had been careless, for several large trees extended their embrace of branches into the space over it. Iydahoe continued his meticulous advance, well aware of the humans cooking, eating, and talking directly below him.

By midnight he had reached a branch that extended almost directly above the cleric's wagon. Here he crept onto the low limb and lay still, twenty feet off the ground, while he studied the surroundings. Gradually the camp fell silent, though the legionnaires—still fearful after the brutally effective ambush—would no doubt remain jumpy and vigilant throughout the night. Several of the nearby sentries slumped listlessly at their posts, and a few of them even began to snore.

Finally, certain that he had located every human within sight—and that all of these were either sleeping or absorbed in their own musings—Iydahoe swung downward, suspending himself by his arms. With a last look around, he dropped to the grassy meadow, collapsing into a crouch that muffled the sound of his landing into an almost inaudible whisper.

Crawling to the wagon, Iydahoe could hear nothing from within. Narrow cracks in the canvas were utterly dark, so the wild elf deduced that the occupants had no lamp burning—a good thing, since the pulling back of the flap would otherwise have cast a sudden, alarming illumination through the camp.

Iydahoe froze, suddenly alarmed by the sensation that someone was very near. Moving his head only slightly, he looked around, his keen eyes penetrating the shadows cloaking the large wagon. He saw no one, but the peculiar apprehension did not go away.

As he reached toward the flap of the wagon, he heard a single word, spoken practically in his ear. With the quickness of thought, he spun, bringing the steel-edged axe up. There, a few feet away, in a space that had been empty when Iydahoe had looked a moment earlier, stood a *human*—the gray-robed mage! The man's finger pointed, as if in accusation, at the frantic wild elf.

Before Iydahoe could swing the axe, he felt gooey strands encircle his arm, quickly expanding into a cocoon around his chest, torso, and legs. Struggling in his fury, he tried to twist away, but succeeded only in tripping himself. The wizard gazed coldly downward, then snapped his fingers. Immediately a bright light emanated from his hand, and, as he held it up, dozens of legionnaires advanced from the darkness to form a ring around the immobilized elf.

With bitter bile in his throat, Iydahoe knew he had been

taken by magic. The web caster must have been lurking beside the wagon for hours, waiting for a chance. The brave even wondered if magic had somehow silenced the sound of the mage's own breathing he suspected that it had, or the keen-eared wild elf would have known of his presence.

"So, Feigh, you've taken the wild elf assassin!" declared a loud voice. A human dressed in a golden breastplate and cloak pushed through the crowd. Iydahoe recognized the garb. It was the same worn by the first man he had killed during the ambush. This fellow's hair was longer and neatly combed, his mustache drooping but well-trimmed. His face might have been handsome, except for a cold vacancy in his black eyes that seemed to absorb every bit of light cast by the wizard's spell.

"Aye, Captain-General Castille. Your guess was correct. The murderous wretch thought to approach the wagon undetected." Feigh, the wizard, spat at Iydahoe as he spoke. "He was easy to capture."

The wizard clapped his hands, and flecks of diamond-like dust flew into the air. The stuff seemed to coat much of the mage's body, sparkling into sight with the man himself when he had cast his web spell.

"These savages never stop to think about magic," continued the gaunt-faced mage, expansively. "I used the same trick to sneak up on their villages, years back when we tried to exterminate them."

Iydahoe stared in mute fury. The wizard's cold gaze met his, and there was a touch of cruel humor around the man's narrow lips. The warrior felt a flush of absolute rage—the mage had *wanted* him to know that he was the killer of the four tribes! And now Iydahoe could only tremble impotently, helpless to strike. The gray robe floated outward, and the elf saw a pouch tied to the wizard's belt. Flecks of the glittering dust clung to the embroidered flap.

"Good killing on that campaign," the commander agreed cheerfully.

"Your men have died twofold for the dead of my tribe!" Iydahoe retorted, feeling the emptiness of the boast even as he spoke.

The man called Captain-General Castille threw back his head and laughed heartily, though the humor did not reach his eyes. Abruptly he crouched and seized Iydahoe's long hair in a heavy hand. Pulling the elf up to a sitting position, he studied Iydahoe's tattooed face, taking care not to touch the gooey strands that still encircled the Kagonesti's body.

"You have killed too many of my soldiers, Elf. If I hadn't stayed in my wagon today, you would have killed me—instead, you took the poor wretch who wore my uniform. For all these reasons, you will die . . . very slowly."

Iydahoe spat into the man's face. The captain-general cursed and threw him back to the ground, standing and wiping his cheek with the back of his hand. "Drive a stake into the ground," he ordered, without taking his eyes off the Kagonesti. "Gather brush—dry twigs, kindling. I want this to be a long, slow fire."

Castille kicked the wild elf in the knee, and Iydahoe stifled a grunt of pain—he would not give this human the satisfaction of visible suffering. Still, as he thought of imminent death, his old, inescapable fear returned with numbing force. How could the tribe survive without him? His bitter need for vengeance had never seemed so foolish—now it would doubtlessly cost them Bakall's life as well!

Abruptly another person stood over him, and Iydahoe recognized the cleric who had stood on the wagon's seat—the House Elf who had somehow compelled Bakall to come down from the bluff.

"I see you have taken your prisoner," the newcomer said quietly.

"Aye! Now give us the other wild elf, Wellerane. Let the two burn side by side!" demanded the captain-general.

"I do not want him to burn," the priest replied, his tone gentle, lacking in the passion that seemed to emanate visibly from Castille and Feigh.

"A pox on your elven superstitions!" cursed the magic-user. "These Kagonesti are no better than animals. I'm only sorry to see that a couple of them still survive."

"There have been wild elves for thousands of years. Why do you take it upon yourself to eliminate them?" pressed the elf called Wellerane, though his voice retained its serene, soothing tone.

"Their time is long past. Now they're obstacles to the Kingpriest. And you've seen how dangerous they are!" snapped the wizard. Feigh looked frankly at Iydahoe. "I thought we did a more efficient job a few years back. I dusted a whole army of the Kingpriest's men. Invisible and soundless, they sneaked up and wiped out every village."

Iydahoe's rage hissed through his body, driving his muscles in a vain attempt to break out of the gummy web. Trembling, frantic with hate, he at last collapsed in utter exhaustion. Yet even in his despair, a portion of his mind heard the wizard's words and remembered the flecks of glittering dust.

"Enough talk of butchery," declared the priest, with a short, chopping gesture.

For the first time, Iydahoe saw Wellerane as an elf. True, the cleric's unpainted skin, his garments of fine cloth, marked him as no better than a human. At the same time, high cheekbones and a narrow forehead, slender ears extending gracefully beneath the strands of fine, golden hair, showed him clearly as a member of the sylvan race.

"Feigh's right," declared Castille. "You should give us the young one, too—nits make lice, after all."

"Nonsense. There is much to be learned from the youngster—he is, after all, a rare survivor of a nearly vanished people. And, as to this one, you must—in the name of Paladine—give me leave to absolve him before his execution."

"More of your superstitious nonsense!" spat the magic-user with a good deal of venom. "Burn *both* the wretches at once!"

"Captain-General, you must realize that this is a political decision." The cleric ignored the gray-robed wizard, speaking directly to the expedition commander. "Your prisoner is a noted villain, to be sure. If the black arrows are any proof, he is responsible for hundreds of deaths—well deserving of execution. But your liege, the King-priest, is ever a man—a *being*—who perceives the pure goodness that is the ultimate gift of the gods. He would take it poorly, I think, if this condemned elf is not given the chance to hear of this ultimate beneficence—*before* he burns."

As the wizard turned away in disgust, Captain-General Castille stared bluntly at the web-shrouded prisoner. Iydahoe met his gaze with a flat stare of his own. He had no care to hear Wellerane's words, to be absolved by the House Elf cleric, but anything that delayed his execution could only increase his chances of escape. Fear still thrummed through his muscles—a certain knowledge that the tribe would come to disaster, that the last Kagonesti on Ansalon would cease to exist if he failed them now.

It was the same fear he had known on the hunt, fourteen winters before, when the taking of a deer had meant the survival or starvation of the tribe. His solution, now, could only be the same thing as it had been then.

Iydahoe would not allow himself to fail.

Finally the captain-general turned back to the priest. He nodded, with an effort. "You can have him for one hour—not a second longer. My men will drive the stake and collect the brush. He'll burn as soon as he comes out."

The priest nodded, but as he turned to enter the wagon Castille made one more addition. "I want Feigh to go in there and keep an eye on him—and I'm sending two swordsmen as well. At the first sign of trouble, they'll hamstring him. He'll sizzle just as well crippled as he will whole."

# Chapter 27

# Wellerane and Vanisia

The wizard spat a word, and the strands of gooey web fell from Iydahoe's arms and legs. Two burly legionnaires took his weapons, then seized his arms, hauling him bodily onto the driver's deck of the wagon. One of them pulled back the canvas flap while the other roughly shoved the wild elf into the shadowy interior, slamming him into a sitting position on a wooden bench.

The wagon interior was lit by two flickering lanterns, though the shadows were thicker than they had been in the glare of the wizard's light spell. Still, Iydahoe remembered that the wagon had seemed utterly lightless outside—it was obviously well screened against observation. Kagonesti eyes adjusting quickly, Iydahoe looked at the wagon's interior, which proved surprisingly spacious. The two legionnaires, swords drawn, laid the elf's axe, quiver, and bow down somewhere out of sight. Now they stood beside Iydahoe's chair, each with a firm hand on the wild elf's shoulder. The wizard Feigh stood somewhere behind them. Before him, Wellerane, the cleric, pursed his lips into a faintly disapproving frown—whether because of Iydahoe or the legionnaires, the elf didn't know.

Beyond the priest, in the rear of the wagon, Bakall squatted on the floor. The young elfwoman who had gathered the flowers beside the trail was partially concealed by a gauzy curtain, but she sat quietly beside the young wild elf.

Iydahoe tried to catch his tribemate's eye, to compel Bakall to look for an avenue of escape, but the younger elf seemed disinterested—he barely took note of Iydahoe's arrival. Instead, his eyes remained fixed on Wellerane, as if the Kagonesti couldn't wait to hear what the priest would say next.

The warrior turned his angry eyes toward the House Elf, but he was unable to forget that Wellerane's intervention had given him another precious hour of life. He only wished that he could put that time to better use. Although the House Elf's face was unlined, the cleric's eyes were wizened, giving a suggestion of many centuries of age. He wore a plain blue tunic, adorned only by a platinum chain, which held a collection of tiny disks. These circlets, also of platinum, jingled slightly when the cleric spoke or gestured. The sound they made was soothing, mellow.

"I am a priest of the goddess Mishakal. In her name I ask you to tell me of your life, to purge yourself of transgressions."

"Who is Mishakal?" Iydahoe was not about to tell this House Elf anything. "Is she the concubine of the Kingpriest?"

The Kagonesti intended to shock Wellerane, but the cleric's only reaction was a curious raising of his slender eyebrows. "Mishakal is not a person of any kind. She is a goddess, wondrously kind, marvelously wise. It is she in whose honor we travel to Istar."

"How can an elven goddess know honor in the heartland of evil humankind?" Iydahoe challenged.

The cleric sighed. "I cannot say that Istar is a place worthy of her goodness, but Mishakal is not merely a goddess of Silvanesti. Her words are for humans and dwarves, kender—and even our cousins, the Kagonesti."

Behind Iydahoe, the wizard Feigh snorted contemptuously. The wild elf felt the tightening grips of the two legionnaires holding his arms, sensing that Wellerane's words distressed these humans.

"Why do you ride with legionnaire butchers?"

"The Kingpriest likes to hear us sing." For the first time, the elfwoman spoke, and Iydahoe had no difficulty believing that her voice could produce very beautiful music. "Every year, a chorus from Silvanesti travels to Istar, to raise our voices in the Evening Prayer. We will sing in the temple itself, at the very heart of the great city."

Only then did his eyes travel to the golden-haired elf-maiden. She leaned forward, peering around the gauzy screen to look at him with frank curiosity. Her eyes were greener than any Kagonesti's, but flecks of darker color suggested a depth of understanding beyond that of the typical House Elf. In the firm set of her chin, the frank and appraising expression in her eyes, Iydahoe sensed that she was a female of great determination and courage. She showed no fear of him, but neither did she seem upset by his arrival. He recalled that her name was Vanisia—it seemed a wonderful and appropriate thing to call her—and that she had earlier gathered flowers by the trail.

Abruptly the wagon sagged under a sudden weight.

Vanisia gasped, and Iydahoe twisted in shock, surprised to see that *another* House Elf now occupied the wagon with them—an elf who had not entered through any way the warrior could see. Adorned in plain clerical robes, the newly arrived priest stood to the side of Iydahoe and bowed serenely to Wellerane.

Feigh gasped and raised his hands as the men holding Iydahoe raised their swords toward the strange elf. Though startled by the stranger's arrival, the Kagonesti was also amused by the expression of terror on the wizard's face.

Wellerane quickly held up a hand as the magic-user began chanting the words to a spell. "Hold your casting, sorcerer!" the priest commanded, so sharply that Feigh halted in midphrase, turning to glower at the priest.

Apparently, the newcomer was known to the elfwoman and the cleric, for both of them bowed deeply before him. Iydahoe took a closer look at the regal figure. The white clerical mantle resembled Wellerane's except for the color. The new elf was older, with strands of silvery hair dangling from both sides of his balding scalp. At his breast he wore a medallion depicting a platinum dragon where the cleric of Mishakal displayed his disks.

"Loralan!" Wellerane gasped, finally raising his eyes. "How do you come from Silvanesti so quickly?"

"I travel swiftly, for I have little time. Indeed, we *all* have little time." The stranger's words sent a tremor of apprehension along Iydahoe's spine, though only later would he grasp their meaning.

Feigh snorted again, but the wizard's sound carried a subtle undertone of fear. "Teleportation is a wizard's skill, Priest! What black magic do you work here?" he demanded.

Loralan ignored the wizard, instead fixing his eyes on the kneeling cleric. "I have come for you, my loyal friend and companion. It is our time."

"Time?" Wellerane was mystified. "But I journey to Istar with the chorale! I must—"

The elder priest held up a hand, and Wellerane fell silent. "It takes more than thirteen days to reach the city—by that time there will be no Istar to greet you. But enough—I cannot speak any more of this. It is time for you to go."

"But Vanisia—my daughter! She must come with us!

She, two, is a faithful priestess of Mishakal. In time, she will be a true and mighty cleric!"

Loralan sighed, his eyes wrinkling in sadness. "I know that you speak the truth, but as I said, there *is* no time."

Wellerane blinked in confusion, looking at Vanisia. The elfwoman stared back, her eyes growing wide in terror, and perhaps the beginnings of comprehension—a glimmering of understanding that went far beyond the grasp of the thoroughly mystified Iydahoe.

Abruptly, both Loralan and Wellerane were gone. They didn't leave, didn't even move—nevertheless, they were no longer in the wagon with the others. Vanisia gasped, then moaned softly. Bakall blinked and shook his head, as if awakening from a dream. Iydahoe tensed, certain that they needed to take their chance to escape now, or it would be too late.

"Go! Take him out to the stake. We'll burn them both, *now!*" hissed Feigh. The wizard seized a stout staff and raised it menacingly, ready to smash Iydahoe's head. Only then did the wild elf see that the wizard's eyes were wide with terror. The disappearance of Wellerane had shaken him badly.

"No!" It was Vanisia who spoke. Trembling, her own eyes darting around as if she expected to see the priest hiding somewhere just out of sight, she nevertheless found the strength to challenge the furious wizard.

"How dare—!" Feigh's rebuke was interrupted by his scream. The staff in his hands twisted into a long, living snake, the tail coiling around the magic-user's waist while the wedge-shaped head strained at the man's face. With both hands the shrieking wizard held the jaws inches away from his cheek.

With the quickness of thought, Iydahoe's hand lashed out and seized a surprised legionnaire around the neck. A sharp tug brought the man down, and the wild elf slammed his head against the wooden floorboard.

The other guard slashed with his blade, but fear made him wild, and Iydahoe ducked away from the attack. A bronzed body flew past as Bakall sprang, knocking the second legionnaire against the side of the wagon. Seeing his axe on the floor, Iydahoe picked up the weapon and bashed it into the man's helmet. With a grunt of surprise, he dropped, senseless, to the floor. Next the wild elf raised the weapon toward Feigh, who had collapsed to a sitting position and still grappled, screaming, with the snake. The animal contorted its bulging, scaly skin, drawing tighter around the now-gasping wizard's waist.

"Wait. Do not kill him." Vanisia spoke softly, more beseeching than commanding, and Iydahoe realized with shock that he did not want to disobey the young priestess.

"Why not?" he demanded after a moment.

"All living creatures are the children of Mishakal. She desires that we not harm each other."

"No goddess of elves would deign to notice these short-lived scum!" snapped the warrior with a great deal more vehemence than he actually felt.

"Please!" Vanisia spoke the one word, and with her eyes on him there was no way Iydahoe could work the violence that still seethed in his heart.

"More humans are coming." Iydahoe couldn't believe that the noise of the fight hadn't already drawn additional guards. "We have no time!"

"This wagon is shielded from noises beyond—and likewise, nothing from within can be heard in the world outside. We *do* have a little time," Vanisia said. Her trembling had ceased, and she spoke calmly and forcefully. Iydahoe suddenly had the feeling that she was not as young as she looked.

Bakall, shamefaced, held a sword ready to stab the terrified wizard. The priestess spoke that strange word again, and the snake once more became a mere shaft of wood. Feigh hurled it from him as if the touch of the wood stung his hands.

"It is a good thing he thought to strike you with Wellerane's staff," Vanisia said seriously.

Iydahoe studied the wizard. Feigh's eyes flashed hatred,

and he remembered the wizard boasting about the destruction of the Kagonesti villages. Only then did he remember the pouch at the magic-user's side. Swiftly the wild elf reached down, roughly snapping the strap that held the stuff. Raising the flap, he took a few of the diamondlike flakes and sprinkled them over his leg.

The leg vanished.

The Kagonesti almost fell to the side, so surprising was the disappearance of his limb. Yet it was still there. He kicked outward, and Feigh grunted as the elf's toe slammed into his leg. The sensation of invisibility was deeply disturbing—but at the same time it might have its uses.

"It may be possible to slip past the guards. Get our weapons," he said to Bakall, nodding at the bows and quivers while his eyes remained fixed on the cowering magic-user.

Iydahoe saw movement in the corner of his eye as the elfmaid came along with Bakall. The warrior realized with a shock that she had declared her allegiance with them. If she hadn't enchanted the staff, Iydahoe might already be burning. Now, without Wellerane to protect her, the legionnaires would make short work of the priestess. Or her end might not be so short, he thought with a glimmer of darker dread.

"You must come with us," he said, surprised by how easily the words flowed out.

"I know," Vanisia said. She stood, adorned in her robe and platinum medallions. A curling seashell, rimmed in gold, served as the clasp of her belt. She wore ornate, golden sandals, which would be impractical for walking, but there was nothing to do about that now. "I'm ready."

"There's no place on Ansalon where your kind will be safe!" sneered Feigh, sensing that he was about to be spared.

"You're wrong." Iydahoe looked at the man, and he saw the burned bodies of four villages, the trampled huts, the slain warriors and women and babes. His hands were trembling as a red haze lowered across his eyes.

The steel axe moved more quickly than the striking snake. In an instant, the wizard's head thumped to the floor, rolling thickly to the back of the wagon. Vanisia, her hand pressed to her mouth, stared in horrified silence at the gory object.

As the bleeding corpse slumped to the floor, the wild elf felt a curious emptiness—the killing had not cleansed his soul of the horror or the fear, but a great enemy of his people was dead, and the one man who might have tracked their escape was no longer a threat.

"He had to die. He was an enemy of the tribe," Iydahoe told Vanisia. With a shudder, she stepped past the bleeding corpse as the brave held out the pouch of magic dust.

"Come," he said. "You are a wild elf now."

# Chapter 28

# The Wrath of the Gods

"Here. There's a door in the floorboards. We can go out that way." Vanisia pulled back an ornately patterned rug, revealing a brass handle and the outline of a small square.

"Good." Iydahoe nodded as Bakall handed him his bow and quiver. He quickly sprinkled the disappearing dust over Bakall, Vanisia, and himself, marveling at the way their flesh vanished. He could see nothing of his companions and was startled when the brass ring of the trapdoor lifted upward from the floor.

"Wait," he told Bakall, sensing the young warrior's eagerness to be gone. He doused the two lanterns that cast shadowy illumination through the wagon, knowing that their spill of light would have drawn the attention of every guard within a hundred paces. "I'll go first," Iydahoe declared in a whisper, touching Bakall's unseen shoulder.

Even through the magical concealment the older warrior felt his young companion's imploring gaze. "Please, let me," Bakall whispered.

The curious trance that had earlier captured Bakall had been Wellerane's doing, Iydahoe knew, but he always felt more confident when he himself was in the lead. Still, he sensed the young warrior's need to restore his own pride, so he reluctantly agreed.

The door rose silently, and Iydahoe heard Bakall drop to the ground. He saw puffs of dust as the warrior scuttled on his belly to the rear of the wagon. Swiftly, soundlessly, Iydahoe came behind.

Vanisia followed Iydahoe out of the wagon, dropping to the ground with surprising stealth. Together they crawled into the shadows beneath the nearby tree and looked around. Iydahoe saw guards gathered around a huge fire, while others still collected more tinder for the execution blaze. Numerous guards were posted around the wagon, and without the concealment of invisibility the elves certainly would have been seen—even by the night-blind humans. As it was, however, none of them took note of the elves' stealthy departure.

Bakall sprang upward and disappeared into the branches. Iydahoe leapt, pulling himself upward, then reached down from the tree branch to help the novice priestess with her initial upward leap. Here their invisibility hampered him. He didn't know where she was until the branch drooped slightly, sagging as Vanisia pulled herself up. Bakall moved on, slipping silently into the darkness, and the warrior worried for a moment that the female would not be able to keep her balance or move without noise among the dense limbs of the forest canopy.

Yet when Vanisia crawled behind Iydahoe on the limb, he could sense that she had no trouble keeping her balance. The Kagonesti warrior felt a glimmering of respect for this Silvanesti female, a feeling that he was strangely fortunate to have her come along with them.

He saw a great ring of legionnaires gathered around a heavy stake. Piles of brush towered nearby, while several branches were thrown around the base of the sturdy post.

"It's time!" shouted a man—Captain-General Castille, Iydahoe saw. "Fetch me the elf!"

"Hurry!" hissed the wild elf warrior, helping Vanisia to slip past him, urging her after Bakall. Iydahoe paused to nock an arrow and draw back his bow. He had a clear view of the captain-general through a gap in the trees.

He sensed Vanisia pausing, knew that she was watching him, even though she couldn't see his skin or his weapon. He could not bring himself to shoot. Confused, he relaxed his bowstring and shook his head. Perhaps this was the practical choice. Killing Castille would only alert the legionnaires to their escape that much sooner, whereas the execution of Feigh had given them additional time to flee. He knew, however, that there was more to his reluctance than this pragmatic concern.

He hastened after Vanisia, following her progress by seeing the leaves that she brushed out of her way. Even though she remained invisible, he knew that her chances would be bad if she fell among the angry humans below. Taking care to avoid the branches directly over the human sentries, the three elves passed from each tree to the next. They followed the middle terrace of branches, thirty feet or more above the ground, sometimes crawling along, snakelike, and in other places standing to scurry down the broad, rounded limbs.

They had barely moved beyond the outer pickets when they heard the cries of alarm from the center of the caravan camp. Iydahoe imagined the human's fury. A grim smile tightened his face as he pictured the discovery of the headless wizard.

"Humans can't see in the dark like we can. Let's run for it!" he whispered to his companions, who voiced quiet agreement.

They dropped to the forest floor thirty paces beyond

the outer guard posts and trotted through the darkness. Relying on their elven eyesight, they avoided the deadfalls, underbrush, and moss-covered rocks that occasionally blocked their path. Furthermore, Iydahoe led them on a roundabout, rough trail in an effort to discourage and mislead any potential pursuers.

As they jogged, Iydahoe was as impressed with Vanisia's endurance as he had been with her stealth. Never complaining, she held the same pace as the two wild elves, though the warrior suspected that her ornate sandals must be causing her no small amount of pain.

Finally, several miles from the Istarian camp, the dust of invisibility began to wear off. In a matter of moments, all three of them could clearly be seen—and since they were well beyond the nearest humans, Iydahoe found their reappearance to be something of a relief. No pursuit was audible, so the warrior allowed a brief rest. Vanisia collapsed to the ground while Bakall, his head held low, muttered something about making a circuit around the place to make sure they weren't observed. Iydahoe sensed that the young warrior was embarrassed by the lack of willpower he had displayed atop the bluff, and didn't want to discuss the matter. Knowing that solitary meditation might be the best cure for Bakall's guilt, Iydahoe agreed.

For a short time, he sat in silence with the elfmaid, but curiosity finally compelled him to speak.

"Why did you stop the wizard from burning me? You spoke of going to Istar, of singing the Evening Prayers. Why did you turn away from that?"

He was afraid that she would be terribly upset, but when she spoke, her voice was strong, her words clear. "Istar is meaningless now—or at least, it will be in a matter of days."

Iydahoe remained silent, waiting for her to continue.

"Loralan has preached this prophecy for many decades, more than a century. I have heard about the spiraling descent of Istar's rulers. The current Kingpriest is the worst, and it was only with reluctance that Loralan consented to allow our chorale to make the journey this year. Then, from things he said in the wagon, to Wellerane—" Here her voice cracked for the first time. "—I believe the end is near."

"The end? Of what?"

"Of Istar—and, perhaps, of Krynn. The wrath of the gods will strike our world, and the legions of Istar will perish. If that happens, and I cannot be with my father, I did not want to be among the humans of that wretched procession."

"In the forest we live with little, by House Elf standards," Iydahoe pointed out.

She smiled slightly. "Little? There are those in Silvanesti who have *nothing* amid the splendor and plenty."

"Spoken like a Kagonesti," the warrior admitted, impressed.

"I've treasured the solitude of the wild places since I was a little girl," Vanisia said. "I chose the fields of Mishakal's flowers over the greatest crystal citadels of our elven architects. Often I slept outside, on the banks of the Thon-Thalas, just to hear the music of the river in the dawn."

"We have no architects in the forest," Iydahoe replied, "but I, too, know the song of flowing water." In his heart, he wondered if she would be able to survive—and enjoy a life—in the mud-and-deer-hide lodges of the Kagonesti. Surprising himself with his vehemence, he desperately hoped that she would. Only then did he wonder if there could possibly be any substance to her fears. There couldn't. She was frightened by the strange disappearance of her father. Surely that was all.

"I—I thank you for taking me away."

"You took yourself away," Iydahoe said with a shrug that was an attempt to conceal his pleasure at her companionship. All this talk of gods' wrath unsettled him, but he could not bring himself to believe that the end of the world was a real possibility. Still, he pressed her on the point. "What words did this cleric say to you, to your father, to make you believe the future is so dire?"

"He has talked of the growing arrogance of the King-priest, of that man's belief that someday he will be able to command the gods themselves. When he tries, the gods will punish him—and all of Ansalon as well."

"How will they mete out this punishment?"

"Loralan did not know. But he said that the true clerics might be summoned away beforehand, and that many days—twelve or thirteen, I think he said—of terror would befall the land. And that none of the warnings could cause the Kingpriest to turn from his disastrous path."

"The priest did say something about that, about the road to Istar taking more than thirteen days," Iydahoe remembered, still unwilling to accept the veracity of her fears.

Vanisia only nodded.

"And you believe that the first of these predictions has come to pass, that the priests have been summoned away?" Iydahoe did not place a great deal of faith in prophecies, but the young elfmaid's words disturbed him nonetheless.

"Loralan came to get my father, just as he is taking the other clerics—the true speakers of the gods who live across Ansalon. I suspect they are all gone now."

"Clerics and wizards of the House Elves may come and go as they wish," Iydahoe replied skeptically, "but other priests still dwell among the peoples of the world. My father, Hawkan, is a shaman who knows the ways of the gods—and he awaits us in our village. We will see him by the end of the day."

"I hope you're right," said Vanisia, and he knew that she meant it.

Yet Iydahoe was disquieted by her conviction, sensing that she would be honestly surprised to find the wild elf shaman in the camp.

"Why do you think the clerics were taken from the world?" he asked, grappling with the mystery.

"I can't say for sure. Perhaps because we have allowed the arrogance of the Kingpriest to grow too strong. Neither elves nor men have been able to prevent his mad condemnation of everything he dislikes. He brands a thing, or a people, as evil—then he has it killed. Dwarves, ogres, even elves have felt this hatred."

"Then why did Silvanesti make a road to his citadel?"

"For more than a century we had shunned Istar, banished all trade and commerce with that realm. But some of our priests—notably Loralan—convinced our rulers that we must try to communicate with the Kingpriest. He felt that only thus could they even have a chance to change his disastrous path."

"We have no need for such superstitions in the wild. You will find that life is simpler in the forest." In Iydahoe's own mind he began to wonder if, too, it might not become more peaceful. How many more humans would he have to kill before the four tribes were avenged? For the first time, he realized that he had embarked on a hopeless task—and he gave real thought to laying aside his quest for vengeance.

"I think this is more than superstition, though I pray that I might be wrong."

They rested uneasily for a few hours, then rose to take the trail in a peculiarly dim and misty dawn. The light seeping through the trees seemed pale, sickly, as though a greenish filter had been laid across the sun. It was not until midmorning, when they emerged from the trees onto a low promontory with a view of hills, valleys, and sky, that Iydahoe understood why.

The entire expanse of cloudless heaven had become a dank, putrid green.

Like a sweep of fetid marshlands, the pale, sickly color stained the sky. It was not in any way a healthy, verdant green, like the budding of spring or the rippling of a lush field of grass. Instead, it filled the upper air with a dead, shadowy layer of rot. The vast space overhead took on a vivid, dire cast, like the skin of a person who had become seriously ill.

Iydahoe vividly remembered Vanisia's words, her predictions of godly warnings that would pace off the days before disaster. Certainly it did not take much imagination to think that this coloring of the sky must be such a warning. Indeed, it could be nothing else!

The three elves did not speak, but took the homeward trail with renewed urgency. Iydahoe was shaken to his core, though he tried not to display his unsettled state to his two companions. Bakall looked around wildly, holding an arrow constantly ready in his bow, while Vanisia became listless and downcast, plodding dully along with her gaze fixed on the ground.

They jogged as quickly as possible, Iydahoe taking the lead, now seeking the shortest path back to the grotto of the small tribe's village. Under the pall of the bizarre sky, he felt that the legionnaires would hasten back to Istar and not waste a lot of time seeking the two wild elves. Undoubtedly the human soldiers, bereft of their wizard and their priest, were reacting with horror to the phenomenon.

The memory of the dead wizard left Iydahoe cold, even numb. Always before the slaying of his enemies had been a thing that gave him satisfaction. Now he had killed perhaps the deadliest enemy in the history of the four tribes —and yet the memory of that justifiable death gave him no pleasure at all.

He wondered if the humans would realize that the Kagonesti had taken Vanisia—or if they would believe that they had abducted Wellerane as well. The Istarians' consternation didn't matter to him, except insofar as his enemies would be too distraught to bother with following the wild elves. This, of course, was a good thing.

Near sunset, they approached the grotto, traveling more slowly than the two Kagonesti would have by themselves. Still, the elfwoman trotted without complaint, though raw blisters were clearly visible on each of her feet. The three hurried among the tall trunks leading to the gorge and the sheltered village.

Vanisia's piercing scream shot through the forest like a lightning bolt, and Iydahoe whirled to see what had frightened her. With a moan, she pointed toward the bole of a tree, sinking to her knees in shock.

As Iydahoe followed her pointing finger, he felt a chill descend into the very pit of his stomach. The bark of the tree trunk had split apart like some kind of festering wound, and from the opening dripped glistening, crimson blood! Streaming onto the ground in a thick, congealing flood, the liquid gushed as if it poured from a fresh, deep cut.

The elves stared in dull disbelief. Vanisia and Bakall recoiled a step, while Iydahoe's fists clenched in impotent rage. What kind of horror was it that could rend the very trees of the forest? He saw the pool of blood expand, pouring over the dike formed by a gnarled root, starting a small trickle along the forest trail.

The bark tore on another tree, nearby, and more scarlet liquid flooded out. All around them trunks ripped, and soon the stench of spilled blood overpowered everything else in the forest. Fueled by steadily growing panic, Iydahoe led the pair through the woods, racing as fast as their feet could carry them. They leapt splashing rivulets of gore, desperately skirted growing pools of the horrid stuff. The warrior ran as if he fled a nightmare, no longer certain of what they would find in the grotto. He no longer felt certain about *anything!*

When they slipped through the narrow, twisting gorge that led to the concealed village, Iydahoe tried unsuccessfully to calm his pounding heart. Finally they reached the clear pool of water, and he saw the small lodges of the makeshift tribe. The young Kagonesti, all the survivors of the Istarian massacre of fourteen years earlier, came running toward them, shouting in relief.

But *only* the younger elves were here. He saw the fragments of the Ram's Horn, sitting as always on the smooth, mossy blanket before his father's lodge. The coals of Hawkan's fire were out, and there was no sign of movement within the shadowed interior of the little hut.

"Hawkan? Where's my father?" demanded Iydahoe.

The boy Kagwallas, who was almost as old as Bakall, stepped forward, his eyes filled with tears.

"A person came last night, a House Elf," he explained. "He took your father by the hand. Together they went away."

"They just disappeared! It was *magic!*" wailed little Faylai.

Iydahoe staggered under the onslaught of monstrous fear, sinking to the ground from unbearable weight, knowing that Vanisia had spoken the truth.

The end of the world had begun.

# Chapter 29

# Thirteen Days of Doom

The terrified Kagonesti huddled around a small fire, watching the woods. At sunset, they divided themselves into the three largest lodges to spend the long, ghostly night. At dawn, they emerged again, rebuilding the fire and watching their wilderness perish before their eyes.

The trees continued to bleed, fouling the streams, polluting the crystal pool in the center of the village. Fortunately, Kagwallas had had the presence of mind to order all the waterskins filled when the trees had first split open, and the tribe did not suffer for water.

Keeping his bow and arrows in his hands, Iydahoe often rose to his feet and paced around the periphery of the village. He felt as though the forest itself was planning an attack, and he despaired that his own vigilance would not be enough to prevent or deflect it.

Kagwallas and Bakall, too, kept watch on the woods, while Dallatar tried amuse the younger elves by making funny faces and performing inept juggling acts. Ambra held little Faylai on her lap, while Vanisia sat among all the wild elves, offering a comforting word whenever she could.

Iydahoe heard a stirring in the woods—the first such noise since the trees had begun to bleed. Carefully raising an arrow, he peered among the gory trunks, certain that something large moved out there. A bulky form crashed heavily through the decaying brush.

A stag lumbered into view, shaking its antlered head from side to side, groggy and confused. Snorting, it fixed bloodshot eyes on one of the lodges. Lowering its rack, the great deer charged, smashing through the bark-and-leather wall of the small hut.

Oddly, Iydahoe's first fear was a concern that the heavy hooves would further smash the pieces of the Ram's Horn, which still lay on the mossy blanket nearby. Overcoming his surprise, the elf raised his bow and shot—a perfect hit, sending the arrowhead deep into the creature's heart. Yet the deer only stumbled, raising its head and snorting as it looked around for the source of the attack. Iydahoe shot again, followed with a third arrow before the animal sank to its knees, then toppled, dead.

Regretfully, the warrior and the older boys dragged the meat into the woods, reluctant to eat a creature that had been touched by such visible and profound madness. That night, Iydahoe trembled on his sleeping pallet, hearing the surreal moaning of the wind, the sighing of the trees, as if each limb, each trunk, felt terrible grief over the wounds that so unnaturally drained them. His nightmares came while he was awake, and his fear blocked him from seeking the only available refuge—sleep.

"Is it true that you have killed many hundred men?" asked Vanisia suddenly, her voice emerging from the

darkness on the other side of the hut. For a moment, Iydahoe didn't even comprehend her question, and when he
did he thought that her curiosity seemed no more bizarre
than the natural chaos around them.

"That's what the human said. I have not kept count of
lives, though I've shot many hundreds of arrows at the
Istarians. And I rarely missed," he added, wanting to be
truthful.

"Why did you kill so many?"

He told her of the day, fourteen years before, when his—
and the tribe's—life had changed forever. It was not until
he finished speaking that he realized he wept, that sometime during his speaking Vanisia had come to his side.
Now she, too, wept as she held him. In the strength of her
embrace he found the only goodness he knew in the
world, profoundly relieved that there was, at least, that
much comfort amid the chaos and despair.

"Why must you do this avenging, this killing?" she
probed gently, after a long silence.

"I—I don't know. Since that day, the tribe has had no
Pathfinder—"

"They have *you*," Vanisia said firmly, and her words
brought him up short. "You will show them the way. And
perhaps that way is not always by killing."

"I am beginning to think you speak the truth," he
admitted. With this thought on his mind, he finally slept.

The next day, the maddened intruders were wild
boars—three of them. The creatures stampeded into the
camp, heads lowered, and charged at the first Kagonesti
they saw. This was Dallatar, who ducked out of the way.
But one of the young girls, trying to run, was tossed high
by a tusked snout and suffered a broken arm. She cried
shrilly as Iydahoe and the older youths finally slew the
maddened animals with spears and arrows.

Once more the wild elves dragged the meat away from
the village and left it to rot. Vanisia showed her clerical gift
as a healer in mending and splinting the broken bone, but
when she prayed to her goddess for aid in healing, those

beseechments went unanswered. All her concentration and effort could not bring a response from the angered deities of Krynn—there would be no miraculous recovery.

On successive days, wolves, hawks, even rabbits and squirrels, dashed into the village in berserk frenzy. The youngest Kagonesti wielded clubs and threw stones, joining the rest to battle the unnatural onslaught. On the seventh night, the wild elves moved from their lodges into a large, dry cave that stood in one of the grotto's walls. There they slept fitfully, always with several sentries posted to keep their eyes on the night's exceptionally deep darkness.

Late in the morning of the ninth day, a bear lurched into the village. The brute drooled, snapping foaming jaws as it peered around with dim, bloodshot eyes. Iydahoe ordered the rest of the tribe into the cave and faced the monster alone. He shot many arrows into the bear before it charged, roaring. Then he chopped with his axe as the bear mauled the elf. The two combatants rolled across the ground, the elf snarling as fiercely as the bear. Claws raked Iydahoe's ribs as the steel axe bit again and again into the crazed animal's side.

It was that keen blade that ultimately saved him, slashing through the arteries in the monster's neck. Iydahoe's tribemates dragged the corpse off the bleeding, ravaged warrior, but the wild elf would not lie still and let Vanisia tend his wounds. Instead, he stumbled to his feet, shaking his bleeding fists at the equally gruesome forest.

"Why do you turn on us?" Iydahoe cried. The pain from his wounds was nothing compared to the spiritual betrayal he felt. His rage was mindless, directed at the woods and mountains themselves. The corruption of tree and wild beast was too much, too vile, to bear.

"Come and kill me—now!" he shrieked. "The bear was too weak! Give me a *real* killer! Or are you afraid?"

He didn't know who he shouted at as he wildly looked around, but suddenly his eyes fixed on a focus for his rage, his despairing sense of abandonment. Blindly he stumbled to the mat where the shards of the Ram's Horn lay.

"Take back your gifts!" he railed. "Useless, pathetic symbols. What use are they to us!"

The elves of the tribe watched in shock as he picked up the shards, threw them by the handful into the woods, cursing and shouting until, at last, he collapsed into a ragged heap.

Deeply shaken, Bakall and Kagwallas carried him into the cave. Finally Iydahoe felt shame, knowing his outburst must have terribly frightened the Kagonesti. Still, there was that bleak, all-consuming despair. . . .

If it hadn't been for the presence of Vanisia, Iydahoe felt that these dire portents might have caused the loss of his own sanity. Yet when his despair seemed darkest, when hopelessness settled over his mind like a burial shroud, she would ask him questions, gently direct his attention back to the mundane life of the tribe—such as it was. Sometimes she just held his hand, and the touch of her soft skin was the strength, the hope that sent a few rays of light spilling through his despair. At other times, they exchanged legends about their peoples. He told her of the Grandfather Ram and Father Kagonesti, while she spoke of wise Silvanos and his long, troubled legacy.

They shared these tales with the young ones and talked of lighter things as well. Vanisia allowed the girls to play with the large, coiled shell that was her belt buckle, explaining that it came from an ocean shore. For hours Faylai and Tiffli listened, rapt, as she told them of beaches and waves and the sea. Then the youngsters held the shell to their ears, listening, imagining the distant surf.

The elves drank water sparingly and slept as best they could. Always after dark the winds came, each night louder, more furious than the last. Shreds of bark were ripped from the roofs of the lodges, and dead leaves swirled into the low kettle of the grotto. One by one the smaller lodges had collapsed under the unnatural onslaught.

Vanisia passed some of the time by making herself a pair of sturdy moccasins, using scraps of hide from the ruined lodges. She was so successful in her endeavor that, in short order, she made footwear for several of the other Kagonesti—and taught the youngsters to do the same. Her silent labors were a source of reassurance, of normalcy to them all, and the young elves brightened perceptibly, wearing their first new clothes in fourteen years.

On the twelfth morning, Iydahoe awakened to a bleak silence. He saw Vanisia sitting in the mouth of the cave, looking outward. When she noticed that he was awake, she held a finger to her lips and gestured that he should join her.

"What is it?" he whispered, apprehensive.

"Look. I don't know where he came from, but he hasn't moved since first light."

Iydahoe was shocked to see an elderly elf standing under the drooping branches of an oak, apparently observing the battered village from the shelter of the forest. The stranger's hair was long and pure white, and he supported his frail frame by leaning on a stout, crooked staff. A pattern of faded ink seemed to darken the elf's skin in places, and Iydahoe wondered if he saw an oak leaf tattoo over the fellow's left eye. If he had been marked as a Kagonesti, the inking had been done so long ago that it had all but faded.

For a few minutes Iydahoe observed the old fellow, noting his ragged robe of deerskin, his bare feet, and his emaciated physique. The stranger looked back, seeing the two elves sitting in the door of the lodge but making no move to approach or retreat.

Finally, Iydahoe rose to his feet. Slowly, with a peculiar sense of reverence, he went outside, under the sickly green heavens. The trees had ceased to bleed, and a stillness had settled over the entire forest. The warrior wrestled with an unsettling sense that he and this old elf were the only two living creatures currently under that oppressive sky.

"Come, Grandfather. You are welcome here," he said politely, using the honorary term for an elder Kagonesti. "We have jerky and dried fruit. Join us as we break our fast."

The white-haired elf simply stared, though his dark hazel eyes sparkled. Iydahoe sensed that he had heard every word, but still the ancient figure made no movement, no reply.

"Do you hear me, Grandfather?" he asked.

"I hear—but do *you*, wild elf?" The stranger's voice was strong and resonant, a surprisingly forceful sound emerging from that frail chest.

"What should I hear?" Iydahoe was puzzled.

"You offer me help, but you cannot help me. Nor can I help you."

"*Is* there any help, any hope?" asked the warrior.

"You call me Grandfather, and this is wrong. Seek *him*, wild elf. Seek the true Grandfather of us all. Know the legends, and you shall know where to find him."

Iydahoe blinked, surprised by the elf's words, and by the serene confidence with which they were spoken. As he tried to formulate a reply, he realized that, in the space of his blink, the ancient hermit had disappeared.

"Did you see where he went?" he asked Vanisia, who emerged from the cave to look around. She shook her head, and he crossed the village clearing to look behind the great oak. Not only did he see no sign of the stranger, but the muddy ground where the elf had stood was bare of any footprint.

"When did you first see him?"

"He was here when I woke up."

"He never moved?"

Vanisia shook her head. "No. He stayed by this tree for as long as I watched him." Her green eyes probed his face, and Iydahoe felt something terribly important, a piece of knowledge that he must, somehow, grasp. "What did he say to you?" she asked.

"He said . . . seek the Grandfather, 'the true Grandfather

of us all.' He means the Grandfather Ram."

"But seek him? Where . . . ?"

Something in Iydahoe's face froze Vanisia's question in her throat. Abruptly the warrior saw with abrupt, crystalline clarity what he had to do—and he feared that, already, he was too late.

"Each of you, pack a bedroll!" ordered the warrior, addressing the young elves who gaped, wide-eyed, from the mouth of the cave. "Everybody take a bundle of jerky—as much as you can carry—and a full waterskin. We're leaving here. *Now!*"

None of the young elves paused to question his directive. Instead, they scrambled to clean out the wreckage of the dozen small lodges of the village, and within minutes had gathered bundles of their most treasured belongings. Bakall, Kagwallas, and Dallatar helped the youngest while Iydahoe and Vanisia filled large rucksacks for themselves.

The warrior never questioned his certainty, his conviction that they were doing the right thing—and that they desperately needed to hurry. He remembered the legends—there was only one place they could go.

The Grandfather Ram had lived in the highest places of Ansalon, that much he knew from the ancient tales. The aged elf had urged him to seek the places of the Grandfather, and finally Iydahoe understood.

The Kagonesti needed to climb for their lives.

In quiet urgency, he led the tribe up the steep slopes leading out the back of the sheltered grotto. Beyond rose the foothills of the Khalkist Mountains, with the snow-capped summits themselves looming into sight just above the nearer crests. These massifs came into full view as, working steadily upward, they soon topped the precipice.

Iydahoe was surprised to see that many of the summits beyond had lost their nearly permanent mantles of snow. Dark, sinister clouds spewed upward from numerous peaks, and though Iydahoe had occasionally observed smoking mountains far to the north of here, he had never seen so much of the noxious vapor, nor had it ever been this close to his home. Now it curled through the peaks like an ugly, pervasive blanket of gloom.

"The mountains look dangerous," Vanisia said as she and Iydahoe waited for the last of the children to come up behind them.

"It may be that they will kill us," he replied simply. "But if we stay here, I believe that we are certainly doomed."

Iydahoe kept his eyes skyward as they climbed. Clouds seethed in ways he had never imagined—not in his worst nightmares. He felt as though he looked into the surface of a vast, bubbling caldron that was somehow suspended upside down and that covered the entire sky.

Several of the younger Kagonesti began to whimper, slipping and skidding on the steep slopes, unable to maintain the pace. Iydahoe took Faylai, the littlest girl, on his shoulders, bidding her to cling tightly to his neck. With each hand he took the tiny fist of another, leading them toward the element of safety, however small, that they might find above. The Silvanesti female also took the hands of younger elves, and Bakall, Kagwallas, and Dallatar aided their smaller tribemates.

They climbed through the long day, and when night fell, Iydahoe shouted and cajoled, convincing the elves that they needed to keep going. The clouds blocked even the pallor of the green sky, but the elves could see enough to scale the ascending slopes as the ghastly night filtered toward an eerie, still dawn.

Dawn of the thirteenth day, Iydahoe remembered.

Still they kept climbing, crossing the lower mountain ridges now, many thousands of feet above the sprawling forest lands and plains of Vingaard. High summits beckoned to the northeast, but Iydahoe steered the tribe due east, where the mountains flattened into miles of rolling, forested plateau. These woodlands had many trails, while the warrior knew that the summits to the north became a maze of canyons, cliffs, summits, and gorges.

"Look!" cried Bakall, suddenly crying out in horror as

he pointed to the northeastern sky. The little tribe was fil-
ing across a clearing—a place incongruously studded
with wildflowers—amid the pine forest of the plateau.

Iydahoe saw the wave rippling along the bottom surface of the oily cloud, as if a great stone had been plopped
into the caldron of liquid he had earlier imagined. The
eerie sky showed through that gap, an even more sinister
shade of befoulment than before. The ground began to
tremble, huge rocks cracking free from the higher cliffs.
The elves staggered, riding a buckling carpet of supple,
boulder-strewn turf, ground lacking all solidity and form.

Abruptly the sky shot through with brightness, green
paling to blue and then to a harsh white light that seared
Iydahoe's eyes and caused Vanisia to moan in pain. Children began to cry, but the warrior could only grip their
hands tightly.

The subsequent explosion was impossibly, incredibly
violent. The rocky ground convulsed, pitching them into
the air. Iydahoe clutched the hands of his young tribemates, the group of them tumbling madly, momentarily
weightless. He felt as though they could fall forever, and it
was a strangely peaceful sensation.

The smash into the bucking ground brought him back
to reality with cruel force. Stone gouged Iydahoe's face,
and splitting pain racked his skull. He heard the youngsters crying, but for several agonizing moments his eyes
brought him only a blur of bright lights and swirling colors—the images of his own pain, he knew.

Then came the onslaught of full, numbing fear—the
knowledge that he had failed, that his tribe was doomed.
How could he fight against this kind of power, world-
racking might that could rock the very fundament of
Krynn? Surely most of his tribe had been killed by this
blast! He knew that he, himself, was broken, his body
smashed to pulp.

"Let's go. Get *up*, Iydahoe!" He heard Vanisia pleading,
but he couldn't move. Why should he? There was no
hope.

He heard more crying, then—the terrified sobbing of many young voices. They came from all around him, and Iydahoe blinked. With a supreme effort, he lifted his head, seeing Kagwallas, Bakall—each cradling a pair of crying youngsters. Vanisia knelt beside Iydahoe, and when he moved, she reached out to touch his face.

"Who's hurt?" he groaned. "How badly?"

He forced himself to look around, seeing past the white spots that still lingered in front of his eyes. The young elves of the tribe were scattered around him in the meadow. Some sat up while others huddled on the ground, crying. Two, the boy Dallatar and a younger girl, lay perfectly still amid the churned sod and rocks.

Then the girl, Tiffli, moaned and rubbed a hand across her face. Iydahoe and Vanisia went to Dallatar. The lad showed no sign of awareness, though his chest rose and fell weakly. In desperation, the warrior crawled to the frail form, while Vanisia and Bakall helped Tiffli to her feet.

But the forest stretched all around them, trees leaning crazily. The bleak clouds had closed in, concealing any view of the horizon or the sky. Which way should they go? There were no heights in view, no clue in the tangled woodland or shattered clearing to indicate where they had been headed before the quake had struck.

Iydahoe, for the first time in his life, was lost.

With that knowledge, he released the tiny shard of hope he had grasped—there was no way to escape this disaster. The tribe had no Pathfinder. He had tried to fill the role, had tried to be that which they needed him to be. He had desperately strived to perform tasks for which he was not prepared.

And he had failed.

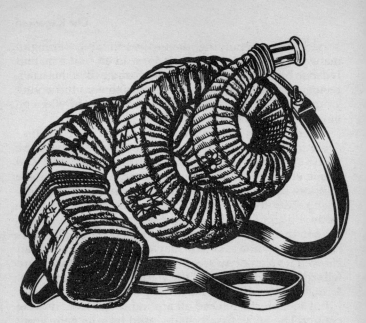

# Chapter 30

# Song of the Grandfather

Despair weighed on Iydahoe, pinning him to the ground, a physical weight that overwhelmed his puny strength. Cataclysm had come to Ansalon, and he and his tribe would die as surely as any insects on a lightning-struck log. If another earthquake wracked the ground, the convulsion would kill the battered elves. Even if the ground remained still, Iydahoe was lost—how could he seek the heights of the Grandfather Ram when he lay directionless on this ruined plateau? Around them stretched a tangle of quake-racked forest. Progress would be painfully slow, perhaps impossible, in every direction.

Abruptly a glimmer of white showed through the chaos of broken trees. The brightness caught Iydahoe's eye—it seemed the only pure and wholesome thing in this night-mare of a day. Straining to rise, the wild elf found that his muscles worked again. Grimly, desperately, Iydahoe stag-gered to his feet and took several steps toward the wood.

"What is it?" asked Vanisia, while Bakall and Kagwal-las looked at him curiously.

"There!" he croaked, as the white patch showed again.

Then he saw the head—huge, with the broad forehead a swath of alabaster fur. The huge, round eyes, soft and luminescent, studied him with a wisdom and compassion that moved Iydahoe to tears. Glowing pale yellow, those eyes touched him in a way that made him stand more steadily, helped him to swallow his fear and clear his head.

Only then did he notice the horns, spiraling to either side of that great head. Triple circles, each of them, culmi-nated in the proud, curling points of a mountain king.

"What are you looking at?" cried Vanisia, stepping after him, touching his hand. Iydahoe knew then that only he could see the Grandfather Ram—and even as he realized this the animal turned, with a flick of its snowy tail, and vanished into the woods.

"Come. Gather the children. I know which way to go." He stooped and picked up Dallatar. The young elf's breathing was shallow, his eyes rolled back in his head, but he still lived.

Iydahoe led them into the forest, picking a route through the felled timber that best followed the elusive white fig-ure. He discovered that, by walking along on the trunks instead of the ground, the Kagonesti could make fairly rapid progress. Gradually the plateau sloped again, a gentle incline signaling the beginning of another ascent.

They broke from the trees onto a grassy slope that extended more steeply upward. The wrenching earth-quake had torn numerous fissures in the soil, but Iydahoe had no difficulty finding a straight, smooth path between these frequent chasms. Soon they arrived at a ridge ex-tending from the north to the south, seeing a deep canyon and then lofty, rugged mountains beyond.

Vanisia instinctively turned north, toward the highest mountains of the Khalkist range and the heart of the smoking inferno that racked the world. Beyond those heights, hundreds of miles away, lay Istar.

To the south, the mountains were not so high, rounded summits and sheltered, tree-lined slopes. In the far distance beyond them lay the southern lowlands of Silvanesti. Iydahoe stared in that direction and felt the warming comfort of a soothing, return embrace of wisdom. Were those luminous eyes gazing at him from somewhere in that distance?

"Wait," Iydahoe said, looking at the seething wave of the cloud. The highest ground lay to the north, but he felt strangely drawn to the south. "Follow me. We'll go this way," he declared, trusting his instincts. Still carrying Dallatar, he led the others toward that more gentle terrain.

The elfwoman's face was streaked with smudges of dirt, her once golden hair tangled with mud and brambles. Vanisia looked at the rising, gentle slopes, then at the tall, black-haired elf. Nodding, she followed, and the youngsters came on behind.

Wind whipped over the ridge, pushing them first to one side, then, sheering viciously, twisting to send them staggering in the other direction. The clouds had risen high, blanketing the land from far above, and now they could see for dozens of miles.

On the vast plain beside the mountain range, the ancient flatland that had been known as Vingaard and Solamnia, the northern horizon shimmered. A white edge advanced, with smooth grayness flowing behind. The ground dissolved into something like sky—a bright, smooth surface that swept steadily closer, obscuring woodlands and fields, roads and towns.

With growing horror, Iydahoe understood. "It's water—the sea flows onto the plain! Ansalon is sinking!"

Again the elves turned and climbed, this time propelled by a clear sense of urgency, moving toward the southern heights on the path chosen by Iydahoe. They trotted along the smooth tundra of the rising ridge crest, gaining altitude quickly, avoiding the cliffs that towered all around.

The flood continued below, a deceptively gentle-appearing blanket drawn over the land. As the wave drew closer, the elves saw an angry fringe of furious white water burying forests, sweeping across pasture lands with the speed of a strong wind. It rushed from the north, swelling to fill their entire western horizon, filling out in a great bay to the southwest. Spray, closely followed by massive breakers, surged against the foothills, inundating the grotto where the tribe had made its village. More and more water flowed into the new sea, and the level of its tempestuous surface continued to rise.

Quickly the surge swept upward, splashing over the slopes that the Kagonesti had climbed only that morning. Waters swept over the ridge, the sea filling the plateau where the tribe had weathered the earthquake. The water churned close now and Iydahoe sensed the menace in the storm-tossed surface. Gales whipped monstrous waves upward, exploding into showers of spray that rose all the way to the ridge crest.

In the saddle behind the tribe, where that crest dipped low, the waves lunged all the way through the pass, showering into the canyon to the east. The sea level continued to rise, and these waves became a steady current, then a thundering cascade forming a permanent barrier between the mountains of the high Khalkists and the tribe's own southern ridge. And still the Newsea grew, chasing the fleeing elves with almost palpable desire—like a predator racing desperately after choice prey.

For hours they ran, though the incline of the ridge lessened for a long time, until they were running along level ground. Higher summits beckoned them to the south, the nearest several miles away, and Iydahoe could only hope that they reached it before the flood swept them away.

Waters continued to cascade into the canyon to the east. It seemed that an entire ocean thundered into the depths, shaking the ground with mighty impact. Still the sea grew, the waters rose, crashing into the mountainous gorge faster and faster, until a great wave filled the canyon to the top, equalizing the water level to east and west.

Instead of a lofty ridge, the wild elves now ran along a peninsula of rock, with angry waves slashing the shore to either side—and steadily rising behind them.

Tiffli stumbled, then collapsed. Vanisia halted beside the girl, trying to hoist her up, but her own strength gave out and she, too, sprawled onto the rocky ground. Halting on unsteady legs, Iydahoe realized that fatigue had stopped him as well—if he put down the unconscious Dallatar, he would never be able to pick the boy up again.

They would lose the race with the sea. A wave, surprisingly chilly, splashed forward until it eddied, ankle deep, around them. The heights to the south were cut off, as higher surges swept across the ridge, connecting the eastern valley to the sea in many places, rendering the once-lofty ridge into a chain of low, rounded islands. The gale roared so high that any one of these spots of land could be momentarily buried below a wave.

With crystalline clarity, Iydahoe saw that the formerly enormous ridge beneath his feet would become a reef of shallow water between two deep basins. He looked to the heights of the Khalkists, still towering to the north. If they had turned in that direction, they might be safe now, working their way into true mountain heights. Yet that strange compulsion he had felt, the penetrating gaze of the Grandfather Ram, had caused him to turn south.

His eyes remained fixed on those lofty summits, watching the smoke and debris belch skyward from beyond the jagged horizon. He blinked, wondering if the ground beneath him suddenly surged upward, for the mountains did not look as tall as they had before.

Then, in a bolt of shock, he understood—the high Khalkists were *sinking!* Landslides rumbled downward in clouds of dust and debris. The remaining glaciers broke free, sliding in avalanche toward the unseen valleys. Then the ridges themselves began to crumble, the summits breaking apart and falling away.

The great mountain range settled quickly, water rushing between the crumbling summits until a series of conical islands jutted upward from the tempest. One by one, these towers of rock disappeared, their foundation collapsing as they melted into the raging ocean.

As the mountains tumbled down, water flowed from the rest of the sea to fill the vast and growing crater. Around the Kagonesti, the Newsea retreated, spilling down the slopes of the ridge and clearing the route toward the forested highlands to the south.

By the time the raging waves settled into a rough chop, the water level remained steady against the ridge, some fifty feet below the level reached by the fleeing tribe. The peninsula extended for perhaps a mile to the north, then ended in a barren, wave-racked outcropping of rock. It was no more than two hundred paces wide for most of its length, though its base widened as it met the mountainside to the south.

"Look! A seashell! Like on your belt!" Faylai exclaimed to Vanisia. "But no!" she pouted. "It's too big!"

The warrior saw the curled shape on the rocks, glistening wet, as though it had been cast here by a wave, before the sea had fallen back. He knew the three spirals, recognized the wide bell with a growing sense of awe.

"Not a seashell." Iydahoe had not seen the treasure, intact, since the years when it had been played by Washallak Pathfinder. "It's the Ram's Horn of the Kagonesti," he said quietly, kneeling to pick up the precious horn.

"Look." Vanisia's fingertip outlined the pattern of tiny cracks in the horn's surface.

Iydahoe nodded, recognizing several of the shapes as fragments that he had recovered from the Silvertrout village. Many more, including some sizeable pieces, he had never seen before.

"Play it—play the horn for us," urged Bakall, stepping forward.

"No! Only the Pathfinder . . ."

"Play it, Pathfinder Iydahoe," said Vanisia, taking his free hand in both of hers.

He put the horn to his lips, and it felt as though it belonged there. When he played, the notes were warm and soothing. Iydahoe was immediately lost in the muse, felt his despair sloughing away. He thought of Istar, and that thought awakened no hatred, no lust for vengeance. There was no enemy there, now—Istar was a place of the past.

The elves, except for Dallatar, got up from the ground. Iydahoe slung the horn at his side and lifted the unconscious youth, relieved by the fact that Dall's breathing had become stronger, and his eyes closed more naturally, as if he were merely asleep.

A herd of deer stampeded southward along the ridge, passing within a few yards of the elves in their fear—but Iydahoe could see that this was proper fear, now, not the madness that had earlier afflicted the wild creatures. The deer bounded along, seeking the tree-fringed range of hills they could see in the distance.

When he saw the herd, Iydahoe knew that the tribe, like Krynn, would survive—their Pathfinder had led them from the greatest threat that had ever wracked the world. He held Vanisia's hand, finally, and led the elves toward the still-verdant forests, where Iydahoe saw towering firs. In the lower valleys, aspen groves shimmered in the wind, a stretch of woodland that promised haven for the weary, frightened elves. Already the deer had vanished there, seeking a new forest home.

Iydahoe knew that the deer would find sanctuary in that woodland, and soon the wild elves would as well.

# Epilogue

For many years after the Cataclysm the tribe lived a life not terribly different from its earlier existence. Indeed, of all the peoples of Krynn, perhaps the Kagonesti adjusted best to the loss of civilization's icons. Cities fell, empires vanished, vast estates were washed away by rains—and still the forests thrived.

Pathfinder Iydahoe played the Ram's Horn to mark the passing of the seasons, the rituals of the hunt, the time-honored celebrations of the tribe. Often he played for no reason other than to raise music to the fact of his people's survival. The tribe again knew health and happiness . . . and love.

Iydahoe and Vanisia were the first to take the vows of marriage, pledging timeless love to each other in a celebration cheered by all the wild elves of the tribe. Shortly afterward, Dallatar and Kagwallas became warriors, receiving their ritual tattoos from Vanisia. The ever-serious Bakall made many journeys into the surrounding lands, becoming a hunter of great skill and, under the tutelage of Iydahoe, patience.

In the decades that followed, Bakall even traveled far to the west, past Qualinesti, and learned that other wild elves lived there—the tribe of the Newsea was not the only gathering of the Kagonesti. Indeed, these other wild elves knew of still more tribes in the east. Bakall returned home as a famous scout, his body covered by the tattoos of a veteran warrior, and he brought with him a young bride from one of the coastal tribes.

Dallatar married Ambra in the same year that Iydahoe and Vanisia's first son was born. Two more births were soon expected, as Dallatar and Bakall strutted about with the universal pride of expectant fathers.

Iydahoe played his horn, and he knew that the Kagonesti would survive. His fear was gone forever, vanished in the same convulsion that had swallowed Istar. But his joy came from an even greater knowledge, the truth that—as the wild elves made new homes in the forest, as they stalked and roamed through lands they had never seen—once more the tribe would know peace and would grow.

# DRAGONS
## of
# SUMMER
# FLAME

**An Excerpt**

**by**
**Margaret Weis and Tracy Hickman**

# Chapter One

# Be Warned . . .

It was hot that morning, damnably hot.

Far too hot for late spring on Ansalon. Almost as hot as midsummer. The two knights, seated in the boat's stern, were sweaty and miserable in their heavy steel armor; they looked with envy at the nearly naked men plying the boat's oars. When the boat neared shore, the knights were first out, jumping into the shallow water, laving the water onto their reddening faces and sunburned necks. But the water was not particularly refreshing.

"Like wading in hot soup," one of the knights grumbled, splashing ashore. Even as he spoke, he scrutinized the shoreline carefully, eyeing bush and tree and dune for signs of life.

"More like blood," said his comrade. "Think of it as wading in the blood of our enemies, the enemies of our Queen. Do you see anything?"

"No," the other replied. He waved his hand, then, without looking back, heard the sound of men leaping into the water, their harsh laughter and conversation in their uncouth, guttural language.

One of the knights turned around. "Bring that boat to shore," he said, unnecessarily, for the men had already picked up the heavy boat and were running with it through the shallow water. Grinning, they dumped the boat on the sand beach and looked to the knight for further orders.

He mopped his forehead, marveled at their strength, and—not for the first time—thanked Queen Takhisis that these barbarians were on their side. The brutes, they were known as. Not the true name of their race. The name, their name for themselves, was unpronounceable, and so the knights who led the barbarians had begun calling them by the shortened version: brute.

The name suited the barbarians well. They came from the east, from a continent that few people on Ansalon knew existed. Every one of the men stood well over six feet; some were as tall as seven. Their bodies were as bulky and muscular as humans, but their movements were as swift and graceful as elves. Their ears were pointed like those of the elves, but their faces were heavily bearded like humans or dwarves. They were as strong as dwarves and loved battle as well as dwarves did. They fought fiercely, were loyal to those who commanded them, and, outside of a few grotesque customs such as cutting off various parts of the body of a dead enemy to keep as trophies, the brutes were ideal foot soldiers.

"Let the captain know we've arrived safely and that we've encountered no resistance," said the knight to his comrade. "We'll leave a couple of men here with the boat and move inland."

The other knight nodded. Taking a red silk pennant

from his belt, he unfurled it, held it above his head, and waved it slowly three times. An answering flutter of red came from the enormous black, dragon-prowed ship anchored some distance away. This was a scouting mission, not an invasion. Orders had been quite clear on that point.

The knights sent out their patrols, dispatching some to range up and down the beach, sending others farther inland. This done, the two knights moved thankfully to the meager shadow cast by a squat and misshapen tree. Two of the brutes stood guard. The knights remained wary and watchful, even as they rested. Seating themselves, they drank sparingly of the fresh water they'd brought with them. One of them grimaced.

"The damn stuff's hot."

"You left the waterskin sitting in the sun. Of course it's hot."

"Where the devil was I supposed to put it? There was no shade on that cursed boat. I don't think there's any shade left in the whole blasted world. I don't like this place at all. I get a queer feeling about this island, like it's magicked or something."

"I know what you mean," agreed his comrade somberly. He kept glancing about, back into the trees, up and down the beach. All that could be seen were the brutes, and they were certainly not bothered by any ominous feelings. But then they were barbarians. "We were warned not to come here, you know."

"What?" The other knight looked astonished. "I didn't know. Who told you that?"

"Brightblade. He had it from Lord Ariakan himself."

"Brightblade should know. He's on Ariakan's staff. The lord's his sponsor." The knight appeared nervous and asked softly, "Such information's not secret, is it?"

The other knight appeared amused. "You don't know Steele Brightblade very well if you think he would break any oath or pass along any information he was told to keep to himself. He'd sooner let his tongue be ripped out by red-hot tongs. No, Lord Ariakan discussed this openly with all the regimental commanders before deciding to proceed."

The knight shrugged. Picking up a handful of small rocks, he began tossing them idly into the water. "The Gray Robes started it all. Some sort of augury revealed the location of this island and that it was inhabited by large numbers of people."

"So who warned us not to come?"

"The Gray Robes. The same augury that told them of this island also warned them not to come near it. They tried to persuade Ariakan to leave well enough alone. Said that this place could mean disaster."

The other knight frowned, then glanced around with growing unease. "Then why were we sent?"

"The upcoming invasion of Ansalon. Lord Ariakan felt this move was necessary to protect his flanks. The Gray Robes couldn't say exactly what sort of threat this island represented. Nor could they say specifically that the disaster would be caused by our landing on the island. As Lord Ariakan pointed out, perhaps disaster would come even if we didn't do anything. And so he decided to follow the old dwarven dictum, 'It is better to go looking for the dragon than have the dragon come looking for you.'"

"Good thinking," his companion agreed. "If there is an army of elves on this island, it's better that we deal with them now. Not that it seems likely."

He gestured at the wide stretches of sand beach, at the dunes covered with some sort of grayish-green grass, and, farther inland, a forest of the ugly, misshapen trees. "Elves wouldn't live in a place like this."

"Neither would dwarves. Minotaurs would have attacked us by now. Kender would have walked off with the boat *and* our armor. Gnomes would have met us with some sort of demon-driven fish-catching machine. Humans like us are the only race foolish enough to live in such a wretched place," the knight concluded cheerfully. He picked up another handful of rocks.

"It could be a rogue band of draconians or hobgoblins. Ogres even. Escaped twenty-some years ago, after the War of the Lance. Fled north, across the sea, to avoid capture by the Solamnic Knights."

"Yes, but they'd be on our side," his companion answered. "And our wizards wouldn't have their robes in a knot over it. . . . Ah, here come our scouts, back to report. Now we'll find out."

The knights rose to their feet. The brutes who had been sent into the island's interior hurried forward to meet their leaders. The barbarians were grinning hugely. Their nearly naked bodies glistened with sweat. The blue paint with which they covered themselves, and which was supposed to possess some sort of magical properties said to cause arrows to bounce right off them, ran down their muscular bodies in rivulets. Long scalp locks, decorated with colorful feathers, bounced on their backs as they loped easily over the sand dunes.

The two knights exchanged glances, relaxed.

"What did you find?" the knight asked the leader, a gigantic red-haired fellow who towered over both knights and could have probably picked up each of them and held them over his head. He regarded both knights with unbounded reverence and respect.

"Men," answered the brute. They were quick to learn and had adapted easily to the Common language spoken by most of the various races of Krynn. Unfortunately, to the brutes, all people not of their race were known as "men."

The brute lowered his hand near the ground to indicate small men, which might mean dwarves but was more probably children. He moved it to waist height, which most likely indicated women. This the brute confirmed by cupping two hands over his own breast and wiggling his hips. His men laughed and nudged each other.

"Men, women, and children," said the knight. "Many men? Lots of men? Big buildings? Walls? Cities?"

The brutes apparently thought this was hilarious, for they all burst into raucous laughter.

"What did you find?" said the knight sharply, scowling. "Stop the nonsense."

The brutes sobered rapidly.

"Many men," said the leader, "but no walls. Houses." He made a face, shrugged, shook his head, and added something in his own language."

"What does that mean?" asked the knight of his comrade.

"Something to do with dogs," said the other, who had led brutes before and had started picking up some of their language. "I think he means that these men live in houses only dogs would live in."

Several of the brutes now began walking about stoop-shouldered, swinging their arms around their knees and grunting. Then they all straightened up, looked at each other, and laughed again.

"What in the name of our Dark Majesty are they doing now?" the knight demanded.

"Beats me," said his comrade. "I think we should go have a look for ourselves." He drew his sword partway out of its black leather scabbard. "Danger?" he asked the brute. "We need steel?"

The brute laughed again. Taking his own short sword— the brutes fought with two, long and short, as well as bow and arrows—he thrust it into the tree and turned his back on it.

The knight, reassured, returned his sword to its scabbard. The two followed their guides deeper into the forest.

They did not go far before they came to the village. They entered a cleared area among the trees.

Despite the antics of the brutes, the knights were completely unprepared for what they saw.

"By Hiddukel," one said in a low voice to the other. " 'Men' is too strong a term. *Are* these men? Or are they beasts?"

"They're men," said the other, staring around slowly, amazed. "But such men as we're told walked Krynn during the Age of Twilight. Look! Their tools are made of wood. They carry wooden spears, and crude ones at that."

"Wooden-tipped, not stone," said the other. "Mud huts for houses. Clay cooking pots. Not a piece of steel or iron in sight. What a pitiable lot! I can't see how they could be much danger, unless it's from filth. By the smell, they haven't bathed since the Age of Twilight either."

"Ugly bunch. More like apes than men. Don't laugh. Look stern and threatening."

Several of the male humans—if human they were; it was difficult to tell beneath the animal hides they wore— crept up to the knights. The "man-beasts" walked bent over, their arms swinging at their sides, knuckles almost dragging on the ground. Their heads were covered with long, shaggy hair; unkempt beards almost completely hid their faces. They bobbed and shuffled and gazed at the knights in openmouthed awe. One of the man-beasts actually drew near enough to reach out a grimy hand to touch the black, shining armor.

A brute moved to interpose his own massive body in front of the knight.

The knight waved the brute off and drew his sword. The steel flashed in the sunlight. Turning to one of the trees, which, with their twisted limbs and gnarled trunks, resembled the people who lived beneath them, the knight raised his sword and sliced off a limb with one swift stroke.

The man-beast dropped to his knees and groveled in the dirt, making piteous blubbering sounds.

"I think I'm going to vomit," said the knight to his comrade. "Gully dwarves wouldn't associate with this lot."

"You're right there." The knight looked around. "Between us, you and I could wipe out the entire tribe."

"We'd never be able to clean the stench off our swords," said the other.

"What should we do? Kill them?"

"Small honor in it. These wretches obviously aren't any threat to us. Our orders were to find out who or what was inhabiting the island, then return. For all we know, these people may be the favorites of some god, who might be angered if we harmed them. Perhaps that is what the Gray Robes meant by disaster."

"I don't know," said the other knight dubiously. "I can't imagine any god treating his favorites like this."

"Morgion, perhaps," said the other, with a wry grin.

The knight grunted. "Well, we've certainly done no harm just by looking. The Gray Robes can't fault us for that. Send out the brutes to scout the rest of the island. According to the reports from the dragons, it's not very big. Let's go back to the shore. I need some fresh air."

The two knights sat in the shade of the tree, talking of the upcoming invasion of Ansalon, discussing the vast armada of black dragon-prowed ships, manned by minotaurs, that was speeding its way across the Courrain Ocean, bearing thousands and thousands more barbarian warriors. All was nearly ready for the invasion, which would take place on Summer's Eve.

The knights of Takhisis did not know precisely where they were attacking; such information was kept secret. But they had no doubt of victory. This time the Dark Queen would succeed. This time her armies would be victorious. This time she knew the secret to victory.

The brutes returned within a few hours and made their report. The isle was not large. The brutes found no other people. The tribe of man-beasts had all slunk off fearfully and were hiding, cowering, in their mud huts until the strange beings left.

The knights returned to their shore boat. The brutes pushed it off the sand, leaped in, and grabbed the oars. The boat skimmed across the surface of the water, heading for the black ship that flew the multicolored flag of the five-headed dragon.

They left behind an empty, deserted beach. Or so it appeared.

But their leaving was noted, as their coming had been.